LIVE WIRE

ALSO BY LORA LEIGH

THE BOUND HEARTS

Forbidden Pleasure
Wicked Pleasure
Only Pleasure
Guilty Pleasure
Dangerous Pleasure

NAVY SEALS

Dangerous Games
Hidden Agendas
Killer Secrets

ELITE OPS

Wild Card
Maverick
Heat Seeker
Black Jack
Live Wire

THE CALLAHANS

Midnight Sins
Deadly Sins
Secret Sins

ANTHOLOGIES

Real Men Do It Better
Honk If You Love Real Men
Real Men Last All Night
Men of Danger
Legally Hot

LIVE WIRE

Lora Leigh

St. Martin's Griffin
New York

This is a work of fiction. All of the characters, organizations, and events portrayed in this novel are either products of the author's imagination or are used fictitiously.

LIVE WIRE. Copyright © 2011 by Lora Leigh. All rights reserved. Printed in the United States of America. For information, address St. Martin's Press, 175 Fifth Avenue, New York, N.Y. 10010.

www.stmartins.com

The Library of Congress has cataloged the St. Martin's Paperbacks edition as follows:

Leigh, Lora.
   Live wire / Lora Leigh.—1st St. Martin's Paperbacks edition.
     p. cm.
   ISBN 978-1-250-03669-8 (paperback)
  1. Intelligence officers—Fiction. 2. Terrorism—Fiction.
3. Man-woman relationships—Fiction. I. Title.
   CPB Box no. 1477 vol. 11

2011507781

St. Martin's Griffin books may be purchased for educational, business, or promotional use. For information on bulk purchases, please contact Macmillan Corporate and Premium Sales Department at 1-800-221-7945, extension 5442, or write specialmarkets@macmillan.com.

First St. Martin's Griffin Edition: October 2013

10 9 8 7 6 5 4 3 2 1

In memory of those who can never come home.

The warriors, the men and women whose courage and determination, whose loyalty and dedication to their country demanded the ultimate sacrifice.

My prayers for your loved ones, your wives, parents, children, and friends are whispered nightly. My dream that your sacrifice was not in vain is an ever-present thought.

Your blood was precious, your laughter is missed, and your dreams, though not realized, will never be forgotten.

You are the ultimate heroes, and your precious light will shine forever in the minds, the hearts, and the lives of freedom you have provided for us.

May heaven hold you in its embrace, as we shall always hold you in our hearts.

Lora Leigh

Special thanks

To Lisa Cesa, thanks for all the help and advice. It's not always easy to find someone willing to give their time and friendship as you have, and it's greatly appreciated.

Uncle Ronnie and Aunt Sug. I've missed you more than you know, and having you in my life once again is a gift I'll never forget.

And to Bret. You're growing up too fast, becoming a man too soon. But my pride and joy in you knows no bounds. Thanks for understanding, for supporting, and most of all, for just being you.

PROLOGUE

Elite Operations Base
Alpine, Texas

She was a vision of beauty.

Too fucking young, but her eyes weren't those of a twenty-four-year-old. They were the eyes of a woman who had seen too much, who had known too much danger, too much pain.

Jordan watched as she went through the strenuous training maneuvers the Elite Operations backup team was putting her through and wondered how the hell he was going to say no to her.

She wasn't strong enough to match the Elite Operations agents in physical strength or endurance, but she was more than a match for them in speed and ingenuity.

"She has no place to go, Jordan. She's spent her life running from her father and her brother. She doesn't have the education or the job skills to step out of this life. This is all she has." Kira Richards stood beside him, the former CIA asset somber, persuasive, as she attempted to smooth over the anger Jordan knew he wasn't hiding.

He'd arrived at the training facility to check the status of his nephew, now known as Noah Blake, as well as the other operatives that were part of his Elite Operations command. He hadn't expected to find this tiny sprite of a woman with masses of red hair, haunted green eyes, and a too sad face sparring with the nephew in question.

"Elite Operations isn't an orphanage, Kira," he reminded her, careful to keep his tone cold, emotionless.

He couldn't show the chink he knew this young woman had put in his defenses the first time he had met her two years before in Aruba during the Diego Fuentes operation. The operation involving Kira's now husband, Ian, and his father, Diego Fuentes, had been rife with danger. And there the girl had been, desperate to end the life of death and misery her father had been waging to find her for nearly twenty years.

Her eyes had been shattered then, filled with desperation and fear that the plot to bring down the terrorist Sorrel wouldn't succeed.

But she had been game. She'd thrown everything she had into revealing the identity of the man who had destroyed her mother and who had tried to destroy her.

"Elite Operations isn't an orphanage, but we owe her," Kira reminded him forcefully. "You know we do. Besides, she would be perfect in base operations. She knows communications, she knows how to organize things. Give her a chance."

He glanced at the woman at his side. It wasn't a request, it was an order. Make it happen. That was what she was saying. Just make it happen.

"You're a contract asset for the Ops, Kira," he reminded her. "This isn't your decision to make. Nor is it up to those men out there." He waved his hand at the training room viewed through the two-way mirror he stood behind.

"The whole team has more or less adopted her, Jordan," she informed him. "You can't get out of this. If you don't take her, then the backup team will."

He grimaced.

Hell, he had very little control over the Elite backup team. He couldn't order Reno or Clint to do shit and he knew it. But he owed them, and he knew that as well. Just as he knew that if she were working with them, it would be a damned sight more dangerous than being confined to the Elite Operations base would be.

"She would fit in perfectly as your personal assistant, as

well as mine, in communications," Kira went on to say. "We've been in operation long enough that you know we need someone to fill that spot. Give her a chance, that's all she needs."

She would be perfect to make him crazy, that was what he knew. The few times he had been in contact with her, his blood pressure had nearly gone through the damned roof, and his cock had nearly burst from his jeans.

The need to fuck her had been so damned overwhelming that for the first time in years Jordan had considered breaking his own rule. Never fuck or become close to his female operatives. He knew better, just as he knew the outcome if the past remained true.

Losing one of them posed the risk of too much distraction. It was a distraction he could ill afford when the lives of the entire team depended on his ability to think straight.

She was eight years younger than he was, she was looking for a life, for a battle to replace the one she had fought for so many years. The battle to bring her terrorist father to justice. But he knew the dangers of not letting her in, the danger to her, and that terrified him.

Sorrel's allies would find her and exact vengeance for the terrorist and white slaver's death. The thought of the hell they would put her through before they killed her was enough to give him nightmares.

He knew the risk to himself as well as the team in letting her become involved. She was young, she had no official training, other than what she had received in her desperation to survive over the years. She was an impulsive redhead, and she was weakness personified.

"She's not Catherine, Jordan. She's not a field agent, and she has no desire to be one."

And of course Kira would know exactly why he didn't want her there.

Jordan turned away from her. She had known Catherine, though not very well. Hell, they had worked for the same damned agency in the same line of work. Except Catherine hadn't survived it, because of him. Because he hadn't been able to protect her and the unborn child she and her husband had dreamed of having. Because she had been a close friend, and when she had placed herself in a situation he hadn't been prepared for, he'd dropped the ball.

"I never said she was Catherine," he stated coldly. "I said we're not an orphanage. Bringing her in would be a risk."

"But you'll bring her in," she demanded, but with just enough respect that he couldn't deny the request out of pride. She was right, Tehya was a perfect fit for the Elite Ops, but she was a distraction to him. And that made her a danger.

Jordan sighed heavily. The knowledge of the debt he owed Kira, her husband, Ian, and Ian's SEAL team was never lost on him, either.

Together, they had saved his nephew, dragged him out of hell, and even now they worked to heal the wounds inflicted on Noah's soul.

Besides that, there was also the fact that they were a working unit now. Elite Operations and its backup team was a cohesive unit, and throwing a wrench in the works over their choice of a base member wasn't in his best interests.

It was the woman in question, and the risk she posed, not so much to the unit, but to his own self-control. The woman who had haunted him since he'd met her in Aruba two years before.

"Bring her in." He heard his voice harden and he knew that the fact that he didn't agree with the choice wouldn't be lost on Kira.

"That's all I needed." Satisfaction filled her voice, and when he turned to look at her, he saw the amusement in her soft gray eyes.

"This is a mistake, Kira," he informed her, knowing the anger was slipping past his careful control.

She stared back at him, her lips quirking as an unholy gleam of wicked laughter sparked in her gaze. "Why? Because you get hard for her? Think of it this way, Jordan, she'll add a little spice to your life." Despite the flippancy in her tone, understanding filled her gaze.

"I don't need spice in my life."

"Sometimes, that's exactly what you need to live again," she said gently. "You're like Noah, almost dead inside. Catherine wouldn't have wanted that for you, and I know her husband, Killian doesn't. She was your friend, Jordan, not your albatross."

As he watched her walk away he felt the familiar guilt, reminding himself that even Kira didn't know the truth.

He was the reason Catherine was dead. And he would never let himself forget that. Because of it, he refused to involve himself in the lives of his agents refused to allow himself a lover he worked with. Especially Tehya. Because she did make him hard. Harder, faster than any other woman in his life.

He turned back to the two-way mirror that provided a view into the training room and watched Tehya again. He had let her into the Ops, but he would never let her into his bed, or into his life.

And he swore he would never let her into his heart. Though, his fear was, she was already there.

Six years later

"Evenin', Da."

Riordan Malone Sr. looked up from the marble gravestone and his silent good night, his fingers caressing the sun-warmed stone as though he could reach the woman fate had taken from him so many decades before.

Wild Irish and soft as a summer morn, his Erin had given his life meaning, then she had given him two sons that a man could be proud of.

Courageous, brave, strong sons.

His eldest, Grant, may have been forced to appear less than honorable, less than courageous for a while, but he had done it to protect his own sons, and the sacrifices he had made were no less than Riordan Sr. would make himself.

His youngest son, however, the one his wee Erin had called her mini-Rory, he was the one Riordan was perhaps the most proud of.

"Jordan." A smile tugged at Riordan's lips. His son always approached him as though he were never certain of his reception. As though he were unaware of the power of a father's love.

He watched as Jordan moved across the small cemetery, his long-legged, powerful form tall and strong as he walked up to his mother's grave.

Riordan watched as Jordan touched the top of the stone lightly as he had done for so many years. In the gesture, Riordan saw things, sensed things he knew his son would never be comfortable with him knowing.

He saw a son's regret, a man's aching loneliness, but even harder to observe was the flash of weariness. Jordan was growing tired, and that was dangerous for a warrior.

"I miss her." Riordan patted the stone gently as he turned his gaze from his son and stared at the marble instead.

She was his talisman, his Erin. She had been his boyhood dream, his teenage love, and finally, she had become his wife. The mother of his sons, the foundation of his soul. She'd made him swear to linger on this earth without her to see to the happiness and safety of her boys. And he'd done as she asked. He had pushed himself through each day with only that purpose in mind.

This son, ahh, but this one, he tested an old man's strength.

He looked toward Jordan's truck before bringing his gaze back to his son. "You've not brought young Tehya with you, then?" he asked.

Jordan's jaw tightened as it always did whenever Riordan asked about the girl. As though Jordan somehow thought that if he didn't speak of her, then he wouldn't feel for her.

Riordan almost chuckled at the thought, but he doubted his son would appreciate it. Jordan rarely saw any amusement in his denial of the feelings he refused to show.

"She's packing." There was a snap to Jordan's voice that had Riordan's brows lifting in surprise.

He nodded. "You told me last month she would be."

He was saddened to see that team coming to an end. They had given Jordan purpose, Riordan had often thought.

And their leaving meant young Tehya would be going, as well, and that, he feared, might be the breaking point for Jordan. Without her, he feared his son would become that cold, unfeeling shadow he so seemed to want to become.

"I have a few things I have to do after everyone's off base," Jordan all but growled. "Do you need anything before I leave?"

Riordan shook his head. "Noah and Sabella, they take care of things." He nodded toward the house. "Those children of theirs may give me gray hair, but I'll be fine. I was just about to bring the groceries inside though."

He had to grin as he thought of the miniature Nathan, or rather Noah as he was known now. Noah and Sabella's eldest son was already the image of his da, though he had enough of his mother's features to hide the fact he was one hundred percent Malone. Noah Blake, unknown to the world, had been Nathan Malone, Navy Seal, husband, son, grandson. Now, he was Noah Blake, husband to the wife Nathan Malone possessed before his "death."

"I'll get them," Jordan said, before glancing down at the tombstone once more.

Ah, the boy had more than groceries on his mind.

Disappointment lanced him, though, as rather than speaking Jordan turned and walked toward the truck.

Watching, Riordan sighed as his son collected several bags and headed to the small cabin beyond.

"Such stubbornness, Erin," he sighed. "He takes that after you, lass. I was never such a hardheaded man."

He knew that if she were still standing by his side, she would be rolling her eyes in amused disbelief.

That had been his Erin.

"Ah, lass, when will he see?" he asked her softly. "Irish Eyes, he has them. He'll never be free from her now."

Only since the redhead had arrived at the Elite Ops base had Jordan gotten that bright sapphire color to his eyes. Irish Eyes.

They revealed more than his son would have preferred. And Miss Tehya . . . well, she was the cause right enough.

Riordan knew his boys, and he knew their hearts. Just as he knew Jordan's heart belonged only to that young lass.

Jordan could pretend he cared nothing for that young woman till hell froze over, but he couldn't fool his father. He was suffering from his stubbornness and his denial. And the suffering wouldn't ease, it would only grow worse until Jordan accepted it.

"What do we do now, Erin?" he asked. "How do we save our boy now?"

He'd been asking his wife that question for far too many years.

His fingers stroked over the stone as Jordan returned, his gaze now calm, though icy cold.

Yes, this was how Jordan handled all those pesky emotions he refused to allow himself to deal with. He froze them out.

"I've got to head back, Da," Jordan told him. "Is there anything more you need?"

Riordan shook his head slowly. "Is there anything *you* need, Jordan?"

Jordan's jaw clenched. "No games today, Da," he warned him.

Riordan chuckled. "I'd like to see the lass before she's out of our lives forever," he said. "Once she leaves, Jordan, she'll never come back without your invitation. I'd like to tell her good-bye." And he'd like to assure her she always had friends, and a home to run to should she need it.

Jordan looked away for a long moment before giving a sharp nod. "I'll let her know," he promised, and Riordan almost grunted in mockery at the promise.

He let his boy get away with it, though. Riordan would find another way to get the message to her before she left.

When the truck had sped away, Riordan turned back to Erin's grave.

"Far too much like you, my love," he whispered again. "Like talking to a brick wall." He smiled at the memories. "But a fine woman you were, Erin."

And God knew, he missed her.

He missed her until he felt withered, lost without her as he struggled to keep his promise to her.

"Work on him, love," he finally sighed. "Lead him in the right direction." This time, his fingers clenched on the stone. "I'm ready to come home to ya, Erin. Help me, just this one time."

He'd never asked it of her before, but he was damned tired.

It had been far too many years since he had seen her, far too many years since he had loved her.

He was ready to go home.

She was a vision of beauty.

Standing in the dim light of the silent communications room of the Elite Operations Alpha Base in the heart of Big Bend National Park, Tehya Talamosi looked like a woman awaiting the lover who would fulfill her naughtiest dreams. A lover who had waited far too long, and left her far too lonely if the expression on her face was any indication.

Nothing could be further from the truth, of course. Tehya was awaiting a lover who would fulfill dreams of forever, not simply those of lusty, heated sex. Tehya was a happily-ever-after woman, and he didn't have happily-ever-after inside him.

Jordan Malone had accepted that long ago. That acceptance had sent him to the SEALs, and life as a SEAL had taught him that nothing lasted forever, and a man never let himself make friends he couldn't bear to lose, or to have lovers that he wouldn't be able to walk away from.

Some rules were broken day by day, but while he was in the SEALs, those were the rules he had lived by.

As the commander of Elite Operations One—the Elite Ops as they called it—, he'd remained true to one rule only. Never let himself get close to his operatives. Only one had been close to him, the nephew he had nearly lost before he'd entered the select, secretive organization.

And he'd almost broken that rule a thousand times over with this woman.

He watched her, the deserted communications room, for some odd reason, a perfect backdrop for the fact that she was barely dressed. That she was walking around looking like sex personified.

They were the only two team members left on the base now, and they both knew it. They had known it the moment the last operative left the base earlier that day.

She stood proud in the central cavernous center beneath the metal catwalk he stood on now and stared below. She would know she could dress down, dress up, or dress not at all, and no one would be aware of it but him. If he saw her. But he was supposed to be in his suite, not here, watching her from the shadows.

Not standing here, aching for her, his gut clenched with such need that he felt as though the agony were rocking through him, the denial fucking killing him.

She was barefoot, dressed in a black silk gown that dropped to her ankles, the tiny straps barely holding it up over her full breasts. She made him so damned hard his dick felt like iron.

She made him so damned hungry for a taste of her that he actually ached with it. His balls tightened painfully and his cock throbbed in demand. A demand that he go to her, that he touch her, that he take her to his bed and just fuck her. Fuck her until the hellish hunger burning inside him was sated, and the clawing need eased.

Instead, he forced himself to simply stand there, to do no more than watch her.

She stared around the room, her gaze touching on the silent computers, the darkened maps, the blank expanse of screen where satellite images had once been displayed.

And she looked lost. She looked as though she didn't know where to turn, or where to go now that this part of her life was over.

Elite Operations One was done. The last agent had fulfilled the eight-year contract he'd signed. Several had been under twelve-year contracts, but they were finished now as well. Five men had gone their own way to live their lives in the sheltering hearts of the women who had ultimately saved them.

And where the hell did that leave him? Where did that leave Tehya?

She had dedicated six years to the Elite Operations. Pulled in at the age of twenty-four because of her contacts overseas, her practical knowledge of communications, she had eventually been given the code name Enigma. She'd been a last-minute hire, a decision made more by the agents than by Jordan, and she had immediately completed a team that hadn't known they weren't whole.

If it had been left up to him, she would have never wasted those tender years of her life within this mountain. She wouldn't have wasted her life staring at computers, or immersing herself in the lives and the missions that had been played out beyond the steel and cement walls surrounding them now.

She should have been living. She should have gone to college, married, and had a house full of babies instead of hiding on the secretive, secure base of Elite Operations One.

As he watched her, she pushed her fingers through the long, heavy strands of red-gold hair that fell to her hips. He rarely saw it unbound anymore. For years she'd kept it in a tight plait, or a ponytail.

Had she worn it loose during the past years as she did tonight, then he wondered if he could have kept his hands off her for so damned long.

That hair tempted, it teased, it dared. And Jordan wasn't a man that could turn his back on a dare.

In the six years she had worked with the Elite Ops, he'd done his best to stay the hell away from her, but he couldn't deny she had made herself an integral part of the unit.

Tehya was the backbone of the communications center, along with Kira Richards. She had also acted as his personal assistant, and he'd be damned if he could think of anyone who could have fulfilled that job nearly as well.

It was Tehya who kept the files intact, mission information flowing, his coffee hot and plentiful, and his dick spike hard.

It was hard now. His balls tight and throbbing, his muscles tense with the effort to stay the hell away from her, to ignore the silent invitation he saw in her eyes too often.

It was an invitation he wouldn't see any longer after the sun rose on a new day. She would be heading out, leaving the base to begin a life of her own. To learn how to simply be Teylor Johnson, a woman who had spent her life working in the back offices of a central database company. One of those nameless, faceless drones that other workers rarely if ever saw, but whom they depended upon for the various files and information she was responsible for. This was her new identity, the safety net Jordan had created for her.

She would be out of his life though. And hell if he knew how to handle that thought.

As he stood watching, Jordan's fingers clenched when she turned, her lush hair moving in a wave of silk that tempted his fingers to tangle in the long, rioting curls.

Those long strands swayed around her as she slowly shook her head and sighed. A slow, heavy sound of regret before she turned and left the dimly lit room, unaware he that he was observing her, unaware of the hunger that tightened his expression.

There had only been a few times he had ever come truly close to Tehya. She had gone covert with him several times because of her ability to hack her way into any system and her overseas connections. During those times they had been forced into close proximity, so close that more than once they had been forced to share a bed.

Needless to say, he hadn't slept much on those missions. And he wouldn't be sleeping tonight, knowing they were alone, and he could have her.

She made him fuck hungry. He lived in a hellacious haze of lust at times, so damned hot for her it was all he could do to keep his cock in his pants.

He was haunted by fantasies of her naked, her eyes dazed

with lust, her face flushed, as he teased and tempted and sated the lust that he knew would explode between them. Imagining her creamy flesh flush, her eyes dilate and darken. Her hips arching, pussy saturated with her juices, swollen and clenched tight, as he worked his dick inside her.

His nostrils flared at the fantasy he couldn't ignore as the heavy steel door below slid open. It closed behind her as she passed through it, heading for the resident suites farther up the mountain.

The communications room was on the deepest level of the base. Ten stories beneath the mountain above them, heavily secured and completely hidden.

Residential suites were located just a single story beneath ground level, each set of rooms outfitted with a bedroom, bathroom, and small sitting and meal preparation area. The Elite Ops agents were well taken care of. They were the heart and soul of the nongovernment, nonmilitary, secretive group of undercover operatives. Operatives who were now gone with the exception of himself and Tehya.

Jordan had seen each operative off with a sense of envy that even he couldn't deny. Despite his determination to remain single and to remain a doting uncle, brother, and son, he'd been envious of the lives his men had waiting for them. The wives, the children. The freedom to laugh and to love.

It was a freedom Tehya hadn't sought out, though each year he had lived in fear that she would, wondering if he could let her go when she made the request.

Hell, letting her go now was something he was finding impossible to do. He was the reason she was still here. He had kept her busy, kept her working, ensuring she had been delayed and the last to leave. Ensuring he didn't have to release his grip on her until the very last possible second before the new team moved in to take over the base.

And why had he kept her there? He'd avoided her this entire, final week. He'd watched her from afar, jacked off at night when the fucking lust was close to breaking his control, and kept telling himself he could let her go.

And still, he was fighting it. Still, he was trying to find

ways to hold her here when he knew he had finally run out of time.

Shaking his head at the futility of the hunger tearing at his control, he pushed his hands into the pockets of his pants and finished his final inspection before leaving himself.

The next morning would see him walking away from the base, perhaps for the last time.

He had the option of returning and heading the new team, with the new commander working as his second in command. Killian Reece had no problems with Jordan assuming command of the base and operations.

It was a decision he had less than a month to make. He could go another twelve years or he could back off, find a place for himself within the world as a civilian and find a life.

The only problem was, he couldn't imagine life outside this mountain, without Tehya running his life to some extent. Without her tormenting him with her pert smile and sassy-as-hell comebacks that made his dick harder than hell with the need to fuck her into submission.

Son of a bitch.

He shifted the hardened length of his cock as he stepped into the elevator at the end of the steel and iron walkway and pushed the button for the residential level. The thought of her leaving had that need ripping through him with a force that damned near cramped his dick. He had the urge to go to her, to jerk her to him, lift her, wrap those incredible legs around his hips and pound into her.

She would walk out those doors when morning came and he intended to ensure he never crossed her path again. But God help him, would he make it through the night without pouring himself into her?

He doubted it.

He had every intention of going straight to his own suite, he assured himself. Every intention of ensuring he didn't tempt himself further where Tehya was concerned.

Instead, he found himself at her door. Dick hard, pulse pounding, his body tense, unrelenting, in the pure addictive-like hunger pouring through his body.

He hadn't told her good-bye. It would hurt her if he didn't say something before she left in the morning. He couldn't do that to her.

He couldn't do it to himself.

Pressing his finger to the button that would announce his presence, he waited. Rather than her voice coming over the small intercom, the metal door slid open instead.

And there she stood.

The black silk flowed over her full breasts. The long red-gold hair spilled around the creamy perfection of her face.

She was thirty years old, but she barely looked twenty-five.

Vivid emerald-green eyes watched him warily, but the nipples beneath that silk hardened, peaked, and pressed against the material as though reaching for the hungry depths of his mouth.

Damn, he should have gone straight to his own suite. He should have never stopped.

He was going to do exactly what he had told himself he wouldn't do.

He was going to fuck her.

"Jordan." His name was a caress on her lips. The soft, sultry sound was filled with an aching huskiness, a question, a hint of hope.

"Are you packed?"

That wasn't what he wanted to say. He wanted to reach out and rip that damned gown off her body, push her back into the room and thrust into the sweet, hot depths of her pussy.

Damn, she would be tight. She hadn't had a lover in the six years she had been with the unit. He knew she hadn't. He'd kept such close surveillance on her that he would have known the second she had so much as entertained the thought.

She'd given her life to the Elite Operations, and what did she have to show for it? She had no family, no friends, no connections or roots. He was throwing her to the wolves and Jordan knew it.

"I'm packing," she finally answered as she turned away, but not before he caught the flash of hurt in her eyes. "Is that all you wanted?"

Hell, no, it wasn't all he wanted.

Soft, supple leather covered the couch and recliner that faced the wall-mounted combination television\computer screen. A small lap table sat at one end of the couch, the wireless keyboard and computer accessories aimed for the screen.

A colorful western throw was laid over the back of the couch. A cup of tea sat on the coffee table, still steaming, as she moved back to it.

A bookshelf filled with books covered one wall. Interspersed with the books were small figurines she'd been given over the years for Christmas or her birthday. Tiny, collectible dragons. Pocket dragons, she called them. It was the only thing Tehya collected. Whimsical, fanciful, the complete opposite of her life.

She hadn't packed them. The books were still on the shelves, boxes in front of them with only a few books enclosed.

"You have a ways to go," he said as he looked around.

The room was incredibly neat. Even the packed boxes were stacked in neat little piles awaiting morning and the team that would load her belongings and transport them to the storage facility she had requested they be taken to.

"I'll be ready on time." She shrugged.

Those wild green eyes flicked over him, making his cock harder, reminding him of all the things he couldn't have. All the things he refused to allow himself to have.

It wasn't that he couldn't have her. He could, and God knew he wanted her until his body felt on fire from the need. But he knew he would only end up destroying both of them if he took her, if he allowed the dominant possessiveness that rode him to have free rein.

"What do you want, Jordan?" she finally asked as she sat down on the couch, one leg tucked beneath the other as she wedged herself into the corner of the cushions. "You're standing there as though you should be doing something. There's nothing left to do anymore." And the regret in her voice echoed through his entire being. As did the loss. He could hear it, feel it. The loss of something neither of them had been allowed to experience.

No, there wasn't anything left to do.

He felt his jaw tighten as he fought back the need to go to her, to push her back along the leather cushions as he came over her.

Five seconds, he thought. He could have her laid out on the couch, that piece of nothing gown she wore pushed to her hips and his dick buried between those luscious thighs in less than five seconds.

And he would be making the biggest mistake of his life.

She was essentially a coworker. He was her superior, even though the Ops were, for the moment, disbanded. She was a woman that needed more than he could give her, more than he could allow himself to give any woman. She already had more of him than he was willing to admit to.

"Jordan, if you don't stop standing there staring at me as though you're ready to strangle me, then I just may begin to worry."

She didn't sound in the least worried. She sounded irritated, restless, a bit frustrated. But worried wasn't in there.

"Do you need help packing?" he finally asked.

He wasn't ready to walk away. Come dawn, the transport detail would be here to load her belongings and ship them out. She would be following behind in whichever of the expensive, fast little sports cars was still parked in the base garage. He'd given her a choice of the vehicles, something he hadn't offered to the other members of the unit.

"I don't need help packing." There was a snap to her voice now, a sense of impatience and frustration that threatened to light a fuse to his already short temper.

"You'll leave it to the last damned minute and have the transport detail packing boxes and running late while you bark out orders," he ground out as that frustration began to eat at him, to get the better of him. "Dammit, Tehya, they're on a schedule."

"As if I'm ever late getting anything done." Her eyes narrowed, an assessing, curious light glittering in them as she watched him. "Tell me a single instance in the past six years that I have ever been late."

He hated it when she stared at him like that. As though she suddenly glimpsed something in his gaze or in his expression that was another piece of a puzzle she was putting together.

He wasn't a damned puzzle. He was a fucking horny man and he was trying damned hard to keep a handle on the lusts raging through him.

What the hell did she expect from him?

"Do you want me to help you pack?" His arms folded over his chest as he glared at her now, channeling all the frustrated lust into irritated anger.

Anger was a hell of a lot easier to deal with than a redheaded little rogue determined to drive him insane.

"No. Actually, I don't need your help." She came to her feet slowly, like a cat unwinding from a favorite bed.

She didn't stretch, but she didn't have to. Laziness wasn't a part of her demeanor at the moment.

"You need someone's help," he growled as he stared around the living area once again. "What about the other rooms? Are they ready to load?"

Her eyes narrowed further. "Everything but the living room. Would you like to check, daddy, and make certain I'm following orders?"

The sweetness of her voice almost had his balls shrinking. Intimidation from a five-foot-four piece of dynamite? It shouldn't be possible.

But he knew this little piece of dynamite could pack a wallop when it wanted to.

Unfortunately, common sense didn't seem to be his forte tonight.

"Don't call me 'daddy,' Tehya. I'm well aware of your feelings when it comes to fathers."

She distrusted them. She even watched the men she had worked with for years with a suspicious gaze once they'd become fathers.

"Don't be ridiculous, Jordan," she replied with a cute little drawl that in no way detracted from the danger glittering in her gaze. "I have no feelings one way or the other where fathers are concerned. I never had a father, so how should I know how they're supposed to act? Sperm donors don't count."

She had had little more than a sperm donor. One that had kidnapped her mother, impregnated her, then attempted to raise Tehya to become a brood mare for her half brother.

"You've had weeks to prepare for this," he reminded her. "You should already be out of here."

Something flashed in her eyes then, something he could have sworn was grief.

If it was, then it was the same grief that seemed to be growing inside him as well. A well of furious denial where it came to walking away from her. She cast him one of those cool little looks that warned of retribution as she stood facing him.

"I dare you," she suddenly stated, her eyes narrowing as she stared back at him.

Every muscle in his body tightened dangerously.

God, no. Don't let her dare him, not when he could sense where that dare was going.

"Excuse me?"

"Are you not hearing so well, Commander Jordan?" A red-gold brow arched slowly as her arms crossed over her breasts, pumping the delicate mounds up, making so damned tempting a sight his mouth almost watered.

"I dare you to actually touch me," she explained, that note of anger in her voice causing his jaw to clench in determination. "You've been a complete prick for six years now, alternating between ignoring me and ordering your men away from me until it's made me ready to pull my hair out. Be a man, Jordan. See if you can handle it. See if you can handle me or get the hell out of my rooms."

There were some challenges a man couldn't ignore no matter how hard he tried, no matter how much he wanted to. This was one of those challenges.

Be a man?

She had no idea who this man was she was tempting.

"Don't push me," he warned her, his fingers curling to fists at his sides. "You may not like the consequences."

"Or you may not," she replied with an edge of pain-filled mockery. "What's wrong, Jordan, afraid you can't walk away from me as easily as you've walked away from the little bimbos you've been fucking for the past six years?"

That flare of contempt that lit her gaze had his jaw tightening, but it was the pain in her voice, that tore at him. He hated hearing the pain, even that blurred edge of it. He'd seen that aching need, that hunger for something more, for years now. Too many years. He couldn't stand hearing it in her voice now.

"I can walk away from any woman, Tehya." He tried to keep his tone soft, gentle. God knew he didn't want to fray those ragged edges further.

Soft lips tightened as the sharp blade of her nose lifted. Emerald-green eyes sharpened to gem brightness, but not from tears; no, Tehya didn't cry easily. Hell, had he seen her cry at all in the many years he had known her? Definitely he hadn't seen her cry for herself.

"Can you really?" Her head tipped to the side. "Isn't that nice, Jordan, to be so certain you need nothing, no one. How superior you must feel to the rest of us mortals."

Sharp, biting, her voice cut straight through the icy disdain he would have shown any other woman. The problem was, with Tehya, there was simply nothing but raw lust and shadowed emotions. That was the reason he stayed as far the hell away from her as possible.

He couldn't project an icy disdain that simply wasn't there. What he did have was a dick so damned hard he could pound iron with it.

"I don't feel superior, Tehya." Frankly, he felt lacking. During the past years, as he watched the happiness that filled men who had once been cold, hardened warriors, he'd finally realized what he'd lost in his life.

It was a loss he had accepted long ago, he reminded himself. He couldn't make the same mistakes he had made in the past. The blood and rage that stained the darkest days of his life were never forgotten.

"The hell you don't." Anger filled her voice, but naked need filled her eyes. "You stood above your men daily, staring down that sharp, arrogant nose of yours as though they were recalcitrant children in need of discipline for actually daring to love. You were mockingly amused at the lot of them."

Surprise burst inside him. Was this what his men thought? What his nephew thought? That he considered himself better than they because they loved?

He'd be damned if that were the truth. He was aware of the choices he had made, just as he knew that his men were in a far better position than he. They had someone to hold on to at night, someone to ease the aching loneliness. He had only the loneliness to keep him company.

"Is that what you really believe, Tehya?" He took a step forward, feeling blistering need and offended anger crowding inside him.

He promised himself before coming here that he wouldn't touch her, that he would simply tell her good-bye.

Good-bye wasn't going to be enough.

"Why don't you just go ahead and leave, Commander Jordan," she sneered, those tempting witch's eyes flaring back at him as the fiery red of her lashes seemed to blaze around the iridescent color. "There's the door, don't let it hit you in the ass. Isn't that what you Americans say?"

A whisper of French, that alluring little accent that only emerged in the most extreme situations, vibrated across his senses.

It may have vibrated across his senses but it seemed to wrap around his cock and squeeze. His balls tightened, the tormenting ache increasing. His self control was disintegrating and he knew it, felt it unraveling.

She did this to him. She made him crazy like this and there wasn't a damned thing he could do to stop it. It traveled through his bloodstream like poison, like a potent drug, stripping away the control he prided himself on and leaving him grasping at the threads of decency as he tried to force himself away from her.

"You don't want to keep pushing this," he warned her.

"Well, hell, you must be enjoying it, Commander, you're still standing here." Her breasts were heaving, the nipples so hard beneath the silken material he swore they were going to pop right through the threads.

The urge to lick his lips was almost overpowering. The need for her was almost as strong.

"I could fuck you," he growled then. "It's what you want, it's what we both want, but have you considered what would happen the morning after?"

"Will there be a morning after?" she questioned him roughly. "Aren't you the one who said you could fuck me, but then you would have to kill me? Double O Seven has nothing on you, does he, stud?"

Stud? She had not just called him "stud"?

Damn her, the woman didn't have the good sense to know when to keep her smart mouth shut or her tender heart safe.

Before he could stop himself, his hands were on her. His fingers curled around her upper arms as he jerked her to him, watching as her eyes widened, her hair seeming to flow around her as the pure silk of her flesh met the callused roughness of his hands.

And then he froze. Because her skin was so fucking soft. Beneath his palms it felt as heated, warm, and soft as a cloud itself. Sensation sizzled at the touch, heated and mesmerized his senses.

Spreading his fingers apart, he touched her with his palms only and watched as he let the inner part of his hand cup the curve of her shoulder.

Hell, he wanted her. He wanted to fuck her until he was mindless with it, until nothing or no one mattered but Tehya. Until the past and the nightmares were obliterated.

She would be the death of him.

That was but a distant thought as he let himself relish the feel of her flesh against his palms. He swore he could feel the sizzle of heat just below the flesh, drawing him, surging through his pores and washing through his system.

"Bad idea." Swallowing tightly, he stared back at her, so focused on the strength of the need surging through him that all thoughts of pulling back evaporated.

The emerald green of her eyes darkened, glittering with need, as he watched her lips tremble.

"Six years," she whispered. "I waited . . ."

He didn't want to hear it. He couldn't hear it. The words she was about to whisper would be words she would regret the moment she realized that it wouldn't have mattered if it had been twenty years.

To hold back the words he covered her lips with his, because he couldn't let himself hear them.

And everything in the fucking world exploded.

Son of a bitch.

He would have frozen if every lust cell in his body hadn't risen in revolt. Because by freezing, he would be stopping. Hell no.

He wasn't about to stop. He had her now, he couldn't stop. He tasted her.

His tongue slipped over her lips, licked at them, and before he could retrieve his basic common sense, he gave in to this one hunger.

It wouldn't go any further. He wouldn't allow it.

But this one pleasure was incredible.

Tehya was terrified to breathe, to whimper in hunger, or to moan in pleasure. She was terrified he would stop if she did. She was entranced by the kiss she hadn't really expected, enthralled by a hunger that suddenly exploded through her system. His tongue stroked against hers, exciting that feminine, sensual part of her that went deeper than she had ever imagined.

But oh God.

She could feel herself trembling, shaking against him. Her hand lifted, fingers outspread, not really touching him. She wanted to touch him. Desperately. Feel him. Her hands were shaking with her need to touch.

He was warm, so warm. The feel of his lips moving against hers, over them, his tongue stroking against hers, sent pleasure racing through her as she lifted, strained to get closer without gripping his arms and pulling herself straight into his embrace.

His fingers curved around her shoulders, held her to him. Her fingers curled, and before she knew it she was gripping the material of his shirt, feeling the rolled sleeves beneath them.

Okay, maybe he wouldn't feel her hands shaking through the material of his clothing. Maybe he wouldn't sense the incredible need that there seemed to be no escape from. A need that had tormented her since the day she first met him in Aruba.

"God. Tey." His hands slid down her arms, gripped her hips and jerked her closer, pulling her against the hard, heated length of his cock.

Behind denim, thick and hard, the hot flesh of his erection was a wedge of temptation, a promise of satisfaction, and it was pressing into her lower stomach erotically. She could feel that promise within her grasp. His hands gripped and kneaded her ass, lifting her, the silk of her gown pressing between her legs as she felt his thigh pressing between hers, the rough denim rubbing the silk against the swollen, sensitive flesh of her sex.

She had never deemed herself a romantic person, but she saw starbursts. She felt herself melting, her knees weakening and her breathing becoming harsh and labored.

His teeth nipped at her lips as she gasped, fighting to draw in oxygen. His lips tore away from hers, the rasp of the day's growth of his beard scraping against her jaw in a caress that had her arching closer to the incredible sensation. Finally. He was finally touching her, kissing her. Finally she was in his arms where she ached to be.

It was exquisite. It was better than she had ever imagined it could be and her imagination was damned good. Years of fantasies were finally becoming reality.

"Jordan." The gasp of his name was a sigh of pleasure as she felt his hand move from her rear to her thigh, his fingers edging beneath the silk of her gown, the callused tips of his fingers stroking up the outside of her thigh. The rasping sensation of his flesh against hers drove her pleasure higher, hotter.

"Is this what you want, Tey?" His arm wrapped around her waist, lifted her, and before she could do more than breathe out roughly she was pressed against the wall as he gripped her thigh, pulling it to his hips as he brought her closer to the incredible warmth of his body.

Her gown fell back from her thighs as she felt his hard, muscular thigh press harder, more firmly, into the sensitive mound of her pussy.

"Jordan," the moan rose unbidden. "I've needed this. I've needed this so desperately."

"More?" he growled. "Do you want more, Tey?"

More? She was ready to beg for more, did that count?

Her clit throbbed. The aching torment of unquenched pleasure rose inside her, burning through her body and dampening her skin with perspiration. Her breasts were swollen and sensitive, her nipples tight and hard. Every cell in her body was screaming for his touch.

"Answer me, Tey." Rougher, darker, his voice stroked over her senses as she felt his fingers curve over the bare flesh of her rear. "Do you want more, sweetheart? Is this what you want?" His fingers curved, pushed beneath her rear, and found the lush, slick flesh of her pussy weeping in need. Swollen, sensitive, the folds of flesh felt too hot, too slick and wet with her juices.

"Yes." It was a hiss of exquisite pleasure the only answer she could give. His fingers stroked, rubbing against the clenched opening of her pussy, and sent rasping flares of pleasure rushing through the sensitive flesh, through her clit and straight to the inner walls of her pussy.

Oh God, she wanted to come. She was so close. She could feel the need throbbing in her clit, rushing through her veins.

It was a pleasure born of emotion, and she knew it. Emotion she'd kept tightly reined, until now. Until his kiss, his touch, had released it.

Until his fingers rubbed against her opening, pressed and parted the sensitive flesh to slip inside just enough to make her entire body burn. To penetrate just deep enough to make her hungrier, to make her moan in rising excitement.

"You've been begging for it, Tey," he groaned, his voice dark and rough, as the tips of his fingers stroked and rubbed sensitive flesh, sending pleasure rocking through her.

"And you haven't?" she gasped, her head rolling against the wall as those two fingers sank just deeply enough to drag an unwilling cry from her throat. "Every time you warned one of your men off . . ." A startled, desperate cry tore from her lips as his fingers jerked back, then plunged forward, stroking inside her with a whiplash of intensity certain to weaken her mind. Stretching, heating, the walls of her pussy clenched desperately as though to hold his fingers locked inside her.

Her hips jerked, trying to force his fingers deeper as she felt her juices gathering, saturating his fingers as he pulled back and thrust inside her again. The shallow strokes were just enough to build the flames of sensual desperation higher.

"If one of my men had touched you, I would have had to kill him," he suddenly snarled, his fingers fucking deeper inside her. Her pussy creamed shamefully around his fingers as pleasure surged through it. "I would have made sure he was gone, Tehya, one way or the other."

He lifted his head and those wild blue eyes glared down at hers, his dark face flushed with lust. She fought to keep her eyes open. It was hard. She wanted to look at him, to see him as he touched her, as heated lust poured into her gaze and tightened his expression.

She had waited so long for this. For his kiss, for his touch. She didn't want to miss so much as a single sensation or one agonizingly pleasurable moment.

He didn't give her a chance to reply. His lips moved back to hers, kissing her with a greedy hunger that had her arching closer as her fingers gripped the back of his neck, beneath the long strands of rich, silky black hair.

She had never known sensations so rich and lush, so incredibly vivid. She had had sex before, but never had it made her mindless, made her so desperate for it that all she could do was hold on and moan incoherently for more.

A keening wail tore from her throat as the fingers lodged inside her began to rub rather than thrust. He chose a spot so ultrasensitive, so wickedly heated, that she began to shake from the sensations. With his finger curved he reach high in the back of her pussy, pressed and rubbed and sent rapture electrifying her clit.

Her entire body was stretched on a rack of such incredible pleasure that she felt intoxicated. Her senses were dazed with the overload of sensations, her pussy clenching, snug muscles tightening on the two wicked fingers stroking her with diabolical torturous intent.

"There, Tey," he panted as his lips slid from hers again. "You're so wet, baby. So sweet and hot. So fucking tight."

Her pussy spasmed again, her juices spilling around his fingers as his head lowered, his teeth raking against her neck while he nipped and kissed the sensitive flesh there.

The low-cut bodice of her gown was pushed aside, her breasts rising to his lips, her nipples hard, aching, as he kissed a path from one to the other.

Tehya swore she lost consciousness for a moment as his lips surrounded the hardened bud and sucked it inside with a tight, hard drawing motion of his mouth.

"Jordan . . . Oh God, yes," she cried out desperately. "It's so good. So good Jordan."

The feel of his lips drawing on the tender tip sent exquisite, flaming pleasure racing straight to her womb. Ecstasy struck at her clit, her pussy. Fire raced through her, jerking her hips, driving her sex against his fingers as she nearly climaxed from the intensity of it.

Nearly. Almost. She was so close to coming. She could feel her orgasm just out of reach, teasing her with the promise of mindless rapture as his fingers slid back and thrust inside her, driving into the responsive tissue and stroking a maelstrom of eroticism in their wake.

"Damn you. Tey. It's not enough. God help me, I need more of you."

Before she could process the fact that he had moved, Tehya suddenly found herself sprawled over the low bar that separated the living area from the kitchen. Jordan's fingers were still inside her, fucking her with forceful strokes as her hips arched, her thighs falling farther apart, while he sucked, licked, and nipped at the tender tips of her breasts once again.

She felt the wildness of his response, the hunger she had glimpsed in his eyes burning out of control as he groaned around her nipple his teeth rasping over it as his head drew back.

The blaze of lust in his brillant blue eyes seared her as he stared down at her.

"You'll destroy us both," he whispered as his lips moved from one nipple to its mate.

She couldn't answer, it was all she could do to breathe. The fingers of one hand held tight to his neck as she gripped his wrist with the other, desperate to force his fingers to thrust harder, deeper inside her. To give her that extra, added sensation she needed to slip over the edge into orgasm.

She just wanted to come. She wanted that heated, destructive release tearing through her before anything could interrupt it, before Jordan could regain his control and pull back from her.

Then his fingers were sliding from her. There was no time to protest the action, no chance to make sense of the sudden desertion. His hands gripped her thighs, pushed them farther apart, and in the space of a heartbeat his tongue licked through the bare, saturated folds of her pussy.

Tehya froze. Her body quivered, so close to orgasm it was agony to wait as she stared down her body and met those wild blue eyes. Then her gaze slipped lower to watch, her breath catching, as his tongue licked around the glistening, swollen bud of her clitoris.

And he let her watch. Watch as his tongue stroked around

and laved the swollen, flushed nubbin. It rubbed against the pulsing knot of nerves, sent clenching fingers of sensation spearing to her pussy, jerking her body tight and dragging a desperate cry from her lips as she tried to arch closer. Dazed, desperate, she whimpered at the burning pleasure, reaching, begging for more.

As he pushed her thighs even farther apart, his lips went lower, flickering over the quivering entrance before he thrust inside suddenly, spearing into the sensitive channel before licking with diabolical greed and wicked hunger and setting a flare to the fuse of her release.

Tehya felt herself exploding. Arching, shaking, her back came up, her fingers clenching in his hair as the rush of flames tore through her body and seared across her nerve endings in violent response.

The rush of liquid heat between her thighs had Jordan groaning into the swollen folds of her pussy.

He'd never tasted anything as sweet, as rain soft as this woman's response to his touch. Her body was tight, shuddering, pleasure tearing through her as he brought her to orgasm, holding onto her, amplifying it with soft licks of his tongue and the little rubbing motion he used against the underside of her clit.

She was jerking in his arms, crying out his name, her voice hoarse, filled with emotion. God, he didn't want to hear the emotion. This was one night only. It was supposed to be one kiss only, but the damage had already been done. They were both so damned hungry for this that he knew there would be no staying away from each other unless this was finished.

Then he could return to showing the world what a cold, hard bastard he really was. He would return to showing Tehya that there was no future to this, ever. That tonight was all they could ever have.

As the final pulses of her orgasm flexed against his tongue, Jordan slid back slowly, lapping at her, filling his senses with the sweetness of her before straightening, picking her up in his arms and carrying her to her bedroom.

He had been here only once before, when she first came

to the Operation center. He had shown her to the small underground apartment, showed her around.

When they had stepped into the bedroom, tension had whipped in the air, even then.

It wasn't much different now. Boxes were packed and awaiting transport rather than awaiting unpacking. The bed was larger, king-sized rather than full as it had once been.

He laid her in the center of the bed, narrowed his eyes down at her as he undressed.

Shedding the last of his clothes, Jordan watched as Tehya tossed her gown to the floor. It would have been a shame to ruin the silk, but he would have torn it from her if she hadn't removed it herself.

Gripping the base of his dick, he fought back the need to simply fuck her. That was what he should do. He should go right to her, thrust inside her, and drive them both to climax.

But he needed more. He ached for more. He had his own fantasies to fulfill tonight, especially this one.

He watched as she sat before him, pushing her hair back, staring up at him with those witchy eyes as she licked her lips slowly.

Jordan eased onto the bed, kneeling in front of her, the overriding lust stripping away what little restraint he had held on to over the years.

His hand slid into the back of her head, delving beneath those silky curls.

"You know what I want," he growled, almost wincing at the sound of his own voice. "Suck my dick, Tehya. Let me fuck that sweet mouth."

Hunger flared in her eyes and he wanted to curse. He hated himself. Hated the needs that tore through him, the dominance that was too much a core part of him, and the hunger he couldn't still for this too delicate woman.

Her lips parted for him, her little pink tongue peeking out to lick over the engorged, flushed head of his cock as rapid-fire electrical impulses began to attack his nerve endings.

Clenching his teeth, he couldn't hold back the groan that

rumbled from his chest. It was so fucking good. Her tongue was a lash of pure sensual delight on the head of his dick, the aching throb of pleasure sending waves of sensation through his balls and then across the rest of his flesh.

His fingers clenched in her hair as his thighs tightened. He swore he could feel his come building in his balls, threatening to erupt.

Holding the base tight, he rubbed the swollen head against her tongue, her lips. Watching as her eyes met his, as the engorged flesh of his cock caressed heated damp silk.

He wanted to sink inside. To feel her hot mouth closing over the supersensitive head of his dick and sucking it in. The anticipation of it was killing him.

"Suck it," he ordered roughly. "Let me in that hot little mouth, baby. Let me fuck it like I've dreamed of for far too many damned years."

He'd had too many fantasies of this. It had weakened him over the years, obviously, because he was damned if he could pull back from her.

Her lips parted.

Jordan didn't wait for her to take him. Her lips parting was permission enough.

Holding firm to her hair, he watched instead as he pushed inside, then shuddered as a wave of heat tore through him as he watched her suck him inside.

Sweet, pink lips were stretched, reddened. Those brilliant emerald eyes fluttered closed as pleasure suffused her face. Her hands smoothed down his flanks before moving up, one hand easing between his thighs, her fingers finding the taut, responsive sac of his balls and cupping it with silken hands.

This was ecstasy.

Ah hell, he was going to lose himself in her and he could feel it. The threat of it was there. The threat of losing every promise he had made to himself over the years had the potential to destroy him.

"Fuck yes!" he hissed out as she began to move, her mouth caressing the engorged crest as she began a firm, erotic suckling with her mouth that he knew he wouldn't be able to hold out against for long. "Suck my dick, baby. Sweet, hot fucking mouth . . ."

His thighs burned, they were clenched so tight as her hungry mouth began to work over his cock. Her tongue lashed against the underside of the head, rubbed. The suckling pressure eased, then tightened.

Flames of hair swayed down her back, over her shoulders, caressing his thighs. Her hands were never still. One caressed his balls, the other clenched at his thigh, her fingertips rubbing against it every so often. Her cheeks hollowed as she sucked the throbbing cock head in her mouth, working it with delicate greed as a moan vibrated over the aching crest.

Hell, he couldn't hold out long. He wanted to fuck her too bad. The need to spill inside her was building in his balls, burning through his body.

"Fuck," he snarled in desperation. He didn't want to stop. He didn't want to lose his hold on the sight and the feel of her taking him so intimately as his hips moved, his cock thrusting against her swollen lips.

The sensual, completely absorbed look on her face ratcheted up the pleasure racing through him. He could feel his entire body tightening to the breaking point, every muscle, every cell attuned to each draw of her mouth, each flick of her tongue, each incredible stroke of her silken fingers against his balls.

Clenching his hands tighter in her hair, he fought to hold back his release, fought to hold back the groan building in his chest.

She was killing him.

Watching her, seeing the fulfillment of the fantasy that had haunted his life since the day he had first met her in Aruba, eight fucking years ago, was wearing away every objection he had used over the years to remain distant from her.

"Tey." He couldn't hold back the groan. "Ah God, baby."

Hell, he swore he could feel his knees weakening further.

His hips jerked against her as he fought to keep his strokes shallow, to keep from hurting her. Damn, it was hard. He needed to be deeper inside the liquid heat of her mouth. He needed to be surrounded by her.

But pulling back from the sweet pleasure of her hungry suckling wasn't possible, not simply because she refused to release him, but because he couldn't make himself do it.

Her mouth tightened as he felt the blood pounding harder through his stiff flesh. His balls were agonized, the shaft flexing, release was only seconds away.

"Tey," he said desperately. "I'm going to come, baby. Move that sweet mouth or I'm going to fill it."

She moaned, a hungry, greedy sound that lit a fire to a sensual fuse that exploded through him with the power to weaken his knees and almost take him to the floor.

His hands tightened further in her hair. He had to be pulling the strands and couldn't stop. The surge of sensation racing through his cock, exploding through the head and spurting from it, rocked him to his soul.

He'd never come so hard. So many years of waiting, fantasizing, and his mind was exploding with his release.

And still, it wasn't enough.

He was still hard, the pleasure tearing through him was like a narcotic, an addiction, and he wanted more.

Somehow, he found the strength to pull her head back, watching as his still hard cock slid from her reddened lips, as those amazing green eyes opened to stare back at him in dazed pleasure while her tongue ran over her lips, the pleasure apparent in her face.

"Lie down." He raked his eyes over the gentle lines of her body. The scattering of freckles across her nose was duplicated in a small area across the tops of her shoulders. Just the lightest hint of them beneath the skin, intriguing him, tempting him to investigate the satiny flesh.

She lay back, her breasts rising and falling quickly, her face flushed, her soft flesh sweat dampened.

"Spread your legs." He could barely force the words out.

Tehya stared up at him, watching the wild blue of his eyes, darker, gleaming brighter than she had ever seen them.

"Beautiful." The sound of his voice was thicker, harsher

as he came to his knees before her spread thighs. "Do you have any idea how fucking beautiful you are?"

She shook her head. She had never seen herself as beautiful. She had never believed she was beautiful. But at this moment, she felt, at the very least, pretty in his eyes. When he stared at her as though he were starving for the taste of her, his cock thick and hard, flushed, the head dark and throbbing as he came to his knees between her thighs.

"How pretty," he murmured, reaching out to run his fingers over the bare folds of flesh.

For a second, nervousness edged at the arousal that had her dazed, almost uncomprehending.

She could see his absorption with the fact that there were no curls there, that her skin was softer, smoother than it would have been if she waxed or shaved.

Naturally bare. She had been bred to have no pubic hair. Her father had known the child he wanted, and he had chosen the perfect woman to conceive that child. And one of his requirements had been a woman whose genetics lacked the gene for pubic hair.

That thought, the memory of that past, threatened the pleasure wrapping around her.

Then he parted the folds, slid against the entrance, and two fingers pressed inside her.

Immediately her hips jerked, sensation slamming through her womb, her clit, rocking through her system with an overload of pleasure.

"So ready for me," he said hoarsely as he came over her, his fingers sliding free as he gripped his cock and tucked the engorged crest against the entrance.

"Jordan." She could feel him, thick and heavy, prepared to penetrate as her lashes fluttered in pleasure.

"It's okay, baby. Everything's okay."

He pressed tighter.

She had waited so long. For so long she had felt teased out of her mind, desperate to have him touch her, hold her, and it was finally happening. Finally, the aching need that had tormented her for so long would be eased. At least for tonight.

Her hands lifted, her fingers gripping his hard biceps as he began to enter her, stretching her, burning her.

Her nails dug into his arms, her hips lifting, lowering, working his flesh deeper inside her as her gaze locked with his.

"Perfect," he whispered. "That's it, sweetheart. Fuck me back."

Tehya shook her head as she felt her juices gather and gush at the eroticism of the command, the sound of his voice, so rich and husky. She was captivated by him, dazed by the surfeit of pleasure rushing through her.

Surging closer, she gasped, bit her lip. He was so thick, so hard, the shaft was almost bruising as it impaled her, separating her intimate flesh and forging inside each time she thrust upward.

Her thighs spread wider, each sensation merging into the one before it, building, coalescing into such sharp, fragmented shards of ecstatic sensation that by time he took control of her and forged in to the hilt, she was crying out with need, begging for ease.

"Look, Tey." His gaze sliced from hers as he glanced down her body, pulling her gaze to the point where they met where his body disappeared into hers.

The swollen folds of her pussy were parted, glistening with wetness, cupping, enfolding the base of the hard shaft penetrating her.

The sight of it had a punch of pleasure tearing through her womb. It jerked her hips tighter against his, lodged his cock harder inside her, the head rubbing against the overstretched depths of her vagina.

She was gripping his cock, flexing involuntarily around the hard flesh. She wanted to hold him just like this forever.

As she watched, he eased back, revealing the glistening shaft until only the thickened crest remained, before pushing back inside her, slowly, deeply. The flared head stroked over ultrasensitive nerve endings, rasped against excited flesh, and sent a flood of sensations racing through her bloodstream.

As though that thrust were a breaking point, Jordan gave

a harsh groan before lowering himself to her, his lips covering hers as his hips began to move with a smooth, steady rhythm.

Tehya fought to hold on to him, to meet each stroke as pleasure seared her senses and flamed through every cell of her body. Her nails dug into his upper back as she thrilled to the bunching of powerful muscles beneath toughened flesh.

Electric heat sizzled through her, fingers of it raking through her womb, her clit, her nipples. Her body was screaming for release. Each thrust of his cock rasped through her pussy, caressing the sensitive flesh with rapid-fire strokes as the agonizing pleasure surged higher, hotter.

As Jordan's head lifted her gaze locked with his; she was mesmerized by the brilliancy of the blue, held in thrall by the hunger and the need reflected in them.

A hunger and need that tore through her, that rose with each thrust, with each forceful entry into the clenching flesh. It was more than lust. She swore she could see more there. It had to be more. The intensity of the pleasure was just too deep to be physical only. To just be lust.

"Tehya." Her name seemed torn from his lips as her legs wrapped around his hips, her nails digging into his arms. "God yes, baby. Fuck me."

His voice was harsher, thicker. He sounded tortured, as seeped in the agonizing pleasure as she was.

Tehya felt the waves of sensation gathering in her womb stealing her breath. The clenching tightness that echoed to her pussy, spasmed through it. Her clit swelling it further, tightening it until the pleasure and pain mixed with erotic desperation.

She could feel his cock, thicker, harder than before, as each thrust began to tighten, shorten.

Sensation began to burn in her clit, her pussy. Her breaths became moans, rising with each shocking burst of pleasure as she felt the pressure tightening inside her, burning, flaming out of control until it suddenly exploded like fireworks gone wild.

His name became a wailing moan as her hips arched. She

felt her pussy tightening, clenching on his thrusting cock a second before the world melted around her.

Ecstasy began to thunder through her. A storm of sensation exploded through her in rapturous bursts, arching her body, shuddering through it as she felt Jordan thrust in hard, deep. He jerked her against him, his hard, muscular body rippling with pleasure, and he began spilling inside her.

Spurting deep and hot, his release swept through her senses as her own release seared her nerve endings and left her gasping at the intensity of her orgasm.

She didn't know if she was breathing. She didn't care if the world itself rained down upon them. Nothing mattered but this pleasure and the white-hot mix of sensation and emotion rising through her.

Emotion.

She had sworn she would never love, but she had known in Aruba, two years before joining the Elite Ops that it was a promise she would end up breaking.

She loved Jordan Malone.

He'd just destroyed both of them.

Jordan stared at the ceiling above him as he held Tehya in his arms and knew the mistake he had made. He hadn't fucked her. He'd intended to, but he hadn't. No. Hell no. He'd come much too close to making love to her.

He'd fought this for years. Fought it and sworn he'd never give in to it, because he knew it had no future. That *he* had no future with her. He couldn't risk his soul to that point. If he kept her, if he gave into his need, then he'd never be able to let her go. He would allow himself to give in to that illusion that lasted forever, when he damned well knew love was the illusion, and forever didn't exist.

And even if he was wrong, even if she was the home-and-hearth type, and the illusion could be maintained there was always the risk that his enemies, those made before his time in the Elite Ops, would find him. And when they found him, they would find his weakness.

Tehya.

She was the weakness. She was the one woman capable of breaking his control.

"Nothing to say?" she whispered from where she lay against him, obviously awake. It was too much to pray she had gone to sleep.

When he said nothing, she moved. Jordan had to force himself to let her go, to refrain from pulling her back to his chest. Where she belonged.

Rolling from his side she rose from the bed, and slowly, wearily, she collected her gown from the floor and pulled it over her head. She looked defeated. That realization tore at his concience, leaving him steeped in regret and guilt.

Wiping his hand over his face, Jordan rose as well, sitting on the edge of the bed as he watched her broodingly. Son of a bitch, this was one of the reasons he hadn't taken her to his bed. Tehya wasn't a one-night stand, and he had known it. Fuck, hurting her was killing him.

Hurting Tehya was something he had tried desperately not to do over the years. In all his life there had never been anyone he wanted to protect more than he wanted to protect Tehya. There had never been a woman so hard to let go.

Something he had known from the beginning that he had no choice about.

Tehya promised herself she wouldn't cry. She fought back the tears but she couldn't fight back the pain clenching her chest and throbbing through her heart.

She had always assumed a broken heart was more figurative than literal, but she could feel it ripping in half inside her chest. Even her bones ached, her ribs felt too tight, under pressure, as though the emotions tearing at her heart were going to burst from her skin, as well.

"I didn't want to hurt you."

Those eyes. That brilliant, almost neon blue stared back at her somberly.

Irish Eyes, her friend Jordan's sister-in-law, Sabella Blake, had told her once. Jordan had Irish Eyes; any woman lucky enough to steal his love would have a true window into his soul. Sabella had told her how she had once "seen" the horror of her husband's torture when he was kidnapped by a drug cartel owner. That she had felt his pain, dreamed of his screams.

Tehya had always wondered what such love would feel like. She had fantasized about possessing this man's love in such a way. A fantasy. That was all it was. A fantasy she had to let go of now.

"I have to finish packing." She heard the hoarseness of her voice and knew she wasn't hiding her emotions as well as she had hoped. She didn't want him to feel responsible, or guilty that he couldn't love her. Hell, her own father hadn't loved her, why would any other man?

"Tehya, I don't want to lose your friendship, either, not because of this," he said as he pushed his legs into his jeans then rose and pulled them over his muscled legs, his gaze somber as he watched her closely.

"Are we friends, Jordan? Were we ever?" She had never felt friendship with him. Friends was the last thing they would ever be. She felt too much for him, hungered too deeply for his touch.

She couldn't define exactly what she had felt from him over the years. She knew her own emotions had been in conflict more than once, but friendship had never been the definition she would used to describe their relationship.

"I hoped we were." That edge of regret in his voice tore at her.

She could almost feel the pity coming, and she really didn't want to have to shoot him. If he dared to feel sorry for her, then that would be the least of the problems he would have.

Giving her head a quick shake, she turned and walked from the bedroom. She couldn't handle this tonight. She couldn't stand here and discuss friendship, see the pity on his face, or confront the fact that the years of dreams had been wasted effort.

God, it had been so long. Ever since that night in Aruba when she had come to Ian Richards to help him capture Sorrel. It had been too damned long. Suddenly, she felt far older than she actually was, and far too tired to fight with herself or with Jordan any longer.

"Tehya?" Jordan followed, standing in the bedroom doorway as she moved to the pile of empty boxes and protective paper stacked next to the shelves she hadn't yet begun to pack. Because packing meant leaving, and leaving was killing her.

Each of the trinkets had been collected over the years. There were pocket dragons, fairies, expensive little keepsake boxes. And there were pictures. Pictures of the team she had worked with, their wives, and a few included the children of those men. In some, there was an unsmiling Jordan. In one, he stood next to Tehya, an arm around her shoulders, as they stared back at the camera.

These were the past six years of her life.

She picked up the picture of her and Jordan first, wrapped it, packed it.

"Why do you think I hadn't taken you to my bed before now?" he asked from the bedroom doorway.

She had always known why. Because once he did, she would have no choice but to leave.

"Why don't you leave, Jordan?" She didn't look at him, she couldn't.

She wanted to cry. She wanted to scream, and she wasn't about to do it while he was standing there watching her as though waiting for her to break apart.

Before she knew it, he was next to her, his hands gripping her upper arms as he jerked her around.

She saw the anger then. His eyes were bright with it, the blue snapping down at her, his expression tight with regret.

"I didn't want to hurt you!"

"And you haven't." She wasn't backing down from him but she was damned if she would cry for him. She wouldn't do that to either of them.

He hadn't done this to her, he hadn't asked her what she felt. And how many times had he pushed her away, done everything but told her that it couldn't happen? She had been the one that pushed for it, that dared him. She had broken her own heart.

It had been her own stubbornness, her own stupidity, that had led her here. She had known better. At least she should have known better.

Sex wasn't love, and she could see now what he had tried to save her from. Sex couldn't change him and sex wasn't going to make him suddenly realize he couldn't live without her.

Yet the anger was there inside her, as well. A feminine fury she couldn't escape.

"Tehya, we're friends," he ground out furiously. "If you ever need me . . ."

"I didn't need you before I came here, and I won't need you after I leave." Jerking away from him, she stalked to the far side of the room and faced him where the sheer power of his presence would hopefully be diluted. "It's been fun Jordan, thanks for the memories and the sex, but you can leave now."

"God, Tehya!" He raked his fingers through his hair, the long, silken strands falling around his face with such male, sensual disarray that she had to clench her fingers at the overwhelming need to run them through it again.

"Don't do this, Jordan." She had to get away from him, she had to hold back the tears. "Don't make this harder for me than it already is. For both of us. Just leave."

Over the years, that was all she had done, held back her emotions, held back her dreams, hell, she had held back her life in the hope, the dream, that something more than blood could fill her future.

She had obviously been so wrong. Her time here was over. The Elite Ops was shutting down and the new team coming in didn't need her. They had their own people, their own specialties. No one needed the daughter of a white slaver. A woman who had no true specialty, no family, and no longer a reason for being there.

She had no special training. She had no true education. She was an outcast, plain and simple. Unlike the other members of the team, she didn't have a happily-ever-after waiting for her when she walked out the doors of the base.

There would be no family waiting for her. There were no friends she could look up. She had a new identity, but she had no idea what the hell to do with it or where to go with it.

She watched as he shrugged his shirt on and buttoned it with quick, angry movements. She couldn't miss the anger, it glowed in his eyes, tightened his body. There was nothing she could do to alleviate it either.

"I don't want to lose contact with you." He seemed to be forcing the words out.

He was placating her and she hated that. The last thing he would want would be to stay in contact with a woman he pitied.

She nodded slowly. "I'm sure we won't. We have friends in common. Hell, you can always call, right?"

She doubted he would, despite the fact that he had given approval for the team members to keep the satellite phones they had been assigned, as well as the numbers.

As she stared back at him, the only other dream she had left rose in her mind. A life that she could build with the new identity she had been given, and maybe, just maybe, there was one other person in the world that she could connect with. The cousin who didn't know her, who wouldn't recognize her. But a cousin she might be able to build a friendship with.

She still had that fragment of a dream. The Elite Ops had at least given her the ability to walk away safe.

"Tehya." The sound of his voice, the regret returning, was tearing her apart.

She didn't want this. She should have never pushed him, she should have walked out of here and kept the dreams rather than the reality.

Touching him, being touched by him, feeling the first orgasm of her life that she hadn't given herself, would destroy her now. Because she knew what it could be. She knew what she was losing, and it would haunt her every day of her life.

"I need some time." She swallowed tightly realizing his

sense of responsibility wouldn't allow him to leave her alone otherwise.

"I can give you time." He nodded slowly. "But not indefinitely, Tehya. The day will come soon when we'll talk about this."

No, it wouldn't. When the transportation team arrived to haul away her belongings, she would already be gone. She couldn't stay here, couldn't bear to see him, even another moment. If she didn't leave before morning came, then she would beg. And God knew, she didn't want to beg for a love he couldn't give her.

"Of course we will." She crossed her arms over her breasts and turned away from him as she moved to the open kitchen. "We'll talk."

They wouldn't talk, because there was nothing for them to talk about.

"I'll see you in the morning," he stated.

And Tehya nodded. It was another lie. They wouldn't talk in the morning, he wouldn't see her in the morning, because she wouldn't be here.

She didn't hear him move, she felt him move. She felt him coming closer to her and tensed, knowing that the connection to him would be severed forever once she walked out of the base.

It was just over. There were no more chances to capture his heart.

She had failed. The most important dream she had ever had, and she had failed.

His hands settled on her shoulders, his hold implacable as he turned her until he could pull her against his chest.

"I should have never touched you, Tey," he whispered as his lips brushed against her hair. "You're too important to me to lose you this way."

Her teeth clenched. She was going to lose it. Tears thickened her throat, pooled in her eyes. The agony racing through her was tearing her apart second by second until her heart felt like a ragged wound in her chest. She wanted to scream, to cry, to beg, and she thanked God her pride held her back.

"It wouldn't have changed anything," she informed him, amazed that she could speak, that she could breathe through the pain. "Just go away, Jordan. I'll have it all together in the morning and we'll forget it ever happened."

She would never forget it. She had thought that if she could force him to admit he wanted her, she would have a chance at his heart. She had never imagined it would become one night only. What a childishly romantic thought. She of all people should know better than to believe in fairy tales.

"Tehya." The grimace that tightened his face broke her heart.

That expression said it all. The tightening of his lips, the chill in his eyes. Dealing with her emotions, dealing with the fact that she had expected more, was a duty he'd rather be well rid of, no matter what he said.

She should have been thankful he had allowed her on the team. She, the daughter of the enemy who had murdered his friend, who had been instrumental in nearly destroying his nephew. She might have killed Sorrel, but she still had his blood. She was still his daughter. And she should have known Jordan would have never been able to love someone so closely related to such an enemy.

"We'll talk in the morning." Her voice was thicker. She was so close to crying it was humiliating. In that moment she hated the emotions that raged through her. She wished she could be hard, cold, that she could feel only that twinge of regret that she didn't have the emotional capacity to care for anyone outside friendship as he did.

She watched as his head turned, his jaw tightened. Then he gave a brief, hard nod before striding to the door.

"We *will* discuss this in the morning," he informed her, then opened the door and left the suite.

And then the tears fell.

The sob that tore from her shocked her. She'd been certain she could hold it in. Her knees weakened to the point that she nearly fell to the floor as her hands pressed tight and hard into the clenching muscles of her stomach.

The emotional pain hurt worse than a bullet.

She could feel the ragged, gaping hole in her chest where her heart had once been, and the agony of it was a horrible realization. She felt as though she were dying inside. As though a part of her soul were being ripped away from her.

She hadn't thought it would hurt this bad.

She hadn't imagined it would be this hard to face.

Returning to the bedroom, she quickly dressed in jeans, T-shirt, boots. A leather jacket was thrown over the duffel bag she had packed in the closet. A smaller backpack sat next to it.

The moving team had the address and instructions for handling her belongings. They would be stored for the time being, because she had no place to go.

All she knew was that there was no way she could face Jordan when morning came. That the ragged pain in her chest would only turn to anger, and she didn't want the love to turn to hatred.

There was nothing left to do but to leave before she was forced to face him again. Before she could push him again, before she could plead with him to love her, beg him to tell her why he didn't.

Before she broke down completely and a lifetime of pain and grief overwhelmed her.

How silly of her to believe he could love her when no one else ever had.

Jordan knew Tehya was gone the second he entered her suite. There was such a sense of emptiness, of abandonment, that it was unmistakable. The effect it had on him was undeniable.

She was gone.

His chest tightened with a ragged pain that had his teeth clenching, his fingers fisting. The need to hit something tore through him, nearly overwhelming his self-control.

A violent, bitter curse escaped his lips before he could cut off the sound.

Breathing out a weary sigh, he shoved his hands in his pockets and moved through the large set of rooms anyway. Just to be certain.

If she had taken anything with her, it wasn't much. Perhaps a few changes of clothes, he thought as he checked the closet, only to see stacked boxes within them marked "Clothes." He found the same thing throughout the rest of the suite. Boxes neatly packed, closed and taped. Tehya's life reduced to less than a quarter of the capacity of the moving van arriving to relocate her.

He found himself swallowing tightly, his throat oddly blocked at the realization of how little Tehya had amassed over the years. Unlike the other agents, she had no secondary home, no family to go back to, no other house in which to store her belongings. She'd had nothing but the Elite Ops.

And now, she had no one.

A hard grimace contorted his face before he could control it, a result of the hard ache that clenched his chest. Fuck, he missed her already. Her laughter, her shy smiles, her almost innocent sensuality and affection for him.

He should have never taken her. Or perhaps, after taking her he should have taken her again, and again. until she was too tired to run

Turning, he strode from the suite and headed for the garage area, wondering which vehicle she had taken.

Standing in front of the empty slot where his favorite had sat, he almost grinned. She had chosen the black Viper over the many more expensive performance vehicles available. His favorite. The one he had driven more often and had claimed over the years.

Had she taken the Viper because it was the only part of him she could leave with?

She had taken much more with her than she guessed. Already he could feel the empty ache, the dark, brutal core of unrequited need throbbing in his soul.

But she was alive, he told himself as that ache threatened to roll over to grief. She wasn't in his life, but she had a chance to have a life now. A chance to live rather than hide from the past that had haunted her.

That didn't stop that ragged hole in his heart from bleeding, though, and damn if he had expected that. He'd expected regret, hell, he'd known he would miss her. But the ache radiating in his chest wasn't just regret. He didn't just miss her.

His nostrils flared as he breathed in hard and turned sharply from the parking area to stride back to his own suite.

He had let her go; holding on to her wasn't an option. Whatever he was feeling would eventually go away, he assured himself. She had been a part of his life for too long, tempting him, trying to draw closer to him, wiggling her way inside him despite his defenses.

And it fucking hurt to lose her.

But he had lost before. Friends, lovers, coworkers. The violence that permeated the life he lived had taken them from him.

He contented himself with the fact that Tehya was alive, she was breathing, and one day she would love someone. She would laugh with him, sleep with him. She would have a life, she had never had the chance to have one before.

He had made certain she would have that chance now.

And it was too late to turn back now.

CHAPTER 1

Nine months later
Alpine, Texas

"She's been located. Hagerstown, Maryland, identity Teylor Johnson, age thirty. Current owner, Landscape Dreams. Someone's tracked her and a team's been sent to the area."

Jordan stared at the horizon while the sun set behind the family cemetery as Travis "Black Jack" Caine finished the unexpected report.

Jordan could feel a sensation akin to a fist in the pit of his stomach as instinct warned him more was coming. Behind him, he could feel his nephew Rory's gaze suddenly trained on him, sharp, suspicious.

"Who?" Who did he need to kill to protect her?

A heavy breath of frustration came over the line. "Ira Arthurs and Mark Tenneyson, former Sorrel associates. They received a message Sorrel's daughter did not die in that explosion in Afghanistan. No word yet on origination of the message. She was identified as Tehya Fitzhugh, daughter to Joseph Fitzhugh, formerly known as Sorrel. A team is being dispatched from France tonight to verify the information, and her location."

"What tipped them off?"

"I can't get that information," the former agent answered. "All I have is someone sent the message from the U.S. An interested party aware of the interest in the truth of her death and-or her location. And supposedly neither can the two men sent to check the report that the explosion was a setup. I have men trying to track the origination of the message, but they're not certain it can be done."

The explosion the Elite Ops had set up had been staged to appear as though Tehya Fitzhugh had been eliminated by several of her father's associates, who were dead now as well.

"Did you verify her location?" Jordan finally asked as the sun dipped farther behind the marble gravestone that marked his mother's grave.

"The location is correct," Travis reported. "I checked it out myself. She's there, living quietly, making no waves. She bought a small landscaping design and construction company just after arriving there. The report I have says a team is being prepped to head out tonight to verify as well as acquire her for an 'interested party.' Details are sketchy, but there's no doubt she's at risk."

"Why?" Jordan bit out. "Sorrel's dead and his organization disbanded. Why the fuck does anyone care?"

"More information I can't uncover," Travis informed him with a frustrated bite to his tone. "I've been working on this twenty-four hours straight, and I can't find out anything more from any of my sources. I've tried contacting her, but her phone goes straight to voice mail and she doesn't return the calls. I tried tracking the sat phone, but for some reason it's not turning up a location and she doesn't have a landline or another cell phone in operation that I've been able to discover. Do you want Bailey and me to head to Hagerstown ourselves?"

Jordan wiped his hand over his face slowly. "I have a team," he finally told him. "I want to get out there first and access, but contact Heat Seeker and the others. You're on call. If her identity is in question, then we could be up the creek here."

It was more than their asses going into the fire, though. It was Tehya. He'd promised her the fear of the past was over, and that no one would know who she was, or where she was.

"That was my thought as well," Travis answered. "I'll put the call out."

Jordan disconnected before turning slowly and staring at the nephew that had somehow grown harder over the years. Rory, named for Jordan's father, Riordan Malone Sr. At thirty-two Rory had finally grown into himself. His body had matured, his blue eyes hardened, his face acquired strong, lean lines. Hell, he was almost a replica of Noah before the reconstruction to his face.

He'd been working with the Elite Ops backup team in conjunction with a group of army Rangers whose commander Jordan had worked with several times.

Ethan Cooper and his team of Rangers had been deemed unfit for service because of various physical injuries. They were a highly fit fighting force, though, and often worked as "assets" to various agencies until Jordan had picked them up to work with the Elite Ops backup team.

Rory had somehow managed to insert himself into that team, despite Jordan's objections.

Rory straightened from his position against the post, his blue eyes narrowed as he glanced around, nearly causing Jordan to smile.

They all did that. Him, Rory, and Noah Blake. They were checking to be certain their grandpop was nowhere close, listening.

"He's at Dad's," Jordan informed his nephew.

Rory's lips quirked for a second before his expression once more became all business. "They found Tey?"

Jordan gave a short nod. "I need to follow up with a few sources before I go to her. I want you to contact Turk and the two of you meet up in Hagerstown asap. I'll have Travis forward the information to you. Watch her, nothing else. Don't take your eyes off her, Rory. If she's taken, then just follow until the team can get there. You're my only link to her if her father's enemies snatch her before I can get there."

"I'm calling in Iron and Casy," Rory decided. "They can back us up if needed. Two men on this may not be enough. I want two sets of eyes at all times and we can relieve each other that way."

Damn, Rory was turning into a hell of a covert operative

for a team of men who weren't even supposed to be in service any longer.

"Head out." Jordan gave him a sharp nod as he mentally began going over the checklist of preparations needed. "I'll call this evening with an update on my arrival. I should be only hours behind you." He paused, and almost grimaced before his lips parted with words he had no idea how to speak. He couldn't find the words to tell Rory how important this was.

His lips clamped shut again.

"No fears, Jordan." Rory took pity on him. "I understand. She's like Sabella, right? Priority."

That was what Sabella had been when word had come through that her first husband, Nathan Malone, was dead. Jordan had known better, but he couldn't tell Rory that at the time. He'd simply told the boy that Sabella was priority. They were protecting her for Nathan, because that was where Nathan's heart survived.

Jordan wasn't going to look into the fact that Rory had picked up on something where Tehya was concerned. He sure as hell wasn't going to search that mishmash of fucking emotions he couldn't seem to get a handle on in his own soul.

All he knew was that nothing could happen to Tehya. He hadn't had a chance to figure out what he felt yet. He hadn't had a chance to decide the pros and cons of a decision he knew he'd been making for the past nine months. He hadn't had a chance to see her smile again, laugh again, or piss her off again. He hadn't had the chance to make love to her again.

And he'd be damned if he'd allow anyone to take those chances from him.

Especially not a past that should have been dead and buried eight years before at the same time her father, Sorrel, had died.

Hagerstown, Maryland

The back of her neck was itching.

Tehya rubbed at her nape, her fingers pushing beneath

the heavy fall of rich red-gold curls as they cascaded down her back. As she glanced around the narrow confines of Friendly's Bar, her lips thinned in irritation.

Nine months away from the Elite Ops wasn't nearly enough, it seemed. The paranoia that had been part of the life she had lived before Jordan had taken her into the group had returned now.

She had officially been free for nine months. It felt like yesterday.

"Your turn there, Tey." Voice slurred, body weaving, the customer she was shooting pool with called her attention back to the game.

"Got it, Casey," she murmured, the music from the juke-box covering her response as she sank the eight ball and shot him a teasing smile before snapping up the wager they had on the game.

" 'Nother game," Casey announced, glaring at the table as though it were the table's fault rather than his own that he'd lost the small wager.

"Not tonight, Casey." She gave a quick shake of her head as she glanced around the room once again. "Sober up first."

She swore she could feel eyes watching her, someone stalking her. She'd felt that way for weeks now. No matter where she went or what she did, she had that feeling of im-pending danger stalking her.

There couldn't be any danger, though. She was as careful, as cautious, here as she had been most of her life. She never caught anyone tailing her or managed to glimpse anyone tracking her. No one seemed unusually interested in her, and no one appeared to be lingering where they shouldn't.

The security systems attached to her car as well as sur-rounding her home never caught anyone sitting in surveil-lance. No one attempted to break in, nor did they attempt to slip onto her property.

The back of her neck was still itching like hell, though. That primal survival instinct was in high gear, making her restless and ill at ease.

Crossing the small, empty dance floor, she headed back

to the bar and ordered another beer as she laid several dollars on the scarred wood slab.

Kyle, the bartender, slid the cold bottle across the bar to her. Gripping it, she lifted it to her lips as she gave the area another quick glance.

There were few people in the bar at this time of night. All were regulars, all had been coming in far longer than she had, and all had passed the background check she had done on them. Well, except Casey. He'd shown up the night before, but her initial check on him hadn't blipped her radar.

So why the hell was her neck itching?

"Tey, you need to get a life." Journey Taite, one of the few young women there that night, grinned back at her from where she sat at one of the high tables against the wall. "It's one o'clock on a Saturday morning, shouldn't you be, like, sharing time with a lover or something at your advanced age?" There was a teasing snicker on the younger girl's face, amusement gleaming in her green eyes.

It broke her heart every time she looked at the other girl, just as it had the day Teyha had hired her. Journey Taite, her second cousin. Tehya had come to Hagerstown to watch over her, never imagining she would have the chance to get to know her.

"At my advanced age?" Tehya's brow arched as she fought back the regret that seared her because she could never reveal her identity to the other girl. "It's called experience, young'un, and learning the value of sleeping alone."

Journey lifted her beer with a light laugh, her gaze more open now than it had been the day she first came to work for the company just after Tehya had bought it.

"Hell, a man would take his life in his own hands sleeping with either one of you," Casey grunted, his expression drunkenly amused. "I'd be scared."

"Naw, Casey, you'd just be drunk. You'd never remember," Journey teased as she pushed back the shoulder-length, ribbon-straight strands of sunlit red and gold hair. Both the red as well as the streaks of gold were natural, blending and

mingling to a color that was unique to the Taite women.
Tehya had darkened her own hair when she left the ops, simply because of that unusual trait.

The red of her hair was darker, the highlights less natural
and applied in her bathroom.

It was attractive, close enough to a natural blend of sunlit
and red-gold hues, but closer to a strawberry blond than that
of Journey.

Tehya tipped her beer to the younger girl as she held back
her laughter due to the little pout on Casey's face.

He was her age, perhaps a few years older. He was cute,
built like a damned tank but acting more like a gentle giant.

He was one of the newer customers at the bar and a recent
employee at the lumberyard next door to the landscaping
company Tehya had bought six months before.

He'd been coming in for the past few nights, since moving
to the area from Florida. A former army Ranger, he'd been
discharged for medical reasons, though it was hard to imagine the heavily muscled left arm had the pins and rods in it
she knew it had. Her investigation of him had been perhaps
more in-depth than others simply because of his military
background.

"Wicked women," Casey grunted as he rubbed at his
cheek before sliding onto a barstool next to Journey. "Ya just
wanna make a grown man cry is all." Chocolate-brown eyes
blinked back at her as he gave her a drunkenly charming
rogue's smile.

Tehya rolled her eyes and Journey nearly snorted the sip
of beer she had taken as laughter choked her.

"And on that note, it's time for me to say good night."
Tehya rose from the barstool, the sensation at her neck becoming a constant irritant.

Casey sighed lustily. "She's desertin' me, Journ. My heart's
abreakin'."

"Your heart's drowning in booze, Casey," Journey accused
him with a laugh. "Come on, I'll cheat you at a game of pool
before I head on home myself."

Casey's eyes widened in pleasure as he staggered to his feet.

"You're on." His grin was slightly lopsided as Tehya turned to leave, her gaze moving around the bar again, touching on faces, searching for anything, anyone, out of the ordinary, and finding nothing.

"Later, Teylor," the bartender called out as she moved to the door, causing her to almost pause, to betray herself with her unfamiliarity with her own name, even after nine months.

Teylor. She still wasn't used to the name. It wasn't familiar, and it didn't feel like her. But it was the name Jordan had picked out, the identity he had wanted her to have, so she had gone with it.

"Later." Lifting her hand, she called out a farewell as she left by the back entrance, entering a small Laundromat before stepping out into the parking lot.

The parking area was small, barely large enough for a dozen vehicles. She didn't dare park the Viper there, she was terrified a customer would leave a little too inebriated and swipe the expensive little car.

It was her pride and joy. The only thing she had that Jordan had seemed to care about. And all she had left to remember her time with him.

A damned car. How sad was that? Even sadder was the fact that having it gave her some small measure of comfort.

Loping across the street, she moved quickly to the shadowed area where she had parked the car as she held the large key she carried for safety between her fingers.

When she stepped to the curb she hit the ignition switch to the Viper remote. Lights came on, the motor revved. Rounding the back of the vehicle, she pressed the door locks and within seconds was sitting securely in the driver's seat.

Before sliding the car into gear, she programmed the security device attached to the vehicle and waited for a notification of any potential devices that could have been attached to the undercarriage.

A tracker or explosives. Either would have been all she needed to tell her that itch at the back of her neck was right.

There was no notification. *"System Clear."* The words flashed against the digital screen, assuring her the car was secure.

She had lived too long in the shadows, spent too many years hiding and worrying before Jordan had taken her into the Elite Ops. That had to be the reason for her growing paranoia now. She simply wasn't used to any sense of freedom.

Accelerating out of the parking lot and pulling onto the street, Tehya tried to tell herself those years were just catching up on her. She didn't know how to relax and live rather than fight and run. She simply didn't know how to be free. Even driving home, the roads nearly deserted, and still, she was searching for shadows.

The drive back to her small house was quick, the lack of traffic on the streets assuring her she wasn't followed. But her neck was still aching, her senses still on alert.

At any other time in the past, she would have left the area once this feeling hit. She would have packed up and run. Hell, this was the longest she had ever lived anywhere other than the suite at the Elite Ops base, anyway. She had lived there for six years. For a while, she had had something resembling a family and a home. She hadn't realized how thin that resemblance had really been, though, until it was over.

Once the team had broken up there had been no contact. Everyone had gone their separate ways, and although she still had the secure satellite phone, the secure number she had been given, there hadn't been a call. They had forgotten her.

Mocking amusement flitted through her mind. Had she really expected anything more? She was the daughter of the man who had ordered the torture of one of their own. Who had aided in the kidnapping of a young woman who had become the wife of one of their own. The man who had murdered the parents of one of their own.

There were days she had been amazed they had even allowed her to live. Of course, killing her own father might have contributed to the tolerance they had given her in the breathing area, but they hadn't needed to allow her to become part of the team.

They had protected her. They had given her a secure life for the time she had been there. She had to admit, she hadn't expected them to desert her once it was over, though. She had thought she would receive a call at least from Kira, perhaps Bailey. She hadn't expected to be forgotten.

Running wasn't an option, she realized. She had grown tired of running even before she had joined the Ops. She had finally put down roots, and until now, she hadn't realized how deep, how firmly entrenched, those roots had grown until now. Until she had begun to sense danger and decided to try to face it rather than running.

As she pulled into the small driveway of her home, the garage door slid open, allowing her to drive smoothly inside. As the doors closed behind the car and the security display once again flashed the words "system clear," Tehya turned off the ignition and set the parking brake.

There hadn't been so much as a Girl Scout selling cookies at her door. Her neighbors didn't visit often, but they did wave when they saw her. Sometimes, when she was cutting grass or pruning her flowers, they would stop to chat. Once, a nice young couple at the end of the lane had invited her to a party they had thrown. Tehya hadn't gone to the party; instead, she had watched from a hidden, shadowed area at the edge of the yard, both amused at and envious of the innocent hilarity that had often erupted. On the outside looking in, she'd thought at the time

It had been everything she could do to hold herself back, to remain in those shadows. Past lessons were too ingrained, though: to stay hidden, to keep everyone at a distance, to protect those that an enemy might strike at if they couldn't strike at her.

It was best not to have friends, but she had neighbors, and she enjoyed that. She saw the same people everyday and the routine was treasured.

The block she lived on was peaceful. It was quiet and serene. In the six months since she had moved into the house she thought she may have felt a part of her soul healing.

So what the hell had her senses on high alert?

Sliding from the car, she closed the door softly before moving to the entrance leading into the kitchen through a connecting door.

The security wired into the house had dim lighting flipping on as she opened the door. She hated coming into a dark house. She hated coming into an empty house.

Maybe it was time to get a cat. Or better yet, one of those little toy dogs she had always wanted. Because if this was paranoia, then she was going to end up driving herself insane.

Locking the door, she reset the security alarm before turning and staring around the open kitchen, dining, and living area of the neat little ranch she had bought.

Hell, she had bought a house. Teylor Johnson had a mortgage. She couldn't run. She had a business, with employees and responsibilities. She didn't want to run. She didn't want to revisit the time in her life that had been a living hell.

She wanted to live for a change.

It had taken a while to decide the type of home she wanted, where she wanted to live. The minute she had seen this little house with its nice little enclosed patio, she had fallen in love with it.

She had come to Hagerstown because of Journey. Tehya had been keeping an eye on the young woman ever since she had come to Maryland from England to attend college. It was a Taite family tradition to send their sons and daughters to the best colleges in America for additional schooling before they married.

Tehya had watched, she had waited, knowing the girl would be arriving. Journey had arrived in Hagerstown from England just before the Ops had been disbanded, moving into the apartment her family had provided, and unlike other Taite daughters, she had immediately set out to find a part-time job. She'd never had a job, she'd told Tehya, when she applied for the opening after Tehya bought the company.

Journey was family. It was something Tehya had never had. Not that she had expected to ever have a relationship with Journey. She hadn't so much as entertained the idea of seeking her out. It was Journey who had found her. She had applied for a job the week Tehya had taken the small landscaping company over and Tehya hadn't been able to resist hiring her. She hadn't been able to resist getting to know the girl, becoming friends with her, and worrying daily that the friendship could endanger the other girl. She had to admit, Journey was a damned good designer. She and Tehya often drew out the landscaping plans together before Tehya worked up the cost, then supervised the implementation

They made a hell of a team. Tehya hated the thought of losing Journey's talent, as well as her friendship if her family learned she was working.

She gave a weary sigh. It hadn't been just Journey that had drawn her here, though. One of the Ops former agents and his wife lived here. Others visited nearby D.C. often. Tehya had wondered if perhaps one of them would contact her. But they hadn't called. No one had called, and she had too much pride to make the move to call them first.

Breathing out heavily, she moved across the ceramic tile of the kitchen floor, to the gleaming hardwood of the open living room and dining room. The warm colors never failed to welcome her, even on nights such as tonight when it seemed she would never be free of the fear that had followed her most of her life.

The warm autumn colors of the couch, sofa, and recliners went perfectly with the earth tones of the pillows and light throws draped over them. Colorful rugs were scattered over the floors and vibrant drapes pulled closed to ensure prying eyes couldn't spy on her. It was her home, and losing it might kill her.

Tonight, she didn't stop to watch television or grab another beer. She didn't stop at the computer to check her e-mail. A quick glance to the telephone showed no messages or missed calls.

God, what a pitiful life she was living. In the six months she had lived there she hadn't made many friends or acquired a lover, and every instinct she had was screaming at her to run, even as another, more vital part of her demanded she stay and fight. Tehya just wished she knew what she should be fighting.

Stepping into the bedroom, she began unbuttoning the white silk sleeveless blouse she had worn with the leather pants. Her mind was on a shower and ignoring the hard, almost panicked throbbing of her heart. It was racing so hard she could barely breathe as panic began to edge through her. The almost nightly attacks were beginning to fray her nerves.

She should have heeded the warning.

As she moved into the bedroom the lights suddenly went out, blinding her with darkness as the door slammed closed behind her.

Seconds. She had only seconds to escape, or reach the weapon on the other side of the room.

She was ducking and rolling as hard fingers glanced her shoulder obviously intent on restraining her. Kicking out in the direction the attack came, she was rewarded with a solid thump, but not a fallen body or a groan of pain. Dammit.

Rolling across the room, she came to a crouch, straining to see through the pitch-blackness of the room to catch a shadow of movement, the gleam of a weapon. She wasn't close enough yet to the nightstand where her own weapon was hidden.

Cold determination replaced panic. There was no fear. She had stopped feeling true fear years ago, long before she had joined the Elite Ops, even before she had put a bullet in her brother's and her father's chests. She had always sensed she wasn't truly free, and this no more than affirmed it.

She was at a disadvantage, though. She was wearing white, and whoever was in the room with her was obviously dressed in black. Fighting an enemy she couldn't see was a bitch. The only positive note was that evidently they didn't want her dead, or she would already be bleeding from a gunshot wound.

She could barely glimpse a shadow if it moved. Damn, she hated being played with and whoever was there was obviously enjoying their game.

She inched closer to the nightstand and the weapon hidden beneath.

Her fingers reached a folded towel she kept there, less than inches from the gun, when she saw a shadow moving swiftly toward her. No warning, just a quick, silent attack.

A hard kick against the thick carpet and she launched herself away from the attacker, almost making it. Hard fingers gripped her ankle as she twisted and kicked out, breaking the hold and rolling to the side before a hard, heavy male weight suddenly came over her. She was pinned to the floor nearly immobile as she began to fight for freedom.

Her fingers curled into claws and moved for his face, only to have her wrists caught and jerked over her head as hard, muscular thighs trapped her legs. In that instance, something familar, some sound, scent, or sensation warned her of what was coming.

"You're wearing white, baby. Didn't I teach you better than that?"

Jordan.

She froze. For a second, Tehya felt her heart stop just before it began to pound with a hard rush of adrenaline and sexual excitement. The cold, hard determination to survive changed. It rushed through her system, became brilliantly hot, sensitizing her flesh, rushing through her and burning away the chill that had been wrapped around her for the past nine months. As though her body were suddenly jerked from deep freeze and infused with vibrant life, making her feel again. And just that fast, she felt too much. She was too hot. Her flesh was too sensitive. Her hunger for this man was too strong.

Jordan's fingers tightened on her wrist as she suddenly bucked against him, the urge to survive suddenly morphing into something she didn't understand. Into a hunger, a need, an anger that terrified her.

"Get off me!" she hissed, uncertain if it was fury or lust suddenly raging through her. "What the hell are you doing here?"

His lips cut the furious words off, covering hers, slanting across them and stealing her anger with the sudden overflow of need that left her helpless to do anything but take the kiss and demand more in return.

Her eyes flared open, then drifted closed. Sensual weakness began to race through her body, surging through her bloodstream with a punch of heat so brilliant it felt blinding. Pleasure wrapped around her and held her in thrall as their tongues met, stroked, then dueled in an erotic dance of delight.

Suddenly, she was starved for the taste and the feel of him. Dying to take back the months she had been so alone, drifting, uncertain what to do or how to feel, because she no longer had his presence to hold onto, or a day filled with at least the sight of him. She arched to him, whimpering need tearing through her, a desperation to get closer to him overwhelming her common sense.

As his hands loosened around her wrists, one hand cupped her face and his tongue possessed her, licking at hers, and a groan vibrated against her lips. She was starved for him, desperate. The world could explode around them and all that would matter would be his kiss.

Tehya arched against him, her legs parting as his hips lifted, and she moved to press against his thighs as he settled between them. The hard ridge of his cock rode against her sensitive cleft, pressing the seam of her leather pants against her clit and stroking it sensually.

Nine months of restless nights, tortured fantasies, and the memory of a touch she sometimes believed had branded her soul, had all but destroyed her. And now in one brilliant second she could feel the life pouring back into her.

Heat wrapped around her, a wonderful, building warmth that bloomed through her belly and rushed to wrap around her swollen clit.

The instantaneous switch from survival to arousal clashed through her. The abrupt halt of one, the rapid-fire emergence of the other. She was thrown headlong into an inferno of sensation that completely overwhelmed her.

She had dreamed of his touch. She'd awakened some

nights crying out for him. Now, Oh God yes, now, just one more time. His body was hard and demanding above her, his cock a thick wedge beneath his pants as he ground his hips between her thighs.

The strokes of the hardened ridge of his shaft over the sensitive bud of her clit sent hunger tearing through her. Her tongue stroked against his, her fingers tightened in his hair to hold him to her, and she prayed it wasn't a dream. She was desperate to implant each sensation into her memory, into each cell of her body, for the day when it would be gone. To remember even the smallest detail, the slightest touch to help warm her when the nights grew cold.

He wouldn't stay, even she knew that. For whatever reason, though, he was here now. He was holding her, touching her, kissing her with the same desperate hunger that had plagued her for so many nights.

His hands were tearing at the blouse, popping buttons to drag the material from her pants as she jerked at his, baring tight, hard abs. Hard, heated, his palm flattened against her lower stomach before smoothing up to the front closure of her bra distracting her from the need to explore the flesh she had found beneath his shirt.

The bra clasp released smoothly, the sheer cups falling away from the swollen mounds of her breasts. Tehya's eyes drifted open as Jordan eased back from the kiss. Harsh, labored, the sound of their breathing filled the room as their gazes met in the darkness. Then his head lowered, lips parting, then covering the hard, needy peak of a swollen breast.

Electricity surged from the contact as he drew the stiff flesh of her nipple into his mouth. Sizzling pleasure attacked her womb, her swollen clit, drawing her hips upward in a tight, involuntary thrust, as she pressed her pussy tighter against the outline of his cock. Pleasure flooded her system, tore through it, burning past her defenses as though they didn't even exist. Against Jordan, there were no defenses. There was only the searing, addictive pleasure of his kiss, his touch—his possession.

Wicked heat surrounded her nipple as he drew on it, his tongue lashing it with damp fire as he plumped the flesh with his fingers. Sucking with deep pulls of his mouth, each draw sent a rush of electrifying sensation straight to the depths of her cunt.

The feel of him sucking at her, his big body covering her, dominating her, was exquisite. For the first time in nine months, she felt alive. She felt warm and safe. She was a woman again, rather than an automation pushing through the days

"Jordan." Arching against him, Tehya whispered his name with hungry demand. "Oh, God. Harder. Do it harder." She needed more. She ached for that fiery edge of pleasure and pain that he had given her before.

Instead he gave a heated kiss against her nipple, his head lifted, the glitter of his blue eyes barely discernible in the darkness of the room.

"Don't stop," she pleaded, demanded. "Damn you Jordan, don't tease me."

"Witch," he growled, his voice dark, thick with arousal, and she felt the short growth of a beard as it raked against the curve of her breast.

Arching her neck, lifting closer to him, her eyes closed as need burned hot and rich inside her. She wanted to touch him. She wanted the feel of him against her, his hard body stroking against her softer one. The heavy heat of his cock filling her.

Memories of the one night she had spent with him tormented her, haunted her. She wanted one more night. Just one more night she told herself. One more memory. Surely then she could find a way to live without him.

As she arched, her hands ran over his back, his shoulders. Moving lower, her fingers went to grip his waist, and one hand gripped his weapon instead.

Tehya froze, as Jordan's quiet curse seemed to echo through her head. Along with it was the knowledge that it wasn't this Jordan had come for.

Jordan only wore his weapon when on a mission. He

didn't wear it for looks, it wasn't a personal accessory. It was for protection only.

She felt him go still against her, his lips pressed to the curve of her breast, before he moved slowly, his head lifting, his eyes glittered down at her through the darkness. She stared back at him in weary resignation. She should have known he wasn't there for her.

She felt it then, that trembling panic that originated in the pit of her stomach. The restless urge to run, to hide, to change her name, her face, her location. That horrifying knowledge that the instinct warning her of danger wasn't just paranoia.

"Why are you here?" she whispered, hearing the trembling of her voice and hating it. "I think we both know it wasn't for me."

Tehya released the weapon when he rolled away from her and sat up next to her on the floor. He sighed, a sound of weary regret.

"I'm here for you," he denied.

"But not for the little play date we're having on the floor?" she bit out with angry sarcasm.

"No," he finally admitted. "That wasn't what I was here for."

Gripping her hand, he pulled her up. "Stay low," he ordered when she would have gotten to her feet. "Get a bag packed, you're leaving."

Jordan couldn't see her face, her eyes, but he didn't have to. He could feel her tension settling in the air around him and he thanked God he couldn't see her face. Sometimes, a man just knew when there were certain emotions he couldn't face.

Seeing the fear flash in her eyes, or watching her expression change would have brought that familiar tightness to his chest, that regret that he didn't know what to do with or where it originated from. She'd been hurt too damned much already. Adding to her pain, her fear, felt like a fucking sin.

He didn't have to see it to feel it. He knew it was there.

"Why do I need a bag?" Vulnerability and fear filled her

voice, something he had never heard when she spoke before. As though her time away from the Ops, her time as a regular person had softened her.

He hoped it hadn't softened her too much to fight to survive.

"Because you're out of here," he told her quietly. "It's time to move you, Tehya."

"No!"

For the briefest second, Jordan had to admit he was shocked. Damn, it had been more years than he cared to admit since a woman had managed to shock him. Hell, since anyone had managed to shock him. And he had to admit he hadn't planned for this.

He always had a plan to cover every contingency. Now found himself at a loss.

He was so damned surprise he couldn't think for the briefest second.

Which explained how she managed to jump to her feet before he could stop her and flip on the low lamp sitting on the table next to the bed. So much for the order to stay low and keep the lights out.

She was naked from the waist up, her breasts swollen and flushed, her nipples hard and such a sweet candy pink his mouth started watering for the taste of them again. Hell, she nearly derailed all thoughts for safety as his cock throbbed hard and painfully.

Rather than wrestling her back down to the floor, though, he rose to his feet, watching as she pulled a black T-shirt from the dresser and jerked it over her head.

Slender, small boned, fragile. She looked as delicate as a china doll with all those strawberry and gold curls tumbling down her back and those wide green eyes glaring back at him. The black T-shirt, black leather pants, and four-inch-heeled black leather boots suited her, though if she were trying for a dangerous look, she was failing. She looked like dynamite. A sexual goddess ready to rumble. Or ready for a sexual tumble. She sure as hell didn't look like a threat to anything but a man's libido and his piece of mind.

Running his fingers through his hair, he fought to drag his mind away from the scenario where he was fucking the hell out of her, and back to the subject at hand. Keeping her alive until he figured out who had known she was alive and where to find her.

"Someone may be watching you, Tey, that's why I didn't want the lights on," he said, "you've had a tail on you for nearly a week now, and they have orders to grab you as soon as possible."

He watched as she glanced quickly away before her lashes drifted down for a second in weary resignation.

"I had a feeling I was being watched. Stalked." The acceptance in her voice only shocked him further. Hell, she was setting records tonight.

Surely she hadn't continued to hang around without contacting him when she knew her identity was compromised? The very thought of it had his entire body tensing in amazed anger.

"You know you're being watched and you're still here?" A slow, burning anger began to simmer inside him. It was no longer a suspicion she was being watched, she was confirming it. "You didn't contact me, or head to one of the safe houses. Why?"

He believed in contingencies in all things. There were six safe houses set up across the nation, and in each of them were hidden weapons, cash, vehicles, and the ability to create new identities until they could contact other members of the team.

But had Tehya taken advantage of them? Had she even tried to cover that very delectable ass of hers?

Her eyes widened in mock surprise. It was a look that made his hands itch to paddle that delectable ass. "Why, Jordan? Because I'm not running anymore. If I had called you or gone to a safe house then I'd be running the rest of my life. I'm tired of it." The last was said with such exhaustion that Jordan felt his throat tighten. She shook her head then rubbed her hand at the side of her face in a gesture of aching vulnerability. "I'm just tired of it, Jordan. I want it to end, one way or the other."

His arms seemed to ache with the need to pull her into them then, to comfort her. How the hell was he supposed to handle this? How was he supposed to make sure she was safe when keeping emotions in check was suddenly so much harder to do than it had been before?

Damn her, she made him feel things, made emotion surge through him as he fought to keep his shields intact. She was the only person, man or woman, who could touch his soul.

"Pack a bag." He wasn't arguing with her now. Her life was too important to him. He would have to figure the rest out later. "We'll argue over what you will or won't do later, once we've stashed you somewhere safe. But you are leaving, Tehya. Either willingly or slung over my shoulder, tied and gagged. Make your choice now."

CHAPTER 2

"Stash me somewhere safe? Don't I feel important?" she said she turned away from him, and the lost-sounding loneliness that echoed in her voice had his fingers curling with the need to pull her to him.

For a moment, her delicate face reflected an inner sorrow he didn't know how to deal with. But as quickly it was gone, and she was turning to face him fully, her expression filled with feminine determination.

"I guess you better tie and gag me then, Jordan, because you're not stashing me anywhere."

Son of a bitch, he hadn't expected such stubbornness from her. He knew she could be stubborn, just not with him.

"Do you know who's watching you?" he asked. Wondering if she suspected and if it would even make a difference to her, or if she suspected and her stubborness stemmed from that.

Her lips tightened, her dark green eyes shadowed. "I assume it's one of Sorrel's associates or one of his former enemies." She surprised him once again with her answer. "Strange, isn't it? The bastard's dead and he's still haunting me."

"We didn't expect this, but we were prepared for it," he reminded her somberly, hating the dark pain reflected in her eyes now. "That was the reason we staged the deaths, hoping it would put an end to the occasional searches Sorrel's enemies have arranged over the years. Somehow, someone figured it out and contacted one of Sorrel's former associates, Ira Arthur with a message that your death was staged. Someone managed to track you down and is in the process of proving your identity as Tehya Fitzhugh. You know how dangerous that could be."

He'd pulled every trick he knew out of his hat to protect her before she had left Texas. How the hell anyone could have proved Tehya wasn't dead was beyond him.

She stared back at him, her expression so still and calm that for the first time since he'd met her, he couldn't gauge her emotions or her thoughts.

"You're not *certain* I've been found, then?" she asked, her voice guarded.

He gave a hard shake of his head as he stared back at her incredulously. "Tehya, it seems pretty fucking definitive to me, baby."

"You said they were in the process of proving my identity." He could see a fragile glimmer of hope in her eyes, and the knowledge that he was going to have to extinguish it made him clench his fists even as a part of him fought to allow her to keep that hope.

"And how long do you think it will take them to prove you're Sorrel's daughter once they find you and grab you?" The thought of it was so abhorrent he had to force the words past his lips.

"There's no verification of who's searching or why?" she pressed. She lifted her hand to nibble at her thumbnail thoughtfully.

"That rumor was enough," he stated tightly. "You admit it yourself, Tehya, you know someone's been following you."

"I'm not certain," she said, her hand dropping as she bit her lower lip instead. "None of my security systems are showing anything. I've caught no one following or watching me. My damned neck just itches." Her tone was irritated. "It could just be paranoia and coincidence, too. You know how former operatives can get, Jordan. They see shadows where none exist."

"It's enough for me, Tehya." Her instincts were so finely honed to survival he wouldn't dare ignore them. "I don't believe in coincidences, and we both know your instincts are too damned good. And you're forgetting, sweetheart. I slipped right in tonight."

"But you know the system." She waved it away. "I'm just so used to running that I'm paranoid." She gave her head a hard shake. "I need a drink."

Stepping in front of her Jordan stopped her. "No system is fool-proof, Tehya. Even yours."

"Neither are rumors," she informed. "Now, excuse me, I really need that drink."

She walked from the bedroom as though they were discussing nothing more than the weather. Leaving Jordan to follow her in frustrated anger.

"Dammit, Tehya, we need to get out of here. I have a team together and a private plane waiting at BMI to get you back to base. I've convinced Killian Reece to let you in on the new Ops team—"

"Oh hell, no." Her head shook emphatically as she stalked away from him. "I'm not going back. And I'm sure as hell not working for Killian Reece."

Damn her.

Jordan clenched his teeth as he followed her to the living room, watching as she strode to the small wet bar on the far side of the room.

The teakwood bar sat next to French doors that led to a spacious, secluded patio outside.

She poured a drink, no doubt the whisky she preferred, then slapped another glass on the wood and poured another, for him, he presumed. He was going to need it.

"How did you convince Killian Reece to take me on?" She flashed him an irritated look. "And why would you? He lumps me right in there with Sorrel, and hated me just as much as he hated Sorrel for the death of his wife."

For a second, Jordan remembered the reason Killian hated Sorrel. Why he refused to trust Tehya. His wife racing through the rain, escaping the warehouse, a young child in her arms as her blond hair flew out behind her. A child Sorrel had had kidnapped with intentions to sell her on the white slavery market.

There had been gunshots, fury, and disbelief as Jordan watched Catherine Rhyan's eyes widen when she fell, her only thought to protect the child in her arms and the unborn child in her womb even as she bled out before their eyes.

Sorrel had killed her, but it had been Catherine's decision to enter that warehouse without backup just as it had been Jordan's responsibility to protect her anyway. Nowhere in there could any blame be attributed to Tehya and Killian fully admitted to that fact.

"Killian doesn't blame you, Tehya, and he's as concerned as I am about this situation. You'll be returning to base." He had to push the words between his teeth as his irritation threatened to explode into anger.

"I won't return to base, Jordan." She gave a brief shake of her head again before downing the whisky without a grimace. "It's going to end here, one way or the other, *if I'm even being watched.* Until I know for certain, I'm not going anywhere." Weariness flashed across her expression. "I'm tired of running."

It would end in her death. Jordan stared back at her for a moment, at a loss how to handle her.

"How did you find out I was targeted?" she finally asked. "I felt as though someone's been watching me for weeks. Was that you, or someone else? Because if it was Sorrel's associates or his enemies, I would think they'd have made a move by now."

The thought of someone stalking her sent ice chilling through his veins. But she was right. If she had been found, it didn't make sense they would wait around as they had. "It wasn't anyone I sent." Damn, he'd hoped John had gotten the information before she had been found. "One of John's contacts got in touch with him with the information that there was a rumor Tehya Talamosi wasn't dead, and certain parties believed she had been found. That contact was aware of your location as well as your new identity."

He could still remember the pure terror that had flooded his system at the thought of one of Sorrel's partners, or possibly his enemies, getting his hands on Tehya.

"And here I am." Her arms spread mockingly before dropping to her sides. "You've warned me, now you can leave."

He almost laughed at the response. "Do you really think I'm going to leave you here alone?"

What the hell would make her even entertain the thought that he would allow her to face this alone? That any of the former team she had been a part of would allow it.

"I don't know, Jordan, it's been nine months," she stated, the mockery thick in her voice. "You don't call, you don't visit. That makes me think you wouldn't give a damn either way." Her eyes widened. "Oh yeah, that's right, you're just here to escort me to the plane. You've pawned me off on someone else." He caught the hurt brewing inside her now and frowned back at her in confusion.

"I'm not part of the Ops anymore, Tehya. Killian has control of the base, not me. He'll make certain you're protected—"

Expressive green eyes flashed furiously.

"Fuck you, Jordan, and fuck Killian. I don't need your help. You couldn't call, you couldn't care less until you thought the identities of the others were at risk. Admit it." Anger glittered in her brilliant green eyes and flushed her face.

"Bullshit." He was almost yelling back at her, completely losing the calm he had maintained over the years. "I've done nothing but worry my ass off since the second I woke up and realized you'd left base without so much as fucking saying good-bye. Now this? Fuck, Tehya, I'm not worried about the identities of the others in this situation because it doesn't apply. They are not at risk. You are, dammit."

"Why lie to me?" she snapped as she moved around the bar to face him furiously. "All you had to do was call the cell, Jordan, at anytime. I was always here. Not a single call from anyone since I left, and I'm supposed to believe you're so damned concerned about me now? I don't think so, stud. The most any of you are worried about is your own damn asses evidently."

His hand shot out, gripping her arm, as she moved to pass him. "I've been calling that damned satellite phone for over a month, every day straight, and in the nine months before that I called more than a dozen times. Kira has been trying to contact you since you left. I don't give a damn what you believe, but it's your fucking ass we've been worried about."

He watched her eyes narrow, her lips thin. "No one has called me, Jordan. I've kept the phone on me night and day just in case, and trust me, I checked it for calls, messages, and texts, and they weren't there."

The rough, aching vein of pain in her voice had him stilling and watching her closely. She was hurt. He could see it in her eyes, hear it in her voice. The thought that none of the team had contacted her in all this time had hurt her. And he couldn't blame her.

"Where's the phone?" But he knew damned well and good he had called her a dozen times or more before the information had come in that she was at risk. And he sure as hell knew he'd been calling almost hourly until he stepped into her home. That didn't count the number of calls Kira and Bailey had both made.

He watched the suspicion darken her eyes before she moved her hand behind her and a second later pulled the cell phone free from her back pocket.

She slapped it into his hand.

"I've checked the security on it weekly," she informed him. "Nothing's come up, so no one has tampered with it. I carry the damned thing with me and use it for business, so I know you haven't called."

She had a computer program that the phone plugged into. The computer ran through the phone's programs for any hidden trackers or cyberbots that could have found it.

Jordan popped the back of the sat phone, knowing something was wrong somewhere. If her security program had come back clear, then that left only one other answer. Someone had done something before it left base with her, after the more secure Elite Ops information had been erased from it. It was the only way it could have been tampered with and only a select few had the ability to do it.

"Kira and Bailey both called you the first week after the group disbanded and left messages," he told her as he popped the battery from the phone to check the only vulnerability left. "I called the morning you left to chew your ass out for leaving without saying good-bye." He flicked her a look that promised retribution for that little trip.

She ignored it.

Clenching his teeth, he turned his attention back to the phone.

He found the problem in less than a minute.

It looked innocent enough. No more than a small metal prong among several others, yet appearing oddly out of place, set within the small programming section of the internal security chip located just beneath the battery pack.

Jordan pressed the tip of his nail against the prong he knew shouldn't be there, breaking it off.

Pulling his own phone from the clip at his side, he found and pressed the button preprogrammed for her number. A second later, the phone rang.

Tehya stared at the phone as he flipped it closed, cutting off the call, and held his hand out, the little piece of metal lying in his palm.

"It's been receiving calls," she said faintly, but she wasn't doubting him. Jordan had no reason to lie to her.

"It's an additional tracker. It allows the master program to track all calls, messages, and e-mails in or out. It can also be preprogrammed to re-route specific numbers or e-mails," he said. "The tracker is used on phones given to assets and contacts rather than operatives, though, and placed in phones belonging to suspects or marks if possible. It shouldn't have been on your phone." It was only used with those whose trust was in question. Tehya's trust was never in question.

"Then someone at base messed with it," she guessed, that

ache in her chest tightening further at the suspicion as she accepted the phone when he handed it back to her. "Now, who would have done that?" she asked mockingly. She could only think of one person who could believe she was capable of betrayal.

Killian and his team had been at the base several times before she and Jordan had left. It had been their job to clean their sat phones of the agency protocols, e-mails, or mission notes before returning them. Only Killian's team and Killian himself had had the opportunity to tamper with the phone.

Jordan sighed. "It was developed specifically for the Ops by our techs. No other agencies have anything like it."

"Well, then, that tells me something, doesn't it?" It told her she was no safer at base than she would be here. Hell, Killian Reece would feed her to her enemies a piece at a time if he could, which meant she was safer taking care of herself.

"I'll know who did it," he told her, his voice icy cold. "I promise you Tehya, I'll get to the bottom of it."

As far as she was concerned, she knew exactly who had done it. There was no getting to the bottom of it. Only one person would have been capable of distrusting her to that extent.

"I think we're both well aware who it was. Why the hell do you think he agreed to have me at base? So he could destroy me and made it stick. Not out of friendship for you, a sense of decency, or anything else."

"I'll find out." His voice couldn't have gotten any harder.

Tehya gave a small, almost silent snort. "And you think I'd be safe there, do you? Killian and I understand each other, and you keep refusing to believe it. He hates me. I stay out of his way and understand that he'll always place Sorrel's sins on me."

She actually liked Killian Reece. He was hard-core, stone-cold, paranoid, and damned dangerous. He was the perfect commander for the new Elite Ops team. And she knew, in his position, she would have felt the same. She respected the hell out of him, but she was well aware of the fact that he saw her as the enemy. She would have seen him as no less if positions were reversed.

Sorrel had murdered Killian's wife and unborn child; there was no way in hell Killian would ever trust the bastard's daughter.

"Tehya, you can't stay here," Jordan stated simply. "You know yourself what could happen if it's Sorrel's enemies that are after you. If it's his associates or allies, then it could be far worse."

"Naw, I'm too old to be trainable as a sex slave," she assured him. "If it's his associates, then they simply want vengeance. I killed Sorrel and his son Raven, and helped to all but destroy the organization. Why would they care now, more than eight years later? It doesn't make sense."

"And you think they'll simply kill you?" His blue eyes seemed brighter, harder. "Tehya, these are men that Sorrel funded, that gave him their loyalty. The same men who were determined to capture you and your mother for all those years. These men aren't out to thank you, baby. They're out to torture the hell out of you and make you beg to die because you destroyed the man and the organization they were so fanatically devoted to."

They hated her because she had killed Sorrel and Raven, men she knew as her father and her brother. She hoped they were burning in hell.

"I've been running since I was five, Jordan." She sighed wearily, exhaustion crashing in on her at the thought of even attempting to live again as she once had.

The last two weeks had been harder than she had realized. She hadn't slept well; the fear that she was being stalked, that she had been found by her father's friends, or his enemies, had weighed on her, she realized.

"Tehya, there are other places besides the operational base. Just let me hide you until we can reset your identity. We'll do a full facial reconstruct and fingerprint alteration. When we're finished, no one will find you, I swear it," he said. And perhaps, if there had been a hint of emotion in his voice, the thinnest vein of desperation, she might have considered it. But that was all she would have done, considered it.

"The fingerprint alterations rarely work, and there's still

DNA. I'm tired of running," she whispered, staring back at him as the heaviness weighing at her soul threatened to weaken her knees and take her to the floor. "I'm tired of losing everything I've worked for because some entity out there has decided I have no right to live, no right to freedom." No right to love or to have the rest of her life to regret what couldn't be.

"So you're just going to sit here and wait for the bastard to strike?" He crossed his arms over his chest, which was never a good sign.

Jordan was possibly the most arrogant, most domineering man she had ever met in her life, and she had met a lot of men. When he took that stance, he was impossible to sway. Even his men knew better than to confront him at such times.

Fortunately, Tehya wasn't one of his men, and confronting Jordan was something she had perfected over the years.

"I killed my father and my brother." She shrugged, knowing that waiting for the strike would be easier than trying to run from it, easier than never having friends, never having a place to belong. "And I haven't had a single nightmare over it. But if I have to start running again, Jordan, then my life will become a living hell again. I simply can't survive that way anymore. And they'll find out, I won't be as easy to capture as my mother was."

Her mother. Delicate, fragile Francine Taite. She had been tortured to death in Nicaragua when Sorrel's men had finally chased her down, ten years after she had escaped with Tehya. Francine had refused to reveal where Tehya was hidden, had given him no information about where he could find the daughter he had chosen to breed.

Her father's family was obsessed with bloodlines. It ruled everything, and nothing was allowed to taint its purity. Huge sums of money, land, and power were made in exchange and sometimes, there was even force. Her father's family occupied a very dark corner of their superbly rich, exclusive world and for the right price, a blue-blooded daughter could be forced into marriage. Her mother was one of those women. Her father had repeatedly raped her until she had become pregnant with Tehya. It was a fate Francine did not want for her daughter.

Sorrel had still managed to find her, though. Through those hellish years he had murdered everyone who had tried to help her, cut her off from all possibility of peace, and in his demented mind he believed she would actually willingly return to him.

"Goddamn, Tehya." Frustration filled Jordan's voice now.

"You trained me well, Jordan," she reminded him. "At the least, I'll have a chance. They won't be expecting someone able to fight back."

She had learned a lot during her years with the Ops. Enough to believe she had a chance.

"I didn't teach you to be fucking stupid," he snarled, those blue eyes darkening to deep sapphire as he glared back at her. "Tehya, you can't face these men alone. Hell, you've seen the merciless cruelties they inflict on their victims. Do you think I'm going to let you become one?"

Damn, she'd never seen him this pissed off at anyone, especially her so quickly. He was, but for that one night, always calm, cool, and fairly unemotional when dealing with her. No matter what she had done to prick at that wall of self-control he possessed.

"Maybe I just learned that one on my own." Giving him a tight smile she turned on her heel and headed back to her bedroom. "Now, if you don't mind, I'm going to shower and go to bed. Just because it's a weekend doesn't mean I don't have things to do tomorrow."

Jordan watched as she stalked through the bedroom door, her head held high, those damned curls making his fingers tighten with the need to sink into them and hold her in place for a kiss that would rock them both to the soles of their feet. A kiss that would ensure she was too weak to fight him.

Son of a bitch.

His fingers plowed through his hair before he jerked his satellite phone from the holster at his hip and keyed in Killian's number.

"I assume you found her," Killian answered on the first

ring. "The protocol on her phone has been disengaged. How did you know it was there?"

Jordan felt his jaw tighten to the point that he wondered if it would crack. Had Killian been standing before him, he might well have killed the fucker. "I didn't, Killian. I tried to call her to give her advance warning of the danger that was already stalking her, only to learn she wasn't getting my calls."

How Killian could have done something so insane Jordan couldn't imagine. He knew that Killian, possibly more so than anyone else, should have known better than to leave her so vulnerable.

"They're already there? They moved faster than you expected then," Killian mused as though he hadn't heard even a hint of the anger in Jordan's tone.

"Why did you fuck with her phone?" Even he heard the animalistic growl in his tone now, the unmistakable fury.

All he could see was Tehya lying in a pool of her own blood, destroyed before he could get to her because he'd had no way of warning her of what was coming.

And that was Killian's fault. The bastard had dared to mess with her only means of communication with the team. Her only way of contacting him if she was in trouble.

Killian didn't answer for long moments. "She's a risk, Jordan," he finally explained, his tone reserved, as though he were carefully choosing each word. "I was merely keeping tabs on her."

Keeping tabs on her? He'd been spying on her calls, tracking her movements, blocking her ability to receive a call from her former unit operatives.

"And when I called requesting your help to protect her, you didn't inform me of this, why?" It was all he could do to keep his tone low, the ice from disintegrating into full, fiery fury.

"I saw no reason to tell you," Killian answered bluntly. "I was only tracking her, nothing more."

"The team's numbers were disengaged and blocked from receipt," he snapped back. "She couldn't have received our warning of the danger if her life depended it, and it just may well have."

"That was unintended," Killian answered carefully. "I didn't deliberately change those features. Sometimes, the secured numbers already programmed in become disengaged for receipt after the tracking protocols are set. She could have called *you*, though, as you well know. I didn't set those protocols and the default doesn't disengage the ability to call out to any of the programmed numbers. It does however sometimes block the incoming features as well as track them."

He hadn't thought Killian could be so fucking cold, so merciless. Jordan prided himself on being able to anticipate the moves of every man he worked with. It was one of his strengths as a commander, and one that had saved his and his men's asses more than once.

He could count on one hand the number of times he had been wrong about an agent he had worked with and each time that failure had resulted in someone's death.

Had his inability to anticipate Killian's actions gotten Tehya killed, then Jordan knew he couldn't have borne the guilt. Or his fury. He would have killed Killian. Hell he was ready to fly back to Texas now just to take his rage out on the other man. He hadn't lost such control of his emotions since he was a fucking teenager.

He had known Killian didn't trust Tehya, but he hadn't expected him to have actively moved to do something so drastic as to have placed a tracking and security protocol on her phone. For nine months Killian had known where she was every minute of the day. He had listened in on her conversations, possibly known every detail of her life, and it was information he hadn't volunteered to Jordan when she became endangered.

"When this is cleared up, and I have a minute to beat the fuck out of you, then I'll be back to base," Jordan said, the violence swirling just beneath the surface leaking into his voice.

It was a promise, and one Jordan intended to stand by.

Even better, Killian knew he would stand by it. Killian would be lucky if he could walk for a week.

"Your emotions are involved here," the other man told him coolly, and Jordan listened, just for the sheer pleasure of allowing the man to dig his own grave deeper. "Once this is over, I trust you'll see things more clearly."

Jordan breathed in slowly. "If she had been taken, Killian, if she had been harmed . . . How long do you think she could have held out before she broke and revealed the Ops? Think about that. Think about the danger you placed not only my men in, but also your own."

Not that Jordan doubted Tehya's ability to withstand things that would break most men. Even her mother had had a spine of steel, one that had kept her from revealing her daughter's whereabouts despite being drugged and beaten, and her feet burned to the bone, her fingers broken.

"Look, I agreed to let her into my unit, didn't I?" Killian snapped. "I wasn't trying to get her killed or captured. I was simply trying to keep tabs on her. Look at it this way, *if* she had been taken, finding her would have been a hell of a lot easier because of the security protocols on her phone."

"Why did you agree to protect her in the first place, Killian?" Jordan asked, suspicion suddenly slamming through his brain. "What was your intent once she got to the base?"

There was a long pause.

"What do you mean by that?" Killian's voice hardened.

"Exactly what I said. How long before you would have tried to send her on a mission that she couldn't have returned from?"

The short laugh that came across the line was cold and bitter. "You think I would have actually made her operational?" Killian asked with a sneer in his voice. "When did you start taking me for a fool, Jordan? She would have sat on her ass in her suite and kept it there. I have no use for her on any of my missions or in my unit. I can think of much kinder ways to commit suicide here. You're so fucking irrational where she's concerned that you would have killed me if she'd gotten even a scratch. God forbid anything more serious had happened."

A lifetime of friendship had just been shot to hell, Jordan thought. In all the years they had been friends Jordan had never asked him for a favor, just as he had never denied Killian any help he needed.

Killian had destroyed those years in a single, thoughtless act. He had refused Tehya the protection Jordan had once extended to Killian's wife without so much as a request from the other man. They were friends; and that had made Catherine's life just as valuable to Jordan as Killian's had been.

Catherine had died anyway. Shot down by Sorrel. He had killed not just Killian's wife, but also their unborn son. A child Killian hadn't known she was carrying until the autopsy. And now, Killian thought he could make Tehya pay for her father's sins, despite her innocence and the hell she had lived through because of her father as well?

"Then it's a damned good thing I didn't send you one of the best communications and logistics agents that I've ever worked with, isn't it?" Jordan said. "I'll contact Elite Command for any help I may need from here on out. I won't bother you again."

"Dammit, Jordan, what the fuck are you talking about?" Surprise filled Killian's voice now. "I've always had your back. That hasn't changed."

"Yes, Killian, it has. It changed when you endangered her life because of your own grief and inability to see past who fathered her to the agent she's become. If that's what you call having my back, then I think I'd prefer to have Sorrel alive and watching it. At least I knew what to expect from him."

There was nothing but silence on the other end. Jordan waited, wondering if the other man would even attempt to present a decent defense. Not that Jordan could think of one, but sometimes the truth had a way of knocking a man on his ass.

"You're making a mistake, Jordan," was all Killian had left to say.

"God forbid I should see you again in this lifetime," Jordan stated icily, "because you may not survive it."

He disconnected the call before Killian could say any more. The rage building inside him didn't leave room for regret over a lost friendship. A friendship that had spanned almost a lifetime, he thought as he contacted one of the only men he knew who could cover him at this point.

"We're on our way to Maryland," John Vincent, a.k.a. Heat Seeker said as soon as he picked up. "Bailey refused to wait for your call. She's been too damned worried."

Bailey Serborne, the heiress John had married, had taken a liking to Tehya during an operation Tehya had worked on with her and two other Elite Ops agents. It had been one of the few operations Tehya had worked off base, and Jordan remembered the nights he had paced the floor worrying while she had been in the field without him.

"Have you contacted Travis?" John asked. "He and Lilly have been just as concerned. They should have landed at JFK earlier and will be waiting for your call."

His men were coming together without being called into operation because Tehya was one of their own. Because they trusted her.

"Call him." Jordan ordered. "The situation here has changed. Too many watching eyes. Tehya's refusing to hide."

"And you really thought she would agree to it?" John questioned in amusement. "Even I doubted your ability to pull that one off Jordan." And here John had taken to calling him the "Miracle Worker" in the past few years.

"If Rawhide makes contact, he's to be considered unsecure," Jordan told him coolly. "Relay the message to Travis and Lilly."

There was a moment's silence.

"That doesn't surprise me." John finally sighed. "Killian can't let Sorrel go, and our girl is all that's left of him. She's all Killian has to punish, if that's his frame of mind."

Both John and Travis had warned him, Jordan thought. When they learned Killian was heading the new Elite Operations unit out of Texas, John had said he hoped that Tehya would never need a haven at the base, as they had all been offered. If she did, John had been certain the doors would be closed to her. Jordan had hoped he was wrong.

"I'll fill you in when we meet," Jordan promised. "Until then, I'm with her, but I don't think she can be convinced to hide."

A moment of silence filled the line before John spoke again, his voice heavy with regret. "After running her whole life, it would get damned old, don't you think?"

Jordan could only shake his head. "Contact me when you meet up with Travis and Lilly. Security is well in hand here for the moment. It should hold until we come up with a workable plan."

Until he could figure out where to stash Tehya and how to convince her to go along with it.

Hell, she was going to turn her protection into a battle, he could see it now.

What he understood, though, was that it wasn't a deliberate battle and it wasn't even a battle he could blame her for. She was thirty years old, and there hadn't been a day in her life that she could be assured of her safety and security other than the years she had spent at the Elite Ops base in Texas.

Disconnecting the call, Jordan moved to the living room closet where he pulled out the bags he had brought in, then secured the door and returned to the central seating area.

The heavy, padded duffel carried a multitude of weapons, just in case. The other carried clothing, while the smaller padded bag held a selection of electronic devices he hoped he wouldn't need.

He had checked the security in and around the house before breaking in earlier. Jordan knew he would have never made it inside without alerting her if it wasn't for the fact that he had more or less built the system with her.

They had installed it at his nephew's and father's homes the year before the Elite Ops disbanded. She had added a few extra sensors he hadn't thought of and a few traps for the unwary that he could only shake his head at. At the very least, she would have a hell of a warning if anyone attempted to break in.

Opening the weapons bag, he lifted another handgun from inside and laid it aside, before breathing out wearily. God, he should have never let her out of his sight nine months ago. If he had kept her with him, kept her in his bed, then he would have known exactly what he was facing.

He carried the duffels to the bedroom and set them carefully on the side of the bed he'd chosen as he tried to figure out the best way to protect her here.

Thankfully, Tehya usually slept on the side of the bed opposite from the one he preferred. If he was going to be forced to protect her here, then he was making damned sure he could protect her effectively.

She didn't want to leave? Then she could put up with him. He wasn't going anywhere without her. He may not be able to keep her but damn if he wouldn't ensure he could keep her safe.

When Tehya walked into the bedroom, wrapped in nothing but a towel, she was greeted by the sight of Jordan obviously making himself at home. And in her bed nonetheless.

He was sitting on the bed checking his weapons and he lifted his head at the sound of the bathroom door opening.

Jordan's gaze darkened with aroused interest the instant he caught sight of her. It flicked over her, taking in the still damp shoulders, and suddenly nervous grip on the towel.

Lust flared in the darkening depths, and for a second, Tehya swore it stole her breath. Instantly, her nipples hardened as a phantom caress to her clit had it aching in need.

She hadn't come earlier. He had teased her nearly to the point of orgasm, only to end up pissing her off once she had felt that weapon at his side.

He hadn't come for her because he missed her, or because he was worried about her. He had come to take her and stash her somewhere safe until her identity could be changed yet again, and her life thrown into complete disarray before he sent her merrily on her way once again. Just as he had before.

She wished he had just stayed in Texas where he belonged. It would have been a hell of a lot easier on her heart.

"What are you doing in my bed?"

She couldn't sleep with him. She wasn't going to sleep with him. The danger of begging him for his touch, for his heart, was still too close to the surface for her to trust herself to that extent.

He laid the handgun carefully on the bedside table, his gaze becoming darker, more intense. "Where you go, I go. Where you sleep, I sleep," he informed her.

The response only infuriated her more. The arrogance and sheer superiority of his response had the anger that had only simmered inside her threatening to flame now.

"No. This isn't going to work." She couldn't allow it to work. If he were that much a part of her life, then there would be no way in hell she could save her heart.

"It's going to have to work," he informed her, his expression bland despite the lust raging in his eyes.

And it was raging. It darkened the intense blue, made it seem brighter, hotter, as he stared at where her fingers clenched around the material of the towel.

She couldn't do this. Her chest tightened with the emotions flooding her. Fear, need, a hunger to belong. For so many years she had convinced herself she had a chance with Jordan. That if she showed him she was nothing like her father, if she was strong, if she trained hard, if she proved herself a worthy partner, loyal and adept, then she would have a chance.

And still, when the time came to leave, he'd had no problem letting her go. They had all let her go. If they had been that worried they would have found her when she didn't answer their calls. They were damned good at finding people, they had known her new identity. All it would have taken was a little effort.

"You can sleep on the couch," she said harshly. "Not in my bed."

He tilted his head to the side, the overly long strands of black hair framing his face and giving him a wicked, pirate look.

"Afraid you won't be able to stay on your own side, Tehya?" he asked softly, his voice chiding. "That's okay, baby. You can crawl over me anytime you want."

Her eyes widened at the deliberate sexual undertones in his voice.

"Now isn't that a change?" she said sarcastically. "Are you sure you're the same man that regretted fucking me nine months ago?"

"It wasn't fucking you I regretted," he assured her. "Why don't you come over here and let me prove it?"

"I don't think so." Oh God, she wanted to. She wanted to sink inside his flesh and feel the heat of him clear to her soul.

He gave a light, mocking chuckle. "Think of it as an educational experience. By the time this is finished, and we've either saved the heroine or we're both dead and beyond regrets, you can walk away without ties, Tehya. It won't hurt anymore, because you won't believe you love me anymore."

Tehya could feel herself freeze inside. Like an animal that's caught the scent of a predator, every instinct was thrown into survival mode.

He knew. He knew what she had stopped hiding from herself, that she loved him, and still it didn't matter.

"And what the hell makes you think I'm in love with you?" A woman had to have some pride.

He shook his head, his expression somber, his gaze alive with emotions she couldn't decipher. "You think you are now. But by the time this is over, you'll know me for the prick I am. You'll see all the reasons why I'd make a lousy relationship choice, or God forbid, a husband, Tehya. Trust me, I'll cure you. You'll thank me for it."

She couldn't believe this. She looked back at him incredulously. She would have been amused under less stressful circumstances. "Is this what you've told your other lovers over the years, Jordan? Has it really been a successful line to use to get them into your bed?" Surely his women hadn't been true airheads?

"You think that's what this is?" His lips quirked with odd

amusement. "No, Tehya, I've never used that particular line before. Does that mean you'll take me up on the offer?"

"I'd end up killing you," she muttered.

"There's always that chance," he agreed as she watched him nervously. "But at least you'll be free of me."

There was something in his voice, in his eyes, that halted her arguments. A somber, grieving "something" that she couldn't quite put her finger on. He hadn't said they would be free of each other. Or that he would be free of her. And Jordan was pretty consistent in saying what he meant.

She had news for him, though. She would never be free of him, and she knew it. Since that night she met him in Aruba, no matter how he played the bastard, no matter how many times she was left feeling as though he never noticed her, still, the need had only grown.

Whatever held her to him had been born that night, eight years ago in Aruba, before she joined the Ops, when he had finally agreed to allow her to be a part of Sorrel's destruction. When he had promised her she could kill the father who had destroyed her mother, and who had tried to destroy her.

"Fine," she snapped. "I'll sleep in the chair tonight. But tomorrow you leave, Jordan. I don't need you in this fight any more than I want the others here. The best thing you can do for both of us is leave. That way I won't be distracted."

She couldn't afford the distraction if Sorrel's men were truly after her. She would need to keep her wits about her. She'd learned that a long time ago.

Jordan's eyes narrowed. "Try to sleep in the chair and I'll tie you to the bed, Tehya. And tomorrow what I'm going to do is upgrade your security and see if I can't find a way to figure out who the hell is stalking you, and destroy them. Until that's accomplished, you can stop protesting, and you can stop arguing. Because you will sleep with me. Whether you like it or not."

Which meant he was damn serious about tying her to the bed. And she was tired. The last thing she wanted to do was fight ropes or cuffs all night. The one thing she wanted, pride

aside, was to lay in his arms, to sleep, just one night, surrounded by him. But she feared that one night would only
leave her hungry for more.

"Tomorrow, you leave," she said, anger and sexual hunger beginning to burn inside her at the thought of sleeping
next to him.

He grunted at the order. "Tomorrow, we see about saving
that fine ass of yours." His gaze flicked over her, the somberness easing and being replaced by a wicked glint. "Because
I have definite plans for it."

She couldn't stop the surge of adrenaline that raced
through her at the sensual warning.

"Revise them," she snapped, suddenly terrified, absolutely certain that facing her enemies wouldn't be nearly as
dangerous as revealing her heart to this man. And if she let
him have her tonight there would be no stopping the reve-
lation.

This was the Jordan she had rarely seen, Wicked, amused,
playful. The one that sent his agents running more often than
not in self-defense when he had that look on his face. He
couldn't, wouldn't be predictable in this mood.

"Tomorrow, we'll discuss it," he offered easily. "Until
then." He patted the bed. "Snuggle in, sweetheart, and I'll
just get my shower. We can iron out the details then."

He rose, moved to *her* closet, and as she watched in outrage, he pulled out his clothes before walking past her, and
disappearing into the bathroom.

Only then did she think to breathe.

As oxygen hit her system, flames erupted through her
body, licking at suddenly sensitive nerve endings and pushing her arousal higher.

Her pussy creamed in excitement, dampening the swollen, sensitive folds as her juices eased around her clit. She
inhaled a hard, deep breath and rubbed at her face desperately. Control. All she had to do was rebuild her self-control.

She might as well cut her heart out now and hand it to him
on a silver platter, if she didn't get control of herself now.

Because as sure as the sun rose in the east, it wouldn't survive sleeping with Jordan. Or working with Jordan. She was too weak for his touch, too desperate for it.

She had to find a way to get rid of him. He had to leave and let her fight this battle on her own. It was her past, and her nightmare, Jordan was her heart. She couldn't fight them both at once.

CHAPTER 3

Stashing her at base would have been a hell of a lot easier on his nerves, Jordan thought the next morning as he watched Tehya move around the kitchen preparing coffee. To fight this battle effectively, he needed to know she was safe, needed to know there was no chance of her being taken. That there was no chance of his hunger getting the best of him and distracting him. As she was now.

Frayed denim cutoffs barely covered the rounded curves of her ass, the threads caressing lightly tanned lush, toned flesh. It was evident she had kept her training up from the appearance of firm feminine muscle beneath her flesh. The snug toffee-colored top she wore molded her full breasts, and thin straps running from her shoulders crisscrossed at her back. She looked even more fragile, more delicate than ever in the skimpy summer clothing. Almost too delicate for the lustful, erotic hungers raging through him.

She didn't wear a bra and the hardened tips of her nipples pressed against the thin material, drawing his gaze and causing his mouth to water. He remembered the heated, sweet taste of them, as well as their sensitivity in her response to his hungry mouth sucking them.

For the moment, he simply watched her as she poured their coffee then slid his mug across the counter to him. The narrow-eyed resentment in her expression was almost amusing, except he hated seeing her this upset

"You bought the house," he stated as he gazed around the neat open area and he searched for a topic that would ease her anger.

He'd been on the computer before she came out of the bedroom. She hadn't just bought the house, either, she'd also bought a small landscaping company that had gone from near bankruptcy to healthy profitability in the six months she had had it.

"I bought the house," she agreed.

She surprised him doing so. He hadn't expected Tehya to put down roots without being forced.

"Why, Tehya? Why did you buy a house rather than renting?" Leaning forward, Jordan was careful to keep his tone even, his expression merely curious. He didn't want to antagonize her this morning. Too many plans had to be made now that plan A was out the window. But also needed to learn more about this side of Tehya that he hadn't expected.

Leaning against the island, she stared back at him with a serene confidence that only made his dick harder. "Why wouldn't I want to buy a house, Jordan?" she asked him. "I thought I was safe from my past. If I had known the truth, perhaps I would have done things differently."

"Then you would have made that decision in Texas," he said quietly. There was just something about the tone of her voice that warned him that buying this house, buying the business, was something Tehya had hungered for only after leaving Texas. After she had felt she had lost her family there. "Buying a house isn't something you do on a whim."

She shrugged negligently and looked around. For a moment, her face softened. For the barest second Jordan glimpsed dreams he had never known Tehya held inside herself. Damn, how had he managed to miss the fact that his Tehya had hungered to put down roots?

"Maybe," she finally murmured.

Maybe. It was a definite. Just as his certainty in the fact that she was in danger.

"Tehya, I'm working on a safe house for you . . ."

"Then you're wasting your time," she assured him, and he knew she wasn't joking. "A safe house is only a delay, Jordan. Changing my identity, moving me, hiding me. It's never worked in the past, it won't work now." Acceptance, bitter and filled with regret, tightened her expression.

Jordan wiped his hand over his face and fought to come up with a new plan on the spur of the moment.

"You know, Jordan," she said as she stared around the house again. "I've been on the run, one way or the other, since I was five years old. I never attended a normal school, I didn't have playmates, and I never had a home." Her gaze met his as her eyes flashed with pain. "Changing my hair, my looks, my name, my fingerprints, or my location never helped. They always found me eventually and they always will. Delaying the inevitable will only give them the chance to surprise me. What you should do is take your men and just leave. Let me face my past and deal with it for good. I know what I'm facing and I know how to deal with them."

Hell.

Leaning back against the barstool, he regarded her silently. Tehya was putting down roots and now she was determined to stand and fight for those roots. He had to admit, he hadn't expected that of her but perhaps he should have expected.

Tehya had never been predictable.

"If I were in danger, Tehya, would you just walk away?" he asked then knowing the answer, just as she should realize he could never walk away either.

"That's different," she answered softly. "As you suspected, I care more for you than I should."

Damn her, she had the ability to slip past his defenses in ways he could never have expected and never failed to surprise him.

"Do you believe I don't care for you?" How the hell had she managed to come to that conclusion?

"Observation," she snorted. "So, did you discuss my phone with Commander Reece?" Pushing away from the center island, she moved to stand across from him. Her brows lifted inquisitively as he fought to find a way to deal with her last comment as well as her abrupt change of subject and the memory of Killian's betrayal.

Jordan felt the familiar anger rising inside him at the thought of what his former friend had done. "Your ability to call the team wasn't affected," he informed her. "There was a tracker pin attached to the programming. He swears the default kicked in and kept calls from sensitive numbers from coming in which is possible, but doesn't change the fact he did it."

Her lips parted, her tongue touching the tip of her upper lip for a second in a gesture unique to Tehya. Mocking disbelief and an edge of hurt.

"Killian definitely believes blood will tell, I guess," she said impassively. "Are we shocked?"

Actually he had been. Shocked and furious. Had Killian been there with him when Jordan learned what he had done, then blood might have been spilled.

"You never called any of us either, Tehya," he reminded her, his voice tight. "You knew you were being followed, you knew someone had found you."

She shook her head, her lips tightening for a second as the long ponytail her hair had been gathered into brushed against her back. "I honestly thought it was paranoia," she admitted bitterly. "I'd never been in one place longer than a few months until I joined your group . . . ." She gave her head a brief shake. "Base was so secure, my suite there completely protected. I worked where I lived. There was no possibility of any danger." Her breath hitched for a moment. "I thought it was a product of being away from that security and being on my own."

She had ignored her instincts and that could have been fatal.

Jordan exhaled roughly at the thought of the danger she could be facing.

"John and Travis are heading in with their wives," he told her. "We need to find out who's behind the search for you and why. The team that's heading here are no more than flunkies.

Ira Arthurs and Mark Tenneyson aren't leaders. Someone has to be backing them."

"I don't need your help with this." Her expression became closed. "I'll deal with it. I told you Jordan. I've been-here-done-this. I don't need your help."

"And you think I'm going to let you?" He was almost amused to think that she would believe that. Amused and fucking offended. "Stop wasting your damned breath."

Her arms crossed beneath her breasts. "What do you care? You were more than eager to walk away nine months ago. Do you really think I need you around now? Trust me, I don't."

No one was able to make him mad faster than Tehya could. Son of a bitch, she was staring right back at him, actually believing the crap spilling out of her lips. As though she actually believed he was going to fucking walk away.

With that knowledge, with that anger, his arousal only surged higher. She tempted him and defied him for the hell of it. It didn't bother her a damned bit to stand there and pretend that her death wouldn't affect him. He knew beyond a shadow of a doubt that it would destroy him.

"I think you're living under the mistaken impression that you have a choice whether or not I stay here and protect that pretty little ass of yours," he warned her as he rose from the barstool, his jaw clenching at the defiance in those incredible green eyes of hers.

"I didn't need you to protect my ass before I met you, and I don't need it now," she informed him, a flush beginning to bloom across her lightly tanned cheeks.

Her nipples were harder, he swore they were. Hell, they were standing there having a serious discussion while their bodies were straining for sex.

It would have been amusing if the situation weren't so damned life-threatening.

"Why the hell do you think Kira pulled you into the Ops, Tey?" he asked her with curiosity, fury beginning to boil inside him. "Do you think it was because she simply liked your pretty face or your charming personality?"

She glared back at him irritably. "I appreciated the help," she ground out. "I appreciated the period of peace. Kira knows that."

But he recognized that flash of fear in her eyes. Tehya knew damned well and good that she had been on the verge of losing the battle she was fighting against whoever had targeted her after Sorrel's death. Just as she had been losing the battle against Sorrel before she killed him and his son.

It wasn't fear for him, or the team she had been a part of, that had her protesting their involvement though.

"You're more scared of this fire between us burning us alive than you are of dying," he said as he placed his hands on the bar and faced her confidently. He knew exactly why she'd rather face her past then have him face it with her.

His dick was throbbing beneath his jeans with an intensity that threatened his self-control more than anything ever had before. The need to taste her, to feel her pussy, so damned hot and tight, wrapped around his cock, was making him crazy.

He'd lain beside her in that bed last night, pretending to be asleep as he listened to her toss and turn for hours. Sleep had been long and slow in coming, and even then, the thought of fucking her had filled his dreams.

He couldn't be with Tehya without wanting her, without the hunger clawing at his guts. And he knew it was worse for her. The illusion of love trapped the senses, the emotions, and infused woman's sexuality like nothing else could.

"I'm not the one scared of it," she all but sneered back at him. "And I'm not the one that regretted the one night we did spend together if you recall. That was you, Jordan."

Yeah, he had regretted the hell out of it because he'd known that forgetting her would be next to impossible. It had been worse than he had imagined it could be. Sleep was impossible most nights; something as insignificant as a breeze reminded him of her touch. The heat of a summer sun, the warmth of a Texas rainfall. No matter where he turned, memories of Tehya haunted him.

"Did it hurt you, Tehya?" he asked carefully. "When

morning came and you knew it couldn't go anywhere, that it was just that one night, did it hurt?"

Her lips tightened. "Not in the least, Jordan. You should have told me just how easy it would be to walk away. I would have left sooner."

The little liar. He almost grinned thinking of the lie that slipped so easily past her lips but didn't quite make it to her eyes.

"I spent six years trying to convince you what a bastard I am." He straightened as he stared back at her. "Hurting you was the last thing I ever wanted do, because you mattered Tehya. Because you hadn't yet figured out that love is the greatest illusion of them all, and I didn't want to be the one to teach you that lesson."

He knew the man he was, and he knew the woman she was. Breaking her heart had broken a part of him that he still didn't recognize.

"I don't need you to teach me anything," she informed him, her eyes narrowing on him. "And I won't give you the chance to prove anything, new. So you're wasting your breath and your time. Go find one of your bimbos, they might appreciate your efforts. I don't."

A dare. It was the one thing she obviously hadn't learned while she worked with him. Never dare him. He was too close to her, too aware of the fact that if he gave her an inch then she had the inner strength to attempt to take a mile and more.

"Oh Tey, there's so much I could teach you though," he crooned, watching her face flush, those beautiful dark green eyes flickering with a surge of hunger at the sound of his voice.

Moving around the bar, he locked his gaze on hers as he neared her. He'd decided now was as good a time as any to show her exactly how wrong she was. Until this was over, illusion or not, she was his woman and she would be his lover. And by God, he'd dare anyone to try to take her from him

Tehya felt her heart racing, a weakness filling her womb

as she backed up, edging into the corner of the L-shaped counter as Jordan stalked toward her.

He didn't move quickly. Eyes narrowed, his muscular body tall and broad, tense and predatory, he focused on her with an expression tight with lust. He came up to her, trapping her against the counter, his hips pressing against hers, the hardened length of his cock shockingly thick and hard beneath the denim he wore.

"What do you think this is going to prove?" She heard the weakness in her voice, the catch of breath, the hunger, and she hated it.

All he had to do was touch her. She was such a glutton for punishment that it didn't even matter that she knew he would never stick around, that she knew he thought she wasn't good enough for a relationship or to love. When he touched her, it didn't matter that the only reason he was back was because of responsibility and duty. All that mattered was that he was touching her. That he was there, that she would have one more moment of pleasure at his hands.

"I think it's going to prove that we both know we can't fight it as long as we're involved in this together," he whispered as his head lowered, his lips feathering along her ear. "Fighting it was easier when we had a mountain to hide in, wasn't it, darlin'?"

She drew in a hard, ragged breath. "I wasn't the one fighting it, though, was I, Jordan?"

She had longed for his touch, ached for it. For nine months she had dreamed of it.

"No, you weren't." His lips caressed her jaw, the rasp of the dark growth of beard sending shards of sensation racing through her nerve endings. "And now, I just fucking don't have the strength to save us both."

A gasp barely escaped as he jerked her to him, his lips suddenly covering hers, slanting over them and pulling her headlong into a maelstrom of wicked sensation and fiery hunger.

One hand cupped her neck, his callused fingers holding her in place as his lips stroked, rubbed against hers, parted them and allowed his tongue to lick against hers as though he wanted nothing more than to taste her.

A whimpering, desperate little moan vibrated in her throat as she buried her hands in his hair. Pleasure sliced through her senses, enfolding her in sensation as Jordan's arm folded around her hips and he lifted her onto the counter. The position was wickedly carnal, and infused with dominant, possessive intent.

Hunger blazed through her as his hands lowered to drag her legs apart, situating himself between them. The hard ridge of his cock ground against her sex as her juices began to dampen the silk of her panties. Her clit swelled and ached, as her fingers plunged buried deeper into his hair to hold him to her. And she began to pray that he wouldn't stop, that he wouldn't pull away. That he would give her just one more memory to hold onto.

"Don't stop." Desperation filled her as he broke the kiss, his lips moving to her neck before spreading a line of kisses to her collarbone. Her head arched back, languid pleasure flooded her body with each touch.

"Not hardly," he bit out, his hands tugging at the hem of her shirt, pulling it up until he bared the tight, aching curves of her breasts. His gaze fell to her nipples, the hunger blazing in his gaze as Tehya stared back at him.

"Jordan." She jerked against him as his hands framed her breasts, fingertips rasping against the tender, hardened tips of her nipples while his head lowered to them.

"Jordan. God yes. Like that. Suck my nipple like that." Neck arching, damp heat surrounding the sensitive peak, Tehya arched closer as the explicit words fell from her lips. Words that had his mouth tugging tighter on the tender tip, his tongue lashing harder.

She stared down at him, shocked and torn by the sensations that were stronger and more powerful than they had been the first time. There had been pleasure with him before, but he had been restrained, more in control of himself. A control he didn't have now, and didn't bother to try to regain.

Staring down at him now, his blue eyes dark, wicked, as

he watched her, his cheeks hollowed and he sucked at her nipple with such hungry demand that Tehya felt the lash of each stroke of his tongue straight to her pussy. The muscles there clenched painfully, spasming with an aching, burning need to be filled. To be fucked.

His tongue rolled and rubbed against the tender tip as each sizzling stroke struck straight to her womb, drawing a ragged moan from her lips. She wrapped her legs around his thighs and arched her hips closer to him, the heavy length of his erection beneath his jeans pressing heatedly into the tender mound of her pussy.

"There, darlin'," he said, his head lifting as he kissed his way to the other sensitive nipple.

Tehya watched as he licked it first, priming it to pleasure. His tongue tipped against the hardened flesh, prodded at it, then licked over it with erotic hunger. Her breath caught as waves of heat rushed through her system. A second later, the rake of his teeth over the tender tip had her crying out again. Her hips arched, grinding against the heavy weight of his cock as it pressed over her pussy.

His lips parted and he devoured the nipple. Sucking, licking, he drew on it ravenously as his face flushed with hunger. Tehya fought to breathe as she felt the harsh, unyielding throb of need centered in the depths of her pussy. She felt the sharp shards of sensation that tore from her nipple to her clit as he drew on it, nipped and licked it. He made a sensual meal of the tender tip as she cried out in pleasure.

It burned through her nerve endings, through her senses. Each draw of his mouth over her nipple sent wicked lashes of sensation to clench at her womb, tightening it with violent pleasure.

"Damn, I missed you, Tey," he groaned as his lips slid from her breast, kissing the curve, his tongue tasting it as his fingers moved to the snap of her shorts and released it with confident, knowing fingers.

"I dreamed of fucking you." Guttural, rough, his voice, his wicked words stroked her senses as the zipper of her shorts slid down. The feel of him removing the shorts left her shuddering in anticipation. She could feel adrenaline sensitizing her further, making her hotter.

In all the dreams she had had of him in the past nine months, it hadn't come close to this. Even that one night couldn't compare to this, to the heat and the pleasure surrounding her.

Her hands moved to his shoulders, her breathing rough, as she watched his lips traveling down her stomach, his hands parting her thighs and nearing the lacy band of the white thong she wore with the short denim shorts.

She had meant to tease him a little, she admitted to herself. She had meant to arouse him, but she hadn't expected this. A hunger burning her alive.

His lashes lifted, and he stared up at her and slowly removed her panties to bare the flushed, slick curves of her sex.

"I've dreamed of eating your sweet pussy," he said explicitly. "That little taste I had before wasn't enough, Tey."

Little taste? He'd driven her crazy as he fucked her with his tongue

Her fingers fisted in the material of his shirt a second before he reached up and removed them. The T-shirt was pulled over his head, revealing his broad chest, the light furring of black curls over bronzed flesh. The sexy, soft mat of hair arrowed down his hard abdomen to disappear beneath of his jeans.

She swallowed tightly. "Don't regret it later," she whispered.

She didn't know if she could bear it, if she could stand to see the regret in his eyes once he was finished. Didn't know if she could bear to see him walk away as though it hadn't mattered.

His eyes darkened further. "I didn't regret it the first time, Tey," he stated. "If there's been anything in my life better than that night, then I don't remember it."

He could have fooled her. Her lips parted to refute that statement. She would have argued the point if he hadn't chosen that moment to run his fingers over the swollen, heated curves of her pussy. Sensation tore through her. It zapped through her, clenched her room and had her pussy creaming further.

"Do you wax? You're so soft here." Approval and pleasure reflected in his voice.

A shudder worked up her spine as his touch sent flames licking around her clit. For the first time in her life there was no shame in the naturally bare flesh that glistened with her juices.

She shook her head. "It's natural."

She could see the surprise in his eyes. Surprise and hunger.

"As soft as a whisper." His fingers stroked along the wet curves, sending the hungry burn deeper into the clenched hungry tissue of her pussy. "As sweet as sugar." A finger parted the curves, eased through the thick juices then lifted.

Shocked, she watched as he brought his finger to his mouth, and tasted her with explicit pleasure. Brilliant blue eyes burned with lust, as he watched her, enjoyed her.

His expression tightened at the taste of her, his eyes darkening until they glowed a brilliant navy blue in his sun-darkened face.

The sexual intent of the act had her vagina clenching with a sudden tightness that nearly threw her into orgasm. Hard surges of sensation were like electric flames tearing through her body, sensitizing her to the point that every touch, every breath became ecstatic.

"Sweet Tehya, you make me drunk on you," he groaned as she trembled, watching, waiting as his head lowered and his lips moved closer to the needy flesh awaiting his kiss.

She thought she was prepared for the touch of his lips, his tongue. "Please," she whispered. "Now Jordan. Don't tease." But when his tongue licked through the seam of her pussy and flicked over her clit, a ragged cry tore from her lips. "Like this, sugar?" his tongue flicked over her clit, rasping it with a fiery rapturous stroke of pleasure.

"Jordan. Oh God, it's so good," she cried out, as lashing sensation seemed to attack every cell his tongue touched.

"It's so good. I need it, Jordan. I need more," she was dying for him.

It was damp heat flaying her too sensitive flesh. It was a lash of fiery hunger that stormed through her senses with destructive heat. It was his tongue lapping at her, eating her with decadent pleasure.

His hands pushed her legs further apart, lifting her knees until he could prop her feet against the edge of the counter and bare more of her to his hungry tongue. His tongue flicked over her clit, around it, creating a storm of blazing sensation that washed through her body in waves of sexual intensity.

"Yes," she moaned, unable to hold back the pleasure, or her vocal appreciation of it. "Jordan. I need you. I need you so bad."

"What do you need, baby? Tell me what you need, Tehya." His fingers parted the folds a second before he laid an intimate, deep kiss to her clit.

The suckling pressure, the feel of his lips surrounding the tender bud, shocked her senses further. She couldn't maintain her position. She sank back, lying along the counter, her fingers curling over the edge to allow her nails something to dig into.

She was so close to coming. She could feel it tightening it her clit with each lick, each suckling kiss. Heat washed through her body, flushing it, causing perspiration to build at her temples as she whimpered with the pleasure.

His lips lifted a second before the explosion could detonate.

"No!" The strangled wail tore from her as her hands reached out for him, locking in his hair as she fought to pull him back to her.

A rough male groan met the protest as she felt his fingers part her further, his tongue licking lower, flickering over the inner folds as his fingers began to circle and caress the opening to her vagina.

She needed him. She needed his tongue fucking her, his fingers. She needed every stroke of possessive heat he had to give impaling her.

She arched to him, desperately seeking that final touch that would send her flying over the edge of ecstasy.

"Sweet, Tehya," he groaned. "I could get drunk on the taste of you, baby."

His tongue moved lower, licking, laving, the tender flesh as her fingers tightened in his hair and fought to hold him in place. If he would just lick a little harder, just a little higher.

"Please," she cried out, agonizing pleasure burning through her. "Give me your tongue, Jordan. Oh God, please fuck me. Fuck me with your tongue."

His tongue sank inside the desperate, clenching depths of her pussy with a hard, hungry stroke.

"Jordan!" Breathless, pleasure screaming through her now, she shuddered beneath the caress. His tongue began licking at the ultrasensitive tissue inside her, drawing her juices to his tongue. He stoked a fire inside her that she couldn't escape. Each impalement of his tongue, each hungry penetration parted her clenched muscles, revealing tender nerve endings, stroking a burning need that only rose with each penetration.

The battle Jordan fought as he tasted her, drew her to him, and felt the ripple of tender, internal muscles caressing his tongue, was one he knew he was losing. The battle to simply pleasure her. The battle to hold himself aloof had been lost before he even touched her.

He had meant to show her she couldn't push him away, couldn't force him out of her life when she needed him. Instead, he found himself spiraling completely out of control. He lost himself. But he was finding himself in the pleasure he could feel coming from her.

The heated, intimate sweetness flowing from her was intoxicating. He was a man possessed, so fucking starved for the taste of her that once it exploded against his tongue he lost the ability to pull back. To hold back.

His fingers tightened against her thighs, holding them apart as he fought to hold his caresses in check. And he was losing that battle as well. His tongue showed inside her, fucking her with deep, heated tastes of her snug little cunt.

Before he knew it he was drawing the sweet, slick essence of her pussy, dragging it lower, caressing and lubricating the tender entrance to her ass. It was a pleasure he had meant to ease her into. A pleasure he couldn't resist giving her.

Tehya jerked, her fingers tightening in his hair, as she cried out his name, her voice broken, hunger throbbing through it. His finger slipped inside the snug anal entrance, felt the tender musles tighten as tongue fucked inside her pussy. Her juices spilled to his tongue, eased past it and spilled to the cleft of her rear where he caught it, eased it further back and used the slick essence to penetrate her snug ass deeper.

His fingers pulled back, gathered more of the rich, lush cream and drew it back again, tucking his finger against that tender entrance as he dragged his tongue back from the sweetness of her pussy. He wanted to watch the intimate penetration, watch her take him with greedy hunger.

"Jordan." She wailed his name again, her hips arching, bearing down against the shallow penetration of his fingertip easing inside the tiny anal entrance.

"God, Tehya," he groaned, using his thumb to drag more of her juices to his finger before easing further inside her. He delivered another heated kiss to her clit, as his finger pulled back then impaled her once again as the tender bud of her clit drew him again.

It was swollen, throbbing, a tempting, pink little sweet that drew his lips, his tongue, as he fucked her rear with gentle strokes of his finger, loving the tight heat that gripped it.

He'd once thought he preferred a silent lover. Until Tehya. He'd watched the restraint he'd always seen her use disintegrate beneath his caresses. Listened to her sultry cries and knew he'd never again be satisfied with less.

Licking the silken, bare flesh of her pussy made a hunger unlike anything he had ever known before build inside him. Taking her rear with his fingers, feeling her, hearing her pleasure stroked his senses. Her fingers pulled at his hair, her thighs parted further for him as his finger slipped further inside the delicate opening of her ass and his tongue returned to the clenched entrance of her pussy.

"You're killing me," she panted, the sound of her pleasure causing his muscles to tense as he fought to hold back the ravenous urges clawing at his dick.

He needed to fuck her. If he didn't get his dick inside her he was going to die from the need.

He had to force himself to pull his finger back from her rear, but he couldn't force his lips from her pussy. Moving back to the throbbing bud of her clit, he closed his lips around it and drew it into his mouth, sucking it, laving it with his tongue as a growling moan vibrated in his throat. He was starving for her, desperate for more.

He felt her orgasm rising. As he tucked the tips of two fingers against the flexing entrance to her pussy, he could feel the fragile tissue clenching, her juices flowing, as her hips began to grind against his lips. She was so fucking close to coming for him that he swore he could almost feel her nearing ecstasy himself.

Laying his tongue against the side of her clit, sucking her more firmly, he began to rub against the sensitive bud. His fingers moved harder, faster, impaling her hot flesh, fucking her harder, deeper in response to the hoarse, pleading cries tearing from her throat.

A second later he felt her explode. Her pussy clamped on his thrusting fingers, milking them as her clit gave a hard, convulsive throb and her juices began to spill along his fingers. Hot cuntal walls rippled, spasmed, locking on his fingers and shuddering in ecstasy.

She was coming for him, melting around him. His lips held onto her clit as she bucked against him, driving his fingers deeper, grinding her clit against his suckling lips, his stroking tongue and thrusting fingers, while he used his free hand to release the tortured length of his dick.

Jordan surged to his full height, his hands gripping her hips as he pulled her to the edge of the counter and directed her legs around his hips.

"Fuck me! Now!" she cried out, reaching for him, her eyes

glowing with emerald fire as he tucked the head of his engorged cock against the cleft of her suckling pussy.

"Fuck you, baby?" He bit out with raging lust. "How much more do you want, Tell me how you want me to fuck you."

He rubbed his thick cock head against her entrance. The heated juices spilled around the thick flesh, searing it with agonizing pleasure as he felt his balls tighten in ecstatic anticipation. This was all he'd dreamed of for nine agonizing months.

"Don't tease me," she cried out, her fingers gripping his wrists as he held her hips in place. "Please, Jordan, fuck me." Green eyes dampened with desperate tears as her fingers flexed against his wrists.

His hips jerked involuntarily, burying the wide crest of his cock just barely inside her. Tight, hot flesh rippled spasmodically, milking at the agonizingly sensitive tip of his dick.

A sheen of perspiration glistening on the fragile column, of her neck as a long, low moan passed her lips. Her pussy was like liquid heat, her juices caressing his cock head as he fought to breathe in, to relish every second of this incredible pleasure.

Slowly, his teeth clenched so tight his jaw ached, he tightened his hand around the shaft of his cock and worked the head of his cock just inside the tight opening of her pussy. The ripples of her flesh around the very tip of his cock were like tiny fingers of electrifying ecstasy.

Staring into her eyes he gave her a little more. Just the barest increase to stretch the snug entrance to her vagina.

"Jordan, please!" Her head thrashed against the counter, her legs tightened around his hips, as she fought to pull him deeper inside her. "Please don't tease me. Please, Jordan. It's been so long. It's been so long." A single tear eased from her left eye.

"Tease?" he groaned. "Ah, baby, I'm not teasing you. I'm giving to you. Giving you every ounce of pleasure I know how to give you."

He drew back, his gaze dropping to her thighs, seeing the sheen of her slick juices clinging to his cock head before he pressed against her once again. A little more. Just a little deeper, stretching the heated vice-like grip tightening further around him.

"Hard." She arched closer as his head lifted, his gaze meeting hers. "Fuck me, Jordan. Hard. Please. I want to feel you. All of you, Jordan. Make me burn."

It was all he could do to keep from shaking, from shuddering and spilling inside her that second. God help him, she was begging for what he wanted more than anything. To give her that edge of pleasure-pain. To take her strong and deep. To possess her. To mark her. And she had no idea what she was asking for.

Tehya stared up at him, dazed, desperate. She could feel that agonizing need whipping through her, burning her. A hunger that pounded at her clit, burned through her pussy and surged through her veins.

"Jordan, I need," she gasped, staring up at him, watching as a bead of sweat eased down his temple as her hips shifted, barely working his cock deeper inside her. "Hard. Fuck me . . ."

She screamed.

Her eyes widened, her upper body jolting inches from the counter, as a hard, fierce thrust sent clenching, furious ecstasy tearing through her senses and his cock buried itself inches inside her.

And it wasn't enough, she didn't have all of him. But he wasn't stopping either.

Suspended on a rack of flames, strangled cries tearing from her throat, she felt each fierce thrust as he went deeper, stretching tender flesh long unused and burning it, branding it, with a rapture she knew she would never recover from. There was no cure for the fever Jordan would leave burning inside her once he was gone.

Their gazes locked. Above her, his features were tight, flushed with a dark hunger, as his hands tightened on her hips, his cock burying hard and deep with furious strokes.

Sweat dampened his face and sun-darkened shoulders. His muscles flexed and tightened as she felt her breathing become hard, shallow. The iron-hard, overly thick length of his erection barging inside her until there was no room left, and still, she took more of him.

Desperate mewls of pleasure slipped past her lips as she felt the fiery sensations tightening through her pussy. Her womb flexed, her clit throbbed in impending release, then spread outward. Her entire body was locked in heated rapture, as she felt her orgasm begin to rage inside her.

"Ah yes, Tey," he groaned, the dark vibration of his voice driving her higher. "Milk my dick, darlin'. Let me feel it, Tehya. Let me feel you come, baby." The strokes became harder, faster. "Let me feel that sweet pussy milking my dick."

Explicit and dark, the sexual words sent erotic rapture whipping through her bloodstream. Her body tightened, pleasure beginning to bloom in shattering, fiery bursts, until she felt her body explode. Every cell screamed in pleasure. It whipped through her mind. It burned through her senses and sank into her soul.

Rapture rocked her. Ecstasy tore through her very being, tightening her muscles as it stole her breath and destroyed her sanity.

Jordan's harsh, male cry echoed through her, but it was the feel of him thrusting to the hilt inside her pussy, his body bowing, then the deep, heavy spurts of his semen erupting inside her, that echoed to her soul.

The heated blasts of his seed threw her higher, extending the harsh explosions of sensation rocking through her until she felt herself disintegrating into pure white-hot ecstasy.

Her eyes drifted helplessly closed as he came over her, his hard body shuddering as his hips jerked against her with each heavy spurt of his release, each burning brand of fiery eruption inside her. It was a brand. A mark of possession she knew she would never recover from.

As the agonizing pleasure began to ease, slowly releasing her from its rapturous grip, Tehya felt her body collapse against the counter, her muscles weaken, and exhaustion slowly overtake her until she drifted in a haze of sated peace.

She had believed nothing could be better than it had been

that last night at base. That despite the pain she had found after the release, that the pleasure couldn't be matched.

She had been wrong. It had been matched, exceeded, and then completely topped. And he had branded her soul.

She had kept him from stealing her soul the night she had left Texas. She had locked it inside her and kept it free of the pain of losing him, of facing a life without him.

But this time, this time he had pushed into it, torn down those walls and filled the empty dark corners that had never known peace, that had never known warmth or a lover's presence.

Until now. Tonight he had broken through, conquered and possessed that hidden part of her.

This time, losing him would destroy her.

CHAPTER 4

Jordan drew back slowly, his jaw tightening at the exquisite pleasure of the snug muscles of her pussy caressing the still sensitive flesh of his throbbing cock. As soft, delicate tissue caressed and milked the still hard shaft, a hard, pleasured grimace pulled at his face.

Damn her. He'd never known pleasure like this. Never known a woman who met him as easily, as heatedly, as Tehya had. For the first time in his sexual life, his knees were left weak after finding a release so fucking strong he wondered if he had nearly spilled his soul into her along with his seed.

Lying back, sated, her arms lying still and relaxed at her sides, Tehya looked like a goddess. Hell, like a goddess sacrificed to a hungry sex god. And he had a feeling he wasn't finished with her yet. He couldn't imagine ever being unwilling to seek the fiery pleasure such as he had just found with her.

Heavy lashes lifted, those brilliant, witchy green eyes stared back at him through the dark slit of her thick, red-gold lashes. Wariness, pleasure, and a sensual glimmer of heat, all reflected in her gaze. In her eyes, he saw what he already knew. It had ended far too soon. The escape she had needed from reality hadn't lasted nearly long enough.

Reality was crashing down on her fast, in more ways than one.

His jeans were around his knees. Hell, he hadn't had his jeans around his knees since he was a damned teenager. He should have felt just an edge of discomfort at that knowledge, at this sign that Tehya affected him in ways that he shouldn't allow her to affect him. Instead, he couldn't help but feel the echoes of the incredible pleasure that still radiated through him.

Pulling his jeans to his hips and zipping them, he reached for her and lifted her until she was sitting on the counter before him, silent, watching him through drowsy eyes as though she expected a blow at any moment.

Hell, after what he'd done to her that last night at base, could he really blame her?

He had known Tehya should never be a one-night stand. Her emotions were too tender, her heart too easily broken. And God as his witness, he hadn't wanted to break her delicate, loyal heart. And he had a feeling that was exactly what had happened. He had wounded her clear to her feminine core.

She hadn't understood why he'd stated that sleeping with her was something that shouldn't have happened. All he'd known at the time was that even then, he'd felt the talons of an addiction piercing his guts. A soul-deep knowledge that he would never be free of her, even as he'd wondered if he wanted to be free of her.

There had been a heavy, overwhelming knowledge that he couldn't escape that undefined emotion he kept fighting where she was concerned. A certainty that if he didn't distance himself and God forbid, something happened to her, then he'd never recover. Unlike Killian, Jordan didn't think he could survive Tehya's demise.

Moving back, watching her silently, Jordan helped her from the counter. Holding onto her until she was steady on her feet, he reluctantly released her.

"Say something," she demanded, her voice ragged.

Turning away from him, she grabbed her clothes from the floor and began to hurriedly dress. There was a certain grace, an innocent sensuality, to each movement that had his cock hardening again. That had the hunger beginning to simmer in his loins and heat his blood with a swiftness that shocked him.

"Say something?" He watched as she pulled her panties up her slender legs, the sexy curve of her ass making his hands itch with the need to caress the gentle curve. But, she wanted him to say something, and he was damned if his brain was working yet. Or if he could figure out what to say. And that just flat fucking spooked him.

"John, Travis, Bailey, and Lilly will be here in about half an hour. What would you like me to order in for lunch? I'm sure we'll be hungry before the meeting's finished and any decisions are made."

He fell back on what he knew, on the only defense he had left at his disposal. Distance. Distance from the confusing jumble of emotions until he could properly restrain them

Tehya straightened. Drawing her shirt over her head, she stared back at him, her gaze narrowing at the smooth drawl in his voice.

This was the commander of Elite Ops One, not the man who had showed up in her room the night before or the one who had just taken her as though he were starved for sex.

His expression was arrogantly determined, his gaze hardening, as she stared back at him. This was the man who was determined not to feel, not to get too close, and to make damned sure he didn't love.

He was so damned stubborn he had her back teeth grinding. She could see the pure arrogance settling around him with heavy determination. The cool distance he kept between himself and the world was pushing her back now.

"You're not leaving, are you?" Pulling her shorts on, she secured them with fingers stiff with irritation. "You're just pushing in and taking over, no matter what I want, or what I think of it. You barge in, make me insane, fuck me until we're both screaming and then pretend it never happened."

His brow arched. "I would never pretend it didn't happen as I fully intend it will happen again. As for Sorrel, his organization was so well hidden that even after authorities confiscated his estate and went through his files, they were certain they were missing high-level lieutenants. We could get lucky and capture one of them for interrogation."

So much for cuddling, sweet nothings or time for an after-glow. Sorrel's past associates that had been captured had been stubborn and arrogant during initial questioning. She'd learned after joining the Elite Ops that those associates had sung like canaries once Jordan had turned them over to Israeli Mossad interrogation specialists.

"Perhaps we'll get lucky and it's just a rumor that doesn't pan out," she said hopefully.

John Vincent's sources were damned impeccable though. He and his wife, a former CIA agent and heiress to billions, had built an information pipeline that spanned several nations.

"I doubt it," and he sounded damned confident.

"There's a first time for everything," she replied with a flippancy she didn't feel. "Just because someone knows where I am, or who I am, that doesn't give them a reason to search for me, or to want to hurt me."

She didn't want to deal with the danger again, the fear, the knowledge that nothing in her life was secure or safe.

Looking around the kitchen, she remembered the feeling that had swept through her when the real estate agent had shown her the house and property.

A sense of belonging had eased through her that she hadn't felt since the day she had walked into the Elite Ops base. She'd stared around the sunlit kitchen, the large open living room, and she'd known she could make a life there. It was the same feeling she'd had when she checked out the local landscaping company for sale.

The employees were willing to stay on if the owner needed them, she'd been told. It was as though fate had laid everything she needed right at her feet, and now fate was taking it away.

"One of these days we'll have a home, Tey." Her mother's smile, weary and showing her diminishing hope, hadn't reached her eyes the night she had held her daughter to her

*as they hid among the bridge people in New York City after
one of the many times Sorrel had nearly found them.*

*Their clothes had been ragged, but they had been warm.
Teyha had been terrified, shaking with fear, and all too
aware of the resignation beginning to edge into her mother's
determination.*

*"Just think," her mother had whispered as she kissed
Tehya's forehead and pulled their blanket tighter around
her. "A real house. With doors and windows and electricity.
We'll have a little garden in the back." Her mother's hand had
trembled, her voice had trailed away. When Tehya had looked
up at her, a single tear had been easing down her cheek.*

*"Momma?" Tehya had whispered, the sight of her moth-
er's tears so rare, they were a frightening thing.*

*"You'll have a house," her mother had promised her, her
gaze suddenly stronger, determined, as Tehya had always
remembered it. "One day, Tehya, you'll have a home."* That
memory, all but forgotten, was almost shocking. A little
house with the perfect garden in the back. A place of serenity
and security.

She looked around, saw the dream she hadn't truly realized she'd accomplished until now. Until she discovered that
her past was attempting to steal it from her. Until she had
realized she would rather face the demons of her past than to
allow them to take her home.

Jordan watched as she surveyed the rooms of her house
and he saw the weary somberness that came over her expression, the sheen of tears she was fighting back. In the haunted
depths of her eyes he saw the realization that she could lose
everything she had ever dreamed of having. It was breaking
her heart, possibly even more than he had broken it that last
night at the Elite Ops base. And watching it enraged him.

Son of a bitch, he couldn't ask her to walk away from this.
He couldn't allow her to walk away, which she may try once
she realized the truth of the situation. He'd been determined
to force her to relocate, to accept a new identity, a new life.
But it would never be the same for her. Tehya would never be

able to trust in her ability to belong again, deeply enough to lay down even the most fragile roots, if she lost this dream to a past that refused to die. A past that had taken every other dream she had ever dared to allow herself.

He had to find a way to save it for her. A way to neutralize those demons once and for all.

"When are John and Bailey arriving?" she finally sighed as he watched her closely.

"Half an hour." He checked his watch absently.

When his head lifted again her expression had cleared, chilled, and her eyes were all but emotionless. Calm, serene. But he knew she was a volcano seething with anger and pain on the inside.

"Why are you doing this, Jordan? Why are you here? Why do you care new when you didn't care before?"

"Do you really fucking believe I didn't care?" he snapped furiously, not bothering to hide his anger. "Dammit Tehya, that team is a fucking family and you know it. All of us. We'd do the same for anyone of them and you know it."

That shocked her. She shook her head. "You don't allow yourself to get close to anyone, Jordan, except Noah."

"I've spent up to twelve years with some of these men and six with you, do you really think I managed to remain that distant? Was I distant when I was fucking us both to orgasm?"

He hid so much, she'd always been aware of that. It was another facet she had learned about the man she couldn't help but love. But she was learning these things too late. He should have given her this chance years ago. At the latest, nine months ago.

Perhaps he would be as protective with the others, she thought, but it didn't change the fact that she hated seeing her friends, the men and women she had protected from base for six years, now risking themselves for her.

"I need to change." She indicated the revealing clothes with a slight wave of her hand along the front of her body as she tried to adjust to too many changes in her life, too fast. "Order pizza or something. I don't have the supplies on hand to cook for more than one, and honestly, I'm really not in the mood for it."

She turned away and strode to her bedroom as Jordan stared at her back in surprise. Hell, he had no idea Tehya knew how to cook. She'd sure as hell never offered to cook for him.

Taking the satellite phone from the clip at his side, he pulled up the local pizza places that delivered before calling and giving the order.

He hadn't told her exactly why Travis and Lilly were arriving. He had hoped Lilly would talk Tehya into leaving, but he knew that the moment the other woman comprehended the depth of pain Tehya would feel at leaving, she would pull back. Just as Jordan was now pulling back as well.

That was the problem with having women on the team, he reflected with a sigh. They thought of more than simple safety. Security had a far different meaning to them than it did to the men whose only thought was protecting them.

At least Tehya had been trained to understand, and to help in the areas required to protect her. And having her involved had the benefit of her knowledge of Sorrel's organization.

He'd envisioned a far different outcome to this meeting with her. He'd assumed that after nine months she would have had a lover at the very least. That possibly she had begun a new life that included dating in her agenda.

He hadn't expected her to have bought a home and a business. To have begun putting down roots, since she had never taken that risk when she was younger or while she had been in Texas.

It made the operation more complicated, but perhaps it was for the best. Hiding her didn't ensure revealing whoever was determined to find her, and it didn't ensure her safety in the future.

At least this way, when he walked out of her life, one of two things would be a certainty. She would be safe, or they'd both be dead. He was opting for safe.

* * *

It was actually closer to an hour before John, Bailey, Travis, and Lilly arrived at the house. Slipping in through the patio doors, the four made their entrances at different stages.

Dressed now in jeans, T-shirt, sneakers, and a bra that did little to hide her still-hard nipples, Tehya prepared another pot of coffee.

She remembered the amounts of hot, rich caffeine the men went through while preparing for an operation while they were all at base. Those planning sessions could take days. Determined to hammer out the first stages and acquire all possible information, they rarely slept until it began affecting their ability to reason. And then they only napped for a few hours before awakening and heading first to the coffee, then back to the meeting room.

When she went to the grocery store, she would have to buy enough to keep them going. She'd better stock up on food as well, she thought in resignation. And there was no way in hell she was cooking from scratch for this crew. She would be cooking night and day. Sandwiches and canned soup would have to work for them. She was making that list of supplies as Bailey and Lilly slipped into the house ahead of Travis and John.

"No wonder we couldn't get a hold of you. I'm sorry, Tehya, I never thought Killian could be such a bastard," Bailey said as she moved around the counter and gave Tehya a quick hug. Lilly followed behind her, both women frowning at her. "He needs his ass kicked."

"At the very least," Tehya murmured, though in all fairness, she didn't think she could blame him. What wouldn't she herself have done to protect her friends, the people she thought of as her family? Killian had done no more than she would have done herself.

"Well, no fears, dearest," Lilly stated with an arch of her brows and a quick smile. "I'm certain it will be taken care of at the earliest convenience." She glanced at Jordan as he, John, and Travis spoke in low tones on the other side of the room.

The two women were as different as night and day in

both mannerisms and temperament, but they were dead ice when it came to a mission, and when it came to protecting friends. She had seen that over the years. Along with Kira Richards, they had kept the base running smoothly, and the men centered, in ways Tehya knew they wouldn't have been without that feminine presence. They had claimed the women being there kept them human.

"Jordan said it was your and John's sources that reported the discovery," Tehya said, turning to Bailey. "What happened?"

Bailey's pretty face tightened into a grimace. "We have several contacts in Afghanistan who knew to listen for any inquiries into the death of Tehya Talimosi Fitzhugh. Several weeks ago two of them contacted us along a secured channel. Ira Arthur and Mark Tenneyson had been sifting through the wreckage of the warehouse we had blown up to retire your identity. Arthur and Tenneyson were overheard discussing the information that you hadn't died as well as your new name and possible location. We still haven't learned who contacted them, but we have people working on it."

"Your contacts have no idea who employed the two men?" she asked as she felt a warning shiver chase up her back.

"None." Bailey shook her head. "But when we arrived in D.C. last night, we learned that Stephen Taite and several of his associates had arrived in the States last week to oversee the purchase of a chemical production plant in Pittsburgh. Arthur and Tenneyson were reported to be watching him as well."

Stephen Taite.

Tehya turned from the two women to drag mugs from the cabinet and hide her response to this information.

He was her great-uncle. Her grandfather's younger brother. When Bernard Taite and his wife had died, Stephen had taken over the Taite estate and business holdings. From what she had learned, he had barely managed to save it after stockholders began pulling out following the deaths of his brother and sister-in-law.

It hadn't been an easy time for the family, and Tehya had

been dealing with her mother's death then, as well as the death of the former marine whom her mother had persuaded to protect Tehya.

How long ago had it been?

So long. The same month her mother had been killed in Nicaragua. Francine had called her parents out of desperation at that time, begging them to help her to send someone for her and her daughter. Sorrel had been so close, Tehya had learned, to both their locations.

Less than twenty-four hours later Bernard Taite had been killed in a hit-and-run on a Paris street. The next day his wife had been found in their bedroom, dead from an apparent overdose.

And her mother had died at the hands of a madman determined to find Tehya for reasons she still didn't completely understand.

Sorrel claimed she was the child he had promised to his son, her half-brother. That all she had to do was return to him and he'd ensure she didn't suffer her mother's fate.

For months, Tehya had contemplated simply giving up and taking her own life. So many people had died trying to protect her that she hadn't dared contact Stephen Taite, her grandfather's brother. She had been terrified Sorrel would kill him and the rest of her family as well.

"After all these years do they actually believe I would contact my family?" she asked softly, keeping her back to the others as she laid the mugs out and pulled sugar and powdered creamer from another cabinet.

"When you aided the authorities in France in bypassing Sorrel's computer security and locating the underground rooms in which he kept the young girls and women he kidnapped, your identity as his and Francine Taite's daughter was revealed to the authorities," Lilly continued. "I know for a few years Stephen tried to contact you, to learn if you were indeed the Taite heir, but you never answered the messages he sent to you through the French authorities."

Tehya shook her head as she turned back to them, hoping she now had her emotions in check.

"I replied and I told him that I wasn't related to him," she said. "That he needed to search elsewhere for his niece and her daughter. He never tried to contact me after that but I had to leave days later when an assassin attempted to get to me while I was still at the estate."

She hoped he had accepted her denial of their kinship. Her grandparents had been murdered because of their determination to help her and her mother. She had no desire to have more of her family killed, or to put them at more risk than when her mother contacted her own father.

"Evidently someone is aware of the connection, though, and believes you will make contact," Lilly said. "I suspect thats why Arthur and Tenneyson are watching him while I suspect others have been keeping tabs on you."

"The report our contact received states that there seems to be a rumor that you've been working as an agent for the goverment since leaving France until you were dismissed just before you staged your death." Amusement gleamed in Bailey's eyes. "Quite the industrious little thing, aren't you?"

"So it would appear," she murmured with a grimace as Jordan, John, and Travis came to the counter for the coffee.

"So, do we have a plan C,D, and E yet?" Bailey turned to the men, her tone patient and filled with amusement as she stared at them.

Jordan had always trained his men to have more than one plan. Tehya was aware she had shot his plans A and B to hell and back. Evidently the others were aware of it now as well.

"We're getting there," John said. The look he gave his wife was one filled with love, devotion.

Tehya had once dreamed of seeing Jordan gaze at her in such a way. It was a dream that had died the morning she left Texas.

It was the same look Travis Caine gave his wife, Lilly. She completed him, and it was more than apparent that he completed her as well. The two couples were the perfect examples of the relationship she had dreamed of having with Jordan.

"What about grabbing Arthur and Tenneyson and allowing

Micah to interrogate them?" Tehya suggested, "Surely they would know who hired them?" She wondered if they could get that lucky? God, she just wanted this over this before Sorrel's men had a chance to hurt her friends as Sorrel had once destroyed anyone who attempted to protect her and her mother.

Including the young nun who had taken her in at the convent just after Tehya had turned six, while her mother had tried to lead Sorrel and his men away from her.

Within months Francine had sent word that Sorrel possibly knew their location. Tehya remembered Sister Mary wakening her, the room so dark she had stumbled as the sister helped her dress, urging her to hurry.

They had left the convent by way of a small tunnel hidden behind the stone wall of the wine cellar in the basement. As they had exited the tunnel into the heavy forest, Tehya had heard gunfire in the distance and a woman's screams. The remaining nuns had died horribly that night.

Within three years the nun had put Tehya under the protection of a former CIA agent she had known while in college. He had managed to keep Tehya safe for only a few years.

He had been killed mere days after putting her on a bus and sending her across the country to a friend who lived in the Washington mountains.

The same scenario had played out so many times. A short period of peace. Then as soon as she began learning how to sleep without fear, it had begun all over again.

Tehya had been fifteen when she had received word of her mother's death. After that she had to run on her own. She couldn't bear to be the cause of anyone else's death. To see more bloodshed for a child who was no more than a curse to anyone who cared for her.

And now it seemed, the past was returning with a vengeance.

The thought of seeing these men and women risking their lives, the love they had found in each other, for her, was too much to face.

"We would try interrogation, but we have enough suspicion they're unaware of his identity that at the moment it's riskier than we'd like. We don't want to tip them off that we're aware of them at this point," Lilly explained.

Tehya clenched her fingers into fists and tried to beat back the fear and the panic. "I can't deal with this!" The exclamation shocked herself as much as it did the rest of them. "You should all leave. You shouldn't be here, risking yourselves this way. For God's sake, go home."

She didn't wait for a response from any of them. Walking past the two women, she strode quickly to her bedroom to escape. She couldn't bear to see the love between the two couples and know what they were risking if they involved themselves in this fight. She'd tried. She'd fought this fear, but it was her only weakness besides Jordan. No one who had ever tried to help her had survived it.

Even more, she couldn't allow Jordan to take this risk. Knowing she had been the cause of his death or any of his family's would destroy her soul in a way she knew she would never survive.

The Elite Ops had given her six years of peace, what more could she ask for? It wasn't their fault that the team had disbanded, that their contracts had run out. It wasn't their fault that she was haunted by a past her father had created.

"Tehya." Lilly's determined tone had her pausing at the bedroom door, her hand on the knob. "We're friends. Wouldn't you help Travis and me if we were in trouble?"

She turned back just enough to see them, her gaze flicking to Jordan. "But I don't have anyone who would give a damn, Lilly, in the way you and Travis care for one another. So that really doesn't apply, does it? Perhaps that's something all of you should think about. You have families. The others have children. You have something to live for. Do you really want to risk that for someone who isn't worth it?"

Yanking the door open, she walked into the bedroom, slamming and locking the door behind her before rushing to her dresser.

Her small emergency backpack was there on the side. A weapon, cash, credit cards, and an extra set of keys to the car were inside.

She doubted there was a chance in hell of getting to the car, but she had to leave the house. She had to get away from the acceptance and love she could feel between the two couples. She was so desperate to have it herself, and the knowledge that they were risking what they had to help her made her die a little inside.

Thinking straight, thinking logically, wasn't going to happen here with Jordan demanding to protect her, and the other four backing him without a thought for their own safety.

She wasn't at base any longer. There was little security, there was no safety, and Jordan wouldn't always be there to protect her.

This was one battle she was going to have to decide whether or not to fight, on her own.

"She's slipping into the garage," John stated quietly as he watched the handheld monitor he carried. The wireless reception from the small cameras he'd installed before dawn came in clearly.

Jordan stood facing the French doors that led to the back patio, his arms crossed over his chest, as he forced himself to stay in place.

"Are Micah and Nik in place?" he asked quietly.

"They're ready to roll," John told him. "They have the same view I have until she leaves the camera's field of vision. After that, all he has is the tracker we placed on her car." He gave a small, amused grunt. "Son of a bitch, it's a good thing you warned me about the electronics detector she slipped out of base, because she's running it over the vehicle now. I was able to modify the tracker so she can't spot it, but damn, it wasn't easy."

Jordan almost had to grin. She'd slipped out several little goodies that the team had used in the course of their missions. The enterprising little thing had squirreled away well over a million dollars' worth of high-tech equipment.

And he'd let her. Despite the fact that he had been certain she was covered, that her new identity was secure, he'd allowed her to take it.

Because he knew it would make *her* feel secure.

"It's nice to know she came out of there with something for the six years she gave you," Bailey murmured, apparently following his train of thought.

Jordan almost winced at the not-so-subtle dig. He knew that for years the women at the base had watched him and Tehya, expecting any day that their relationship would develop into something more. When it hadn't, their disappointment in him had been apparent.

"Door's up and she's pulling out, Jordan," John reported. "Micah and Nik are on her ass."

Maverick and Renegade would make sure she was protected.

Jordan had known she would run. Once John, Bailey, Travis, and Lilly had shown up, she'd panicked, just as Kira had predicted when he had called and apprised her of the situation before arriving in Hagerstown.

He was praying that in allowing her to run they would at least catch a glimpse of who was tailing her here. If they could identify who it was then perhaps they could get lucky and trace them back to their employer.

Kira had known Tehya far longer than the rest of them had, and during that first year on base, she had kept Tehya centered on her job when her fears had almost had her running more than once. It had taken nearly a year for her to settle into the idea of being safe.

Staying in one place wasn't something Tehya had ever done. Most of her life had been spent running, barely managing to stay one step ahead of her father, or the men he continually sent after her.

Settling down and accepting safety hadn't been something Tehya could adapt to overnight. And as Kira had known, once she had accepted it, the agents with the Elite Ops had become her family.

The thought of endangering them, like those who had

tried to protect her as a child had been endangered, had sent her back into the panicked running mode.

Those protectors had all died within weeks of hiding her with someone else. Her father had caught up with them, tortured and murdered them. For months after Tehya had moved into base quarters, her screams had echoed into the steel-lined hall outside her bedroom from the nightmares that haunted her. More than once Jordan had been unable to resist going to her, pulling her from her suite and putting her to work to exhaust her.

"What if she doesn't come back?" Lilly posed the question worriedly.

"She'll come back." Jordan turned back to them. "She has roots here now, Lilly." He gazed around the house and thought of the small business she owned. "She's never had roots before. They'll tie her to this damned house when nothing else could have."

Lilly shook her head, her gaze somber. "There are no roots strong enough to hold her if her friends are endangered or if you are."

"Then Micah and Nik can drag her back," he said icily. "Either way, she's right, it has to end here, once and for all. And hiding her isn't an option any longer. If she doesn't face it, if she's not a part of her own protection, then she'll never feel secure." And he hated realizing that. Hated having her in the line of fire.

He had assumed the malevolent shadow of her father had died the night Sorrel had been killed. He had been certain she would be safe then. Until she was attacked in France while she had been aiding French and American authorities in going through Sorrel's estate.

This threat was coming from either her father's former allies, or from his former enemies. Though why, Jordan hadn't been able to learn. Sorrel was dead, there was no leverage Tehya could provide his enemies. The Sorrel organization had disbanded, and those not in prison had gone on to much more lucrative ventures. Those men had no reason to want to strike out at her. It didn't make sense, but there was too much proof that somehow, somewhere, this was coming from her ties to her Sorrel.

"You shouldn't have let her go off alone," Lilly said, the distinct, feminine arrogance of her European accent emphasizing her displeasure. Lilly had no problem expressing her displeasure when she felt it warranted.

His lips thinned.

"Enough," he said coolly. "I'm no knight in shining armor, Lilly. I can't be her savior. All I can do is try to get her through this alive."

Lilly gave a delicate little snort as her husband cleared his throat. It was more than obvious he was covering a chuckle.

"There's a difference between being her savior and her lover, Jordan," Bailey said. "And don't even try to tell me you weren't, or aren't interested."

Jordan glared at John, then at Travis.

John held his hands up in surrender. "Hey, man, she has a mouth of her own. I just try to protect it when she pisses too many people off."

Hell. He didn't need this crap. He should be out there following Tehya, ensuring her safety rather than leaving the task to others. For now, she was his woman, his lover. She was his responsibility.

Not that they weren't fully capable of protecting her, but the male protective instincts rising inside him didn't care. She was his. He didn't trust anyone to protect her as he knew only he could.

"I did get around to researching the landscaping company she owns," Finally Bailey had something to say other than the subtle recriminations she and Lily were prone to aim at him. "I reached the previous owner before we came in this morning. He's retired and living the life in Florida." She rolled her eyes. "The company had been up for sale for over a year before Tehya bought it. There's nothing suspicious there. He absolutely adores her, though. She negotiated the price down by several thousand dollars despite his best efforts. He said it was like stealing money from his own kid until he dropped the price for her." Amusement and affection filled her voice.

Jordan could believe that. Saying no to Tehya was damned hard, even for him.

"It was near bankruptcy when she bought it," Lilly said, taking over. "It's now thriving. She has quite a few customers, many who began with simple, small projects and then ended up calling again for other projects as her flair for design became known. When I called them, supposedly for references, he sang her praises and all but demanded I hire her."

"She has an excellent head for business," Travis said, taking his turn. "I went over her accounts when I hacked her office computer this morning. She's building slowly, taking her time and ensuring she's not overreaching. As stated, she's a damned good designer and she has a some good employees."

"Losing the business would break her heart," Lilly said as she stared back at him, her gaze hard, as though he were somehow endangering the business their friend so loved.

Hell, the two women weren't going to stop.

"I'm not asking her to walk away from it, Lilly," he reminded her, irritation hardening his tone. "You know that."

Her lips thinned as she turned away from him. It was evident the two women were somehow blaming him for this situation.

Much more, Jordan admitted, and he would have to rethink his decision to bring the couples in. He may end up having to send them back to their own lives.

"She's stopped, Jordan." John interrupted his thoughts as a report came through to the Bluetooth communications set he wore at his ear. "A bar in Hagerstown."

"Friendly's." Jordan gave a short nod. "She's been going there for a while." Rory and his partner Casey had been watching her there for nearly a week.

"And she had a tail." John turned to him as Jordan felt his body tighten with furious tension. "They pulled back for some reason, though, when she pulled into the bar. Micah's certain he and Nik weren't spotted, but when she pulled into the parking lot across from the bar, the tail turned around and disappeared."

"They knew where she was headed," Jordan guessed. "There's someone either waiting at the bar or heading in behind her. They'll wait to see who follows her in."

John gave a tight nod. "Whoever's following her here are damned good Jordan. That's the only glimpse thats been caught of them. They're careful."

"Too damned careful and too damned quiet. We don't even know how many are watching her, who's hired them, and not even a peep regarding their agenda," Lilly crossed her arms beneath her breasts as she frowned back at them.

John shook his head as his wife, Bailey, moved closer, and he wrapped his arm around her. "They can't remain hidden forever though. Sooner or later, they'll have to make a move, and when they do, we'll be there, waiting."

Jordan stared at the two men and their very capable wives as they stared back at him, and thought of the two men following her, as well as the one winging his way to Maryland even now. He'd called in the best help he could find to save the only woman who had mattered to his soul since he was a boy.

He'd called in the first, and the best, Elite Operations team that had ever existed.

His team, to protect his woman.

CHAPTER 5

"Hey, Teylor, you're here early," Kyle the bartender called out as she entered the dim interior of the bar and looked around.

The Saturday afternoon regulars were there, no more than half a dozen. Journey was there as well, a plate of Wing Dings, the bar's exceptional chicken wings, and a glass of soda sat next to a heavy text book she had been reading. Friendly's had become her only hangout, Journey had told Tehya a few weeks before. It was the only place she felt comfortable, she claimed.

Journey lifted her head and a smile crossed her face as she raised her hand in greeting before turning her attention back to her book, obviously more interested in studying than socializing.

Shoulder-length fiery gold hair fell over a delicate face as she frowned fiercely at whatever she was reading.

"This is the wrong place to attempt to study," Tehya chided her in amusement as she caught Journey's nails tapping against the table in time to the music. "I hope the test isn't being given anytime soon."

Journey grimaced as she lifted her head and pushed the book away. "A very boring dissertation on an even more boring poet. I'm still trying to convince grandfather to allow me to drop the English major for one of graphic design."

"She'll make a lousy English major with that attitude." Casey stated sympathetically from the table next to Journey. "She needs to simply do what she wants and tell the rest of them to kiss her ass."

"Is that your best advice, Casey?" Tehya shot him a look of amusement that took effort. "Maybe you should give her tips on pissing her grandfather off."

"I would, but she keeps throwing that damned boyfriend up at me." He shot her a quick grin. "I keep telling her Sebastian's a sissy name and there's no way he'll stand up to good ole grandpop with her."

Tehya gave a low, easy laugh. Another response that she didn't feel. Journey had begun seeing Sebastian several weeks before, though she had only mentioned him to Tehya a few times and never with a last name.

After getting his beer, Casey came back to the table and Journey, who was still staring at her book.

Tehya headed over to the bar and accepted the cold bottle of beer Kyle set in front of her. She moved beside Journey as she remained silent, gripped the bottle and sipped.

Hell, why had she run here? Tehya wondered as she looked around the small bar. Journey was studiously ignoring Casey now as she always did when he teased her over Sebastian.

"Hey, Tey, you're quiet today." Casey looked over to her a few minutes later as he sipped at his beer, his brown eyes curious. "Everything cool?"

She nodded absently. "Fine, Casey. Just at loose ends at the moment."

Tehya didn't work Saturdays and Sundays. She usually cleaned house, took care of the yard, or did paperwork. Normally, she didn't arrive at the bar until late for a drink, and to watch other customers while pretending she was a part of the joviality that existed among them.

Friendly's was just what its name implied. No one put on airs, no one pretended to be superior to the others. It was simply a nice little place for a beer, friendly company, and a chance to unwind.

And still, she felt out of place. And today, she definitely

wasn't unwinding, while the sense of not belonging felt sharper than normal.

Always on the outside looking in.

Always dreaming about life, but never living it. She'd never had a chance to live, to love without fear, or to work to realize her dreams. And she hated that.

A shaft of light speared through the side entrance, drawing her gaze as she lifted the beer to her lips, pausing before taking a sip.

Tehya wanted to groan in frustration. Instead, she pretended not to see the new arrival as he strode to the table and pulled out the chair before sitting down.

That didn't keep the few women in the bar from turning to stare. After all, he was tall, broad shouldered, arrogant, and had an air of sexy, dominant danger about him.

He was dressed in jeans, a casual dark shirt, leather jacket and boots, and there were probably no less than half a dozen weapons hidden on his body. Breathing out wearily she stood from the table, ignoring Casey and Journey's curious gazes as she moved to the bar, followed by the silent, dark-eyed male everyone seemed to be watching. His arrival told her far more than words ever could. Jordan was serious about this unsanctioned operation. And he was serious about making certain someone was watching her.

He slid onto the barstool beside her. "Give me what she's having," he ordered the bartender, nodding at her beer.

Kyle shot her a surprised look before filling the order and taking the money tossed onto the bar.

"What do you want?" she asked, her voice low as she lifted the bottle to her lips. "And who do you have following me? I know it wasn't you." She would have seen him. Micah wouldn't have tried to hide from her.

"Nope, wasn't me." A flash of white teeth in sun-darkened flesh, the glimmer of devil's black eyes.

Micah Sloane, aka Maverick.

She sighed. "You should be home with your family."

What the hell had Jordan done, pulled in the whole freakin' team?

"Seen the pictures lately? I'm telling you, that little rugrat is hell on wheels." Pure pride filled Micah's voice as he pulled a photo from his inside jacket pocket.

Tehya almost rolled her eyes at the proud papa move.

Laughing, radiant. It was almost as if the picture itself were infused with the love shining from his young blond wife and the toddler, black-haired, black-eyed Trace, she held in her arms. Micah sat beside her, his arm around her, and in his free arm he held an infant dressed in pink. Six-month-old Emmaline Allegiance Sloane.

The boy had a mischievous grin on his face, the daughter innocently content in her father's arms, and the mother stared back with a secretive Mona Lisa smile. She was a woman who knew the joys, the secrets of being loved by a strong, powerful man.

He tucked the photo away again.

"They're beautiful," she said, taking another long sip. "Why aren't you home with them?"

From the corner of her eye she watched as he reached up and scratched his jaw while staring at her profile. Black eyes were gentle, his expression compassionate.

"Well, see, I have this friend," he confided, his voice low enough to carry to her ears only. "She's in trouble and doesn't want to accept help. Then I have this other friend. He's lost his heart and doesn't want to accept it. I'm here to help both of them. I'm a nice guy like that."

And she wanted to cry, because he truly was a good friend like that and thought nothing of endangering himself to help a friend.

"Your friend hasn't lost his heart," she said, knowing exactly who he was talking about. "Trust me, it's right there in his chest, just as hard and cold as it ever was."

Micah chuckled.

"Hey, Teylor, this yahoo botherin' you?" Casey's voice came from behind her. It sounded more aggressive than she had ever heard him, and filled with a warning to Micah. Lord love him, Casey had no idea the weapon he was close to challenging.

She could only shake her head wearily.

"Hey, man, I got this," Micah assured him with an amused, patient smile. "Go find a little plaything of your own, why don't ya?"

Tehya choked as she fought back a weary groan. She really didn't need the male posturing right now.

"It's fine, Casey," she turned and said to him. "What my friend means is that he's a smart-mouthed ass, but he's cool all the same."

"Oh." Casey looked at Micah, narrowing his gaze on him, his expression forbidding. "He looks like bad news to me, Tey."

"Naw, he just likes to bring bad news," she told him. "Everything's fine, Casey, I promise."

Casey scratched his head in confusion, as he looked from Tehya to Micah and back again for a long moment.

"I should just go back and aggravate Journey some more maybe?" he suggested, though Tehya could see the suspicion still darkening his gaze.

Tehya's nodded somberly. "Yeah, I'd do that, Casey."

He gave another glance toward Micah before grunting irritably and returning to a still-silent, studious Journey.

"You know, Tey," Micah drawled, "your choice of friends here is a little immature. Sure you don't want to come out and play with the big boys and girls again?"

She gave a heavy sigh. "I guess you're parked here until I leave, right?"

He leaned closer, his expression becoming serious. "It's like this. I followed you from the house. You had a tail keeping well back for the better part of the way. When you turned in here, they drove off and simply disappeared. Now, what does that suggest to you?"

That she was in a shitload of trouble. That the panic building in her gut wasn't simply paranoia, it was danger. The kind of danger that had murdered her mother, her friends, and had made her life hell until six years before. It told her she was in over her head here.

"Either his partner is here, or he would have arrived within minutes after I did," she answered painfully.

He gave a subtle nod. "And I didn't see anyone come in after you. Did you?"

She shook her head slowly. There were three entrances, impossible for one person to watch unless he were inside. Tehya had been inside and no one had entered after her, except Micah.

"No one came in," she said softly, painfully. "They've been watching me long enough to know my habits, to be able to guess my moves."

"Long enough to know if you have any weaknesses," he reminded her.

She swallowed tightly, but forced herself not to look around. She knew everyone here. They were all regulars. That meant whoever was watching her had been here from the beginning. She had run a very thorough background search on everyone here, and they had all been above suspicion.

If Micah was right, someone was backed by a hell of a lot of money and power to be able to pull that off. Those commodities were essential to building a background that would pass a check like the ones Tehya was capable of making.

She let her gaze rove discreetly around the bar once again as regret built inside her.

She had needed to feel a part of something, and she had chosen this place because she had believed it was neutral enough, that it was safe enough. Had she been more wrong than she could have ever imagined? Who here had managed to fool her to that extent?

"The situation is delicate, then," she murmured as she lifted the beer to her lips. "Explains why you're in covert mode."

She had wondered, when she had first seen him, about the slight differences in his cheekbones, the longer hair, the scar slashing down the side of his face that he didn't really have. If a picture were taken of him, it would show other differences that she wasn't catching in the dimness of the room.

Differences that would disappear once he returned to his wife and children. Enough differences that he would never be mistaken for Micah Sloane, a personal security expert in Atlanta, Georgia.

"Yeah, that explains it," he agreed as he turned his head and looked back at her. "Doesn't explain why you're here rather than safe at home helping everyone come up with the plans, the contingency plans, and countercontingency plans the boss man always requires, though."

She was almost amused. Jordan definitely believed in contingency plans, and the countercontingencies.

She finally sighed. "All of you need to let me handle this myself." Though she was beginning to suspect it was far worse than she imagined.

"Aw, darlin', you know that's not going to happen, right?" Gentle affection filled his tone. "You're family, Tey. We don't turn our backs on family anymore than you slacked on the job when we needed you."

She had to swallow tightly to hold back her tears.

"I don't know if I can do this again," she said when Micah said nothing more. "I don't know if I can bear losing everything I've built here." She could feel the grief tearing at her chest.

"I think we both know it's too late to back out. You can run and hide, or you can stand and fight. There's no in-between, Tey."

Yeah, she knew there was no in-between. That didn't mean her choices didn't suck.

"He told me to warn you that if you run without him, he'll have your car targeted and disabled," Micah continued with quiet sincerity. "And I'd help him. It's too late to run."

She propped her chin against her hand and stared over at him morosely. Just what she needed, Jordan finding ways to dictate to her and he wasn't even there.

"That's just exceptionally wrong," she muttered. "He knows that's just exceptionally wrong, Micah. That's my car. It's not his any longer."

He rose slowly from the barstool, his black eyes glinting in the dim light.

He bent down so his lips were close to her ear. "I'm going to fade back into the shadows now," he said softly. "Head home soon, darlin'. You're closer than you know to possessing everything you've wanted for the past six years. Don't give up just when you've received the chance to enter the fight."

She almost shook her head at his advice as she watched him stroll casually to the exit, sunlight flooding the darkened bar as he opened the door, then abruptly disappeared as it closed.

If he meant Jordan's heart, then he was so wrong. Jordan had showed her during that last night at base that, at least where she was concerned, he didn't possess a heart. Now didn't count. Jordan felt he had to be there with her. He hadn't come for her because he had needed her for himself.

What he possessed instead was a sexual appetite that set fire to her own, and only drew her closer to a broken heart.

"Hey, Tey." Journey sidled up to the stool next to her. "Who was that piece of hot stuff you were talking to?" She flashed Tehya a wicked grin as she waggled her brows suggestively.

"Someone with a complex," Tehya sighed as she wondered who in the bar could be the enemy. She was a fool, because she couldn't believe any of them could be a danger to her.

She had learned as a teenager that the enemy could pose as anyone, even a friend. Yet evidently, that lesson hadn't impressed itself upon her effectively enough.

It could be Casey, it could be Kyle, or even Journey. Tehya had known the other girl was a risk from the beginning, but not the type of risk Micah was watching for.

"Someone with a complex and a seriously nice ass," Journey laughed.

"More than a seriously nice ass matters, Journey," Tehya said. "And on that note, it's time for me to leave."

She had to get out of the bar, away from whoever was there

specifically to watch her, to betray her. To complete Sorrel's mission and destroy her.

It wasn't as safe here as she had believed it was. For all her careful surveillance and background checks, somehow she had still managed to fuck up. Still, she had allowed herself to be fooled.

That, or she had been located within those first two months of moving to Hagerstown and was being watched even as she was watching those around her.

That would have allowed whoever was following her to put someone in place and prepare a proper background. Especially if she had been led there, or if her enemy had known her well enough to guess where she would head.

The thought that she was under surveillance for months and had never guessed until the past few weeks, had a chill of terror racing through her.

Looking around, she didn't catch sight of Micah or anyone else. She felt the eyes on her, though. God, she should have paid attention to her instincts and run that first night she had felt the back of her neck itch.

Two weeks ago.

But if her suspicions were right, if Micah's were right, it had been too late long before that. But why hadn't she felt the danger then? Why had she only begun feeling those eyes on her in the last two weeks?

Slipping the small electronic key fob from her jeans, she started the ignition to the car before crossing the street. Once she got to the vehicle, she walked around it, watching the screen on the fob intently for any sign of electronic devices or explosives.

The screen showed clear.

Once inside the vehicle she sat still and quiet and stared out the windshield, as she tried to get a grip on the fear building inside her, and the final realization, the acceptance that her father truly was reaching out from the grave to drag her into hell with him.

She wouldn't get rid of Jordan or the others. If he had pulled the team in before he had showed up on her doorstep—

and it appeared he had done exactly that—then he'd intended to learn who was searching for her on his own once he had placed her at base or in a safe house.

She knew Jordan; He didn't do anything without a carefully thought out plan. He would have shipped her off to the Elite Ops base and then gone after anyone that seemed to be interested in her. He would have attempted to take care of the matter on his own.

What he couldn't have realized was the moment she disappeared, her shadows would have disappeared as well. And eventually they would have found her again. They always did. And someone always died.

How many times had someone ended up dead because they thought they could fight her battles for her? Because they thought they could save her or her mother, no matter the odds.

However, unlike the others, Jordan had come prepared, and Tehya knew he had. She knew how he worked, how he planned, how he waged war.

Pulling out of the parking lot, Tehya headed home. Watching the rearview and side mirrors carefully, she drove around for a while, hoping to catch sight of anyone that could be tailing her. At least, perhaps she would give Micah a chance to catch sight of them, though she doubted whoever it was would be so careless at this late date.

She knew Micah was most likely behind her somewhere, but she couldn't catch sight of him, either. Had she lost her edge? There had been a time when her instincts, her ability to draw out a tail had been so much better than this.

By the time Tehya pulled into her garage she was frustrated, irritated, and riding a temperamental edge that she rarely allowed herself to visit. Fear did this to her. It made her crazy with the need to run, to hide, to draw the danger away from friends or acquaintances.

When she was too weak to control the fear, her mother used to tell her that her redheaded temper would get her in more trouble than what they had following them.

She'd had a horrible temper as a child when under stress.

She had believed she had conquered it as a teenager, though. Hell, she hadn't had a choice. It was control her temper or risk her mother, or a protector's life. But now, she could feel it rising inside her like a storm that couldn't be stopped. She felt as though she were being infected by the fear. As though it were crawling inside her, burning her guts.

Parking the car in the garage, Tehya got out and walked into the house only to come face-to-face with more people than she had left there.

Jordan and the two couples were waiting, but with him was his nephew, another former Elite Ops agent, Noah Blake. Micah and Nik were slipping through the patio entrance even as she locked the door between the kitchen and the garage.

"Did I give you enough time to catch my tail?" she asked Micah as she leaned against the door.

A grin quirked the hard line of his lips. "Not this time. They followed you in, but they didn't follow you out. We crisscrossed behind as well as ahead of you and didn't glimpse anything or anyone suspicious."

She turned to Jordan. "You didn't tell me you brought the whole damned team in." She then glared at his nephew. "Isn't Sabella close to giving birth?"

Noah's wife was pregnant with their second child, and she knew from the first pregnancy that he became a temperamental son of a bitch if he even suspected a mission would interfere with his ability to be with his wife during the birth, or in those first weeks afterward.

"I have permission to head home if I need to." Noah grinned back at her, his dark blue eyes amused yet concerned. "I have an understanding boss this time around."

The last time Sabella was close to her due date just as a mission had ended. Jordan had found himself sporting a black eye hours later when he had mockingly asked Noah for a written report on the mission before he left for home.

"Did you learn anything while I was gone?" she asked Jordan.

He sat at the kitchen counter in front of John and Travis, and now Micah and Nik. Noah took the seat beside him.

The two women were on the living room couch working on several laptops they had set up on her coffee table. Her living room was now a fucking command center.

"We're working on it," he stated coolly, but the tension radiating from his body was impossible to miss. He was furious that she had run out as she had.

"Well, I see you made yourselves at home. Should I find a place for all of you to sleep?" She straightened from the door and moved farther into the kitchen. "I hope sleeping bags will do."

Jordan stood up, his broad shoulders appearing wider. His eyes bluer.

"Are you finished running?" he asked, his voice low, dangerous, and filled with a blatant challenge.

Tehya's brows lifted and she came to a stop in the middle of the ceramic tile floor, aware that all eyes had turned to her and Jordan.

Surprisingly, the moment she had walked into the house and caught sight of Jordan she had felt a spark of life suddenly flare inside her that hadn't been there before. A glimmer of hope perhaps.

Adrenaline, anticipation. A flare of hunger, she couldn't extinguish if she wanted to.

"Probably not," she said, her tone flippant as she fought the anger she knew she couldn't hide if she tried. She glanced at Micah. "Or at least not until I can find a way to outrun the Rottweilers you sicced on me."

A bark of surprised, amused laughter burst from Noah and Micah.

"I think he's more like a junkyard mutt," Noah said, laughing at Micah.

"You've always said that," Micah agreed with a grin. "I prefer her description though."

Tehya felt a tug at her heart. It was almost like those days back at the base. The camaraderie, male-bonding bullshit, and insanity that she had always loved watching.

"They're all dogs," Lilly piped up as she tossed her husband a wicked grin. "Aren't you, darling?"

Travis gave a low, sexy growl. Tehya glanced at Jordan, only to find him looking back at her, and she felt the tension between the two of them rise.

Did he envy the others as well? Was there a part of him, as there was in her, that hungered painfully for that same emotional bonding. A hunger she knew no man could sate with the exception of Jordan.

Sometimes, she felt as though she had been cursed by him. No matter how she had tried in the months since leaving the ops, she couldn't get him out of her head, or out of her heart. He was a weakness she now knew she had no chance of resisting. Just as she knew he had ruined her for any other man.

"You have your orders," Jordan stated to the others, his gaze still locked with hers. "Make the necessary contacts and we'll get this started."

Jordan used the tone that everyone knew meant business. It made the team jump and head for the nearest safety zone. It just made her hot. It always had. It made her wet and never failed to keep her pussy throbbing in need.

Everyone was leaving except Lilly and Bailey. They rose gracefully to their feet and came into the kitchen while the men gathered files and prepared to leave.

"I contacted Ian and Kira, Tehya," Lilly told her. "They've been in D.C. for months. Kira said she's been trying to reach you since you left base. I'm certain you'll be hearing from her soon."

A heavy breath escaped her and she closed her eyes. She didn't want anyone else involved in this.

"I wish you hadn't called them," she said.

"Darling, Kira would have killed me, and made sure it hurt. Badly," Lilly told her, clearly amused. "But never fear, we have several excellent plans here that Ian and Kira conferenced with us on. We're going to have such fun saving your temperamental little hide. You'll actually thank us later."

Laughing lightly, Lilly kissed her cheek and then Bailey gave her a quick hug. "Take care dear, and we'll be seeing each other again soon."

Tehya remained still, watching them warily now. She'd

seen these two play their little high jinks on the men of the
unit, but this was the first time she had been a recipient. It
wasn't a pleasant sensation. Now, she almost regretted the
plots she had helped them with.

Within minutes, the small crowd had dispersed, slipping
silently from the house, and leaving her alone with Jordan
and the hunger heating between her thighs again.

Tehya wasn't used to having neighbors, so the fact that
her house was in the middle of a large block had been her
opportunity to learn how to live among people. It wasn't a
crowded block, though. The houses were spaced a good distance apart, ensuring privacy. Her house sat in front of a line
of sheltering trees and the two neighbors on the left of her
were related and currently vacationing together.

Walking into the living room while Jordan locked up,
Tehya pulled the heavy drapes carefully over the French
doors, ensuring there wasn't so much as a crack between the
material for prying eyes to see into the house.

"So, you have plans C, D, E, and F?" she asked as he
turned to her once again.

"G, H, and I, as well," he informed her coolly. "You can
never have too many plans, Tehya."

Arrogance settled around him like a royal cloak.

"So you say." She shrugged, crossed her arms over her
breasts, cocked her hip and stared back at him, her brow
arched.

"Don't give me that look," he warned her. "You could
have stuck around to contribute to planning your own protection, rather than running off as you did."

"Well, it was leave or commit murder," she told him
archly "Has anyone told you that you're damned arrogant
Jordan? Or that you could make a saint conspire to murder?"

"Only every day you were around," he snorted. He dropped
his arms and stared back at her with a look of pure, hard
dominance. "Why did you run, Tehya?"

She hadn't expected him to question her.

"I've all but lived with you for six years, and you can't
guess that one?" she asked with a hint of sarcasm. "Do you

have any idea how hard this is for me to accept? Sorrel is supposed to be dead!" she suddenly cried out, surprised by the vehemence that tore from her. "He's not supposed to haunt me like this."

Jordan heard the pain in her voice and once again fought the tearing at him, that urge to just *do something* to make her pain go away. It killed him to see or hear her pain.

Hell, she'd always had the power to do this to him. She forced him to feel emotions he didn't know how to handle. She made him feel as though he were betraying both of them by being unable to what she made him feel when it rose tight and hard inside him as it did now.

"Tehya, the people who helped when you were young weren't qualified to go up against Sorrel, and neither were you." He braced his hands on the counter and forced himself not to touch her. "You were a child, not an adult, and it was no fault of yours. There was nothing you could do to change any of it."

She turned her head away from him, her tongue peeking out to touch the point of her upper lip. Somber grief tightened her expression as she gave a little shrug, as though the explanations, the reasons why, really didn't matter.

Her fingers raked through the heavy hair at the top of her head, causing those long, riotous curls to bounce around her shoulders, down her back and tempt his fingers. "It will never be over," she whispered, her voice harsh. "He swore he would never release me, and even in death he's managing to keep a hold on me."

"It doesn't matter how far you run, Tehya, or how hard you fight it, you're going to have to realize the only hold Sorrel has on you is the one you're allowing. I won't let the past destroy you. And neither will your friends. But we need you to see, to believe we can do this together."

She rubbed the back of her neck. She was irritated, frightened, and he was damned if he knew how to help.

The need to do something though, anything, to wipe that fear from her eyes clawed at the heart he didn't know he still possessed until he met Tehya.

Her lips tightened as her dark green eyes seemed to glow in the frame of her pale face. That little spattering of freckles stood out in stark relief on her nose, clearly visible despite the tan that he knew covered her entire body.

"When Mother first escaped, she hid with me in a convent with Sister Mary, a friend she had known since she was young. She stayed only for a while, then left to make certain Father's men hadn't followed her. She called Sister Mary late one night, about three years later. Sister Mary pulled me from my bed and we ran. As we ran through the forest, I remember hearing gunshots. His men raped several of the sisters. The Reverend Mother had been tortured before they killed her. Horribly."

He knew that. He had the file on the horrendous murders of the sisters at the Holy Blessings Convent.

"Sister Mary and I ran for several years," she continued. "I saw Mother only rarely. Then one night we met with an ex-marine. Matthew Thomas." She rubbed at her arms as though suddenly cold.

"Matthew slipped me into America, and I thought I would be safe with him. I thought he could defeat any monster, he was so strong. He and Mother had evidently had a relationship. I think they may have even loved each other." She swallowed tightly her gaze stark with painful memories. "Several months later, Sister Mary's body was found. She had died just after handing me over to Matthew. He and I both knew she would have told Sorrel who I was with, and where I was. She was so fragile, Jordan. So tiny."

She stared back at him with those eyes so haunted it broke his heart. "When Matthew sent me to his friend Boyd in the Washington mountains, he told me he was going to take care of the problem once and for all. Then he would bring Mother to me, and we would be safe." The pain in her face had his fingers aching to clench into fists. "Two months later Boyd pulled me out of bed in the middle of the night and we were on the run." The first tear eased down her cheek. "Matthew's body had been found. He had been skinned alive."

Jordan couldn't stand still another moment longer.

"Goddammit, I have the fucking files," he bit out furiously as he took her in his arms and held her to him with an overwhelming need to take those painful memories out of her head. "I have the files, Tehya."

"Then you know." She sobbed, anger, fear, and desperation in her cries. "If these are Sorrel's men, then you know what they are. You know what they're capable of doing. Why, Jordan? Why won't they let me go? Why won't they leave me alone?"

His hands gripped her upper arms as he pulled back and stared down at her before lifting one hand to wipe the wetness from her cheek.

"Tehya, sweetheart," he whispered. "We kept you hidden rather than taking care of this when we should have. Sorrel isn't haunting you, but it's obvious someone associated with him believes you have something they want. We'll just have to figure out what that something is."

It was the only thing that made sense.

She shook her head. "I didn't take anything from the estate while I was there. I even left the clothes I had brought myself the night I was attacked there."

"We'll figure it out," he promised her. Nine times out of ten it was something as simple as a file she may have seen, or some insignificant piece of information Sorrel had given her before the night he died.

For now though, all he could do was hold her. All he could do was comfort her and ache for the years of her life that had been stolen from her.

"I'm fine." She gave a hard shake of her head as she pulled away from him and moved to the counter before turning to face him once again.

Letting her go wasn't easy, but it was easier than seeing that pain in her eyes.

"You'll be fine," he promised her. "We'll see to that, darlin'."

Jordan saw the determination on her face, the pain, the belief that somehow she could protect herself, protect her heart, if she had just found a way to defeat Sorrel when she was younger.

"Will you?" she asked then, her expression closing on him, her gaze becoming shuttered. "Will it be better, Jordan? Or will the past steal the rest of my life?" She gave a hard, brief laugh. "I guess it's a good thing I didn't buy that puppy I wanted. This would be a hell of a life for a little dog, wouldn't it, Jordan?"

A tear slipped down her cheek. "It's just a puppy." Her breathing hitched. "I can't even have a fucking puppy."

Before he could pull her to him again she swung away, her hand pressed to her mouth, more tears obviously following as she rushed to her room for a second time that day.

And hell, he hadn't even known she wanted a puppy.

CHAPTER 6

The situation wasn't going to change. Her friends were sticking by her side, and Tehya had to admit that knowing that she wasn't facing this alone eased the tight, panicked pressure in her chest and lifted the fatalistic feeling that she may not live to see her next birthday. But the fear of losing someone else reopened the ragged wounds of the past.

The world wasn't a pretty place, she thought, at least not for her. Her life had been an endless battle and each day of freedom had been paid for with the blood of others.

Now, as day faded to night and she sat at the computer completing the last of the payroll checks that would go out on Monday, Tehya realized that the distant thought of escaping and running alone wasn't a course she could take, either. The time for running was over, just as she had told him when he first arrived.

Her life had been a series of paths leading here, to whatever battle fate had planned for her.

Shutting down the accounting program, she gathered the checks and tucked them into their individual envelopes. Penning the final name, she stared down at it silently.

Journey Taite.

She sighed, sliding a finger over the letters.

Journey had somehow broken with tradition and had managed to escape notice as she found herself a job. Taite daughters didn't work. Francine Taite had once stated that fondly. It was a tradition. Taite daughters were protected from the world at all costs. The youngest of Craig Taite's daughters, Stephen Taite's granddaughter, was evidently determined not to be protected.

They were second cousins and Journey had no idea Tehya even existed. But Tehya had known about Journey. The moment the other girl had arrived in America Tehya had known, and she had made it a point to watch out for the younger girl, even from Texas.

When Tehya had left to find another home, she had found herself in Hagerstown, close enough to ensure a chance meeting. And because of Journey, Tehya had found herself watching the bar she was so fond of now.

Had she endangered the other girl as well? God, she prayed she hadn't.

And then there was Jordan.

He was on the couch in the living room working silently, not even a shuffle of paper to betray his presence. However, she knew he was there, and she knew she would have to deal with what he had said earlier.

She hadn't even wanted to know what the plan was after returning to the house. But now, hours later, she found herself wondering about it despite her best efforts to remain unaffected.

She straightened the envelopes before turning and tucking them into the leather briefcase sitting on the floor by the desk. Her employees would be waiting for their checks when she arrived.

There were a dozen employees, fewer than she needed, but she had wanted to wait before adding to the business. She was glad she had. Fewer to suspect, fewer to worry about protecting.

"What do I do about my company?" she asked quietly as she rose from her desk.

Jordan looked up from his laptop, his intense blue eyes lasering in on her.

His brow lifted mockingly. "Are you ready to listen now?"

She deserved the comment. She had cut him off each time he had tried to discuss the situation with her.

"You know, Tehya, you surprised me." Disappointment laced his voice. "We're here for you. The entire team came the second they learned you were in danger and each member of the backup team has offered their help. And you don't even want to hear how we're going to keep you alive."

There was a thread of anger in his tone, and she couldn't blame him.

"Does it matter now?" Finally, she sighed and walked over to the recliner facing the couch. "I'm ready to deal with it now Jordan. I wasn't capable of accepting it earlier." She rubbed roughly at her face as the weariness made her feel weak, almost too tired to face this discussion. "Perhaps, Jordan, just once in my entire life, I wanted to believe I was safe. I wanted a home, a life. Perhaps a cat or a dog." Weary acceptance filled her at that realization. She'd wanted a pet. "How pathetic is that? I've never had a pet."

"Understandable." Despite the sympathy, his voice hardened. "Now we have to fix it so you can have one. But I can't do it without help."

Her shoulders bunched defensively. "What more can I do, Jordan? I won't run again. I'll do whatever is needed, just as I always have."

This was the commander of the Elite Ops. Hard, cool, so damned logical he could have been a damned robot as he stared back at her.

"We need to consider the determination this shadow has shown since Sorrel's death. The occasional searches, and the obvious interest in your death that we set up. I happen to be someone who knew why you were so important to Sorrel."

"Then they would know more than I do." She sniffed. "And that would mean it would be someone close to Sorrel, Perhaps another son? A brother? Because he trusted very few people." Though as far as she knew her father hadn't had family. "He was rumored to be an only child. When he died, no one came forward to claim the estate."

"Because he left that estate to his son and his daughter," he reminded her. "You and Raven. With his son dead, that only left you. Coming forward would do no one any good at this point since the French government confiscated the estate as recompense against Sorrel's victims. But that doesn't cancel out the revenge angle against for his death."

That was what she was scared of, though she had assumed a former associate rather than a family member. "But no matter which, how do we draw them out?"

His lips tightened in frustration. "You won't like it, but I want you to promise to hear me out."

She nodded and said, "Okay, but before you dive in, keep in mind that I'll also need to know what to do with my company. My employees can't afford to be without work, Jordan, and I don't want to lay them off or suspend business."

"The company is easy," he assured her. "Tomorrow, you'll give the information needed to Clint and Morganna when they arrive. They're flying in tonight from Atlanta. They'll be here by dawn. They'll take over for you until this is over, while supporting the rumor that you're considering selling the company." He lifted his hand as she started to speak. "This will keep anyone from targeting the company or your employees. Their covers are simple. They're coming in as themselves, and we'll have no contact with them after the initial meeting. Once this is over, then you can return and simply say you changed your mind about selling. The employees may be concerned, but I believe they'll handle it okay if Clint and Morganna promise no one will be fired because of the sell."

Her lips tightened as she gave a quiet nod. She didn't like it, but he was right. If the person or persons behind Arthur and Tenneyson were the same as in France, or worse, someone fanatically dedicated to Sorrel's memory and his cause, then they would target the business and her employees if they thought it meant anything to her.

"Is that the only part I won't like?" She had a feeling it wasn't.

"No, it isn't." He sat forward, his gaze meeting hers, locking with hers, and she felt that familiar heat curling in her lower belly.

"Then what is it?" she asked shortly. "Go ahead, Jordan, strip me to the bone quickly, don't draw it out."

His lips almost quirked into a smile before his expression stilled.

"We're going to use the Taite family to draw them in, Tehya. It's time for you to face your family."

She jumped to her feet, astonished fury erupting through her. "The hell it is."

Jordan came to his feet slowly. "You know, Tehya, this temper of yours could get you into trouble, sweetheart," he warned her with an air of forced patience.

"Go to hell, Jordan!" she snapped, her fingers raking through her hair as she fought to make sense of this supposed plan of his. "What the hell makes you think I'm going to face them simply because you dictate it, when I haven't done so in all these years? Who the hell do you think you are?"

"I'm the man trying to save your pretty ass," he bit out furiously. He jerked her into his arms.

"I will not allow you to sacrifice my family," she raged bitterly. She couldn't believe he would suggest such a thing. That he would even believe she would consider it.

"By God, I will sacrifice Stephen Taite, his son, and a hundred more like them to protect you!" Savage determination hardened his expression. "Don't doubt that for a fucking minute, Tehya. No one, but fucking no one, matters as much to me as you and your safety."

His anger barely registered. All she could feel was her own, her complete rejection of ever revealing herself to her family.

Even her mother had refused to go to them. Despite their wealth and power, decades after her abduction her mother had vehemently opposed contacting them anytime it was suggested. Until Boyd had been killed. Then, she had contacted her parents, and she had paid for it with her life and with theirs. Tehya vowed she wouldn't make the same mistake.

Now Tehya would not go to them, and she wouldn't have them pulled into her battle.

"Too late, Tehya," he told her, his tone harsh, the cool logic lost as his eyes flamed with blue fire. "You can go along with it or we'll go on to the next plan. Anonymously informing both Stephen Taite, as well as the press, of your existence and your whereabouts. Now we can fight this battle privately or, by God, we can do it publicly. Take your damned pick."

He was furious.

Tehya had never seen him so angry, his eyes glittering with fiery emotion. But she couldn't remember the last time she had been so pissed off, either.

Rage bit into her, fueling the aggression rising inside her.

"How dare you barge into my life and think you can make such autocratic decisions where I'm concerned! You are not my father and you're not my husband, so you can fucking back off."

"But I am your damned lover now and I won't back down. I didn't back down for Sorrel and I won't back down for whoever the hell thinks they can continue to torture you. And I sure as hell won't back down for you."

Her lips parted to rage at him, to spew the fury boiling inside her, when he abruptly jerked her closer and his head lowered, his lips suddenly covering hers with a dominant, furious hunger.

As though the touch, the kiss, filled with his own fury and protectiveness had lit a fuse inside her own lust, Tehya began fighting, not for release, but for control of the kiss.

She nipped at his tongue as he licked hungrily at hers, his lips slanting over hers as her hands moved suddenly from his chest to his hair.

The force of her teeth against the sensitive flesh had him jerking back, but only momentarily. A second later his hand gripped her jaw, holding it as his lips covered hers forcibly once again.

The dominance, the incredible seductive force of the action, had a hungry moan passing her throat as her fingers clenched in the material covering his chest.

Buttons popped. The material parted and a second later the sexy mat of curls on his chest tingled against her sensitive palms.

It was incredible. Force meeting force as he groaned and the kiss deepened. Her nails rasped over his chest, her hands caressing, lowering along his abdomen to the low band of his jeans.

Beneath the tough denim material, the hard ridge of his cock tempted her, causing her to flatten her palm over the heavy width as a desperate cry vibrated in her throat and she returned to tearing at the metal clasp.

She wanted to taste him, to own him. To control all that hard strength and dominance for just a moment. To feel the hunger and the need that she knew he couldn't deny when held in that intimate caress.

Finally the metal snap released, allowing her to work the zipper over the thick length.

Wickedly hot, the heavy flesh met her touch, sending trails of heated sensation to whip across her nerve endings.

Her nipples ached, felt too tight, too sensitive. Her clit throbbed in agony and her vagina clenched with emptiness. Need sizzled over her flesh, making her body ultrasensitive, receptive to even the slightest touch, aching for it, as she felt his hand slide into her hair and clench the heavy curls.

Fiery pleasure-pain whipped through her scalp. Heated need tore through her, striking at her clit, at her pussy, and causing her hips to jerk against the hard contour of the thigh suddenly pressing against her clit as she slid her hand lower and cupped the taut sac drawn tight against the base of his cock. Wicked, carnal, Tehya whimpered with the hunger to taste every part of him.

"Damn." His lips jerked from hers as he stared down at her, his expression savagely hewn, reflecting the power and possessive heat of his lust.

"Take what you want, baby," he dared her, as the grip on her hair tightened and he began to draw her down his body. The feel of his hands in her hair, the strength and dominance sent a sensual weakness flooding her body.

She became intoxicated. Rage, pain, and fear disintegrated beneath the freedom to kiss, to caress the hard contours of his chest. The hard flat disc of his nipple that elicited a groan from him and his fingers tightening to tug erotically at her hair, pulling her down his body. Her tongue darted out to flick against the hard abs flexing beneath her lips and tongue as the wild male taste of his flesh exploded against her taste buds.

His response was instantaneous. His grip tightened in her hair as a harsh groan rumbled in his chest. The response sent a spike of anticipation racing through her.

"Ah, sweet Tehya," he moaned, his voice rasping. "Damn, baby, I love that hot little tongue."

Kissing, licking, stroking, she went even lower, slowly going to her knees as she attempted to wrap her fingers around the too wide flesh of his cock. Flushed, dark, silk over heat-infused iron, the heavy shaft throbbed beneath her fingers.

Enclosing it in her hand wasn't happening, but still, she stroked and caressed the heated flesh as she allowed her tongue to reach out and flick against the damp, engorged head.

"Hell, yes." The broken sound of his voice only made her hotter, made the act sexier. "Suck it, Tehya. Suck my dick, baby."

His hips pressed forward, the flared crest pressing against her lips, pushing between them, as she sucked it slowly, teasingly into her mouth.

Staring down at her, Jordan fought to hold back the overwhelming hunger to push her to the floor and just fuck her. Never had he known a need for a woman as he did for this one. She was like a flame burning inside him, the conflagration spilling from her, into his veins, across his nerve endings, and burning straight to his soul.

As those sweet, pouty lips parted, stretching around the width of his cock, he felt pure lust explode through his balls, tightening them further. Carnal, blistering in its heat, feverish hunger struck his senses. It had been too long since he'd had her, too long since the pleasure he'd only found with this woman had torn through his senses.

His fingers tightened in her hair, a convulsive, almost involuntary movement, as he filled both hands with the fiery curls. Holding her head in place, he controlled the impalement of her lush lips. Watching her take him so intimately, with such pleasure and hunger, spiked the dominance that raged through him.

Needs that he normally had complete control over went haywire the moment he touched her. The moment she touched him. Nothing mattered but the pleasure that raged between them and the burning heat they shared. He watched as her cheeks hollowed, her face flushed, and pleasure tightened the muscles of his thighs painfully.

Damp heat enclosed his cock head as her nimble little tongue swirled around the tip of the engorged head of his cock, before moving beneath to rub against the exquisitely sensitive spot located there.

Staring down at her enraptured expression, he held her head in place, his hips shifting, moving slow and easy as he fucked her swollen lips, barely holding back a snarl caused by the near violent ecstasy rushing through him.

Son of a bitch, it was so fucking good. Addictive. Pure hot lust licking over his flesh. Her mouth was like damp fire, searing his flesh, shredding his self-control. Pleasure tore through his system, laying waste to any precautions he could have taken to remain emotionally distant from her let alone controlling the addictive need for her touch.

She was his weakness, it was something he had sensed she would be for years. The one woman he couldn't walk away from or bear losing. She was his pleasure, his pain, and if he didn't fuck her, soon, then she would be the death of him.

Tehya wanted to protest as she felt Jordan's hands gripping her shoulders, drawing her to her feet. Her lips parted to speak, but at the same time his hands moved to her jeans, strong fingers releasing the metal buttons that held them on her hips.

Her gaze jerked downward, her attention suddenly held

by the fact that she was being undressed. That Jordan was undressing her. For some reason the thought of it was powerfully arousing.

"Get those sneakers off," he demanded, his expression hard as he stared up at her from where he crouched in front of her.

She toed off her shoes, her breathing heavy and labored as she felt her body preparing for more, begging for more. Her pussy ached, her clit rasping against her panties as her hips shifted.

Within seconds, he had her naked, standing before him, flushed, her body silently begging for his touch.

Staring at her swollen breasts, he drew his shirt from his powerful shoulders, the heavy muscles moving erratically with his breath.

As he leaned against the side of the couch, he removed his boots, then shed his jeans before straightening, his hard fingers gripping the base of his cock.

"I've never been so damned hard in my life," he groaned as he moved to her, his hand gripping her hip as the other cupped her cheek.

His head lowered, his lips brushing against hers. A deep male groan filled the air and the kiss became deeper, causing a heavy fatigue to invade her limbs as her thighs clenched in response to the surging ache between them.

"Sweet baby," he whispered as he eased her back.

The edge of the chair pressed against the back of her legs.

"Sit down for me, Tehya."

God, it was so damned sexy. Wicked.

She eased into the chair, the soft, expensive leather cushioning her as he knelt in front of her and spread her legs.

"Come here," he said gripping her hips and easing her forward until her hips rested on the edge of the chair, giving him easy access to her.

His lips pressed to her thighs, first one, then the other. His tongue licked against her flesh, heating her further as her clit throbbed and seemed to become more swollen.

"Stop teasing me!" The harsh cry was thick, desperation

echoing through it, as his fingers trailed fire to the bare folds of her pussy.

"I'm not teasing, sweetheart," he assured her. "I definitely intend to deliver."

His hand pressed beneath her thigh, lifting it until her leg folded over his shoulder.

Tehya's breath caught. Pleasure lashed through her system with the power of a whip, striking against her swollen, sensitive clit and causing her hips to jerk involuntarily.

Heated and damp, his tongue flicked over the tiny bundle of nerves as she felt his fingers slowly rim the clenched entrance to her pussy.

Her fingers tunneled into his hair, gripping the strands as she strained closer, her lashes drifting closed while shattering waves of sensation washed through her body. She felt drugged by the sensations, pulled into a dazed state of sensory overload that she needed to leave.

"There, baby, just lay back there and let me have you." His free hand slid up her torso, callused fingertips finding the hard tip of a nipple and gripping it in an erotic vise.

A convulsive wave of electric pleasure tore through her, her body jerking with the extremity of it. Her pussy tightened and clenched, her juices weeping from the entrance as his fingers slid in, rasping against the delicate inner muscles as he caressed nerve endings grown ultra sensitive.

His tongue licked, probed, and caressed her clit as pleasure built in a burning arc that threatened to consume her.

Her nails dug into his scalp as she tried to get closer to the burning caress of his tongue circling her swollen clit.

The slow, measured strokes of his fingers fucking inside her pussy had deep, desperate cries rising in her chest as she thrust up to meet his fingers. She fought to gain a deeper, harder thrust inside her clenched vagina, a firmer, hotter pressure against her clit.

"Jordan, please." The whispered need was rife was desperation as lips eased from her swollen flesh while his fingers slide from the tight grip of her pussy.

Her lashes lifted, watching in dazed anticipation as Jordan

gripped the heavy weight of his cock and rose between her thighs.

The thick head pressed against the folds as his lips moved to the tender tips of her breasts. The combined sensations rocking and exploding through her with rapid-fire percussion.

As he sucked the tight tip into his mouth, his hips pressed forward, his cock stretching, working its way into the snug sensitive depths of her pussy.

"Ah hell. Tight. God, Tehya, you're so fucking tight." His lips pressed to the curve of her breast as he fought to breathe, to drag enough oxygen into his body to beat back the light-headed, drugging effects of the pleasure tearing through him.

He could feel her, the snug tissue rippling over his flesh, milking his cock drawing him in as he felt perspiration bead along his spine.

"Jordan!" The whispered cry stroked his senses like a physical stroke of ecstasy. Desperation filled her tone, the rising need for release in it matching the flex and hungry strokes of her pussy over his cock head as he worked slowly inside her.

A final lick to her nipple and he lifted his head, watching the hungry glow coming from beneath her lowered lashes.

Her neck arched, her hips flexed upward, her fingers digging into his shoulders as a whimper left her lips.

"Fuck me, Jordan," she whispered as those dark, emerald-green eyes lit with an inner fire and glowed up at him, hungry demand flashing in their depths.

The wickedly sensual demand lit a fuse to his lust and sent a powerful, overwhelming wave of hunger tearing through him.

He'd waited too long. The knowledge of that was only a distant thought. He'd suffered this damned hard-on through the night and all fucking day. The hunger had torn at his guts, and now he'd waited too long to take her.

A hard, involuntary thrust of his cock buried him inside the gripping depths of her pussy as feminine muscles clenched tight and hot with urgent demand.

Fiery and erotically slick. Control was forgotten, and nothing but the race to ecstasy remained.

Tehya felt her back arch at the forceful, dominant thrust of his cock inside her. Flames tore through her vagina, raced around her clit, and through her system as Jordan began thrusting inside her.

The powerful arcs of sensation were explosive, detonating through her as the exquisite pleasure-pain began to erupt through her pussy.

"God. Tehya." His voice was a harsh, guttural cry, as it rasped over her senses, spurred her pleasure higher and hotter.

She strained against him, her breathing hard, the feel of his chest hair prickling her nipples, his lips slanted over hers, his tongue licking, probing, his cock stretching and burning her inner muscles.

It was building. Flares of heat, surges of electric, agonizing pleasure. Her clit was a living flame, each stroke of his pelvis against her driving spikes of pure white-hot sensation through her womb.

Her entire body pulsed and throbbed.

The feel of his erection, thick and heavy, forging its way into her pussy.

Waves of rapture began to surge.

She gasped for breath, her eyes flaring open, widening to stare up at Jordan in dazed, ecstatic euphoria. Convulsive, destructive, her orgasm began in the pit of her belly, tightening and blazing out of control as she felt the first, furious explosion of release.

Her pussy contracted on the shuttling flesh between her thighs. A rivulet of perspiration ease down his temple, his expression sharpening to savage angles.

The first agonizing surge of release slammed through her. She felt Jordan thrust in hard, deep. Throbbing, pulsing, his cock exploded inside her, shuddering through his body. Her vision dimmed, her breath stilling inside her lungs before a low, wild whimper escaped her throat.

Deep spurts of semen were triggers to her extended

release. It seemed never-ending, each shuddering pulse of ecstasy tearing through her, tossing her into brutal waves of elation.

Her head thrashed against the back of the chair. Her nails dug into his arms, and she swore that had to be her trying to scream.

Or was she actually screaming?

No, she couldn't have, she wouldn't have.

That wasn't her voice crying hoarsely "Oh God, Jordan, I love you . . ."

No.

She wasn't that insane.

CHAPTER 7

Long minutes later, lying in her bed, her back to his chest, his arms wrapped around her as she felt the slow steady beat of his heart against her back, Tehya realized she didn't want to risk this. "This" being the sated languor she couldn't shake off.

It sank through her, glowed inside her, and warmed her with a heat so comforting she didn't want to move.

It was *this*.

The physical satisfaction, the emotional upheaval, the sense of finally being where she belonged. Held in Jordan's arms. It was a complete and total sense of inner committment.

She must have managed to keep the insanity of her emotions inside her during her release. Jordan hadn't mentioned a lapse. He hadn't advised her against loving him or expecting him to stick around once the mission was over. He wasn't lecturing her on illusion, adrenaline-inspired emotions or any other subject guaranteed to ruin this incredible moment.

Perhaps the declaration of love had been a silent one. She could only pray it was, because she would be damned if she wanted to face one of Jordan's all-knowing, love-is-an-illusion dissertations.

He had simply picked her up and carried her to bed where

he now lay close to her, the warmth of his body wrapping around her.

One muscular calf pressed between hers, his forearm lay against her stomach, his chin rested atop her head. Intimacy wrapped around them and infused every breath.

She felt wrapped in security, safe and settled.

It was a feeling she hadn't experienced even when she bought her first home, or her business. Never in her life had she known this feeling, though it seemed she had ached for it most of her life.

It was a feeling of almost complete peace. It would have been complete if not for the knowledge that once she was safe again, he would ride off into the sunset.

Wasn't that what the white knight always did?

There was always someone else to save wasn't there? She wasn't the only damsel in distress in the world.

"You're not sleeping." There was a lazy, relaxed quality to his voice. A sense of male satiation that sent a surge of feminine pride racing through her.

But sensual pride, intimacy, or a hidden love couldn't sustain her. Reality washed it away quickly enough as she remembered exactly how they had ended up here, and the argument that had spurred that kiss.

Dominating, domineering, and arrogant. He had made his plans and he was determined to follow at least one of them. Unfortunately, all of them involved the same family.

Her family.

"Why are you involving the Taite family?" she finally asked, rather than facing the emotions tearing through her or a feeling she knew she couldn't hold on to.

His arm moved, his fingers caressing across her stomach before coming to rest against the top of her thigh.

The physical caress sent waves of warmth washing through her. A warmth that invited her to lie back and bask in the aftermath.

"For several reasons," he finally said quietly. "One being the fact that the two men who checked into your death in

Afghanistan are watching Stephen Taite. Someone is obviously waiting on something where you and your family are concerned and reporting to someone. The best way to get a response is to give them something to report."

"Someone really knows I'm alive, then and that I'm Francine Taite's daughter," she whispered painfully. "Nothing lasts forever, does it?"

"Some things do," he said with a sigh. "Unfortunately, this didn't."

Tehya licked her lips. The nervous energy surging inside her should have been enough to force her out of his arms. Instead, she was still lying there, still trying to make sense of what she should do versus what she wanted to do. And how she was going to handle the fact that she was no longer as safe as she thought she was.

"I won't reveal myself to them," she stated, fighting back her tears knowing she couldn't bear to face them or to endanger them. "This has to be done without their knowledge. It's too late for me to go back, Jordan. It's too late to be a part of a family that's doing fine without me."

Jordan remained quiet behind her. Her eyes closed, pain twisting inside her at the fear that it was what he had planned. That his intentions all along had been to bring Tehya together with her family.

He might not love her, but Tehya knew he cared for her. Years before, he had suggested that she go to her family, that she let them know she was alive. She'd refused then, and she wouldn't change her mind now.

"I wouldn't force such a decision on you." The clipped words assured her she had managed to offend him. "Do you believe I would hurt you in such a way, Tehya? That I would risk your future like that now, while I know your past hasn't yet been resolved?"

It wasn't her future that frightened her, it was the rejection she knew she would face and the possibility, slight though it was, that the dangers she faced would risk them as well. Besides, the last thing the Taite family would want would be her return.

And Stephen Taite knew his family would lose Taite Industries to Tehya and her heirs if she returned. When Bernard Taite, Tehya's grandfather, had been forced to change his will after his daughter hadn't been found, he had named his only brother, Stephen, as his heir. But there was a codicile in the eventuality that his daughter or her heirs were ever found.

If they were, his estate, in its entirety, would be turned over to her and his brother would be regulated to CEO of the business only.

It would breed resentment and discomfort. Whether Tehya claimed everything or not.

There was also the small matter of an inheritance that only Tehya *could* collect.

Bernard Taite had created the wealth the Taite family enjoyed, but for the past fifteen years, Stephen Taite and his son Craig had called it their own. They wouldn't want to relinquish it now, and she couldn't blame them.

It would give them a reason to reject her. A reason to fear her.

She could turn the companies over to Stephen or his son Craig, but there was a portion of the inheritance, held in reserve that had been set aside in case Taite Industries had ever failed. An inheritance that would, in cash, gold, and bonds, total far more than Taite Industries was worth by now. An inheritance Tehya was determined to hold on to in the eventuality that her dream of being a mother herself was ever realized or that the danger she faced was ever defeated.

"How are you going to manage this without the Taites knowing who I am?" Her fingers curled into the pillow as she held back her tears. She was absorbing the fact that she would have to face the family she could never allow herself to have and possibly to accept.

"You've already made a first contact, Tehya. Why are you so frightened to face the rest of the family when you employ your second cousin and have obviously become friends with her?" he said, as she felt her heart sink.

Micah would have run a background check on everyone

that walked into that bar before the team ever arrived. Tehya should have thought of that.

"How long did it take you to find her?" he asked when she said nothing.

She closed her eyes. She had wanted to keep that connection to herself, to enjoy it, to relish even this small contact with at least one family member. She hadn't wanted it tainted by the danger she faced.

"I knew before I arrived," he revealed. "How long were you planning to make contact?"

"I've kept an eye on her for years," she revealed. "I learned she had come to America to go to college just before the team disbanded." She almost smiled. "She's as wild as the wind, Jordan. I didn't want her getting into trouble."

"So you came here to watch over her?" he guessed, his tone carefully controlled, as though he knew any show of anger would only ignite another confrontation between them. "She's a lot like you. She has your temperament. Micah's report on her is like reading your life if you had been born into that family. A rebel. Independent and stubborn as hell, she and her grandfather are rumored to go head to head often, and according to my sources, the only reason she wasn't sent to a private girls' college was because the Queen of England herself intervened and 'requested' her father uphold the Taite family tradition of sending the girls to America to complete their education."

Yeah, that was Journey. She was so young, so damned determined. It made Tehya proud as hell to know her. And she was damned calculating in getting her way as well.

She suddenly realized couldn't lie there in the bed any longer. That nervous energy building inside her wouldn't be denied.

Rising from the bed, she glanced over her shoulder, barely glimpsing his curious expression in the dim light of the room.

"Why, it really doesn't matter, does it?" she asked quietly. "But if your plan is to use Journey in this little plot of yours, then perhaps you should reconsider it. I believe I would be truly upset over that Jordan."

Jordan almost grinned at the protectiveness Tehya felt for the sharp-tongued Journey Taite. And it didn't surprise him. The other woman had no idea how much she was like her missing cousin. They were so alike Micah had remarked that they were all damned lucky they didn't resemble each other. Because there would be no way to hide their familial relationship if they did.

Propping his elbow on the bed, he rested his head against his hand and watched her patiently, waiting for more.

"She looks just like my mother did as a young woman," Tehya finally said softly, the loss she felt over her mother's death echoing in her voice. "Sometimes I let myself imagine what our lives could have been like if Sorrel hadn't destroyed her. Mother would have been happy, I think. She would have made everyone around her happy. No matter how horrible the running could get at times, Mother always had a way to make me smile."

"She passed that gift on to you, Tey," he assured her.

He watched as those fiery curls moved gently when she shook her head before she asked, "What are you going to do to pull the Taites into this? Using Journey would be wrong, Jordan. She deserves more than that."

And it would break Journey's heart if she learned Tehya was the daughter of the deceased Francine and hadn't revealed herself. If Journey was anything like her, she would be hurt because Tehya hadn't confided in her. She would be more than hurt, she would be furious.

"Actually, we're using someone else to bring you in contact with the Taites," he said. "Kell Krieger has decided to go into politics. With the help of his father-in-law, Senator Stanton. He and his wife are hosting their first series of campaign balls and luncheons to allow the senator's backers to get to know him and his wife, Emily. One of those backers is Jordan Malone." He grinned self-mockingly. "I'll be arriving with my new lover, Teylor Johnson, to support my good friend and fellow Navy SEAL."

Tehya collected her robe from the chair by the bed and pulled it on slowly as she allowed the information to process.

She was going to end up with a headache before the night was over. She could feel it building just behind her eyes as she fought back the tension rising inside her.

"You're not going in covert? You're risking not just yourself but your family?" She couldn't believe he would do such a thing. That he would possibly ever bring the Malone name into an operation.

"Too many people know me too well, especially in D.C. Creating a cover will only cause more problems than it can fix."

"I don't like this plan." She gave her head a hard shake. "God, Jordan, you're risking Grandpop? Sabella and the children?"

"There's no risk," he answered definitively, almost convincing her. Almost. "If anything, that risk will be confined to myself only."

She shook her head, her lips parting to speak.

"Tehya." His voice sharpened. "Why would they bother to strike out against my family? It would serve no purpose. Even Sorrel wouldn't have bothered to go so far out of his way. And once they've been neutralized, all they'll know is that an operation targeting them by a law enforcement agency succeeded. Jordan Malone will never be tied to it."

She was shaking her head as she spoke.

"You're insane," she snapped.

"We could always go back to plan A." He shrugged. "As I said, the SEAL base commander in Florida has expressed a lot of interest in having you on his team once he learned Killian wouldn't be acquiring you."

She threw him a glare before sitting on the edge of the bed and turning to watch him furiously.

"Fine. I'll go to Florida." A lifetime of hiding. No true friends, nothing that could truly belong to her. An underground suite without windows again, the knowledge that she never truly belonged. On the outside looking in.

She couldn't do it, but more to the point Jordan knew she couldn't do it.

His smile was tight, knowing. "It won't change the plan," he told her softly. "But I'll have you transported out at daybreak if that's what you want."

"You could go back to retirement." She swallowed tightly. "Go home and help raise your nephew. You've always said if you're not around then Noah and Sabella will spoil him to death."

Of course, he was usually telling Noah that. Noah and his wife Sabella were completely crazy about their son. They would be even worse over the coming daughter, whom they'd already named Mira.

He shook his head slowly. A negative movement that matched his mocking grin.

"In three days, the game begins. We'll leave for D.C. tomorrow evening. There's a suite reserved for us at the Four Seasons in Georgetown. We'll begin a series of carefully coordinated social events until someone bites. We're going fishing sweetheart."

Fishing.

He'd explained that saying before. Carefully coordinated outings where they played the bait and waited to see who would bite. It was a game she had played in the past with Sorrel's men, and she hadn't liked it then: she liked it even less now. "It leaves too much to chance," she argued. "And the risk is too great."

He rose from the bed, naked and powerful.

Tehya watched as he moved around the bed until he reached her. Gripping her shoulders, he pulled her to her feet and unbelted the robe slowly.

"It's time to sleep, baby," he told her gently as he removed the silk and pressed her back down to the bed. "Come on, Tehya, lie with me just a little bit longer. We'll argue the pros and cons of the game on the way to D.C."

He pulled the sheet over them after he climbed in beside her and wrapped his arms around her once again.

"We need to discuss this," she argued helplessly as he held her to him. She had never been very good at arguing with Jordan when he refused to argue back. "Jordan, you're being too damned stubborn."

"I'm being logical. I'm really good at that Tehya, I promise."

She lay there, staring into the darkness, listening to the heavy, sluggish beat of her heart, the panic threatening to choke her, and knew that the final battle she had been putting off all her life was nearing.

But as he said. Jordan always really good when it came to the logic thing and to his plans. He checked every angle, and then every nook and cranny that those angles could present. He was her best chance at survival and she knew it, but that didn't mean she had to like it.

Jordan was aware of the fears that haunted Tehya. As he held her close, simply sharing his warmth, he tried to give her the time she needed to come to grips with the operation they were preparing for as well as the past she had been trying so hard to avoid.

He could feel her heart beating hard and heavy as he stroked her back, and he knew the urge to run, to hide, was nearly more than she could fight. That was all Tehya had ever known for safety, to find a hole and dig in.

The time for hiding was over, though. Whoever had found her, whoever had taken the time and the effort, not to mention the danger, of looking into the explosion in Afghanistan, wouldn't stop.

They had tracked her to Hagerstown, and then had decided to watch her rather than striking. They wanted something from her. Otherwise they would have struck by now. Jordan had run enough ops both as a SEAL and as commander of Elite Ops team, that he recognized the signs.

Tehya wasn't seeing it for what it was because the memories of the past, the blood and death, were all she could see.

Jordan was considering everything, though, and the fact that there were no answers, that there were no clear avenues to follow, sent a chill racing up his spine. Hiding wasn't as easy as many thought it should be. Especially when one hired henchmen like Arthur and Tenneyson. Someone somewhere, a rumor, a drunken employee. There should have been some kind of information, at least one name to indicate who was behind it.

"Why are you here now?" she whispered into the darkness, confusion thick in the soft question.

"Why now what?" He allowed a finger to wrap around a silken curl that trailed down her back.

"Why are you in my bed now, Jordan? And why are you so determined to save me?"

The confusion in her voice was genuine, as though she couldn't understand why he would care. Damn her, he was going to end up with gray hair where she was concerned.

"Why do you think I allowed you into the Elite Ops?" he asked quietly. "You were a civilian, Tehya. The daughter of a known terrorist and white slaver. You could have been a hell of a risk. Why would I allow that?"

He felt her tense in his arms, and hated knowing that the question reminded her of things he realized she wanted to forget.

"Because it was what Kira and Ian wanted." The decisiveness in her tone indicated that she fully believed that.

He chuckled lightly. "Yes, they definitely pushed for it. But Tehya, I could have said no. They wouldn't have liked it. They would have been pissed, but they would have still done their jobs."

He felt her tense marginally, as though she were considering his explanation.

"Then why did you?" Once again her voice echoed with her bemusement.

She truly didn't know.

"Because I wanted to ensure no other man touched you," he said, his hand tightening on her hip to drag her back against the hardening shaft between his thighs. "Because Tehya, as much as I fucking hated it, I couldn't get you out of my head."

And it was no more than the truth.

He could have easily told Tehya no. He wasn't above it. Nothing should have come above the team itself. But Tehya had, and for six years that had been the only defense he had against her. The knowledge that she was his weakness.

As she moved to turn to him, a screaming, high-pitched alarm began tearing through the house.

"Someone's coming in." Tehya was moving instantly, adrenaline kicking in, fear driven out by carefully programmed instinctive responses. The instinct to survive, combined with six years of rigorous training exercises.

Following Tehya, Jordan rolled from the bed.

Within seconds they were both dressed and rushing for the bedroom door.

Weapons were held ready in their hands as they each slung a smaller pack that held extra weapons and ammo over their shoulders. Tehya had grabbed her go bag from the closet, while Jordan slung the large pack, with the more powerful weapons, over his shoulder with the smaller pack.

Jordan jerked a set of communications links from the side pocket of the bag. He activated them quickly before handing Tehya one, a second before attaching the small earbud into his own ear and activating the line, even as they raced from the bedroom.

As they raced through the doorway, the sound of the alarm abruptly stilled, and at the same moment glass exploded into the room as the sound of an explosive charge filled the room.

Jordan felt the bite of icy fury surging through him as he pushed Tehya quickly ahead of him, covering her with the automatic Uzi he carried over his shoulder.

Micah was barking satellite heat signatures into the communication link as automatic fire was returned, blasting through the shattered patio doors and tearing into the drywall and wood that covered the walls.

"Move!" Tehya yelled, surprising him from her position at the door to the garage as she began laying cover fire from an obviously converted P-90 Personal Defense Weapon.

He didn't make her wait.

Throwing himself across the kitchen, away from the flimsy protection of the refrigerator, Jordan rushed through the doorway before pulling her after him.

Just in time. The return fire tore chunks from the door-frame, pelting them through the exit as Jordan threw them both to the floor.

Tehya felt a sharp bite in her right shoulder, but she didn't cry out.

In the next second he gripped her arm, pulling her along the floor as quickly as possible to the exit.

"Micah, are you in place?" he barked into the link.

"We're pulling in now," Micah responded sharply.

"We're at the door. Do you need assist?"

"Get ready to roll, they'll be right behind us."

Gripping the doorknob, the door was pushed open as the metal door on the other side of the room exploded inward.

Helping hands jerked Tehya into the armored black Hummer before Jordan followed, throwing himself as Micah hit the gas and tore out of the driveway.

"They were watching for assistance," Noah reported as automatic gunfire hit the outside of the Hummer before Micah took a sharp curve, putting trees, homes, and vehicles between them and the gunfire.

"We had to take out three of the bastards to get into the driveway," Noah continued, turning in the passenger seat to stare back at Jordan. "We were delayed getting to you because of that."

"Satellite imagery borrowed from a nearby base showed four coming in from the patio, three through the bedroom window, three moving along the driveway entrance, two heading to the garage, and two covering the enclosed van parked on a back street just down from the house. We were able to take out the van, those at the driveway and moving on the garage. There was no way to halt the attack on the house." Noah looked at Tehya where she sat between Jordan and Nik as he apologized.

Jordan watched as she gave a sharp shake of her head.

Her hand lifted to cover her shaking lips. "It's okay, Noah," she whispered hoarsely.

But it wasn't okay, and Jordan knew it.

"Noah, monitor the police channels. Did you leave bodies?"

Noah stared back at him with knowing mockery. "I left trackers on the vehicles."

Of course he hadn't left bodies, just as they hadn't allowed any of the assailants to see who had shot back, wounding their men. A few possibly fatally, but they would still have enough life left in them to get out of the area before witnesses arrived.

"They were moving into the driveway when Noah and I slipped in," Nik said. "I couldn't get in position fast enough so I elected to take those coming in behind the garage instead."

"They moved in stages, Jordan," Micah reported. "They were looking to see what defenses she had. They hit the patio first, then moved into the driveway exit, then the back garage door. It was well coordinated, armed, and manned, with about two-minute intervals set between each."

"Did they suspect we were there?" Noah questioned. "Ten men is a lot for one little girl."

The pain was like an inferno tearing through her sensitive flesh, but it wasn't the first time that had happened. She had taken her first flesh wound at age twelve and her first bullet at fifteen. She hadn't forgotten what it felt like. But this time, it didn't incapacitate her.

"You can thank the little girl for that," Micah grunted, glancing in the mirror once again. "Until her disappearance into the Elite Ops, Tehya Talamosi was well known for her ability to do serious harm to the men sent after her."

Jordan glanced over at her once again to catch the quick blinking of her eyes and the sheen of moisture on her cheeks.

"They suspected I had help. Then next time, they will come prepared."

"They suspected," Jordan affirmed. "There's no doubt in my mind they knew. I'm just very, very curious how they knew, because it's not possible we were seen."

He knew his men.

"We never saw them either," Noah pointed out. "Yet, they knew when she left the house."

"They know too much," Jordan agreed. "It's time we figure out how they know, what they know, and who they're telling."

As they discussed security, logistics, and plans, Tehya found herself deliberately blocking them out. It was that or begin screaming, howling from the pain, both emotional as well as physical.

The flesh wound on her right shoulder was nothing compared to the agony tearing through her heart, though.

Her house. Her home.

It was destroyed.

Her little patio, her beautiful little kitchen.

Her wide open living room.

It was all ruined.

She stared straight ahead and tried not to think about her house. The thick, soft rugs she had spent so much time searching for, the comfortable furniture she had bought with relaxing laziness in mind, the gleaming wood floors that she polished once a week.

It had been her haven, and now that haven had been taken from her.

Her throat was tight with unshed tears, her insides vibrating with rage at the thought of strangers tromping through her home.

Her home.

She had had so little in the past that she could call her own. For the first time, she had believed she could finally live rather than simply exist.

How wrong she had been.

"Are you okay?" Jordan was looking down at her. Obviously becoming concerned as she sat silently beside him.

Could he see the paleness of her skin, possibly the glitter of tears in her eyes? At least he couldn't see the blood slowly easing down her arm.

"I'm fine." It took effort to make herself sound normal.

To hold back the tears that wanted so desperately to fall. She sounded hoarse instead, and a few tears had escaped.

She'd learned long ago, a lifetime ago, that tears didn't help, the pain didn't abate because they were shed. Not the pain in her heart or the pain from a gunshot.

"Sure?" His fingers tucked beneath her chin in a gesture that she should look up.

"I'm fine." She pulled from him easily before staring ahead once again.

From her side, she heard the subtle little growl from Nik, an indication of disappointment, or disapproval. But thankfully, if he had glimpsed the wound, he was keeping his mouth shut.

"Boss, long-range link." Noah handed Jordan the larger satellite-connected link. "We have backup online."

"Who's backup?" she asked Nik quietly, wondering if the team attached to the Elite Ops for ten years was the same team providing backup now.

"We have a small team of marines currently on leave. Emergency backup. We've had them waiting in case they were needed."

For a group that wasn't government backed or government funded, the Elite Ops had always had several military groups as well as advanced weapons at their disposal.

"They got away." The satellite-communications link was jerked from his head minutes later and thrown carelessly to Noah who caught it easily. "Son of a bitch. That would have never happened if Clint and Reno were here."

They got away. Everyone of them.

Tehya stared through the windshield ahead and drew in a deep, shaky breath.

Whoever had invaded her home, whoever had torn aside the shield of safety and security that she had built for herself over the past months, had escaped.

"The team has the house secured and are checking the doors for prints but my guess is they're going to come up empty," Noah spoke then, obviously listening on his own link. "The team commander is dealing with the authorities as Tehya's cousin. Everything's covered."

Tehya gripped her arm tighter. The hard thudding of her heart was pushing blood through her veins and straight to the wound. She could feel the liquid dripping to her jeans, dampening her thigh. She could feel her heart breaking, raging. They had dared to attack her home.

"Head to D.C.," Jordan ordered Micah. "Let's get her secured, then we can figure out the rest of it."

Tehya shook her head.

She felt her breathing hitch, felt the tears want to fall. She could feel the blood at her temple as it eased down her cheek from where the splinters from the bullet striking the door frame had slashed her skin.

The wound in her chest hurt worse, though. Her heart.

Someone had stolen her home from her, not just invaded it.

"Why wait this long to strike?" Micah asked as he hit the interstate heading to D.C. "She said herself she felt she was being followed for weeks. Why not attempt to take her sooner, before she had help? Or hell, when she least expected it?"

"They know she has help." Tehya felt Jordan lift his arm to rub at the back of his neck in irritation. "I was careful coming in and I haven't left her house since arriving. Either they saw one or more of us going in or the house is wired."

"The house isn't wired. I checked while she was at the bar," Noah said.

"We're not going to figure this out now." Jordan's tone was savage. "We will figure this out though, and we'll figure out who's behind it."

"Then we really get to have fun," Micah mused as they sped toward D.C. and the plan Jordan had obviously decided to put in place.

Tehya stared down at her lap, her eyes closing momentarily.

Someone was playing with her, she decided. A cat-and-mouse game in which they had decided to raise the stakes with this attack because they feared she would soon have protection. They had to have suspected or known Jordan was there, that was the only answer.

"Whatever they have in mind, let's see if we can't up the ante for them," Jordan decided.

"We weren't seen," Noah assured him. "We were still pulling together the backup team when her alarm went off, triggering the alert I placed on my cell phone. We barely arrived in time to catch that second team. We wouldn't have if we had actually moved farther than just down the street."

"They knew when to attack," Tehya stated faintly. "Are you certain we're not being followed?"

"We're not being followed." Micah gave a quick shake of his head. "We were out of there before anyone could catch us. Trust me, Tehya, no one's following us and there's no tracker on us, you should know better than that."

Yes, she knew better than to doubt the fact that the team knew exactly how to protect her.

"I knew better, Micah." Her smile, directed at the rearview mirror, betrayed her by shaking perilously. "I'm sorry."

"We're an hour and a half from D.C.," Noah said then, quietly. "You can make it up to me when we get there by making Jordan chill out for the night. You know how he tries to work us into the ground just because he's pissed."

"I'll be sure to do that," she promised, her voice still too raspy.

"An hour and a half is too long."

Tehya felt her breath stop in her chest as Nik spoke up then, his voice a harsh, dangerous growl.

Jordan shifted to stare over her head at the other man.

"She's been shot, Jordan," he said.

CHAPTER 8

She was fine.

She was fine.

Jordan had to keep repeating the words to himself as he they made the drive to D.C.

A quick stop to ascertain the damage, then Nik had taken the front passenger seat for Noah who moved to the far back as Jordan quickly bandaged the arm while Micah drove.

Had the assailants meant to strike her?

Jordan couldn't help but think that they hadn't. For some reason, the bullets had seemed carefully placed. As though the wound was meant to confuse and frighten her, nothing more. Make her vulnerable and easy to capture.

The low-level explosion in her living room had been more for effect and noise than anything else. Each move had been designed for one purpose, to corral her. To weaken and disorient her.

As Noah drove to their destination, Jordan let his fingers play with the curls that cascaded over the arm wrapped around her shoulders.

He'd managed to get a painkiller in her by lying and telling her it was an antibiotic. The dosage had been more than enough to knock her out and force her to rest during the drive. There wasn't a chance in hell she would have taken it otherwise. Tehya detested taking pills for any reason. Even the brutal headaches she often suffered were simply dealt with rather than drugging up, as she called it.

She would be madder than hell once she awoke, though. The last time he had slipped a painkiller into her, she had suffered from a brutal headache that lasted more than a week. That last day he'd gone to her suite to check on her and found her nearly incoherent with pain. At that point he had simply had enough.

But she had awakened without a headache. She'd been mad enough to throw a glass at his head, but she had been refreshed and clear-eyed rather than weeping in pain. It was a choice he made easily. Especially this time. What he saw in her eyes made him insane. He had to find a way to force her to rest.

Force her to close those haunted emerald eyes and ease the pain that filled them. Force the ragged, uneven breaths that were holding back sobs to even out.

She was breaking his heart.

From the moment those wide eyes had met his as they realized someone was attempting to gain entrance into the house, they had shattered with the knowledge that her security was being stolen.

Knowing she had been found, knowing someone was following her, wasn't nearly as destructive to her as the attack on her home. What they had done to her tonight, Jordan could easily kill over. The men who had violated her home had damaged it so severely, that they might have irreparably damaged the roots she had finally found the courage to put down.

"We're ten minutes out," Noah said quietly. "Nik is texting Kell Krieger."

Jordan gave a brief nod. "I want to get her to the Four Seasons. We can't layover at the senator's place. The risk to Kell's family is too high."

"We haven't been followed," Micah protested irately. "Damn, has Tehya's lack of confidence in me, fucking affected you too, Commander?" There was no heat in his voice, but there was definitely irritation.

"Would you bet Risa and your children's lives on it?" Jordan asked him. "Would you take us into your home if you had any other choice?"

Jordan stared into the rearview mirror, watching the former agent's expression. He knew Micah's training, and he knew they weren't being followed. That didn't mean they couldn't be tracked.

Micah grimaced. "Four Seasons," he stated.

"I thought you'd see it my way." Jordan nodded. "Our only contact with Kell or Senator Stanton will be no more, no less, than required as a close acquaintance and business associate unless we have no other choice. Our first contact will be made at the party tomorrow night."

"Mikayla has Tehya's wardrobe nearly completed. She was able to use the sizes from the weekend attire she made for her just before we disbanded." Nik was proud of his wife, a successful dressmaker whose name was increasingly being shared among the elite as "unique" and a "must-have" when it came to their social attire. Fortunately, with the additional seamstresses she'd hired, she was able to get the dresses Tehya would require completed quickly.

Jordan gave a short nod as he forced himself not to hold Tehya too close. He wanted to pull her close enough that she melded with his flesh. That he could heal her pain simply by wishing it done. Damn, he couldn't bear what he knew tonight had done to her.

"Stanton and Krieger are going to require updates as well as mission planning," Noah said quietly. "Arranging that could be difficult if we're going on acquaintance only and using your real identity."

Jordan gave a shake of his head. "We'll invite them to lunch at the Four Seasons to discuss various business concerns Kell and I share. We can take care of everything there."

"We'll need to come up with explanations for our presence as well," Noah reminded him.

"We weren't expecting this, and you didn't plan for it." There was an edge of smugness in Noah's tone.

"Don't bet on it," Jordan snorted. "When we arrive at the

Four Seasons, contact John and Travis; they're already there and you'll find our suites are waiting for us."

Nik chuckled lightly. "Haven't you given up trying to catch him without a plan, Noah?"

Noah snorted. "Not in this lifetime. One of these days, I'll catch him, though."

Jordan's lips quirked at his nephew's response, but Noah wasn't kidding. He'd been trying to catch Jordan without a plan for as long as he'd been walking. Thankfully he just hadn't been around to see the effects when Jordan overlooked an angle. There was a reason he was so fucking careful.

"I wouldn't bet on that," Micah chuckled. "Hell, you're just like him, Noah. We all are since working with him. One of these days it will be our kids trying to catch us without a plan."

Noah and Nik both responded with amused groans, but Jordan couldn't regret the training he'd drilled into them for so many years. Even Tehya hadn't escaped, and the proof that she had listened lay in the carefully packed emergency bag she'd had ready when it came time to run.

Just as Noah had proved himself when he contacted a nearby retired Special Forces commander and two of his men to move into the apartment over his garage and watch over his home and family on the small rise next to it. And the others had made arrangements for their families as well. Just in case.

"Make sure the men we hired to cover Grandpop, Sabella, and Grant are in place," Jordan told his nephew. "I don't expect trouble there, but I'd rather be safe than sorry once we begin flushing out whoever is giving the orders here." Contingency plans, back up positions. He was accused often of being a paranoid son of a bitch, but that was preferable to the alternative.

"We're moving up on the Four Seasons," Micah said as he maneuvered the Hummer through the streets toward the exclusive hotel.

"Contacting John and Travis," Nik announced, his harsh voice darker, deeper than normal as he glanced back at Tehya sleeping in Jordan's arms.

She was like the kid sister of the unit, Jordan knew. During the months they had been out of touch with her, they had tried to maintain their distance, believing it was what she wanted.

None of them had ever imagined that Killian had used the time he had been at the base, before the group had disbanded, to reprogram her phone.

The satellite phone and the Viper had been "gifts" from the Ops that would allow them to always be in contact with her. Just in case their identities were cracked or the team were somehow threatened.

"Travis and John are taking care of camera surveillance at the hotel while Lilly and Bailey are running interference," Nik reported as he held his phone to his ear. "We'll pull up to the rear entrance where Lilly and Bailey will get you to the suite without being seen. Micah, Noah, and I will take care of the Hummer and collect another secured vehicle."

Jordan gave a tight nod before maneuvering Tehya carefully in his arms, wincing at her mumbled moan.

The small, drowsy whimper pierced his heart. The painkiller he had given her was a powerful one and still, the pain had slipped past it enough to pull a low cry from her as he moved her.

"In ten, Jordan," Micah advised him. "Ten, nine, eight . . ."

At one, the vehicle slowed to a crawl as Jordan pushed the door open and stepped from the vehicle with Tehya in his arms.

Lilly Harrington Caine, Travis' wife, was at the door, swinging it open as Jordan rushed past her. Just inside, John Vincent's wife, Bailey Seaborne, a former C.I.A. agent waited patiently.

"We have twenty seconds on surveillance interference," Bailey told him quietly. "We're using the staff elevator."

They stepped inside the open elevator as Lilly followed then quickly inserted an electronic key, overrode the normal controls, and hit the button for the top floor.

"You have the Presidential," Bailey told him. "John checked you in night before last. Micah, Nik and Noah have the attached suites on each side. We've received the intel on the attack on the house via Commander Reece and we'll have that to you as soon as John and Travis return."

"Reece?" Jordan questioned roughly as he shot her a furious look. "And how the hell did he get anything on it, let alone intel?"

Bailey gave a brief shake of her dark head. "I have no idea. But he was in contact with your backup team within seconds of them going in and coordinated satellite and strike intel with them. He wants contact ASAP and he's questioning his exclusion from the Op."

"Fuck him," Jordan muttered as the elevator slid to a halt.

"This way." Lilly, moved quickly along the thickly carpeted hall to the open double doors of the suite just above the elevator hallway entrance.

She closed the door as he stepped quickly inside the room and headed to the bedroom at the far end of the suite.

"A physician has been contacted," Lilly informed him. "He'll be here within the hour and slipped in as well."

Jordan stepped into the bedroom and headed for the large bed across the room

Cloud soft, gleaming white, the comforter had been stripped back to reveal a protective covering that had been placed to keep the blood from the silk sheets below.

Laying Tehya on the bed carefully, Jordan drew the serviceable sheet at the side over her.

"She's sedated," he told Lilly as she stood at the end of the bed, her dark, moss-green gaze concerned as she watched Jordan lay Tehya down carefully. "It's only a flesh wound, but . . ." He wiped his hand over his face. How the hell was he supposed to tell her that he just couldn't bear to see the pain in Tehya's eyes any longer?

He was a hardened soldier, but Tehya just did thing to his heart.

"But she breaks your heart when you have to look in her eyes and see the shattered dreams," Lilly stated softy, her aristocratic face drawn into an expression of concern and sympathy. "I completely understand why you would sedate her Jordan. It's likely the only way she would have slept.

"Is everyone aware of what she does to me?" he smiled with an edge of self mockery. "And here I thought I was hiding it."

Lilly's smile was gentle, soft. "Everyone but Tehya, I would guess," she said. "And I believe she has a problem seeing beyond her perceived beliefs of why she isn't good enough for you to see the truth of what you do feel. Besides, being Sorrel's daughter is a tremendous burden to her. She's terrified it will become a burden for you as well."

Jordan shot her a sharp look.

"She knows being Sorrel's daughter isn't something I give a damn about." He shook his head faintly. "There has to be another reason why she was so determined run."

Lilly gave a bitter snort of laughter. "No, Jordan, trust me, once you accept that you came from pure evil, getting past it is never easy. If I hadn't had Travis to keep me centered when I learned that lesson, I might not have survived."

Lilly had been forced to face the fact that her own mother had considered her flawed, broken. And that she had carefully planned her own daughter's murder.

"Contact Travis and John, make certain everything is going as planned," he ordered her as he looked around the room, searching for anything that would indicate a problem. "And tell him I want the Intel Reece provided, ASAP."

Lilly had begun to give a quick nod when Bailey stepped into the room.

"John and Travis are here," she told Jordan. "The doctor's ETA is twenty minutes. He's being met by Nik, Micah, and Noah. They'll escort him through the rear entrance and up here."

Jordan glanced down at Tehya, hating like hell to leave her alone.

"Go, I'll sit with her," Lilly told him as she moved to the comfortable recliner next to the bed, and smiled back at him. "I promise, she'll be fine with me."

He knew she would be, and it wasn't as though Tehya's problem was life-threatening. Still, pulling away from her and stalking into the main portion of the suite was nearly impossible.

When she awoke, she would be groggy and pissed the hell off. And strangely enough, he wanted to ensure he was the one with her. The only one to watch out for her until she was feeling herself again.

As he stepped into the combined living and dining room, John and Travis turned from their discussion, their gazes flickering in concern to the open bedroom door.

"She's still asleep," he answered the unspoken question in their eyes. "Fuck, I knew it would happen, I just didn't expect it so soon." Travis raked his fingers through his dark blond hair in frustration. Jordan almost wished he could just tone down whatever he was feeling to that level as well.

"Always plan for the worst," Jordan sighed. "Though to be honest, I didn't expect it to happen this quickly myself."

"The backup team we were lucky enough to have in place in Hagerstown did manage to get a few prints," John injected. "As soon as we have a hit on those from our contact at the FBI, maybe we'll have a better idea who or what we're looking for."

"Remnants of Sorrel's organization," Jordan informed them. "I'm almost certain of it. I just can't figure out why, after all these years. What kind of threat does she represent that has someone going to the trouble, not to mention the expense, of launching such a search and attempted capture of her?"

As Jordan spoke, Travis shot John a hard look.

John grimaced at the obvious message in the other man's gaze.

"I know you wanted Killian excluded from this," he said as he reached to the table for the heavy file. "A courier dropped this off about half an hour before your arrival. Evidently there has been some movement over the past few years to reorganize and revive Sorrel's operation."

"By who? And why do they need Tehya to do this?" Son of a bitch.

Tehya was right. Somehow Sorrel was reaching out from the grave to haunt her.

"According to the information Killian has managed to pull together, whoever's behind it believes Tehya is a key to the funding the operation." John moved to the table and pulled out the chair in the front of the file.

Casting a quick glance to the bedroom door, Jordan followed.

"Here's the will Tehya's grandfather, Bernard Taite, left before his death." A stack of legal papers was pulled from the file. "According to this, if Francis Taite, or one of her children, were ever found, then their inheritance would be incredible. The Taite main estate, which is currently occupied by his brother, Stephen Taite, and his family, would be immediately turned over to the heir. That includes two large estate homes, four guest cottages, various cars, limos, servants, jewels, you get the picture." John waved his hand to the will.

"The Taites are one of the richest families in France," Travis picked up. "They're related to both the French and English crowns, with Stephen Taite holding the position of not just the third cousin to the king but also included on his board of advisors."

"How much would Taite industries pay to have their heir back?" John asked. "Better yet, how much would any or all of them pay to see her disappear forever?"

"How much would she be worth if she could be brainwashed to obey the whims of her captors instead, if they had managed to capture her that night?"

The sun was rising beyond the narrow slit of the heavy curtains across from the table.

Travis sat back and stared at the will for long moments.

"As the legal heir to the Benard Taites fortune, the amount would be more than I want to sit and figure up for them."

Neither did Jordan, but the amount would be enough to make any man risk the attempt.

"Any word in there concerning who contacted Arthur and Tenneyson concerning the true details of Tehya's death?"

John picked up the papers in the file and rifled through them for a moment before pulling the printed report free.

Jordan accepted the page, his gaze moving to read the detailed report, as a frown pulled at his brow.

"Origination, Hagerstown, Maryland," he murmured, then looked at each man. "Did you track the number?"

"The number went back to here." Travis pulled the report free.

The number had originated from Room 714 of one of the better hotels in town.

"At the same time, Tehya was registered there while she was having interior work done on the house."

"The caller didn't reveal her location, though why he bothered to keep it quiet made no sense," John grunted. "Because they revealed her name."

"Be too helpful and you can sabotage yourself," Jordan pointed out. "The caller gave just enough information to ensure the story was checked." He tapped his finger against the file. "How did Killian acquire the information?"

"He sent a four-man team to Afghanistan after you discussed returning Tehya to base. He asked that you contact him concerning that, by the way," Travis stated mockingly.

Jordan gave a quiet snarl of disgust.

"Yeah, that's what we thought, too," John approved. "But he had a team still working this. They're currently in France attempting to put together a list of known associates for Ira Arthurs and Mark Tenneyson. Maybe we'll get lucky."

Jordan shook his head before leaning back in the chair and glaring at the curtains covering the windows across from him.

Some habits were impossible to break. He still kept the blinds pulled securely in his apartment in Texas. He had noticed, though, that Tehya kept the curtains over the kitchen sink open. She had been attempting to break the habit.

"You won't find the person behind this on any list," he finally told the other two men. "If Arthurs, Tenneyson, or anyone else sent after her knew who they were working for, then their name would have already shown up."

John's muttered curse just about summed it up.

"Travis, pull together our contacts in France," Jordan ordered. "What I want to know is, who among the elite moneyed set had ties to Sorrel that weren't found until after his death. Anyone related to him who would have the means to pull this off, or anyone among his social set who could reorganize the business or revive it. I'm betting we'd find the name on that list."

As he moved to close the file, he caught a shadow of movement from the bedroom doorway.

Turning his head, he caught the sign from Bailey that Tehya was waking up.

"This is connected to the Taites, their money and influence," he finished as he rose to his feet. "Arthurs and Tenneyson are watching the Taites, and it's obvious they're watching for Tehya. Let's see what happens when we give them something."

He didn't wait for their opinion. Moving across the room, he headed for the bedroom and the woman too many damned men seemed way too interested in.

"She's waking up." Lilly nodded to Tehya with a soft smile, as Jordan entered the bedroom. "Doc will be here in a few. See if you can get her to cooperate. We all know how much she loves the medical profession."

"Which means not at all," he grunted, his gaze moving to the bed and the woman in it.

Lilly's brows lifted, waggled, and a knowing grin crossed her face as Tehya's lashes flickered open. The door closed softly as Lilly and Bailey returned to the front room.

Staring down at her, Jordan held back his grin as that first drowsy irritation crossed her face before her gaze adjusted, knowledge filtered through, and irritation turned to a spark of anger. As she caught sight of him.

"You drugged me," she breathed out heavily. "Asshole."

"We have a doc heading in to check the wound," he told her. "You were in pain, Tehya."

She gave a weak little snort. "This ain't my first rodeo, cowboy."

No, it wasn't. She'd been wounded before.

She amazed him sometimes. One minute she was in tears over the invasion of her home, and in the next second so blasé about a fucking gunshot wound that the thought of the past she had lived had sweat popping out on his brow.

"It may not be your first rodeo, but you were too weak and you'd lost too much blood for my comfort level," he informed her. "You needed to rest until we could safely stop, check the wound, then call a doctor in to look at it. You may need stitches."

The weak little glare she shot him was almost amusing. It would have been, except for the anger he glimpsed in her eyes. That look assured him there might be hell to pay once she managed to regain her strength and lost the grogginess.

To a point, sometimes, he could maneuver her, but there was no controlling her. Especially when she was pissed. And Tehya was edging very damned close to pissed where he was concerned.

"And if we had been attacked while on the road? What then?" She struggled to sit up in the bed, her expression irate before she winced at the pain to her arm

"Let me help you." He reached for her, only to have her slap his hand away with a glare. "Dammit, Tehya, you're going to cause yourself to start bleeding again then you'll really need stitches if you pull the adhesive I used loose."

Tehya slowly pushed herself from the bed, the grogginess in her head making her teeth clench.

She really didn't like being drugged. And she had no problem letting anyone know when there was something she didn't like.

She'd learned quick enough that Jordan and his men did not care if she suffered her anger in silence.

She ignored him, pushing herself up with her good arm until she was sitting on the side of the bed and glaring at him. "Answer me," she bit out, her voice strengthening marginally. "What would have happened if we had been attacked on the road and I was unconscious? I would have been dead weight, Jordan."

"Good thing you don't weigh much," he quipped, then watched as she dropped her head, shaking it slowly. She wasn't even considering the other side of the coin. She would have been vulnerable to enemies with an unknown agenda. All she was considering was whether or not she would have slowed him or the team down.

"I had everything covered, Tehya," he promised when she said nothing more. "It was an hour-and-a-half trip and you were hurting like hell. You've lost sleep, and you're riding on nerves. I wasn't going to let you suffer like that when I knew the pain medication would help. Besides, there was an antibiotic with it. You have a head start on fighting back an infection."

Tehya lifted her head and stared back at him, outraged. She couldn't believe he had drugged her. How dare he have taken such a decision out of her hands?

"I fucking hate drugs," she snapped, realizing her voice was still too weak to really hold any force. "And I was fine. It hurt. I was pissed off that my home was invaded, but if you had trusted me you wouldn't have drugged me. What did you have to do, Jordan, that you didn't want me to see or hear?"

Jordan always had plans. He was especially good at those contingency plans that no one was aware of but him. Had that had something to do with the reason he had drugged her? Was there a part of what was going on that he didn't want her to know?

She watched as his gaze narrowed, his expression tightening with a hint of anger and disbelief that she had asked the question. "I've always trusted you, Tehya."

"Whatever," she snorted back at him as though it didn't matter, and she didn't believe him in the least.

But she wanted to believe him. God, she needed to believe him right now, because she felt as though her entire world were being jerked out from under her. "Where's the shower? I stink of blood. God, I hate that smell."

She needed to clear her head and clean the feeling of betrayal from her senses. Even more, she wanted to escape the memories that the scent of blood triggered.

Her mother's blood, fresh, oozing from a knife wound that was too deep and refused to clot. "I'm okay." The sickening iron stench invading her nostrils as she tried to help her mother apply a tourniquet. "It's okay, sweetie. See, Momma is fine." Her mother, so weak and still trying so hard to smile despite her pain.

It was too much. She didn't want to remember, she didn't want to feel what she had felt each time her mother had nearly been caught.

"Let me help you up." Jordan didn't take no for an answer. Before she could evade him, he moved to her and all but lifted her from the bed.

She pushed away from him as soon as she was standing steady on her feet, the irritation combining with the drugged, out of sorts feeling. If she had the strength, she'd kick his ass. She wished she just had the strength to kick him.

Well, she'd try to kick his ass. She might consider it anyway. Threaten him. She wouldn't get far.

"Drug me again, Jordan, and I'm out of this little game. I'll show you and my would-be captors exactly what I've learned during my time in hiding and disappear for good."

She hoped he believed her. She prayed he did. Because if he ever did anything so asinine again, she might very well end up trying to kill him herself.

"Tehya." His hold became firmer on her arm as the expression on his face hardened to pure make dominance. "Don't threaten me. And don't run. I promise, if you run on me I'll make damned sure you understand the error of your ways within twenty-four hours flat. Are we understood here?"

She stared back at him furiously.

"I'll tie you to a bed and fuck you until you can't consider running ever again, sweetheart. I'll make sure you're so tired, the memory of pleasure so deep, the ache for more so ingrained inside you that even the thought of running will be erased from your mind."

Her brow arched. "If I had known that, Jordan, I would have run years ago," she told him, her voice lowering as she allowed her gaze to rake over him suggestively.

He wasn't the only one that knew how to use the hunger burning between them

He was aroused. His cock was pressed hard and tight behind the zipper of his jeans. And she remembered clearly, *very* clearly, exactly what it was like to have him buried inside her. To have his cock stretching her until she was certain she could take no more, thrusting inside her, throbbing erotically against nerve endings that felt fully exposed.

As her gaze returned to his, she watched the blue darken, glitter with hunger and dominance. And just that fast her pussy was aching and wet, and all too ready for him. God, what was she going to do when he was gone. How would she survive losing him a second time when even the dream of a home wasn't there to fall back on.

Slowly, he drew back, rather than following through with the threat. Disappointment clenched her chest and had her drawing in a ragged breath.

"The doctor will be here within the next twenty minutes," he warned her, his tone low and dark with a hint of sex. "Be careful Tehya, or he'll see more than either of us want him to see."

Tehya escaped to the shower though she would have preferred his touch. The suite they were in was gorgeous, elegant. Marble floors in the bathroom with a walk-in shower and large Jacuzzi tub. Heat lamps lit up above her as she flipped the lights on, spreading an edge of warmth through the room as she undressed, adjusted the temperature of the water, and stepped beneath the heated spray.

She was careful to keep her arm out of the spray. Stepping back from the stream of moisture, she washed her hair awkwardly. To rinse it, she turned her side to the water and worked the lather from the long curls.

It took twice as long as usual but when she was finished, she felt as though she might actually be able to think clearly soon. The warmth of the shower helped clear some of the drowsy lethargy from her head and though she still felt weak, at least she didn't feel as though she would fall asleep on her feet.

Wrapping a towel around her, she held back the wince at the sharp pains to her arm as she finished. Painkillers would be nice if they didn't knock her on her ass. Unfortunately, that was exactly what they did. They left her feeling worse than the pain did, without the benefit of being aware of what the hell was going on around her.

As she stepped from the cubicle, she came to a hard stop her breath suspending in her chest as excitement began to rage through her body once again and anticipation dampened her pussy.

Jordan stepped into the bathroom.

He'd obviously showered as well. His thick, black hair was still damp, and he had changed into a pair of sweatpants and a T-shirt.

God, his feet were bare.

A man shouldn't have sexy feet, but he did. To be so damned big, they were strong, male, and powerful. Even his damned toenails were perfect.

"What do you want?" she asked, her voice husky, breathless from the hard fierce throbbing of her heart in her chest.

He should be illegal. He should have to wear an ugly disguise when he was in public to weaken his effect on the female of the species. Because she wasn't the only woman to grow immediately wet at the sight of him.

"Doc is here," he told her, the lazy drawl in his voice filled with knowing arousal as his gaze slid over her body. "Keep the towel on. He'll need access to the arm though."

Tehya rolled her eyes, but she wasn't stupid. She knew the wound had to be checked. The towel was large enough that she was well covered, but it still left the heavy slice on the outside of her bicep accessible.

Thankfully, the doctor was old enough that she felt reasonably comfortable, and he was well supplied with all the tools of his trade. One of those tools was a numbing cream that he used on the wound before bandaging it.

Within minutes the worst of the pain eased, giving her some relief without the grogginess of the pills.

"You need to pack that stuff in your bag." She informed Jordan. "Steal it or something."

"The wound isn't too bad," the doctor assured them as he and Jordan both ignored her. Though, bless his heart, he left the tube on the table as he repacked his bag and stared down at her with kind eyes. "You should feel right as rain once you've slept for a while and the wound has a chance to start healing. Keep the cream on it, keep both cloth and adhesive bandages. Don't use the arm any more than you have to and you shouldn't have any problems."

He laid out a small bottle of medication. "It's not too strong, even for your system." His lips quirked in a grin. "Mr. Malone explained your sensitivity to painkillers. It has some pain medication and antibiotics. Once every four hours unless you want a nasty infection."

She stared at the packet and clenched her teeth in frustration. She detested pills and medications of any sort. No matter what they said, the stuff always made her groggy at the very least.

"Take one now, my dear." The doctor laid one of the oval pills in her hand. "Have you ever seen gangrene? I'm certain one so pretty wouldn't want such a nasty infection."

She swore he was in league with Jordan.

She took the pill. If it knocked her out and she managed to wake up safe and sound, then she would make certain Jordan paid for it. And the look she shot him promised retribution, because she knew, somehow, he had found a way to man-uever this pill thing.

As the doctor left the room and the door closed behind him, Tehya gathered up the change of clothes Jordan had laid out for her.

Soft lounge pants, a loose T-shirt, and warm socks. She kept them in her go-bag. A girl never knew when she was going to need to be comfortable. That and makeup, and she was usually good to go in almost any situation.

Pulling her make up bag from the pack, she took out the moisturizer before placing the bag on the chest.

"What are you doing?" He stepped in front of her as she headed for the bathroom.

"I'm going to get dressed, Jordan," she said sarcastically.

"It's time for bed, Tehya," he shot back in return. "And you don't need to get dressed for that."

Hell, when he dropped his voice like that he made her stomach clench in hunger. There were times when loving him, needing him as she did, could be a terrible distraction. And this was one of those times.

"I've already slept, remember?" She argued as she shot him a glare.

"That was no more than a nap," he scoffed as he blocked her way once more.

What the hell was his problem?

"I'm too restless to sleep." She narrowed her eyes back at him suspiciously. "Go away, Jordan. Surely you can find something better to do than aggravating me to death." If he couldn't think of anything, then she was certain she could.

Jordan grinned. "That's okay, baby, I have a cure for that."

The towel fell to the floor as Tehya felt her breath catch. Her body flooded with heat and sensitivity. The cool air of the air-conditioned room washed over her. It was an additional caress as she felt Jordan step behind her. The warmth of his chest warmed her, creating a feeling of security even as she felt the arousal beginning to surge out of her control, as his hand slid slowly down her arms, gripping the hand of her good arm and guiding it up until she curved her fingers along the nape of his neck.

Jerking against his grip she almost escaped, only to be pulled back into his arms as he chuckled wickedly and replaced her hand. Why was she fighting him? Oh yeah, that's right, he had drugged her, deliberately, when he knew she hated it.

"Stop fighting me, Tehya. You don't know what you're doing."

He obviously hadn't expected her to try to escape again. This time, she made it free of his arms and turned to face him. She had every intention of telling him exactly what she thought of his high-handedness. Despite the fact that there wasn't a time that she didn't crave his touch, that didn't mean he had to be so confident that she was his for the taking.

The she saw something in his eyes that had the juices spilling from her pussy, lubricating the bare folds and sensitizing her clit. A blazing dominant lust that all but glowed in his eyes and tightened his expression in intense, carnal, burning arousal. A powerful need she could already feel herself weakening to.

She had always suspected it lurked there. That overwhelming, pure dominance gleaming in those sapphire blue eyes as his gaze raked over her body.

"What am I doing, Jordan?" she asked, her lips parting to breathe in roughly as she dared to challenge him. "Refusing to put my head down and obey your every whim? Is that what you require in your women? Submission? Damn, and here I don't do submission so well? Perhaps you should spank me." She licked her lips slowly "Or something?"

She was naked and defying him, and there was a thrill racing through her that made her feel intoxicated. For now, a sense of power began whipping through her. A knowledge, an instinct where her lover was concerned. Where her own hidden, unrealized needs had once lain dormant, she could now feel them rising fast and out of control.

Jordan watched the challenge building in her eyes, the steamy seductive heat as it made her expression drowsy with sensual hunger and a need for that challenge to be met and conquered.

He was going to fuck her until they were both gasping for air and too weak to move. Until there wasn't a chance in hell she could forget exactly who her very beautiful, very aroused body belonged to.

Tehya stared at him, her breathing heavy and rough as she sensed that sexual edge sharpening inside him. The look in his eyes sent a chill of anticipation racing up her spine. She had never seen that expression on his face before, never done more than catch a fleeting glimpse of the powerful needs he had hidden so carefully.

"You're mine," he bit out suddenly, forcefully, shocking her with the depth of the declaration. "As long as we're in this together, by God, you're mine and you will survive this, Tehya. No matter what I have to do to ensure it. And you will not fight me further where your protection is concerned."

Oh, she wouldn't?

"Kiss my ass," she retorted, knowing damned well the affect it would have on him.

His lashes lowered, blue fire erupting in his gaze as the words slipped past her lips, and reacted on his senses.

"Oh baby, with pleasure. It will be my absolute pleasure."

As pure unadulterated lust exploded in his eyes, he gripped her wrist and pulled her quickly to him, straight into his arms, his grip unbreakable as he held her snug against him.

Her nipples were so hard, so sensitive, they throbbed with the swollen response that tightened them as they rasped against the material of his T-shirt. Her sex flooded with warmth, with the slick essence that prepared her body for his possession. The reaction was so quick, so strong it swept through her control and laid it to waste with immediate response. Her breath caught, a gasp parting her lips and giving him the opening he needed.

Jordan took complete advantage. His lips lowered and the kiss shattered her defenses, if there had been left against him. His lips possessed and marauded stroking over her lips and throwing her headlong in desperate need. She met the kiss, suddenly so aroused, so out of control that she met his kiss with the same forceful need that he spilled into her.

They ate at each other's lips. Tongues dueled, fought for control of the kiss, and for control of each other

The wound on her arm was forgotten. Whether it was the cream or the drugs or the lust, or a combination of the three, she wasn't certain. She also wasn't hurting for anything but Jordan's touch.

Straining to get closer, to feel the touch of him against every cell of her naked body, Tehya moaned in distress. She couldn't get close enough. She couldn't kiss him enough, couldn't taste him enough.

She couldn't claim him hard enough or fast enough for the hunger raging through her. Her hands pushed beneath his shirt, finding hard male flesh and curling her nails against it.

His arms were around her, clasping her tight to him as she fought to touch more of him, to holding him closer to her. She felt herself lifted, moving, until she felt the bed against the back of her legs. She felt sensations brewing, whipping inside her. A storm she couldn't resist and pleasure began whipping through her.

Jordan tore his head back, his blue eyes flaming as she met his gaze.

"Kiss your ass?" he growled. "Oh baby, I'm going to do so much more than that to your gorgeous tight little ass."

CHAPTER 9

Tehya felt the bed at her back as Jordan lowered her to the mattress, before standing in front of her and stripping until he was as naked as she was. Hard, heavy muscle flexed beneath his chest as he came to her, his knees pressing into the bed as he came to its center, his head lowering until his lips could brush over her collarbone, his tongue licking a trail of pure heat across her sensitive flesh. The touch had a low moan escaping her lips as she arched closer to him.

Flames began to spread through her system as the exhilerating kisses moved over the curve of a breast, and his hand smoothed up her side to the swollen undercurve. He cupped it dominantly, his lips descending on the tight, hard tip of her nipple.

The ultrasensitive swollen bud throbbed in pleasure as he sucked it into his mouth, drawing on it and pulling every wracking sensation of need from her nipple to the tight, aching nubbin of her clitoris.

With his free hand Jordan stroked down her abdomen, his callused fingertips rasping over her flesh as exquisite bliss began to rock through her body. She was to the point of shaking, shuddering with the powerful carnal rapture building inside her.

His fingers trailed to her thighs, stroking, caressing as her hips lifted, desperately seeking his touch against the swollen, needy folds of her sex.

She would have screamed for more if she had the breath, if she could find enough oxygen to do more than whimper as she tried to beg for more, for a firmer, rougher touch.

Her clit ached with an intense demand, pinpoints of electric sensation sizzling to the aching bud before whipping through her vagina with agonizing need.

She couldn't bear it. She needed his touch there now, his fingers stroking, caressing, driving inside her, fucking into her with a force that would send her flying into orgasm.

Strange, mewling little cries vibrated in her throat. She'd never heard such a sound coming from her own lips. It pulsed with hunger, with need, a reflection of the sensations racing through her, out of control.

As his fingertips finally eased between her thighs and stroked through the burning folds to rasp against her clit, she lost her breath. There was no strength, no will to do anything but strain against him and fight for the touch that would throw her headlong to the edge of ecstasy.

There was no oxygen to scream, let alone cry. There was only the feel of his fingers caressing her cunt, sliding through the slick slit, between swollen folds to circle the agonizing throb of her clit. The firm circular motions sent vivid ribbons of clashing sensations whipping through her body.

His teeth nipped gently at the tender bud of her nipple, arching her tight against him as her nails bit into his shoulders. Her hips writhed beneath the caress of his fingers, pressing closer, fighting for a deeper, harder penetration, for the stretching heat, the pleasure pain that Jordan knew how to give her.

Waves of sensation washed through her as she fought to hold on to Jordan. The vortex of pure bliss rushing through her was like a tidal wave swamping her control.

Just when she thought she could hold on to that last remaining ounce of reason, a scream tore from her lips.

Two fingers, thrust into the tight, slick depths of her pussy, nearly throwing her over the edge of release. It clenched in her womb, spasming warningly and shocking her senses.

Pulsing flames shuddered through her as his lips lifted from her nipple, kissed the curve of her breast, then nipped at the fragile flesh.

His fingers eased from her clenched sex before he moved, drawing away as she fought to hold him to her, fought for more of that incredible pleasure as his touch deserted her pussy.

"Come here, baby," he groaned, lifting her as he lay back, bringing her to her knees. Her rear faced him, her head poised over the straining length of his cock as he gripped the base of the heavy flesh.

Heavily veined, the head flushed dark, the thick shaft rose to his abdomen as the fingers of his free hand slid to the long curls that fell over her shoulder, clenched, and pulled.

Tehya's breath caught at the eroticism in the possessive action, as he silently demanded the incredibly intimate act.

"You know what I want, Tey," he groaned, his tone rasping with a dark sensual caress against her senses.

As she moved to turn to face him, a hard hand at her hip held her in place. Oh God, she knew what he wanted, just as she sensed what he was planning to do. A sexual act she'd never participated in before. One she had fantasized about sharing with him

"Like this," he demanded as he drew her hips toward his shoulders with one hand while the other tugged erotically at her hair once again. "Just like this, baby. And we'll see who loses their mind first."

Trembling she licked her lips as her head lowered to the flushed crest of his engorged cock head as he gripped her knee, lifting her leg over his face until her pussy was poised, bare flesh saturated with her juices, above his lips, while the hard tips of her breasts rasped against his lower stomach. Heat spread through her system as she gripped the base of his cock, unable to surround it, but holding it in place as her head lowered.

She fought to breathe, to draw in oxygen as she felt

Jordan's lips at her thighs. Heated kisses and hungry licks had her hips shifting as she fought to press the swollen folds of her sex to his lips, struggling against the the firm grip holding her from her goal.

Her tongue licked over the swollen crest of his erection, a hungry moan passing her lips at the taste of male heat and hunger that glistened on the swollen, throbbing, head of his cock.

She was drowning in pleasure. Her lips parted, drawing the wide, blunt crown between them, filling her mouth with the hard, delicious heat. Her tongue flickered over the blunt tip, to taste, to relish the strength and hunger she held in her hands.

His tongue licked over the swollen, soaked folds of her pussy. With wicked, probing licks his tongue stroked and explored. Rimming the clenched opening of her vagina, he gave a firm, loving lick before thrusting inside for a quick taste before retreating.

Tehya wanted to scream, she needed to scream, but the sound was muffled by his dick as his tongue swiped through the slit of her pussy and circled her clit with quick agonizing strokes. It was like liquid fire feverish and intense. An inferno circled the sensitive bud, throbbed to her womb, and sent crashing waves of sensation through her every nerve ending in her body.

To counter the destructive effect he was having on her, Tehya had to force herself to think, to use the sensual instincts rushing through her, to concentrate on Jordan rather than the pleasure he was giving her.

Working her mouth over the wide, flared cap of his erection Tehya's hand stroked the heavy shaft, palmed the tight sac beneath it, and alternately raked his thighs with a firm rasp of her nails. Sucking him deeper, she tucked her tongue beneath the flared edge of his cock head, stroked and rubbed, glorying in the hard, muted groan that rumbled into her sex.

Jordan's hips jerked, pushing his dick harder against her lips as he lost control of the growl he'd been holding in his chest.

His tongue licked, caressed, and probed at the entrance to her pussy. Drawing her juices free, he tasted the sweet rich essence, before licking to her clit and allowing his fingers to find the heavy cream easing from her.

Tehya, shuddered as she felt his fingers press slowly inside her, withdraw, then press inside her again. It was a pattern intent on driving her crazy with need until he made his intentions fully clear.

His fingers began drawing her slick juices of her pussy back to her anus. Once he reach the nerve-laden entrance, he used the rich essence to lubricate the tender hole before his fingers began to push slowly, gently inside the forbidden entrance.

Her flesh stretched and burned, the overwhelming sensations scouring across her nerve endings.

His fingers retreated, drew more of her juices back and began easing his fingertips slowly, gently inside as she felt the arousal, the hunger burning higher. As though the need were beginning to build a bond she couldn't resist between them one that refused to release her.

A bond bred from his need for sexual dominance, and her sudden hunger to just submit. To give him anything and everything he could want from her at this moment.

His tongue moved over the swollen curves of her pussy, licked between them, then probed at the entrance of her vagina.

Tehya lowered her hips further, trying to get closer to his lips, his tongue as she let her fingers move lower, let them caress and cup the heavy weight of his balls as the heat inside seemed to surround her on the outside.

His tongue, wicked and fevered, fucked into her pussy, burying inside it as she cried out at the smooth penetration, the flaming licks. The feel of his hand at her hips, holding her in place as he pleasured her with each driving stroke of his tongue.

His cock throbbed in her mouth. Sucking him almost to her throat, she was so hungry for him, the taste of him, the touch of him that created a vortex of frantic pleasure. Her nails kneaded at his thighs. Her hips writhed in his grip, pressing against his fucking tongue, as she fought to breathe. She felt the sensations begin to build, to overtake her, enflaming her as she cried out his name pleadingly.

She was so close. She could feel it just out of reach. She was going to come. It burned in her clit, the strokes of his fingers in her rear, the scissoring of his fingers stretching her, sending bursts of pleasure pain tearing through her. Those strokes in her ass were as destructive as the hungry licks of his tongue screwing inside her pussy, with fierce strokes.

Panting for breath, her mouth moved on his cock, feeling it tighten as his fingers slid back, then slowly, oh so slowly and gently, began to spread the entrance to her ass with an additional finger.

Her moan vibrated around his cock as she stiffened violently, sharp claws of forbidden sensations racing through her veins on fiery flames.

It was there. The heat began to bloom to an overwhelming height. Tehya shuddered with the ecstasy of it, her body tightening violently as she was flung brutally toward the edge of release.

And just that fast, it was gone.

"No!" She tried to fight as he lifted her quickly from him, attempting to turn, to confront him. She had to return to that edge.

Damn him, he couldn't stop now.

Pushing against his hands, gasping for air, she fought to straddle his thighs and impale herself on the straining length of his cock.

Instead, she found herself on her knees, his heavy hand between her shoulders, pressing them down until her face rested against the comforter and he was rising behind her, his hands palming the curves of her ass.

"Now, let me show you what I'm going to do with that gorgeous little ass, Tehya," he growled as he came over to her, his teeth nipping at her shoulder. "Let me show you just how perfectly fuckable I've always known it would be."

Jordan couldn't control the need any longer. Every confrontation they'd had over the years, every time she had dared him to take what they both wanted coelesced into a brutal ache of desperation.

Now, he couldn't deny it.

Reaching to the bedside table and the small bag there, he pulled the tube of personal lubricant free as he moved more fully behind her.

"You're killing me, Jordan," she groaned, her tone husky, hungry.

Tehya had known this was coming. The moment she had realized it was him holding her down on her bedroom floor, she had known this was imminent.

"What do you think you do to me, sugar?" he said, the growl in his voice heavy with intent as his hand caressed the curve of her ass. "I use to fantasize this, Tehya. Fantasize about you leaned over as I watched my dick disappear up your tight little ass."

Tehya's eyes closed as she dragged in a hard, gasping breath. Behind her, Jordan pressed his lips to the side of her ass as his fingers parted the ripe curves.

Cooling yet heated, his fingers spread a heavy slick gel over the entrance to her rear before his fingers began working inside her once again.

This time his touch wasn't as slow, or as exploring. He'd already prepared, her body was screaming for it as her nails dug into the sheets beneath her.

"Jordan," she cried out weakly, her thighs spreading further as she felt the weakening lust sapping her strength and leaving her at his mercy.

"Such a tight little ass," he groaned as two fingers slipped inside her. "I've watched you walk, watched you run, watched you bend over whatever equipment you were working on, that pretty ass tempting me until I felt as though I'd die from the hunger for it."

Tehya shivered as she felt the sense of dazed submission mixing with a powerful flame of hunger. She was caught in a whirlwind she couldn't control. One she had no idea how to handle. It whipped through her senses and flung her into a fiery blaze that threatened her sanity.

As his fingers worked inside her, stretching her, preparing the tender tissue that had never known a man's touch as a heavy shiver raced up her spine.

She could feel the juices of her pussy dampening her thighs now. The need rose so high that there was no pain, there was only burning, clawing hunger. Desperation rose inside her, so deep, so dark, it was blinding as she cried out for him, cried out for more.

"Now, Tehya." His fingers slipped free as she tried to back into them again. She was on the verge of begging for more. "Stay here for me, baby."

His hand caressed her hip as she felt him move, shift. A second later the the heated, engorged head of his cock pressed against the tight opening of her anus. Her breath caught in her chest, a moan escaping her lips as her fingers curled into the comforter beneath her. She felt him begin to press forward the heavy, flared head of his cock slowly parting her flesh.

Pleasure and pain.

Her flesh stretched, wrapping slowly around the swollen cap of his cock as he pressed inside her ass slowly. The iron-hard, iron-hot width of his erection burned her, stretching the entrance open as she cried out, her senses rocking with an agonized pleasure.

White-hot, blazing sensation wrapped around her as, the heavy width of his flesh pressed into the tender, untouched entrance of her anus.

It was unlike anything she could have ever imagined it would be. It was an agony she wanted to hold on to forever, a pleasure she never wanted to end.

Tehya hadn't been a virgin when Jordan took her to his bed the first time. She had been far from a virgin. Yet, she had never known how incredible a man's touch could be. She had never believed she could feel more with Jordan than she had felt before or imagined she could feel.

"Ah, Tehya," he growled behind her, his voice dark and rough as his cock breached the tight ring of muscles that flexed and shuddered around the blunt crest.

"Jordan." The whimper in her own voice sent another

shudder through her, the realization that she could feel herself falling deeper into the maelstrom created by his touch, by his possession, rushed through her.

As Jordan felt the snug muscles of her ass clamp around his dick, he had to grit his teeth to hold back the groan of pure male pleasure. He could feel himself losing control. And control was something he prided himself on. It was something he never lost, not with any woman especially not during this act. Until Tehya.

He could feel the perspiration gathering on his forehead, his shoulders. He retreated until only the throbbing head of his cock remained inside her and fought to drag in a ragged breath.

It was exquisite. It was a conflagration racing up his spine as his hands tightened on her hips, once, twice, before he completely lost himself inside her.

He thrust forward, buried deep and groaned as her ass flexed around his cock. Pushing his fingers beneath her, Jordan buried them between her thighs and found the swollen, slick folds of her pussy, then the tight, hard bud straining forward.

Her clit was a hard little bud, throbbing as brutally as the head of his cock. Her juices lay thick and heavy on the heated curves as he found the drenched, tight entrance of her pussy and worked two fingers inside the satiny depths.

The walls of her pussy rippled around his fingers as he fucked them inside her. The muscles of her anus gripped him, milking his dick and pulling him deeper inside her as he fought to catch his breath. He knew it was too late to worry about holding onto his control. Much too late to worry about what he might be losing.

Something as important as losing his heart. A heart he had never suspected he possessed.

He gave his head a hard shake. Either from rejection of the thought or in desperation as he fought his loss of control.

Unfortunately, it was too damned late to hold anything back.

His cock, his fingers.

His fucking heart.

Before Jordan knew it, he was thrusting inside her like a man possessed by a demon of carnal need. As she cried for more, he gave her all he had.

He wasn't taking her easy, he wasn't taking her with the tenderness he'd wanted to show her.

Hell no.

There was no time for finesse, no time for tenderness or grace. His balls were so tight they felt tortured, his cock so fucking hard it was steel.

His fingers screwed into the ultra-tight depths of her pussy fucking her hard, just as he felt her tightening in nearing release.

Sweet heaven have mercy on him, he was fucking her ass with heavy thrusts, feeling her milk him, her ass sucking at his hard flesh like the hottest, tightest little mouth.

The pad of his palm pressed into her clit, feeling the swollen bud heating and throbbing as his fingers moved inside her.

Her pussy tightened.

Her ass tightened with a bite of pure rapture around his dick flexing and stroking every thrusting inch as he drove to the hilt inside her.

Hell, she was going to come. He could feel her orgasm building. Her body tightened, and in that moment, nothing mattered but Tehya's pleasure. Nothing mattered but her satisfaction, and ultimately holding her to him as she began to explode around his flesh.

Pleasure was agony. Pain was ecstasy.

Liquid rapture, white-hot and searing, flowed through Tehya's veins as she heard the cries tearing from her throat. She was lost to reason and lost to reality as it exploded through her.

"God yes!" Behind her, Jordan thrust hard and heavy inside her, his cock burning the depths of her ass, the stretching, heavy ache building to a rapture she couldn't resist.

She wanted the edge. She wanted to leap into the pure, blinding ecstasy she could feel just out of reach, hovering, awaiting her. She was there, tiny eruptions rocking through her as she kept climbing, kept fighting for that ultimate release.

"Better than my dreams," Jordan snarled behind her as his fingers fucked her harder reaching inside the depths of her pussy. His fingertips caressed high and up, stroking that small bundle of nerves just behind her clit, a hit-and-miss caress that kept her teetering, kept her flying.

Liquid flames licked over her flesh now, reached into her veins.

"Jordan." She clawed at the comforter, her hips thrusting back to him, driving him harder inside the sensitive entrance as she felt the rush of adrenaline and exhilaration surging through her.

She needed. Oh God, she needed so bad.

"Please," she cried hoarsely.

"Not yet." His voice was thick, heavy. "Hold on Tey. Just hold on, baby. Let it build. Let it burn for me."

Burn more?

She was dying. She couldn't bear it if it burned more. If the flames licked hotter inside her.

"Now," she cried out, begging, ready to plead.

Oh God, she was begging.

"Not yet. Tehya, baby, you're so tight. So exquisite."

Her womb clenched, her pussy rippled with impending orgasm.

She needed it. She had to come. If she didn't come then didn't know if she could survive it.

She needed release so desperately that the agony of waiting had perspiration slicking her skin, had her juices spilling from her vagina. They eased past the fingers thrusting inside her with ever-increasing strokes.

She couldn't bear it. She couldn't survive another minute.

Suddenly, burningly, as his fingers pressed more firmly, rubbed, caressed, she exploded.

Every muscle tightened, her bones locked, her head tilting back as a wail tore past her lips, and she began to shudder violently with the orgasm that tore violently through her.

Pleasure was the center of an internal sun imploding. Heat, flames, a burning crescendo that overwhelmed her and sent pure, intense sensation ripping through her body.

Behind her, Jordan thrust into her, elevating her orgasm, prolonging it, and finally sending another sharp burst radiating in the middle of the first as she felt his release suddenly begin spurting inside her.

The final, hard thrust inside her was followed by the deep fiery spurts of semen filling her rear. Each pulse was followed a hard jerk of his body against her. The fingers at her hip tightening, the ones buried in her pussy caressing that sensitive little spot deep inside her.

It seemed to go on forever.

She wanted it to never end. She couldn't survive it much longer, but she wanted to hold it inside her forever.

"God! Tehya!" Growling, savage, the sharp exclamation came as the final burst of his release filled her and the last hard explosion of pleasure tore through her body. Ripples of heat, her nerve endings pulsing, her pussy clenched and milked him as the final shudders shook through her.

Tehya collapsed against the bed.

There wasn't an ounce of energy in her body. All but the most necessary brain impulses shuddered to a stop. She could breathe, that was it. She hoped she wasn't required to do much more.

Her eyes closed and she simply drifted.

Behind her, Jordan lay over her, his weight braced on one arm as she felt his fingers ease from her gripping pussy.

She shivered at the additional pleasure, shocked that there was enough energy in her body to do that much.

His lips brushed against her shoulder.

His chest heaved at her back at he fought for breath with the same desperation she felt.

She could feel *him*.

Inside her.

Not just inside her body, not just buried in her rear, his cock still throbbing and hard. But *inside* her. As though he had found a way to penetrate her very spirit, to steal it, to possess it in ways she knew it could never be possessed again.

"Sweet Tehya," he whispered, moving slowly away from her and pulling a cry from her as she felt him withdraw until his body was no longer locked to hers.

She was glad her face was buried in the blanket, glad he couldn't see her expression, or he would have seen the tears she had to blink back.

Oh God, she loved him.

No, she had always loved him. From the moment her eyes had met his in Aruba, years before she was inducted into the Elite Ops, she had loved him.

No other man had touched her since that night. No other man had possessed so much as a dream or a fantasy in all those years.

She belonged to Jordan Malone, a man she knew didn't want or need the heart she had given to him. A man who believed love was no more than an illusion.

"Sweet Tehya." He brushed her hair aside as his lips pressed to the back of her neck in a lingering kiss before shifting from her.

She lost his possession of her. She lost the warmth of his body even though he moved no further than to lie beside her.

"What am I going to do with you?" he whispered, his voice so low she almost missed what he had said.

She certainly had a few ideas there.

Her head turned slowly as she forced her eyes to open.

"What did you say?" She had heard him, she just wanted to be certain he had said what she thought he had.

He stared back at her, his eyes such a brilliant sapphire blue she was instantly lost in them.

If she could just live here forever. Just like this.

His lips quirked slowly. "I hope I didn't hurt you," he said then.

Tehya frowned. She could have sworn she had heard something more, something akin to regret in his voice. And she was damned certain that was not what he had said.

He brushed her hair from her face, the heavy curls trailing around her as she laid her head on her arms and stared up at him. He reclined beside her, using the palm of his hand to hold his head up, a grin almost quirking his lips.

"I'm fine," she assured him, though she knew better.

She would only be fine until the day he walked away from her once again. After that, God only knew if she could survive intact. Walking away, or watching him walk away, would be the second hardest thing she had ever done in her life. The first was walking away the first time.

His fingertip eased over the curve of her face.

"You burn me alive, Tehya," he said, his voice low, as he stared back at her.

She remained silent, her heart leaping in her throat, hope digging sharp claws into her tender heart.

He breathed out slowly, heavily.

"You do the same to me, Jordan," she whispered back, her need to hear more almost a physical hunger.

His gaze flickered and darkened.

"It starts tomorrow," he said his expression growing, not exactly distant, but no longer as soft as it had been. "The senator's first party to introduce his son-in-law to his backers will be held at the Stanton estate."

Her throat tightened. She didn't want to discuss this right now.

"I'd prefer to glow just a little longer," she told him with false amusement. "Let's talk about this later, okay?"

When her heart wasn't breaking because the sweet nothings hadn't lasted long enough after the most incredible orgasm of her life.

"Tehya, we don't have time to wait." His fingers tightened on her face as she moved to turn away from him. "I have to know now, can you handle facing the Taites? Can you endure an introduction and pretend you don't know them? Can you bear to walk away from your family without . . ."

"They're not my family." She had no idea if they were even likeable. She couldn't miss what she had never had.

It was that simple. She wasn't going to argue the point.

"Tey, look at me." The gentleness in his tone nearly broke

the fragile shell of her defenses. "Why? What's holding you back from taking what belongs to you? Your family, and your inheritance?"

Did he sincerely want to know? Why did he want to know? God, he wasn't supposed to switch gears like this. He was supposed to maintain some kind of consistency, wasn't he? There was nothing worse than someone who switched gears that easily.

"Look." She breathed out wearily. "Right now, they're none the wiser and neither am I. Any heirs my mother had are assumed dead. I'm assumed dead. If I return, they'll always fear I'm there to claim my inheritance. They'll never believe otherwise. They'll never trust me. It's a no-win situation, Jordan, and I'm tired of fighting. I just want to rest for a while, nothing more. And returning to, or should I say, trying to enter, the bosom of my family, isn't something I've put on my agenda this year."

She was tired of fighting, she was tired of being alone, and she was tired of the shadows that refused to allow her any peace.

She was simply exhausted, and once this was over, she wanted to hide and heal the wounds gathering in her heart.

Staring back at him, she realized she wanted only to rest in his arms.

"Come here, baby." His arms tightened around her, drawing her to him. "I'll be there with you," he promised. "Lean on me if you have to. But when this is over, it's a discussion we'll have again. This decision isn't set in stone."

Unfortunately, it was. She had set it in stone long ago, and she intended to keep it there.

CHAPTER 10

It was set in stone. In cement. In steel.

It was a promise she reaffirmed the next evening.

Tehya reminded herself that she had made a promise to her mother and to herself. After her grandparents' murder, she had sworn to her mother that she would protect the rest of the family by staying away from them. That she would also protect the single secret her grandfather had given her mother unless she had no other recourse, until the threat of all danger had passed.

That secret, a set of numbers, was more than her own legacy, more than the legacy that had been stolen from Francine Taite, when Sorrel had kidnapped her. It was an inheritance set aside by Bernard Taite for his missing daughter. Cash, gold, bonds, family jewels, and a portion of Taite Industries profit per year, after Bernard Taite's death. It was a legacy set aside by her grandfather, and Tehya couldn't claim it until she either married, reached forty years old, or decided to return it to the overall estate for a very small portion of the whole. That inheritance was all she wanted from the Taites. As far as she was concerned, she deserved every tiny bit of it.

"Your gown will be here in about an hour." Jordan stepped into the bedroom where she stood in front of the large, well-lit mirror, that hung on the wall behind the dresser completing her makeup. She hated vanity lighting, preferring the more natural light in the bedroom instead.

Dressed in thin shorts and a camisole top, barefoot, freshly showered and still trying to come to grips with the night before, Tehya avoided his gaze as she brushed a finishing powder over the completed accents to her face, before returning her makeup to the bag lying on the dresser.

"Fine," she answered shortly as she checked the feature-defining job she had completed on her face. Smoky eyes, defined cheeks, the darker eye shadow highlighting and darkening the emerald green of her eyes.

Hell, she didn't look like Teylor Johnson any more than she looked like the missing Tehya Talamosi Fitzhugh. Which was the effect she had been working for. Makeup was indeed a girl's best friend.

Jordan paced across the room to her as she watched him carefully from the corner of her eye.

He wore black silk slacks, custom-made leather shoes, and an Egyptian cotton white shirt so expensive she was almost amused by the price. She knew the Malone's were incredibly rich, each son provided a healthy inheritance when Erin Malone died. They rarely showed it though, which only made it more shocking when she saw proof of it.

The matching evening jacket was lying across a chair in the other room. She knew his habits, and she was certain he had taken just as much notice of her own.

"You don't seem particularly concerned about the party tonight," he commented as he stood behind her, his gaze going over her face, taking in the expert application of makeup.

"Should I be?" she asked, her brow arching.

"This is the first time you've been face-to-face with the Taites, other than Journey. I know it's a complication you weren't looking forward to," Jordan said.

Her lips twisted bitterly. "True, but life is nothing if not a complication, wouldn't you say, Jordan? Why should one more matter? Besides, they have no idea who I am, and no one at the party who matters has any idea who I am. Why should I be nervous?

Jordan leaned against the edge of the dresser, crossed his arms over his chest, and stared back at her.

"The whole Taite family will be there, Tey. Stephen and his wife, Lauren. Craig and his wife, Melisande, as well as the children. Craig's son and heir, Royce, his daughters Alexa and Journey."

She turned with a frown. "Isn't that unusual? Stephen Taite had one child, Craig, but Craig has three."

"Unusual." His lips pursed thoughtfully though his gaze was amused. "Perhaps Craig didn't enjoy being an only child."

"Mother said Craig was quite determined that there be no other children to share his parents' time with him." She remembered this as bits and pieces of conversations with her mother emerged. "She always appeared very fondly amused by the memory. Evidently, Craig was quite possessive of not just his parents, but also any inheritance he would receive when they died."

"What's your point?" he asked curiously.

Did she have a point? Other than the fact that she truly wasn't nervous and was only now realizing how very little she knew about her family. Even though their youngest daughter worked for her, Tehya refused to listen to Journey discuss them.

"No point," she finally shrugged as Jordan continued to watch her. "I've just always found that rather strange, I guess."

"Why would it seem odd or strange to you if you have no intentions of revealing yourself to them?"

Tehya propped her hands on the dresser and stared back at herself in the mirror for a long, intense moment, before dropping her eyes and turning to stare back at Jordan.

She couldn't bear to see the emotions in her own eyes, or the haunted dreams she had never been able to give up on.

"Mother adored her family," she said softly, frowning as her chest tightened with the pain of everything that had been lost over the years. "That was her only dream, to find a way home. The last call she made, before Sorrel caught up with her, after her parents' deaths, she sounded broken."

She had been broken, Tehya amended silently. She had heard it in Francine's voice, the agony that couldn't be healed, the knowledge there was no home left to return to.

"Trust no one, Tehya," she had whispered without inflection, her voice hoarse, ragged, yet lacking emotion. "Swear to me you'll never risk the rest of the family. But when you're old enough, Tehya. When you reach your inheritance age, swear to me. Swear you'll claim all that is left of what should be yours. Swear it. And when you do, you'll find him. You'll find the son of a bitch that helped Sorrel. You'll make him pay. Swear it, damn you!"

Tehya had sworn. She had wanted to beg her mother to do it. Francine had been thirty-three years old. She'd had only seven years to go. At forty she could have claimed the inheritance and found her own vengeance.

Her mother had lived long enough to claim enough. Within a week of her parents' death, Sorrel's men had found her. They had found her, they had tortured her to death, for her.

Her mother had died protecting her.

"You were her family, too." Jordan's voice pulled her back from her memories. "You were her daughter."

"I was her albatross," she whispered, the muted grief that haunted her reflected in her voice, despite her attempt to hold it back.

"She cherished you," Jordan reminded her. "If you had been her albatross then she would have let Sorrel have you."

"And she lived in hell to protect me." She couldn't forget that. She couldn't fail. She couldn't let the past destroy her, or her mother's death would have been in vain.

"She made me swear I would never involve family in this." She turned to him, praying she was making the right choice in allowing Jordan to draw them in, even to the small extent he was involving them.

And now she was pushing it by going to a party the entire family was attending. A party where everyone would be speculating about the landscaping company owner and what she was doing with one of D.C.'s favorite sons, Jordan Malone.

"You're not calling your family begging for help," he pointed out. "You're meeting them as someone totally unrelated to the great-niece Stephen Taite has no idea how to locate."

And rumor was that he had searched for her for several years after her grandparents' and mother's deaths. She'd never understood why though.

Turning back to the mirror, she fluffed the curls that fell nearly to her hips and checked the smoky shadow that accented her eyes. She needed to break away from the sapphire blue of his gaze, from the unspoken questions that seemed to lurk there.

"Do you expect Ira Arthur and Mark Tenneyson to be there?" she asked after several moments' silence.

"They actually have invitations."

Tehya turned back to him in shock. "How did they manage that one?"

"Through the French Embassy." Jordan's lips tightened. "We're still trying to track down the particulars of that invitation. Until we do, stay close. See if anything is mentioned about the attack on your house."

"They know about that? So much for a life of fucking anonymity, Jordan. What the hell is going on here?"

"We've managed to contain most of it," he assured her. "But you know how rumors work, Tehya. Someone will have heard about it."

"No doubt." She breathed out roughly. "What's the story then?"

"Your cousin, Denver Roberts, was staying at the house when someone tried to break in. Things got out of hand and shots were fired. That simple."

"That simple," she breathed out roughly.

She didn't want to think about her home. She didn't want to think about the damage, and she didn't want to discuss it.

"Fine." She lifted her hand in a denial of the conversation

going further. "Maybe I'll get really lucky and no one has heard about it."

"Tey, you're worrying too much," he told her somberly. "The meeting will be short, an introduction, no more. Just enough to give the men watching the Taites, as well as you, something to report back to their employers. I want to know who is pulling the junkyard dogs' chains; and how the hell they managed to get an official invitation to a Senator's party."

"It's D.C.," she reminded him. "Invitations are traded like baseball cards."

His head inclined in agreement. "I guess we have to find the collectors then," he told her.

"Do we have any idea who the dogs are working for yet?" She rather liked the analogy in regards to Arthur and Tenneyson.

Jordan's lips quirked "Not even a clue. As I said, I'm hoping they'll lead us to them after the party. If nothing else, put us a few steps closer."

A few steps closer.

"Well-funded, well-hidden, and well-connected," she murmured. "We won't know who it is unless they manage to actually take me."

He moved quickly behind her, his gaze meeting hers in the mirror.

"Let that happen, and once you're safe, I promise you, I'll make damned sure you regret it."

She heard the anger in his tone and grimaced as Jordan dared her.

"I haven't been running for all but the first five years of my life just to let them take me, Jordan."

"Make damned sure of it," he growled. "The last thing I need is to lose you, Tehya."

His choice of words had her glancing in the mirror to catch his reflection. He turned away though before she could see anything, and she had the feeling it was deliberate.

"And those words coming from the man who allowed me to walk away nine months ago," she said calmly. "Tell me,

Jordan, did you even think about me before you learned my identity had been compromised?"

She couldn't leave well enough alone, no matter how she tried.

"I didn't lose you," he stated coolly as he turned back to her. "I knew how to find you, Tehya."

Her lips tightened. "Yes, all you had to do was contact Killian."

Another thought had her turning around to face him.

"How convenient that my phone had been tampered with just before this happened," she stated mockingly. "Perhaps we should launch our own investigation, Jordan. Into Killian Reece and whether or not he betrayed me."

Killian hated her because Sorrel was her father. He would have no problem turning her over to Sorrel's enemies. As far as he was concerned, blood would tell, and he had no compunction saying it to her face.

"It's already begun," he promised. "But that doesn't change our present situation so stop attempting to change the subject. Are you ready for this party, Tehya? Will you be able to handle meeting the Taites?"

"No, Jordan. I'm not. But just as with anything else in the past, it doesn't appear as though I have a fucking choice does it?" She fought to throttle her fury.

She swung away from him and stalked across the room, intending to pass him, to move into the living room, to get away from the reality of what she could never have, as well as the realization that she was moving closer to them with every second.

"I've never seen you like this." He caught her arm as she would have passed him. "You're not focused, nor are you trusting me as you used to, Tey. What happened?"

Confusion swept over her as she glared back at him.

"What do you want from me, Jordan? How else do you expect me to be? For the first time in my life, I thought I was safe, only to learn I wasn't. My home was invaded. I'm being thrown into a situation where my entire life once again is out of my control. Should I simply be calm and collected and expect you to take care of it all?" The anger that burned inside her filled her voice now.

She couldn't help it. She was moving too quickly into unfamiliar territory and was unable to get her bearings fast enough. It had been three days since she had lost the small measure of peace she had found, since the security she had unknowingly craved so desperately had been taken away from her.

"You've always trusted me to protect you."

She was confused by the darkness in his tone now, by the glint of anger in his blue eyes.

"This has nothing to do with protection, Jordan," she argued, desperate now to escape this conversation.

"What does it have to do with?" He questioned her rather than releasing her as she tried to jerk her arm from his grip. "Tell me, Tehya, since when do you believe I would allow anyone to dare to harm you."

Jordan couldn't explain why her belief in him was so damned important. Why he had been watching her for three days, probing at her trust, pushing her limits.

The night before he had broken through the reserve she had held against him where her body was concerned. That step had been imperative. Though he had no idea why. He couldn't explain it to himself and prayed she didn't demand explanations. It had forced her to probe those emotions. It had forced her out of that shell and placed him in a position to help her rebuild it.

She had lost too much, he couldn't allow her to lose faith in him as well. When this was over, when the time came to rebuild her life, yet again, he didn't want her shying away from her dreams.

Unfortunately, it had come with more emotion, with more pain than he had wanted to see her facing. That pain was beginning to make him want to commit murder, even as he wondered how her trust was surviving.

That ultimate trust, from a woman to her lover, was the same trust that came with the illusion of love. And with love, there always came heartbreak. God knew he didn't want to break her heart, but that pain was preferable, he thought, to losing the dreams of her home.

"I've always believed in you," she finally answered, her eyes flashing with a vulnerability that surprised him, and a glimmer of emotion he hadn't expected to see. Not yet. A part of him went icy cold, denial snaking through his brain.

She believed she loved him, and the ache in his chest at the knowledge of the pain that belief had brought her, that it would bring her, tightened through him. Even now he could see the grief she felt, and her fear that emotion would never be returned.

It hurt more than he had thought it would.

"I'll protect you, Tehya," he whispered, his free hand cupping her cheek, his thumb brushing over her lips. "In all the years we've worked together, I've never lost an agent, have I?"

"Never," she answered, staring back at him painfully, her gaze haunted with so many hopes and fears, and the realization that dreams were just never meant to be.

He wanted nothing more than to erase the pain in her eyes. To see a smile in her gaze, to see just the smallest glimmer of happiness. In that moment, Jordan realized he would do whatever it took to give her a chance at that happiness. Even if it meant destroying the illusion of emotion she thought she felt for him.

Her lips parted against the pressure of his thumb as those incredible green eyes flashed with exactly what he wanted to see. Mixed with the vulnerability, the emotion she believed was love, he saw that moment when her heart, her brain, her senses locked into the emotion and her trust in him cemented.

For a moment, he let himself bask in that emotional heat, a response he was certain, absolutely positive, she was even fully unaware of.

And it had been achieved with an ease that indicated the depth of emotion she had felt for him before ever leaving the base in Texas.

That knowledge tightened his guts. In a split second he was hard, and filled with such remorse that it shocked him.

Just because he knew the love she thought she felt was no more than an illusion, a cruel, vicious, emotional prank, didn't mean she would ever accept that fact. It didn't mean she believed in it any less.

From the moment she had arrived at her home and found him there, he had pushed her toward one end. Toward the complete and total trust he needed her to feel. And now that she was there, he felt nothing but disgust for himself.

"Protect my family, too, Jordan." A hint of steel flashed in her gaze then. The trust was there. That belief he had needed so desperately to ensure she would work with him rather than against him. But with it was also a warning. Tehya could make a formidable enemy, and if her family was harmed, that was exactly where this course would lead.

He let his lips quirk into a small smile as he forced the lie of amusement into his gaze. A lie because amusement was the last thing he felt.

Unlike his precious Tehya, he knew exactly how to lie with every cell of his body.

"Your family is completely protected," he assured her. "I promise, I even have plans B, C, and D where their safety and protection is concerned."

He was all about his plans. For a moment, just a moment, he wished he could be more about believing in love than about believing in reality.

To keep that regret harnessed, his head lowered and his lips brushed against hers, gently, but with a restraint that made his body tighten and ache with renewed hunger.

As her lips parted, as the fiery heat and infusion of emotion filled her kiss, Jordan wished, for the first time in too many years to count, that he too believed in love.

Tehya's lashes drifted open as the kiss slowly eased away, her senses immersed in the pleasure of a contact that shouldn't have had such an effect on her.

She loved him, though. The emotion she had never been able to restrain welled inside her as she stared up at him, wishing she could hold the heart of the man that held hers so easily. A man who refused to believe love could be more than an illusion.

As her lips parted to speak, a heavy knock at the bedroom door echoed through the room.

"Hey lovebirds, we have a delivery out here." Nik chuckled in amusement.

Tehya almost swore Jordan was ready to roll his eyes.

Staring down at her, Jordan backed away slowly. "I'll go out and talk to him." His lips quirked in amusement. "For some reason, it bothers me that Nik would see you half-dressed, in our bedroom."

Shocking. And Jordan didn't often shock her.

There was the faintest hint of male possession in his tone, as though he had already laid his claim to her. As though he intended to keep her.

Tehya gave her head a hard shake as he left the room to talk to Nik, the sound of the possessiveness in his voice still rocking through her senses. How she had needed to hear that, because Jordan never felt possessive. She had never known or heard of him to be jealous of any woman.

She was checking her appearance at the mirror when Jordan stepped back inside minutes later. "Mikayla delivered the dress." Entering the room fully he laid the ball gown over the bottom of the bed before turning back to her

His gaze was darker, less a sapphire blue, perhaps closer to a navy. As though in the moments they had been apart, some dark memory had filled his senses.

The soft, shimmering folds of the dark violet material looked like a splash of vivid excitement against the white comforter. It was just as she had envisioned it when she and Mikayla had discussed the design. Strapless, with an empire waist and yards of violet silk falling to her feet over the white silk underskirt, it was both romantic and sensual.

The bodice cupped and loved her breasts, while the rest of her curves were hinted at and teased the senses. An illusion of height was added, then given a boost by five-inch matching heels that had been delivered with the dress.

A soft, matching cape with a white silk lining, and a white clutch purse for essentials, and Tehya knew she would be drawing gazes. Thankfully, the flesh-colored bandage Jordan had somehow procured, normally used for wounded operatives on covert assignments, hid the wound on her arm.

That had been one of Jordan's requirements for the dress, that it be eye catching. That it please his senses and arouse him. When he had seen the drawn design, his lashes had lowered, and Tehya herself had become aroused by the look of latent lust in his expression.

"We'll be arriving a little late," he informed her as she ran her fingers over the shimmering silk. "I prefer an hour. Tonight, entrance means everything. The invitation list went out to all the guests and we've already begun receiving other invitations from those my family and I are acquainted with as well as associates of the Taites. We're here only to support Senator Stanton and his son-in-law though."

She nodded slowly. "I understand." His friends would wonder about her, and ask questions later, when she was no longer a part of his life.

Of course, he would be uncomfortable with that. Jordan rarely chose a lover in the position of associating with his family. She let her fingers run over the material of the dress once again. She wasn't going to allow his reluctance to take her around his friends affect the memories she was making.

It was the thought of the Taites though that had her chest tightening.

"Tehya?"

It was her silence that had him moving closer to her, watching her expression as she lifted her gaze to meet his.

"Would they have liked me, Jordan?" she asked, her voice almost too soft to hear, her expression so vulnerable, so filled with a hunger to belong that he wanted to kill Sorrel himself. She was so damned beautiful, kind, compassionate. Any family would be proud of her.

"Tehya, they wouldn't be able to help themselves." It was

in that moment that he knew he was in serious trouble where those unnamed emotions for her were involved. They rose like a tidal wave inside him and threatened to swamp his normal good sense.

His arms went around her, drawing her close to him as he suddenly realized all the emotions she had hidden through the years. She had kept to herself, staying in her suite as he had done when there was no work to bury himself in.

She had fought for the same distance he had, and for similar reasons. Because the pain was too intense when the illusions were ripped away. Or, in her case, when she lost those she loved.

He should have never allowed her to hide in such a way, Jordan admitted.

"It's too late," she whispered against his chest, her fingers curling against his shirt to hold on to him. "It's just too late."

It was too late to go home. Too late to be a part of a family that would never understand the woman reality had shaped. And in a way, Jordan agreed with her. Unless they had an idea of the world that had created her, then they would never be comfortable around her.

"Perhaps you can never go home," he whispered. "But that doesn't mean you can't forge your own place, as Teylor Johnson." Easing back, he stared down at her once again. "You don't have to admit to your familial ties, Tehya, to be a part of a family. All you have to do is be willing to be a friend."

She would be an asset to any friend or family she chose, he thought. The honesty and compassion that was so much a part of her would always draw others to her, like a moth to a flame.

As she drew him. There were days he wondered if he would ever escaped the tangled web of emotion he knew she would wrap around him if she could.

Love. Hell, that illusion was stronger, was more than he was and he knew it.

Finally she gave a short, sharp nod before turning and heading to the bed where her dress was laid out.

Letting her go was the hardest thing he had ever done. He wanted nothing more than to hold her. And to give her the one thing he swore he'd never give anyone. The illusion he suddenly wished he could convince himself of.

Love.

"I'll finish dressing, then," she told him quietly as she glanced at the clock. "We should have just enough time for your preferred arrival."

He frowned back at her suspiciously. "It doesn't take an hour to put a dress on, Tey."

She almost smiled at the doubt in his tone, and in his face.

"True," she agreed. "But it often takes longer than that to finish the look, Jordan. Stockings can't have runs, the skirt has to lay just right, my makeup will have to be adjusted for the color because I didn't expect the depth of the shimmer once the gown was completed."

She was trying desperately to maintain her control, and Jordan had no idea how to ease the pain in her eyes. That left him with the only option at hand. A strategic retreat until she needed him to hold her, to assure her once again that there was no reason why she shouldn't be loved.

"Enough said." He lifted his hand to halt the subtly mocking explanation. "I'll leave you to dressing while I discuss the security layout and the guests with the others." He indicated the door to the rest of the suite with a sharp turn of his head. "Just let me know when you're ready."

"I'll be sure to do that," she promised as she moved to the head of the bed and loosened the material from the padded hanger it was secured to. "As I said, an hour, perhaps a bit more."

For just as long as she could draw it out.

For some reason, Jordan seemed determined to bring her face-to-face with her family, and she had a feeling it had more to do with his belief that she should align herself with them than the belief that being there would allow him to identify who gave the orders to the men threatening her.

As much as she craved family and connections, she knew that connection had been broken with her grandparents' deaths. All the wishing, all the tears, or all the regrets in the world couldn't change that.

"Just be yourself, Tehya," he reminded her again, suddenly behind her when she had expected him to leave the room.

One hand gripped her hip for a second as his head lowered and he placed a soft kiss at the curve of her shoulder. "I promise, no one could help but to love the person you are."

Everyone but him.

"Of course." She tried to convince him she believed it, though they both knew otherwise. "I would just prefer that it hadn't come to this."

He nipped her flesh, causing her to jerk and turn her head to stare back at him in surprise.

"I wouldn't have missed this for the world." He grinned. "We're just getting ready to have some fun, baby. Where's your sense of adventure?"

Before she could answer him he was drawing away from her and moving from the room. The bedroom door opened and he disappeared through it, closing it behind him with a decisive snap.

There was definitely something to be said for the days when he spent more time trying to ignore her than to seduce her, she thought with a sigh.

At least then the knowledge of her future hadn't been so clear-cut.

Now, she was certain, no other man but Jordan would do, which meant that after he was gone, she was looking at a very lonely existence.

But she wouldn't have missed it for the world.

"There you are." Travis Caine was preparing to knock on the bedroom door when it opened.

Stepping through, he was ready to close the door when Travis stopped him and handed him a small cellophane pack.

"Flash bandages," he informed Jordan. "Covers the wound and hides it. Lilly thought she might need it with the strapless gown. And there's enough for several uses there."

Jordan frowned back at him. "Those are damned hard to come by, Travis." And he knew they were; they were items he'd had problems acquiring even during his time as Elite Ops commander. He was right though, Tehya would more than appreciate it.

"Thanks, Travis." He nodded back to him. "I appreciate it."

"Eh, thank Lilly, she thought of it." He inclined his head back toward his wife.

"I should have known that," Jordan quipped before crossing the room to where the others were waiting.

Jordan faced the men awaiting him in the parlor of the suite, his gaze narrowed, any amusement or sense of fun that he may have given Tehya evaporating.

Getting the team back together hadn't been hard. The moment they had known Tehya was in danger they had come running, several of them with their very dangerous wives in tow. Those wives were there now, in full party dress, like goddesses of beauty sent to tempt mortal men.

"What do we have?" He glanced at his nephew, his unofficial second in command.

"Everyone has received their guest lists and everyone's buzzing. Hell, Jordan, maybe we should socialize more," Noah reported, his darker eyes amused at the knowledge that others were excited at the prospect of a Malone being in town. A testament to Riordan Malone Sr.'s popularity when he was younger. "The Taites are fairly quiet, though Lauren, Stephen's wife, has extended a lunch invitation to the Malone party." His lips quirked mockingly. "Speculation is going wild over the identity of your guest, Teylor Johnson, though. Even the Taites are making inquiries. Within hours, they were aware of the fact that you were indeed the same Jordan Malone that refuses to sell the Malone property in Ireland, that they're so desperate to acquire."

Jordan had been aware of that for years. Unfortunately for them, he had no intentions of selling the Malone family properties. Not in Ireland, nor in America.

"And they're normally the ones to care the least," Lilly Harrington Caine, the daughter of an English lord spoke up.

"The Taites abstain from gossip mongering and concentrate instead on their various charities and on family. To have them asking anything about anyone is a major coup." There was no sarcasm in the words, simply a statement of fact.

"It's Jordan's charm." Noah grinned. "They simply crave having Jordan tell them 'No'."

Jordan almost grinned. The Taites were persistent if nothing else. A trait Tehya had definitely inherited.

"We'll see if they bring it up face-to-face," Jordan said. "Perhaps they'll believe me when I say it isn't for sale this time."

"Stephen Taite believes everything is for sale," Lilly cut in at that point. "He's quite determined to own that castle, Jordan. He learned Travis perhaps knew you, within hours of his arrival in the states this week. He's already contacted us again this morning, wondering if we could arrange a meeting for him. We've declined, by the way."

Jordan snorted at her cheeky grin.

"He only wants it because it's something he's been refused," he growled as he moved across the room to the bar.

"You've picked up tails here at the hotel." Nik changed the direction of the conversation. "Tenneyson and Arthur and their backup team are dividing their time between here and the Taites'. We believe they have the Taites' rented estate bugged, but we're not certain yet."

"Of course it's bugged." Jordan knew he would have had it bugged if he were Tenneyson and Arthurs. The electronic listening devices would allow the team to easily split their time while still being assured no potential players slipped past them.

"We haven't learned who's hired them yet," Noah said. "We're still working on it."

Nodding, Jordan poured himself a stiff drink before knocking it back and relishing the burn in the pit of his stomach. Nothing could sear away the disgust eating at him, though, or the restless anger at the game he was playing with Tehya's emotions. The excuse that it was for her own good wasn't helping in the least.

"Find out who these bastards are." Jordan diluted the furious snap in his voice for the women's sake.

There was no sense in pissing their husbands off because he knew he was getting in over his head with a woman.

Still, they stared back at him, uncertain why this mission suddenly counted so much more than all the others before it.

"We're searching, boss." Micah was the only one brave enough to answer. "Until then, we have Tenneyson and Arthurs covered."

"Something else seems to have come up, though." John Vincent had sat silently at the conference table until now. "We have a new player."

Jordan turned to him with a heavy sigh. "And who might that be?"

"Journey Taite's boyfriend arrived," he drawled. "Several years older than she. Beauregard Grant. He's a third cousin to Andrew and Melissa Grant."

"And fifth cousin to England's Lord Lowden Grant," Lilly added. "He's considered a black sheep, though. Dropped out of college, joined the military for a while. He was discharged for unsatisfactory performance of duty and conduct unbecoming."

"I'm surprised Taite is allowing him anywhere near his daughter," Jordan murmured.

Lilly's smile was all teeth and disgust. "He's still royalty, my dear Mr. Malone. As fifth cousin to Lord Grant, he's also somewhere around twelfth cousin to the Queen Mother."

Jordan's brow arched. "Lineage, huh?"

"Lineage." Lilly rolled her eyes. Anyone related to the Queen Mother placed a stamp on that kinship and proclaimed it far and wide.

"Beauregard won't be a problem," Jordan said. "Journey knows Tehya's identity as Teylor Johnson and nothing more." He looked at each man in turn. "Don't take your eyes off her. Tehya is of primary importance, and tracking down whoever gave the order to attack her home is imperative. I want it over." His voice hardened. "I want her safe."

And as each man stared back at him he knew they understood, and they agreed.

Nothing mattered more to them than the protection of their wives, just as nothing mattered more to him than the protection of his . . . He gave himself a mental shake. Nothing mattered more than protecting Tehya and returning her to the life she had chosen for herself.

Because any life she chose would be far better than that of a life with a man who had learned long, long ago the perils of believing in love, and in happily ever-afters.

Nothing lasted forever.

CHAPTER 11

Tehya could think of far better things to do than to make an entrance at a party of politicians and their supporters. A root canal. A broken bone. Hell, being in the middle of a violent conflict in the most dense of jungles. And she hated the jungle. She hated it almost as much as the political parties.

But she had to admit there was a sense of excitement, a flare of pure feminine pride as all eyes turned to view their entrance, especially those of the women.

Like Tehya, they couldn't take their eyes off Jordan.

Savage and dangerous, a sleek mature male animal, confident and primal, he was an instinctive draw to any female with hormones. And the women here seemed to have plenty of hormones if their sudden interest was anything to go by.

Walking down the short flight of steps, her hand placed comfortably in the crook of Jordan's arm, she let herself pretend for the moment that they were a true couple. They were simply there to support a friend. There was no danger, no haunting past. There was nothing to worry about, no reason to be concerned or frightened.

He had asked her earlier to trust him. What he didn't know, what he didn't understand, was that she had always trusted him.

"Jordan Malone." Senator Richard Stanton stepped forward, a warm smile on his face as his blue eyes twinkled merrily. Hand outstretched, he welcomed Jordan's handshake with obvious familiarity before clapping him on the back and turning to Tehya. "Teylor Johnson, you're as completely gorgeous as ever."

"Senator." Face uplifted, she accepted the brush of his lips against her cheek as a real smile tugged at her lips.

She had always enjoyed the meetings she attended where the senator was in attendance. As Jordan's personal assistant for the past six years, she had had the pleasure of working with the older man often in his capacity of a committee member of the Elite Ops Command.

"You've met my daughter and son-in-law?" The senator turned to Kell and Emily Krieger.

"Hello, Tey." Emily greeted her cheekily, her blue eyes sparkling merrily at the obvious knowledge that Teylor wasnt her real name.

Kell's welcome was just as warm, his dark green gaze amused as he observed the interest they were drawing.

"It's wonderful to see you again, Jordan," the senator declared with robust friendliness. "Come to the bar with me, we'll get a drink and see a few people I know are eager to meet with you."

As the senator accompanied them across the room, Tehya watched as the crowd parted, as avid gazes locked on to them. And she saw the two young women standing together. One fiery haired, the other blond. One familiar yet confused, the other coolly composed, her expression arrogant.

Journey and her sister Alexa. They were as different as night and day. Journey with her red-gold hair, and Alexa looking like an ice princess. Next to them was their handsome brother Royce, his hair and eyes dark, his expression cold. His gaze was harder, almost dead. It wasn't even icy. It was just empty as he watched. There was no interest, no curiosity, and no boredom. They were simply dead.

As the senator led them to the bar, Tehya watched from the corner of her eye as Stephen and Craig Taite moved casually in a parallel line to meet them.

Both men had their gazes on Jordan, eyes narrowed, their arrogant, thin faces drawn into similar lines of predatory intent.

The castle Jordan owned in Ireland had been a bone of contention for years. The Taites seemed especially determined to possess it, claiming it had once been a part of their lineage as well. They had tried to meet with Grandpop Rory, with Jordan's brother Grant, and once they had even flown to Texas in an attempt to meet with Jordan.

Now, they were pressing Jordan at every opportunity to sell the property via both e-mail and snail mail. And Jordan flatly refused, if he deigned to answer at all.

"What can I get you?" The senator turned back to them as they reach the long, dark-wood bar.

Jordan ordered for himself as well as for her before she politely rolled her eyes and turned to the bartender. She ordered her favorite whisky. Turning back to Jordan, she toasted him with the shot glass. Tipping it back and finishing it with a single swallow.

Heated, she felt a surge of bravado as fear receded at the whisky's warmth. When her eyes opened, she found herself staring directly into the disapproving gazes of the great-uncle and the cousin she had never known.

The smile she flashed them was patently false. She didn't dare show the hurt she felt at the disapproval her cousin showed, or the sudden flash of disgust in her uncle's eyes.

"Stephen," Stanton murmured. "I'm glad you could make it tonight."

Stephen inclined his head regally before turning to Jordan. "I thought it time I met my adversary," he said cordially. "We seem to still be locked in a silent duel over a piece of property he's in possession of."

"A piece of property I own," Jordan reminded him as he moved closer to Tehya, his arm going around her waist to pull her closer to her side. "And it's still not for sale."

"Of course it isn't," Craig's tone was just arrogantly superior enough to grate on the nerves.

The younger Taite's blue-green eyes were chilly while the elder's darker, moss-green eyes were frankly curious.

"It amazes me that you're so determined to hold on to such barren property." Stephen finally smiled back at them, though the smile didn't reach his eyes.

This was her family?

"And it amazes me that you would want to buy such barren property," Jordan pointed out, his tone definitely more cordial and less confrontational.

Suddenly, Tehya was seeing the Taites without the rose-colored glasses of nonassociation. She had never imagined such snide prejudice, such superior arrogance. How much worse would it be if they knew the truth of her?

"Jordan, excuse me, darling." She turned to him smoothly, her smile all teeth. "I'm feeling a bit unsettled. Perhaps it's something in the air. I'll just step into the ladies' room to clear my head, if you don't mind?"

"Of course, love." Chiding, knowing, his tone was still warm and caring. "I'll be right here."

He lifted his hand and gave a subtle signal to Travis and Lilly Caine. The two came instantly, following Tehya as she moved for the hall that led to the ladies' room.

Jordan turned back to Stephen and Craig, allowing the anger surging inside him to ice his gaze as he flicked a glance over them before turning back to the senator. "Breeding leaves something to be desired in the manners department," he commented.

Craig Taite straightened his bony shoulders beneath the silk evening jacket he wore. "Was that an insult, Malone?"

"Why, yes, I believe it was," Jordan said, his tone low, careful to keep their conversation where it was, just among them. "You've insulted Teylor, Taite. That could end up being a very bad mistake on your part."

Craig sniffed delicately. "Her manners are atrocious, Mr. Malone. A lady doesn't swig whisky in public."

"Only in private to endure the ass she's with, huh?" he taunted the other man, well aware of Craig's wife's inability to attend many social functions with him because of her love for the inebriated state.

It was said in such a way that Craig couldn't be certain of the insult.

"It seems we were perhaps faulty in believing a meeting would help in building an intelligent discourse for the future," Stephen Taite sighed regretfully. "We have many business interests that coincide. I had hoped we could work together."

"As far as I know, we have no such business interests," Jordan pointed out. "The only thing we have in common is your determination to acquire that which doesn't belong to you."

And would never belong to them.

Stephen Taite had sold the estate to Joseph Fitzhugh just before his niece was kidnapped more than thirty years before. He hadn't cared enough to hold on to the once crumbling castle until Jordan had come along and restored it to the savage beauty it now possessed.

"And shouldn't have been sold to you," Stephen said with a weary sigh. "Such is business, though. It seems you are taking offense to what may be no more than friendly banter, Mr. Malone. That's unfortunate. I admit, I do feel rather possessive of it. Fitzhugh acquired it at a time when I was young and relatively less appreciative of my own belongings."

Jordan had acquired the estate after Fitzhugh's death from the French authorities, months after Tehya had killed him. The property had at one time been Malone land, owned by Jordan's grandfather before the Malone family came to America. "I assure you, I rarely misunderstand a situation, Mr. Taite," Jordan assured him. "I've based my business on knowing exactly how to read others."

Taite's brows lifted. "And what exactly would that business be, Mr. Malone? I must admit, I've never fully understood it."

"I must admit, I've never fully explained it," Jordan said dismissively before turning to the senator. "If you'll excuse me, I believe I have some business to discuss with your son-in-law, Senator. As soon as I collect Teylor."

Tehya could be a part of this family. Their determination to acquire his land should have clued him into their personalities. Personalities that Tehya could never endure for long.

She could never fit in with the pompous arrogance that defined the two he had just met.

Their greed was only surpassed by their own sense of superiority. And it was all he could do to rein in his anger and not inform them of the very formidable enemy they had just made.

He couldn't ignore the looks they had given her that had sent her running, their disgust for her preferred drink apparent as it sliced through her confidence.

Bastards. They'd insulted him well enough over the years; he wouldn't allow them to insult her. He'd just never imagined her family could be all bad.

The estate they coveted had been all but given to Fitzhugh at a time when Stephen Taite and Joseph Fitzhugh had been friends during their youth. Jordan's acquisition of it had been a stroke of luck.

The estate was run by caretakers for the most part, a couple whose own safety depended upon their cover and their ability to maintain that illusion.

Stepping into the hall, he moved to the upper end and toward the ladies' room Travis stood outside of, leaning against a wall, his shoulders tense, his expression drawn into hard, forbidding lines.

Travis stepped up to Jordan and whispered, "I can't believe she shares that bastard's blood. He managed to insult her and Lilly all in the same breath. As though his blood were somehow far richer than others'."

Jordan snorted at the thought. "It was in the dossier we had on him." He finally shrugged. "We should have been forewarned."

Travis shook his head. "Hell, Lilly was raised with the damned family. She warned us. For the past year, I've moved in his society and never even been introduced, and now I understand why. Son of a bitch. Tey is so fucking down to earth, and just *kind*."

Knowing Tehya it had been hard to imagine the Taites were such as holes though.

"Because he avoided it," Jordan murmured knowingly.

Travis's jaw clenched. "Bloody bastard doesn't know who he's dealing with. I could have out-blooded him as well as out-moneyed him at one time. Hell, I still could I believe."

Travis had been an English lord himself once, Jordan remembered. Before he'd lost it all and turned to vengeance instead.

"Do you miss it?" Jordan asked him, suddenly curious. "You gave up a lot to join us."

Travis's lips quirked in a slow, crooked smile as his gaze suddenly lit with a flare of humor. The door opened then, and Lilly stepped out, her gaze meeting her husband's as a smile transformed her, lighting her face and the very air around her with warmth.

"Hell no." Travis sighed. "Look at what I gained."

Jordan's attention had fractured though, the response meaning little as Tehya emerged behind Lilly. His gaze met Tehya's and he saw the weary somberness in it.

Travis and Lilly moved toward the ballroom as Jordan pulled Tehya to him and pressed her head against his chest, feeling her take a deep, uneven breath.

"I'm fine," she told him. "It's like having the rug pulled out from under your feet, I imagine. It just takes a moment to get your breath."

She hadn't imagined they could be so carelessly cruel, even though her mother had regaled her with tales of the society she had once been a part of. A world where best friends were no more than backbiting enemies and trust was an illusion that only children were allowed to believe in. Rather like the tooth fairy.

She pulled back from him slowly, lifted her face, and gave him a careful smile. Another illusion. The lie that she was fine and it would only take moments to get over the shock.

She felt flayed, her flesh stripped to the bone as the family she had dreamed of for years had looked down their noses at her.

Had her mother ever been like that? Her grandparents?

Suddenly, she was incredibly glad that she hadn't been raised to cherish and miss such a life as her mother had.

Francine Taite had grieved for the life and the family she had been stolen away from. The rare times she and Tehya had had together after their escape from the Fitzhugh estate, her mother had dreamed aloud of returning one day.

Until her parents had died, and within days, Francine had died as well.

"I believe this is why we avoid such events," she whispered with amused conspiracy to him as he slowly released her. "So we don't have to put up with the likes of the badgers such as Stephen and Craig Taite." The hurt was there, thick and heavy, though carefully hidden.

She could joke about it, she could even pretend long enough to convince Jordan, that it didn't hurt.

But Tehya knew better. It sliced her heart to ribbons.

His lips parted to speak when she caught a hint of movement from the corner of her eye.

It wasn't an assassin, it wasn't an attacker, a journalist, or any of the hundreds of people she would prefer to avoid.

Rather, it was the single member of the Taite family who seemed to have a heart rather than marble where a heart should be.

"Teylor." Twenty-two, and suddenly uncomfortable, Journey Taite stood before them, dressed in emerald green chiffon and satin. The ball gown she wore was at once innocent and incredibly sexy.

Her long, wavy red-gold hair fell below her shoulders in thick, luscious waves, a far cry from the braid Journey wore at work.

"Hello, Journey." Tehya felt Jordan's hand at her back, comforting and warm.

Journey gripped the small clutch purse she carried with desperate hands as she stared back at Tehya, who knew exactly why the other girl was so apprehensive.

"We have a deal, Journey," she assured her. "I won't break it."

The promise Tehya had made that she would never reveal to anyone that Journey worked for her, except the IRS.

Journey let out a slow, hard breath and within a blink of an eye, the natural vivacity that seemed to be so much a part of her, gleamed in her eyes once again.

"I'd hate to give Grandfather or Father, either one, a stroke," she whispered confidentially. "Or do anything to dislodge the sticks up their bums."

Jordan gave a small cough, an obvious attempt to cover his laughter.

For a moment, Tehya had to fight back tears, though. This girl was everything she had hoped her family would be. Warm, charming, filled with laughter and generosity.

"Are you adopted?" Tehya asked as they turned and headed back to the ballroom. "There's no way you're truly related to them."

Journey grinned at the accusation before sobering. "Actually, my mother tells me often that I remind her of grandfather's missing niece. She says I'm too much like my cousin Francine. Enough so that she worries one day that she'll lose me as well."

Tehya wanted to weep. She'd never really exchanged confidences with Journey for a reason. This reason. Because her memories of the past were still too painful.

"She's missing?" Tehya asked as Jordan's fingertips rubbed against her lower back in comfort.

"She was kidnapped more than thirty years ago," Journey told her, her expression saddened. "She was killed about fifteen years ago. There's rumors she had a daughter, but despite the family's attempts to find her, she remains lost as well."

Tehya made a noncommittal sound, listening rather than speaking as Journey discussed her family.

"I never met my cousin Francine, but Papa says I look a lot like her."

Did she? Tehya stared at the younger woman for a quick second before looking out at the crowd on the ballroom floor as they reentered it.

"She must have been very beautiful then," Tehya told her sincerely.

Journey's smile was hopeful, though it lacked the confidence someone of her looks should have.

Journey did resemble Francine Taite, quite a lot actually. Tehya had seen pictures of her mother when she was young. A fragile, delicate young woman whose smile had been filled with infectious humor and charm. Journey could have passed for Francine's daughter, perhaps more than Tehya could.

Finding one of the small seating areas, they sat down in a sheltered corner where they could watch the crowd and still talk. Tehya noticed Micah Sloane in his role as an independent bodyguard staying a careful distance from her, but close enough to ensure her protection.

"I don't care much for the new managers of your company," Journey said, thankfully switching topics.

Tehya had to control the urge to chuckle at the other girl's pouting expression.

"Why's that?" she asked.

"The McIntyres are nice enough." Journey shrugged. "But they don't have your vision, Teylor. I don't think they're going to make a profit like you would have."

"And the difference is?" Tehya asked her, genuinely curious now.

Journey played with the ends of a heavy swath of hair that had fallen over her shoulder as a thoughtful look came over her face.

"You naturally pull in clients. They become as excited as you do at the prospect of your designs, while the McIntyres don't truly seem to be taking it seriously. They actually seem more like drill sergeants."

Her poor landscaping company. Tehya had to force back the grief at the thought of losing it completely. She loved the design aspects and the clients that always seemed to love the efforts she made to bring color and life to the property they hired her to fix.

"They'll work out fine," she finally promised, with absolutely no confidence that they could hold on to her clients.

Because Journey was right; she seemed to have an affinity for the clients she met as well as the designs that would best suit them.

"Why are you considering giving up the company, Teylor?" Journey asked, sounding concerned. "Is the reason financial? I'm certain I could help you find backers . . ."

"Journey. No." Tehya laid her hand on Journey's arm. "It has nothing to do with money and I haven't made a final decision yet anyway. Lets wait and see what happens."

The words nearly stuck in her throat from the painful realization that as much as she wanted to she may never be able to return to the life she had begun building for herself.

Journey's head lowered before she lifted it and looked around. There was something on the other girl's mind, and for a moment Tehya saw the sadness that filled her.

She would have asked about it if Journey's face hadn't gone through a quick, conflicting change of expressions.

At first, there was frustration, anger, then a glimmer of involuntary interest mixed with the English reserve Tehya always found so fascinating.

Following her gaze, Tehya watched the powerful form of Beauregard Grant as he made his way from the bar over to them.

At twenty-nine, Beau Grant was a tall, formidable vision. He wasn't handsome in the conventional sense, rather he was dark and brooding. A closely cropped beard and mustache covered the lower part of his face, as well as a fine webbing of scars from a fiery car crash he'd been involved in years earlier.

His familial connections to England's queen made him a much sought-after guest wherever he was staying, though his ties to several criminal elements made him a force to be wary of.

The fact that he was involved with Journey was something Tehya knew she would be losing sleep over.

"Journey." He moved to the seating area, bent and kissed the younger girl's cheek warmly. "I was wondering where you disappeared to."

"I met Miss Johnson in the ladies' room," Journey lied smoothly. "We were discussing dresses."

His expression was bland, neither believing nor disbelieving as he flicked a careless look toward Tehya.

"Your father's looking for you as well," he stated. "And I'm ready to claim that dance you owe me." His tone didn't encourage a refusal.

Tehya's gaze narrowed on the couple as Journey rose to her feet with a small sigh of resignation. "Perhaps we'll have a chance to discuss clothing designs later." The unconscious wariness that descended over her worried Tehya now. "Good evening, Miss Johnson."

"Miss Taite," Tehya murmured as the couple moved off.

Grant's hand settled at Journey's lower back in a gesture of possessiveness and control that had immediately set off warning bells in Tehya's mind.

He was too dark, too dangerous, and much too experienced for the demure child Journey still was in so many ways.

As she stood, Jordan moved beside her, his progress from the bar and the group of men he had been talking to made with deceptive laziness. He had been waiting for the other two to walk away.

"Interesting," he murmured. "I personally would have chosen someone much lighter natured for my daughter if I were her father."

Tehya turned and stared back at him in confusion. "Meaning?"

"Rumor is circulating tonight that her father and Mr. Grant have come to an agreement concerning various interests in exchange for Craig's approval and subsequent agreement to force Journey into marrying him. An arranged marriage, I believe it was once called." His icy gaze held hers. "What are his chances of forcing her into it?"

Tehya sighed heavily. "Excellent. Journey hasn't developed the strength to fight against her father yet. Hell, he still controls damned near every aspect of her life that he's aware of, to the point that she's hiding the fact that she's working."

Tehya made a mental note to meet with Journey soon and

discuss this. If her cousin wanted out of that marriage, if she wanted a way to disappear from such a cold-blooded family, then Tehya would help her.

"Genetics are a bitch," Jordan said, his tone low. "It's hard to imagine you're from the same gene pool."

"No kidding." She could only shake her head at the thought of the arrogance and superiority that had oozed from Stephen and Craig Taite's pores. How different they were from what she had imagined. There was none of the warm humor that Journey possessed, none of the charm she seemed to use unconsciously. It was even harder to imagine her mother was related.

"I'll make sure I find out what Journey herself wants," she told him, her gaze glittering with suppressed anger. "I won't let her be forced into anything so important as marriage."

There was his Tehya. Jordan felt a spurt of pride at the pure determination and protectiveness rising inside her.

"We'll see," he agreed. "I believe my business has been conducted for the evening, though. I would like to claim a dance from my very beautiful lover before other things get in the way."

"Expect things to get in the way," she informed him as she laid her hand in the crook of his arm once again and allowed him to lead her to the dance floor, where other couples were now moving in synch with the slow, seductive music the band had slipped into.

"Of course," he agreed with her.

"Have our watchers taken the bait yet?" she asked as she placed her head against his shoulder, his head bent to her.

"They haven't moved." His tone hardened. "But I hadn't expected them to during the party. They've made no phone calls though, which I didn't expect. I was hoping for a number to trace."

"They've been careful all these years not to tip their hand, Jordan." Weariness and a sense of impending doom was beginning to grow inside her once again. "They're not going to slip up that easily."

"I didn't say it would be easy, now, did I?" he pointed out with an edge of amusement.

A smile tugged at her lips. "True," she agreed, "you never promised it would be easy."

His fingers tucked beneath her chin and lifted her head, his gaze staring down into hers. "They have to go through me to hurt you, baby. Me and the entire fucking team," he swore.

Him and the entire team. He took care of those he considered his own. His agents, their wives, their children if needed. He claimed his shoulders were broad.

The fact was, she was still just a part of the team. It was nothing special. It was nothing romantic nor was it something he would allow them to have forever.

She had now though, she reminded herself. She had a chance to make some memories, a chance to gather his warmth, his passion to her and hold it for the cold, dark days ahead.

As he held her chin up, his head lowered to brush her lips with his. The latent hunger in the action sent heat surging through her body and hunger knotting her womb with such fierce heat it felt blistering.

God, she loved him. So much that she would walk through fire, a hail of bullets, or face her family simply because he felt it was for the best.

As his head rose, her hand lifted, her fingers touching his clean-shaven jaw. She didn't care who watched, she didn't care the conclusions they drew. She had to tell him, it was burning in her heart and in her soul, that need to whisper the hunger she knew would never ease.

Whatever happened, whatever the growing panic building inside her meant, she didn't want to leave this world without him knowing. . . .

As her lips parted he laid his fingers against them, leaned close, and simply whispered. "I know."

Chapter 12

It was midnight before the senator's party finally began to wind down and Jordan decided it was time to make their exit. The hours had been spent dancing, chatting, and socializing. The Taites were present, moving around them yet never actually confronting Jordan again.

"Ah, I see you're leaving, Jordan." Still bright-eyed and energetic, the senator met them at the wide double doors as they neared them.

"It's that time, Richard," Jordan answered with a grin as he drew Tehya closer to his side. "I have several meetings tomorrow that I'd prefer not to be late to."

"I completely understand." The senator gave a quick nod before bending his head to kiss Tehya's cheek fondly. "Come see us soon, Teylor. As always, you're missed."

The farewell was a message as well. That she didn't have to wait until the operation was over to visit. That they were friends.

"We would love to see more of you, Tey." Emily Krieger reinforced her father's invitation, using the shortened version of her name to remind her that Emily knew not just who she was, but also who she had been.

"Perhaps," Tehya murmured, though she returned Emily's hug firmly and thankfully.

She knew that once this was over, if she survived it, that

she would need a friend. Someone who could understand without reaching out to Jordan with a guilt trip where leaving Tehya was concerned.

Tehya knew exactly how the unit worked and the friendships that had been built because of it. They were, in many regards, like a family.

"We'll see you soon, Richard," Jordan promised again as his hand tightened at Tehya's lower back to draw her from the house. "And thanks again for the invitation."

Guests were already milling on the mansion's marble front stoop and wide steps that led to the curved driveway and the limousines slowly pulling around.

As Nik pulled the limo to a stop, exited the vehicle, and moved to the back door, Jordan led her slowly down the steps. Her hand lay in the crook of his arm comfortably, the warmth of his body against her side.

Behind her, she felt eyes watching, piercing.

The feeling was stronger than it had been before Jordan found her. The panic was beginning to tighten her chest, building inside her, warning her that the storm brewing around her was going to explode at any time.

Turning slowly in the seat, she sat sideways, facing Jordan, her gaze moving to the crowd gathering on the marble stoop.

Standing out from the other guests, instantly drawing her gaze, their eyes locked on Jordan's limo, were Stephen and Craig Taite.

Staring into Stephen Taite's face, she saw his resemblance to the pictures she had seen of her grandfather, and a slighter resemblance to her mother. Craig Taite resembled her mother more, though. His tall, lanky form was a harder, more masculine, male version of Francine Taite.

Thoughtful, perhaps confused, Stephen's expression was almost enigmatic as his gaze remained locked on the back of the limo, as though he were attempting to sort out a puzzle.

His son's expression was more disapproving, though tinged with interest and a hint of—was that somber sadness and knowledge? Or was she simply seeing what she wanted to see? Seeing a family when there was none?

She forced herself to turn away, to let the sight of them go as her mother's secret whispered through her mind. She held the key to the destruction of the Taite empire, and she had forced herself to remain aloof from them, to push away every dream she had ever had, to ensure not just their safety, but also the balance of financial power they had maintained.

Her family.

Her mother had grieved for her family. Tehya remembered the few months off and on that she and her mother had been able to actually be together, and she remembered hearing her mother cry.

They had been lost in the world, separated when Bernard Taite and his wife had died. Francine had been too terrified to call on what remained of her family after her parents' murders certain that they too would suffer if she did so.

"Tey." Jordan's voice was soft, despite its roughness as he pulled her to him. "It's going to be okay."

She shook her head as she fought back her tears. "Mother grieved for everything she had lost over the years. She called when she learned of my grandparents' deaths, hysterical out of her mind with guilt because she had called them, begging for their help. Their deaths were made to look like an accident with the hit and run that killed my grandfather. It appeared my grandmother committed suicide. Even the officers investigating knew there was more to their deaths. There was just no proof."

Was she shaking? She could feel her stomach trembling where that sense of panic was building.

"Tehya, stop this." Strong, broad fingers suddenly gripped her waist as he lifted her, pulling her to his lap before a hand cupped her cheek and turned her head to face him.

His eyes were a brilliant sapphire, staring into hers, locking her soul to his.

"No one knows who you are. They may suspect, but I promise you, no one will strike out at the Taites because of that suspicion."

Her hand gripped his wrist, desperation beginning to grow inside her, clawing at her until she wondered why she hadn't run, why she hadn't escaped the moment she had known she was being watched again.

"I'm terrified, Jordan," she finally admitted painfully. "I don't want to lose anyone else. I don't want anyone else to die because of me. I've already lost too much."

The men she had worked with during their contract to the Elite Ops were her friends. She was friends with the wives, she had gotten to know their children through pictures and knew their hopes and dreams. She was closer to them, and to Jordan, than she had ever been to anyone else in her life. Even her mother.

And Jordan. Her hand tightened on his wrist as his thumb caressed her lips, sending flares of exquisite sensation washing through her.

In the midst of rising panic, those sensations had the ability to still the storm raging inside her. Fear retreated beneath the warmth that sparked to a flame and hunger turned to a raging need in a split second.

"I don't know if I can survive . . ."

"Shhh." His fingers covered her lips. "We're going to fix this, Tehya. All of it. When it's over, you'll never have to hide again. I swear it."

She knew what he was doing, though. His fingers were holding back the words she knew he didn't want to hear.

He wanted her. She could see it in his face. He wanted her body, her touch, but he didn't want the heart she had given him years before.

This was all she had, and, she promised herself, she would make it be enough.

She shook her head slowly as his fingers slid from her lips, along her jaw, down her neck to her shoulder. Like a whisper of heat, the subtle touch of flames.

"Touch me." If he didn't touch her, if he didn't distract her, then how was she supposed to hold back the emotions?

No, she wasn't holding back the emotions. If he didn't want her to whisper them, then he had to give her another way to express them.

Through her pleasure.

Her head fell back against his arm slowly as she felt his free hand lift the skirt of her dress, his palm cupping the side of her ankle before sliding heatedly to her knee.

Callused and experienced, his fingertips slid to the back of her knee, caressing in tiny circles, causing her leg to tighten as heat pierced her womb.

"Touch you how?" he whispered, sensual promise tightening his voice.

Her eyes opened, her stomach clenched in rising need at the pure, sexual hunger on his face, in his eyes.

Reaching down, her fingers curled around his wrist as she lifted his hand and brought it to her breast.

"They ache," she whispered, her voice trembling.

And they did. Her nipples were on fire as the need for his touch, the heated dampness of his mouth surrounding them, began to tear through her.

"They ache, love?" he asked, his arm shifting behind her back to lower the zipper of her dress.

The bodice loosened, slid slowly over the swollen, tight curves of her breasts and revealed the painfully hard buds of her nipples.

The wash of air over the sensitive peaks sent a shudder racing through her. Anticipation surged, heated and spiked with sexual adrenaline.

"How pretty." The rough pad of a finger slid over the ultra-sensitive tip, causing her body to jolt in response as pleasure became a hunger so intense it bordered on agony.

"Don't tease," she breathed out roughly, her lashes heavy. "I want your mouth on them. Please, Jordan. I want to feel your tongue."

She would be shocked at the explicit demand later, when she had the ability to think. Thinking right now was pushed aside in favor of feeling, experiencing. Burning.

Watching, her breath caught as his tongue licked over his lips, dampening them as his head lowered, lips parting.

The first heated lick of his tongue against the berry-ripe flesh had her nails biting into his arm as she shook her head, fighting against the loss of control, against the weakness flooding her limbs.

His lips covered the tight nipple, his mouth sucked at it, his tongue lashed it.

"So good," she whispered breathlessly, hearing the words, knowing she should clench her teeth against them, but unable to.

His tongue curled around the tip, licked it with slow relish before his head lowered further and his lips surrounded the aching flesh.

The moan that escaped her lips was tight, filled with desperation and a fight for breath. Pleasure seared her nerve endings and burned through her mind. The heated draw of his lips against her nipple was fiery and exhilarating.

Wrapping her arms around his neck, Tehya lifted her head, her lips finding the tough lobe of his ear and the sensitive flesh beneath.

The taste of him was heady. Slightly salty, all male.

Tunneling her fingers through the long hair at the back of his neck, feeling the slightly coarse roughness, the cool caress of each strand, added to the sensations whipping through her.

She wanted to feel him all over her. His tongue licking her, oh, yes, just like that.

His tongue rubbed at the too-sensitive peak of her nipple. He licked as though he loved the taste of her. His lashes lifted and the brilliant blue of his eyes was like a flame, burning in the center, filled with hunger.

For her.

"Jordan." His name whimpered past her lips.

She would have said more. She needed to say more. But before the words could form, his head lifted, his lips covered hers, and her senses became swamped with a sensual pleasure that burned straight to her soul.

His arms surrounded her, held her tight to his chest as she turned to him, the heated tips of her breasts brushing erotically against the material of his evening jacket.

A hungry moan escaped her, fed into their kiss as she

struggled to move, to turn, her desperation to hold on to him, on to the pleasure only building.

And he gave it to her.

Jordan could feel the rising flames whipping through both of them. She was like a flame herself, flaming in his arms as he tugged at the skirt of her dress, jerking it over her thighs as she straddled him, her hands in his hair, her lips beneath his, her tongue licking at his.

His cock was so damned hard it was a living ache, tortured and desperate as his hips jerked upward when the hot dampness of her pussy came over the heavy wedge. Nothing protected her from his possession but the material of his pants and the ultra-thin silk of her panties.

The naturally bare folds of her pussy beckoned him, drew him. The lush heat radiating between her thighs had him nearly insane for her.

How easy it would be to lay her back on the seat, spread those pretty thighs and tear the thin silk of her panties from the slick flesh awaiting him.

The need to fuck her was clawing at him.

His balls were tight, agonizing lust tore up his spine and clenched through his muscles.

He was burning for her and only the possession of her would still the fire.

Fuck that.

The fire for her was never stilled.

Tearing his lips from hers, Jordan quickly pushed his fingers into the long, silken curls of her hair, clenched, and held her in place as he stared back at her, watching as those beautiful green eyes opened with drowsy wonder.

She looked as innocent as the day she had walked into the Elite Ops base six years before. She looked untouched, though he knew damned good and well she wasn't. He'd taken her every chance he had, and still he hadn't had enough of her.

Would he ever touch her enough, take her enough, taste her enough to still the hunger that raged through him for her?

"Don't stop." The longing in that soft whisper sent a shaft of pure lust jerking through his dick.

"Not yet." It was all he could do to force the words past his lips. "In our room." Where she would be safe. Where he could take his time, where he could have her as he wanted her, every way he wanted her.

Her lashes fluttered as he pulled at her hair again, pleasure washing through her expression.

"It almost hurts," she almost whimpered as near ecstasy transformed her face for a moment. "Just right there on the edge, Jordan."

His teeth clenched. Damn her. He didn't know if he could wait. The pressure building in his cock was becoming agonizing, making the battle to hold on to his control one he wasn't certain he would win.

"I need you inside me, Jordan." She rolled her hips, her pussy stroking over his cock, and he swore he felt rockets exploding in his head as his blood pressure hit the roof.

A second later, her lips lowered, brushed against his, and whispered, "Fuck me."

His eyes narrowed.

She was lost in her own need, he could see it, feel it as she moved against him.

Her head tilted back, a moan vibrating in her throat as his hand tightened in her hair, the other going to her hip, clenching. Every intention he had of waiting flying out the window.

If Nik hadn't chosen that moment to pull into the hotel, Jordan knew he would have been lost.

"We're here," Jordan groaned

Moving quickly, he adjusted her dress, zipped it, and lifted her from his lap as he watched her fight to assimilate to the sudden change.

Turning to her, he caught her face in his hand, held her still, and growled down at her. "The moment we're in the room, that dress is going to your hips and that silk you call panties will be ripped from your thighs. Then, Tehya, I'll fuck you. I'm going to bury myself inside you so deep, so fucking hard, that nothing else will exist for either of us."

"Nothing else exists for me now."

What the hell was he supposed to say? To explain to her

the lesson the past had taught him well? To make her see, to understand that he couldn't live the illusion, no matter how desperately he wished he could.

Thankfully, he was saved from saying anything when the sound of the door opening drew him back to reality, to the existence of the world, and the danger surrounding them.

His fingers caressed her cheek as he drew back, then slid from the car. Pausing to survey the area around them for a long second, Jordan then reached inside, gripped her hand, and helped her from the car.

Tiny and graceful, her fingers tucked into his palm as she stepped into the cool night air.

Like a sprite coming out to play. The violet hues of the gown flowed around her, emphasizing the abundance of mussed, long red-gold curls and mysterious green eyes.

Lush, swollen lips, flushed cheeks. Sensuality bloomed around her, gleamed in her gaze, and transformed her features in a way that had every cell in his body throbbing in need of her.

With Nik moving in behind her, Jordan rushed her to the door of the hotel and across the expensive lobby to the elevators.

As they entered the hall, Micah straightened from his position against the wall, nodded to Nik, then took his place at Tehya's back.

Nothing left to chance.

He couldn't lose her. He could leave her. The time would come when he would have no choice, when the danger was over, and it would be time for him to go. He could do that. What he couldn't do was survive if Tehya wasn't breathing.

Stepping into the vacant elevator, Jordan pulled her close to his side, feeling the fragility of her, the delicacy of her slight body, despite the stubborn will that he knew had turned her backbone to steel.

"Noah's checking the room," Micah stated quietly as the elevator moved to the upper floor. "We had a bit of interest before you arrived. Our friends from Afghanistan attempted to slip upstairs."

"Did you catch them?" Violence swirled on the outer edges of the lust.

"Unfortunately not." Micah shrugged. "We will, though. They're getting arrogant."

Jordan glanced at the top of Tehya's head. Tension was building in her now, and it wasn't the tension he wanted her to be filled with.

Casting Micah a speaking look, he remained silent.

He was thirty-eight years old. For more than twenty years, he'd been learning how to be the hunter and how to be the prey. He'd been no more than fifteen the first time a neighboring rancher and his hands had thought they could use Jordan as target practice.

A lot of years, a lot of experience and knowledge.

They would make their move soon, he knew. He was waiting on them.

He'd felt it at the party. He could sense that the danger surrounding Tehya was beginning to escalate.

The men watching them were watching things too closely now, there was a steadily growing tension beginning to mount around them.

What they would attempt to do, he wasn't completely certain. They were definitely after Tehya, and not to harm her. At least, not at first.

There was something they wanted, and no matter how he tried, Jordan couldn't figure out what she could possibly possess that they could want.

They would be aware she was protected now, and they weren't letting that bother them. They were too confident. As Micah said, they were too arrogant.

As the elevator eased to a stop, Micah stepped in front of them, his corded body tense and prepared as the doors slid open.

Only Noah awaited on the other side, though. Jordan's nephew was watching him closely, blue eyes narrowed, suspicion tightening his expression.

"The suite's clean." Noah nodded as they stepped into the hall. "We have the two rooms on each side of you and the suite across from you." He indicated the appropriate doors.

Jordan gave a sharp nod as he led Tehya to the double doors.

"Get some rest," he ordered both of them. "We'll meet at breakfast and go over the information we have. Let's see if we can't do something to liven things up a bit tomorrow."

He had several ideas. Most importantly, he needed to force the men watching them into acting. Once they were off balance, the chances of them leading the team to their employer were greater.

Opening the door he stepped inside, looked around, then drew Tehya in as well.

Once the door closed, watchers didn't exist. Danger didn't exist. There was no threat, there was no reality.

He had her in his arms, lifting her, bearing her to the wide conference table that sat in the middle of the room.

There wasn't a chance in hell of making it to the bed.

Hell, she was lucky he had made it this far.

Setting her on the cool wood surface, he slid the fingers of one hand into her hair once again, clenched in the soft strands, and forced her head back.

"Stop thinking," he growled, determined that the pleasure they had shared in the limo would pale in comparison to the heat rising between them now.

"Jordan." Worry darkened her eyes.

"No." Forceful, filled with furious lust and white-hot demand, he glared down at her. "Not tonight, Tehya. Tonight, you're mine. No worries, no fear. Just this, damn you. Just this."

This.

His lips covered hers, his tongue pressed between them, and his hands moved from her hair to the gentle swell of her hips as he forced her thighs apart and stepped between them.

Staring down, Jordan watched as his hands, dark against the lighter violet hues of the dress, gathered the material and began dragging it slowly up her legs.

"Tonight you're mine," he growled again as he felt the

raging hunger building inside him. "Right here, right now, Tehya, this is all that matters."

The skirt revealed her legs, her thighs, the violet smoke of her stockings, the lacy elastic edge that stretched around her thighs.

His breathing accelerated. His chest tightened as each breath became ragged. Never in his life had a woman affected him this way. Never had anything looked so damned pretty, or been so important to him outside his family.

"Fuck, look how damned pretty." He lifted his gaze, staring back at her, watching her eyes, her face as she became immersed in the sensual pleasure. "Watch me, Tey. Watch me touch you, baby. Enjoy you . . ." He almost said more.

He almost betrayed himself.

He almost gave in to the illusion that between him and Tehya, there was so much more than lust. So much more than pleasure.

If love existed . . .

CHAPTER 13

Tehya could feel the heat rising in the room, or was it just rising in her?

Reclining, she propped her weight on her elbows and stared back at him, the hunger to tease him, to tempt him becoming overwhelming.

She wanted her own memories to store away, but even more, there was something inside her pushing her, demanding she ensure he never forget her either.

As he stared down at her, she lifted enough to release the zipper at her lower back, loosening the gown as she watched his expression tighten.

"Help me." She could barely speak, her breathing was so heavy, excitement flooding her system as his hands moved to the bodice of the gown and began drawing it down her body.

The feel of the silk underslip sliding against her flesh was exquisite, almost painful. The need to feel his hands was rising by the second.

Lifting her hips, she watched his expression as he drew the material over them, then down her legs to allow it to drop to the floor.

His jaw bunched, flexed. His hands slid up her legs, to her thighs, then to the band of the tiny thong she wore.

A second later, less than a second, the material was torn from her body and tossed to the floor. Gripping her arms he drew her up, one hand buried in her hair as the other flattened against her back and his head lowered, his lips possessing hers with a hunger so fiery she felt singed by it.

The sensual impact of the kiss blazed through her senses as arousal began to consume her with a power she didn't have a hope of fighting.

Her arms tightened around his neck, desperate to hold on to him now, to hold on to that dark, unspoken "something" that bound her to him in ways she couldn't explain.

Mixing with each touch, each kiss, each spark of pleasure that fanned the flames higher was a burning knowledge that he was becoming essential to her. That he had already marked her soul, claimed her.

She arched into the kiss, her thighs spreading for the full width and impact of his hips thrusting determinedly between them.

The material of his pants rasped against the tender skin of her inner thighs as the steel hard wedge of his cock pressed against the bare folds of her pussy.

Liquid heat spilled along the sensitive flesh as Jordan nipped at her lips, a harsh groan rumbling in his throat as Tehya whimpered at the need rising inside her.

Her neck arched tilted back as his lips slid from hers and rasped a path of destructive arcs of sizzling sensation down her neck, moving to her breasts, finding the tight, tender peak of her nipple once again.

Swollen, enflamed from his earlier caresses. The feel of his lips drawing on the sensitive peak tightened through her back and pulled a cry from her lips.

Her nails dug into his scalp as her hips moved beneath his, desperate for every stroke of pleasure, every touch, every ounce of sensation.

Her hips lifted to him as she tried to curl her legs around his waist, tried to get closer, only to have him push them apart as he lifted his head and straightened from her.

"Don't stop." She had to force the words past her lips.

"Never." The hard, dark rasp of his voice intensified her pleasure. The knowledge that he was just as affected, that he needed just as much as she needed, sent pulsing excitement whipping through her.

Staring back at him, breathless, Tehya watched as his lips lowered again, this time to the flesh between her breasts. Heated kisses and hungry licks blazed a path of destructive pleasure down her body.

His tongue swirled around her navel, dipped in with an erotic lick before wandering over the soft flesh of her lower belly.

His hands stroked along her thighs, her hips. Each firm caress pulled her deeper into a maelstrom of ecstasy.

"You taste as hot and sweet as hell, Tehya. Damned addictive, sugar."

Her breath caught at the pleasure in his expression, his voice. The slight Texas drawl assured her he was losing himself as much as she was in the pleasure, and that he was forgetting all that careful control he always exerted over himself.

He pushed her thighs farther apart as she trembled with anticipation.

His tongue licked, he kissed. He held her legs apart, whispered a breath over her clit, and she swore she was so close to coming she could touch it.

Lifting his head he gazed at her her through the slit of his lashes. Sensual knowledge burned, male dominance tightened his expression, and pure wicked lust gleamed in his eyes.

She could hope he was losing control, and perhaps he had lost a small part of it. But the sensual, sexual animal he was still maintained enough of his senses to control her.

His fingers moved up her thigh, stroking against her flesh. Anticipation spread through her as her clit swelled with agonizing pleasure.

"Jordan," his name slipped past her lips in a desperate plea.

"Do you need me, Tey?"

Oh, God, she needed him so bad.

"Always." Her fingers moved to his hair again, desperate for something to hold on to.

"Have you always needed me, Tey?" His fingers moved

between her thighs, parted the folds of her pussy, and just rubbed.

Her hips jerked, her muscles tensed until she felt as though she would break.

"Jordan, I've always needed you." Every part of her needed him. Ached for him. Dreamed of him. "I've needed no one like I need you."

Jordan stared back at her. He was losing it. That part of himself that he had always managed to hold aloof. That part that had always been cold, that refused to acknowledge weakness, emotion, or hunger. That part of himself that he had kept carefully hidden away was coming for her.

Staring up at her, he lowered his head, the taste of her sweet pussy exploding against his tongue as he parted his lips, laid them over the swollen bud of her clit, and kissed.

Her hips jerked against him the cry that spilled from her lips slicing across his control.

She was addictive as hell. Liquid heat, sensual nectar met his lips, as he rolled it over her clit and felt it flex against his tongue.

She was close. So fucking close. He could feel the need for release pounding against her clit as her soft juices spilled to his lips.

He knew what awaited him. The pleasure. A pleasure that burned brighter, hotter than anything he had ever known before.

Sucking her clit into his mouth, he drew on the swollen bundle of nerve endings as his fingers moved lower, finding the clenched opening of her pussy and pushing inside the silky, slick entrance.

Immediately the snug, silken tissue clamped on the two fingers working inside her. A cry shattered the silence of the room and the heated glide of her juices washed over his fingers.

And it only made him crave her more. Made him hungrier. Made that part of himself that he kept hidden strain closer to her.

His cock pounded, his balls were so damned tight with

the need to come that it was nearly unbearable. With each taste of her lush little pussy, the hunger only grew. He found himself no longer caring that he ached for that illusion he was always warning her about.

Drawing his fingers back, he worked frantically to release his cock from the cloth binding it. Toeing off his expensive leather shoes, he quickly shed the pants, then rose just enough to remove his shirt.

Straightening, his gaze moved slowly over her as he gripped the base of his cock to hold back the release that threatened to explode despite his best intentions.

"Let me see, Tehya," he growled, his voice harsher, darker than he intended. "Touch yourself, baby. Let me see."

And God, he loved watching her.

Her hands rose, delicate, fragile fingers cupping the undercurve of each breast, lifting them as the tip of a finger stroked over each tight point.

Her eyes raked down his body, her gaze locking on the sight of him gripping his cock as her hips arched, her face flushing with a surfeit of sexual hunger.

"I want to watch, too," she whispered as her hands slid from her breasts to caress lower, to stroke her midriff before moving to the flesh just above the slight rise of her pussy.

Bracing his feet against the floor, he let his fingers move over his cock, stroking it slowly, grimacing as his balls throbbed with the need to come.

The effect on Tehya was far more than he expected. The sight of him stroking himself drew a harsh moan from her throat as her fingers slid into the folds of her pussy to circle the swollen bud of her clit.

Her hips arched. Her juices gathered on the peaches-and-cream curves, glistening with an excess of feminine arousal.

Stretched across the table, her delicate feet still in the wickedly high heels, the violet smoke hue of the stockings still encasing her legs as she propped her feet on the arms of the two chairs to each side of her, she looked like a modern-day sacrifice to lust.

Lush, velvety flesh. Emerald eyes glowing. Graceful fingers thrumming against her clit as he stepped closer, the engorged head of his cock throbbing at the nearness of her pussy's sweet, hot juices.

He could feel the heat of her. The remembered feel of the tight grip milking his dick was nearly enough to make him come as he watched her fingers slide through the swollen, flushed curves.

She parted her flesh, stroked the small, clenched slit, then he watched, his breath stilling in his throat, as the tips of two delicate fingers slid inside.

"No." Before he could stop himself he gripped her wrist, pulling her fingers back as he stepped closer.

Lifting her hand he brought the glistening fingers to his lips, his tongue peeking out to lick the heated, feminine syrup from the tips as the head of his cock pressed gainst the slick entrance.

Their eyes locked.

He'd always been so careful in the past to ensure that he didn't stare at his lovers' faces. A man couldn't lose himself in a woman if he didn't stare into her eyes.

He'd also known instinctively, though, that there hadn't been a chance of ever losing any part of himself until he met Tehya. Until he had seen in her eyes the hunger he denied in himself.

He couldn't deny her anymore. Not inside. Not where that inborn knowledge of a man's mate rested.

He might not believe in the illusion of love as others saw it. But he did believe in a man's knowledge of the one woman created for him. Not love. Much more than mere lust.

It was a claiming.

And he was claiming her.

Watching her, her wrist still held in his hand, his hips bunched, his cock tightened impossibly further, harder, as with a single hard thrust he buried the painfully tight flesh several inches inside ecstasy.

There was no stopping him.

Finesse was gone.

Pure male hunger filled his mind, his senses. He released

her wrist and his hands gripped her hips as he began moving, working the engorged length of his dick inside the impossibly tight depths of her pussy.

Fiery muscles clenched and milked his cock as her legs wrapped around his hips. Her hands flattened against his abdomen, slid up his chest and to his neck as he came over her.

His lips pressed against hers, his tongue slipping past them and he lunged inside her, shafting inside the tender depths of her pussy as he felt her juices gathering around him, searing his flesh.

Gripping her hips, he lifted his head as he forced his eyes open. Forced himself to stare into hers. And felt himself sinking inside her.

What he didn't expect was to feel her sinking inside him as well.

Tehya's breath caught at the deepening blue of his eyes, the savagely honed features, the dark swirling, shadowed emotion she recognized with feminine instinct.

Each hard thrust inside her body seemed to deepen that dark swirl of emotion even as it built the fiery pleasure racing through her body.

His hands moved from her hips to her thighs, pulling her legs from around his hips as he dragged them to his chest, her feet resting against his shoulders as his thrusts began to increase.

Tender nerve endings rioted with sensation at the feel of the engorged, flared cock head raking over them. Sizzling flames enveloped her clit with each stroke of his pelvis against it as he buried inside her full length, filling her, overfilling her, the thick, hard flesh almost bruising in the power of his thrusts.

The pleasure was agonizing. Her fingers curled over the edge of the table, her nails digging into the wood. His hands gripped her ankles to fuck her harder. His hips slammed into her thighs, flesh pounding against flesh as she felt the sudden, blinding rise to orgasm.

When it hit her, Tehya felt her senses exploding with it.

Her breath caught in her chest, hips arching, a strangled cry trapped in her throat as seismic tremors began to race through her body.

Each shattering explosion jerked her body tighter against his as her pussy clenched further, milked harder, and then exploded in a second flash of rapture as she felt him coming inside her.

Each heavy throb of his cock, each fiery pulse of semen inside her heightened her release. It threw her into a brilliant wash of color, sensation, and pleasure so intense she wondered if she could ever recover from it.

And through it, her gaze remained locked with his, and, she swore, her soul became a part of his. She had been his since the day she met him. He'd marked her that first night that he'd taken her, but this time, this time, she felt his possession to the depths of her soul.

This time, Jordan became a part of her.

"Oh God." The shattered breath of sound escaped her lips, and this time, she knew what she was saying. "Oh God, Jordan, I love you."

Silently, meticulously, Jordan helped Tehya into the wrinkled material of his shirt, buttoned it carefully, then stepped back and fixed his pants.

A part of him felt shattered.

He couldn't explain it, and it sure as fucking hell didn't make sense. His nerves felt on edge, and that coming from a man who had nerves of steel. He felt a curious fury burning inside him, or was it something else?

Whatever it was, his soul felt lashed by it, bruised by the violent waves of whatever conflict raged inside him.

"Jordan?" She whispered his name as he zipped his pants and turned from her to stride to the wet bar across the room.

God, he couldn't talk to her right now. The kindest thing he could do was walk away. He needed to walk away before he ended up destroying them both.

Lifting his hand, he blew out a weary breath as he rubbed

at the back of his neck. Escape was futile. There was no escaping her, no matter how much distance he put between them. He'd already learned that lesson the hard way.

"I'm sorry." The heartbreaking regret in her voice sent a shaft of some white-hot emotion burning through his chest.

God dammit. What the hell was he feeling? Anger? It felt like anger. Like helplessness. And by God he didn't do helpless well.

"Don't apologize," he finally blew out roughly as he turned to her, praying she wasn't crying.

And hell no, she wasn't crying. Her chin was lifted stubbornly, her gaze defiant, but he could see the regret shadowing the green depths of her eyes.

"I would say it slipped out, but that would imply I was trying to hold it back, wouldn't it?" Her lips quirked with a strangely amused self-mockery.

"I can always trust you to be amazingly blunt," he sighed. "And it's not the first time it's slipped out."

Damned near every time he had taken her the words had slipped past her lips and dug sharp talons into his soul. Each time, he had tried to muffle the words with his lips; but still, the sound of them had slipped free enough to allow him to make them out.

A shrug lifted her shoulders as she tucked a heavy swath of hair behind a delicate ear.

Red-gold curls tumbled around her face and shoulders. The disarray caused by his hands, by the tossing of her head as she orgasmed beneath him, had given her a wanton, decidedly lush appearance. But her expression, the vulnerability in her gaze, made her appear too innocent, too easily hurt.

He knew Tehya. He knew her compassion, he knew the woman she pretended to be as well as the woman she truly was.

"I don't want to hurt you, Tey, but if you allow yourself to believe you love me, if you give in to that illusion, then that's exactly what I'll end up doing."

There was that strange little smile again. Part teasing, part mocking. It was one of those looks that never failed to put him off balance. He'd be damned if he could tell what she was thinking when she had that look on her face.

"Don't worry about hurting me, Jordan." She brushed back her hair again as she turned from him and headed for the bedroom. "It was too late for that a long time ago."

She almost made the bedroom before he was on her. His fingers curled around her upper arm, dragging her to a stop as she jerked around, unable to hide the anger in her eyes before he saw it.

Jordan paused, surprised, watching as her chin tilted in determination and stubbornness and her cat's green eyes narrowed back at him suspiciously.

"I've heard the lecture," she informed him as she glared back at him. "I've heard you tell your men how love is an illusion, and how they need to watch their backs before that illusion bites them on the ass, so many times it sickens me. Unless you have something original to add to it, then I don't want to hear it again, if you don't mind."

Yes, it was a lecture he had given his men often. Hell, they were his men, his team. They were his family. He felt it was his responsibility to warn them at the very least. Not that he didn't like their wives. Hell, they were damned good women. But when a man allowed himself to live a lie . . .

"You're fooling yourself." He had to force the words past his lips. "You're letting lust and pleasure betray you, Tehya. It tricks you. When it fades, all you have left is either friendship or enmity. It's the enmity that worries me, the knowledge of all the little ways you can destroy one another with the knowledge you've gained. I don't want us to go that route. I don't want you to hate me."

The thought of losing her had his guts clenching in dread. The thought of her hatred, of never seeing the hunger in her eyes and feeling the need in her kiss, had his jaw clenching in imminent fury.

"Who destroyed you, Jordan?" Her arms crossed over her breasts as her lips set mutinously. "Who ruined you before I ever had a chance at your heart?"

The question wasn't asked in regret or in pain. Hell no,

not with Tehya. She was too damned confrontational, as though it were somehow his fault that he'd had a life before he met her.

It took a second to process the question as well as the anger in her expression now. How was he supposed to answer her?

"You're making me pay for what another woman has done." Her lips tightened, her gaze glittered furiously as she made the statement.

"This has nothing to do with another woman, Tehya," he growled.

He wished it had something to do with a single woman, with a broken heart, with a young man's disillusion. How much easier it would then be to give in to the dark hunger he could feel brewing in his soul.

Kira had always accused him of giving up on love because he couldn't save Killian Reece's wife, Catherine, and their unborn child. That he had blamed Catherine, and Killian's love for her for the change Killian had undergone after her death.

That had been a deciding point. It wasn't the whole reason.

"What does it have to do with, then?" Her eyes sparked furiously as he almost gave into the lust beginning to rise inside him once again.

Damn her, he'd no more had her than he wanted her again.

"It has to do with reality," he snapped. "It has to do with watching friends betray friends, countries betray their own soldiers, and lovers turning their backs on the very love they've pledged themselves to because the battle has become too difficult or because their own pride was more important. That is where it comes from."

She shook her head, her gaze filled with pity. "You've watched your men love, Jordan. You've watched their wives give all they have to them. You've seen loyalty, Jordan, and love, and you deny it."

He reached out and touched her cheek, her silken flesh heated and warm, beckoning him. "And sometimes," he said, "the illusion is stronger than the truth. For a while."

Tehya shook her head, mocking anger enveloping her as

she read the belief in what he was saying in his eyes. He truly believed love didn't last forever.

"I've met your father," she finally said softly.

A dark frown drew his brows together. "What does Dad have to do with anything?"

"He still mourns your mother's death. He goes to her grave daily, and he still weeps for the woman he lost."

She knew Riordan Malone, the father who looked over the Malone sons and grandsons that his union with his Irish bride had produced.

Jordan's jaw tightened as the battle to find an argument against her raged in his brilliant blue eyes.

Tehya shook her head. "I'm going to bed, Jordan, but perhaps you should consider this. It's not reality that destroys the dreams, it's your lack of faith. And it's your own fears of facing what you believe your father and Killian Reece faced. The loss of that dream and the only woman who could touch their hearts."

She turned, pulled her arm from his grip, and moved through the doorway to the bedroom.

She wasn't arguing with him, she wouldn't fight with him. She would fight for him, she would fight over him, but never would she battle him over something she knew he had always refused to face.

The loss of his mother had been hard enough, but for years Jordan had watched the aching loneliness and Riordan Malone's inability to ever lose the bleak sadness that had filled him with his wife's death. Catherine Reece had disobeyed Jordan's order during an operation involving Sorrel and a young girl he had kidnapped. She had managed to get herself killed as Killian and Jordan watched in horror, unable to stop it.

No, it hadn't been a broken heart that had destroyed Jordan's belief in love. It hadn't been any single woman who had disillusioned him. The woman who had broken his father's life, as well as his with her death, and the friend who hadn't known how to survive, had given him the belief that no love could truly last forever.

Moving through the darkened bedroom, Tehya shed the shirt he had given her and crawled between the chilled blankets. From where she lay, she could see the light from the door, and Jordan as he stood in the doorway, simply watching her.

He was at his most dangerous when he was so still and silent. When he was plotting, planning, or worse yet, when he was thinking.

He had a wicked, devious mind. He was a man who believed what he believed, and there would be no forcing his beliefs to change.

"You're wrong." His voice reached across the room, so icy, so emotionless, that a chill raced over her soul.

"Of course I am." She swallowed tightly and fought back the tears she would have shed if it would have done any good. If it would have won her the heart of the man she loved, she would have cried a river.

"I care for you." The sudden, fierce sound of his voice, the underlying fury in it, had her eyes closing in pain as she fought the hitch in her breath that would have been a sob. "I don't want to lose you, Tehya. Not your friendship. Not . . . this." The snarl in his voice assured her that he meant much more than whatever relationship they had had at the base.

"Then keep me, Jordan." She stayed, in the bed and refused to look directly at him. "But you can't do that either, can you?"

She couldn't be weak. She had felt something earlier when he had taken her. She had felt something from him that she didn't understand, something she didn't know how to describe.

She wouldn't fight him, but that didn't mean she was giving up. Sometimes, a person just had to give Jordan time to think, to find the truth himself.

Even if it meant letting him walk away to find it.

"Good night, Jordan," she said softly when he said nothing more.

He stood in the doorway, still watching her, the shadowed contours of his face appearing more savage, his eyes bluer as they gleamed in the low light reflecting behind him.

Sometimes, there were some things that just weren't meant to be, she told herself. She was prepared for that. But that didn't mean she couldn't hope, that she couldn't pray that when this was over, when the past was finally defeated, buried, and destroyed once and for all, then just maybe, she would have a chance at holding his heart.

A Malone man, he loves, not just with his heart, but with his soul. She remembered Riordan Malone's words years before when she had met him in Alpine, Texas, the small town the Malone family had lived in for decades. *Remember that, Tehya. It's not their hearts that lead them, it's their souls. And such a love is never easy. Such a love is never truly won but by the faith of a woman's very spirit, and her ability to understand the battle she faces.*

At the time, she hadn't understood why he had told her that. Now, though, she knew. Riordan had to have seen what she had already begun to feel. He had to have known exactly how stubborn, how completely bullheaded his son could be.

Just as she had known how dominant, how powerful, and how incredibly gentle Jordan could be as well.

Jordan was a man who had made his decisions and faced his understanding of the world years before. He'd created the defenses he needed and survived the only way he knew how. By not believing, by not loving. But the truth was, Jordan had loved far more than he would ever admit.

She didn't understand the battle she faced in claiming what her soul ached for. And she had no idea how to fight it.

All she knew was that she was terribly afraid she couldn't live without him.

CHAPTER 14

The bedroom door closed, stripping the light from the room and leaving Tehya to stare into the dark.

She listened as he undressed and checked his weapon before laying it on the bedside table, then slid into the bed, all without the aid of the light.

Once he settled in, a moment of tense silence filled the room before he spoke.

"I was sixteen, she and her family were visiting from England, with a neighbor. She was blond, delicate, and beautiful, and I fell like a ton of bricks for her.

"The affair lasted until the end of summer, when her parents found out. They had the neighbor's ranch hands beat the hell out of me, and when that didn't work, they locked her in her bedroom, refusing to let her out until arrangements could be made for her to return to England. And I thought I could rescue her." The tone of his voice warned her that perhaps that young love hadn't died, but had instead contributed to killing the belief in love Jordan had once possessed.

"I slipped into the house, picked the lock to her bedroom door, and slipped in."

He paused and Tehya wondered what he was thinking, remembering. The silence wasn't as heavy as before, but it still held the weight of the scars she knew he carried deep inside.

"She had been playing with us all," he finally sighed. "It was a ploy to force her parents to return her to England rather than have her attend the private school they were considering in America. She wanted to be with her Irish lover." Mockery filled his voice. "She considered me an acceptable stand-in for the summer, though."

Sixteen. God, how that must have twisted his male pride, as well as his heart.

She felt him shift in the bed until he turned to face her, the gleam of his eyes in the dark pulling her, giving her a connection to him that she desperately needed.

"It was nearly ten years later before I saw her again. I was commanding a small team, working with the British in routing a terrorist cell in London. We managed to strike during a meeting being held by their Afghani commander. Their second in command was there as well, an Irish national who had led the cell for years. They were in interrogation when I had a visitor. At first, I couldn't believe it was her. She didn't just act older, she looked older, more coarse, less like the lady she had pretended to be when she was a teenager. And she needed a favor." It wasn't anger or pain in his voice, instead, there was a heavy vein of mockery overlying the amusement. "She thought she could give me a little fuck for old time's sake and I would help her gain her lover's release. The Irish second in command was the stable hand she'd played me and her parents to return to. I looked in her lying eyes as though they were windows into my own career. We knew there was a link from British Intelligence into the terrorist cell, and we hadn't been able to find it. I was staring at it. She was the daughter of one of the highest ranking intelligence directors in MI-6 and she was the terrorists' link. But I wanted proof. I wanted it, and I betrayed her to get it without a moment's hesitation or guilt. At sixteen, I would have died for her. For years after that, I compared every woman I took to bed with her. But I betrayed her in less than a heartbeat and I didn't feel a damned thing for her as they led her away in handcuffs two weeks later."

"Jordan, she betrayed you," she whispered. "It's not the

same when two people love each other. When they're together, when they're working toward a future together."

"Isn't it?" He reached up and touched her cheek again, as
though that connection, as small as it was, was needed.

"Mom and Dad were working toward a future. They had
three sons, they had a life together, and they were committed to that ideal of love that they professed was so strong."
Now, there was anger, pain. "Dad loved her until nothing
mattered to him as much as his wife. When one of the young
families that worked for us on the ranch was targeted by rac-
ists, she fought back for them. She didn't tell Dad what she
was doing, and she didn't tell her sons, who were nearly
grown. She didn't tell anyone she was driving out to rescue
them and take them to a friend's house in the next county.
When her vehicle went over a cliff and exploded, the sheriff
ruled it an accident. There was no investigation, no questions
asked, despite the fact that there were three adult bodies and
a child's in that vehicle as well. We had no idea what the hell
happened until her friends slipped into the house late one
night and told us what she had been doing." A shard of bitter
laughter filled the room for a second. "She loved so deeply
that she didn't care about risking her own life, the life her
husband and children depended upon."

What was she supposed to say? She stared back at him,
her eyes burning with tears.

"The same as you and your men are forced to risk your
lives protecting and saving the world," she finally pointed
out huskily. "How is it any different, Jordan? She wasn't just
helping that small family, she was imagining her own family in the same danger, and had no choice but to react."

"You know, that's the same bullshit excuse I gave Killian
when his wife Catherine disobeyed orders and slipped into
the warehouse where Sorrel's men were holding a young
girl they had kidnapped. We had to wait on orders to go in
and they were getting ready to move the kid, but we still had
time. I was on the line with my director and we were getting
the order to go in. It was coming," he snarled. "We told her
it would get there in time. But she went in. She went in, she

got the girl, and she was running out of the warehouse with her.

"They shot her before she made it to safety, before we could get to her. She protected that kid, covered her body with her own as she went down and kept her alive until we got there. But she died, Tehya, and she took Killian's unborn son with her. A child she hadn't even told him about. And they gave him the same useless argument. A mother's instinct. The need to protect."

He came over her, pushed her back to the bed as she stared up at him, eyes wide, her breath catching.

"If you ever, ever fucking endanger yourself like that, then I will walk away," he snarled. "I won't watch helplessly, Tehya, while you destroy yourself. I will not let you kill me inside because of your damned stubbornness."

"Then you'll live by the same rules." She was back in his face, teeth bared, furious, aching, hurting for him and yet drawn into the emotional vortex she could feel swirling out from him. "Wrap me in cotton, Jordan. See if I give a fuck. Because you'll be right there with me or you can kiss my ass good-bye."

Jordan stared down at her. He could barely see the outline of her face, but he could see her eyes. Wicked, witchy cat's eyes that glared back at him, that demanded, that refused to back down.

She had an answer for everything.

She made him want to believe in love. Made him want to believe in that unspoken emotion he couldn't seem to get a handle on inside himself. That illusion he had always disdained in the past.

She made him want to give her the world, and even when he'd been sixteen, when he'd been dick dumb, he hadn't truly wanted to give any woman the world.

What did she do to him? He wanted to walk away, because he knew she was a weakness. He wanted to keep her at a distance, remain aloof, but it was damned impossible. She was tying his guts up in knots and at the same time, finding a way to keep his attention focused squarely on her.

And he couldn't figure out how she managed it.

"While we're together," he stated. "When this is over." He had to force himself to breathe through the words. "When it's finished, Tehya, I don't want to walk away. At least, not immediately."

She was silent, still. He could feel her hurt, he knew she had expected more.

"Don't walk away, Jordan." Thick, heavy with unshed tears, her voice whispered through the darkness. "For as long as you can, don't walk away."

He lay back down beside her before pulling her into his arms, her head resting against his shoulder.

He held her, his chest heavy with words he had no idea how to say. Hell, he didn't even know what the words were, just that they struggled to be free. That something inside him felt trapped.

As he stared into the darkness, he wondered, for the first time, if the illusion of love were cared for, if it were cherished, was there any way it could be preserved?

Sleep hadn't come easy for Jordan. The soft weight of Tehya in his arms had felt too natural, much too right for him not to question it.

He'd slept with many women over the years, lovers, mistresses, and never had he slept well with them, let alone lain comfortably with them in his bed.

He realized as he held her, though, that each time he had fallen asleep with her in his arms, it had simply felt right.

She was changing him. He felt it, and he had to admit there was an edge of discomfort in the knowledge. There was the realization that the consequences of losing her would be far different than those of losing anyone else.

As sleep settled over him, he allowed himself to push aside the questions and the concerns. For now, there was nothing he could do but accept it. There was no other option when it came to keeping her close to him. So far, the men shadowing her were too damned good at staying just out of reach. He wasn't about to risk having her taken from him.

There were safeguards built in just in case. Eyes were watching twenty-four-seven, always keeping Tehya in view on the off chance that Jordan hadn't covered every angle.

Those eyes were his last defense against the loss of the one woman he knew he couldn't bear to lose.

Because he could sense the danger coming.

He just didn't expect it to come so soon.

He was nudged from sleep by the awareness that something just wasn't right. A sound, a feeling, a shift in the air that wasn't natural.

It was an awareness, a warning that something threatened Tehya.

He had, before slipping into sleep, tucked his Glock beneath his pillow rather than leaving it on the bedside table.

Lying on his side, one arm around Tehya, he slid the other slowly beneath the pillow, his fingers curling over the butt of the gun as he felt Tehya shift by just the slightest degree, just enough to slide her arm over the side of the bed, the movement hidden by the blankets.

She was awake and ready to move. He had known that same awareness would awaken her as well. She had been on the run for too many years before she came to the Elite Ops. Those instincts didn't die.

Senses open, Jordan listened, fighting to determine where the danger was coming from. He'd left the lights on in the front room; the glow beneath the door had given the room the faintest bit of light.

It wasn't there now. The lights had been turned out, allowing the danger to slip into the room without alerting him by flooding the bedroom with light.

It must have been the click of the door that awakened them.

Rather than moving as he would have at any other time, Jordan paused. Listening closely he opened his eyes just enough to check his peripheal vision. And there they were. The faintest of shadows, not just one. Fuck, there were two.

He had to find a way to take both out at the same time, or to disable the first before drawing the fire of the second and praying he was fast enough to avoid the bullets.

The two shadows shifted, positioning themselves until their weapons were trained on him, not on Tehya.

He almost let his lips curl in satisfaction. They were trying to take him out, to separate Tehya from any hope of support or protection. That wouldn't happen. No matter what happened to him, his men would never allow her to be taken.

But he had no intentions of allowing himself to be taken out so easily.

He could feel Tehya. She was ready to move, tense, and on the verge of panic. Where her back rested against his chest, he could feel her heart racing furiously, the danger of the moment speeding adrenaline through her body.

His hand tightened on her hip where it had rested as they slept.

It was coming. He felt it. The weapons were trained on him, the assailants were ready to take the shot. But now he also knew where the bastards were. Two. They had come in as a team, one to take him out, the other to go after Tehya. He doubted they had plans to kill her.

He was running out of time.

Jordan watched the shadows shift again from the corner of his eyes and knew his time was up.

He moved.

As though Tehya's instincts were directly connected to his, she moved with him as the sound and red flares of silenced weapons discharging popped through the room.

He went for the first would-be assassin. Slamming the butt of his weapon into the head and feeling him fall, he turned and prayed the first was disabled long enough for him to deal with the second.

The pop-pop of bullets discharging from a silencer again echoed through the room again as Jordan rolled. They slammed into his pillow, where his head had been.

"Keep the lights out," he snarled, just in case Tehya was going for the lamp. "Get behind something."

Protection. Tehya had to be protected. That one instinct, that one imperative thought drove his every movement.

He needed the darkness now. The flare of light would blind his senses, leaving him defenseless for precious seconds. It would give the assailants an advantage, perhaps the chance to do as they intended. To kill him.

Eyes narrowed, his gaze pierced the darkness as he threw himself to the side again, drawing the gunfire his way, rather than Tehya's.

He was trusting her to take care of the assailant on the floor while he disabled the other. Discarding his weapon, Jordan threw himself at the second assailant. Rage was a fever rushing through his system, burning into mind and lighting a fuse to danger-induced adrenaline.

Stupid bastards, he thought. If he knew he were going into a darkened bedroom he would have worn night vision hardware. He would have never gone in as blind as his prey.

A shift in the shadows alerted him.

Jumping to the side, Jordan rolled as the blood-red streaks of light flared in the darkness. Catching the assailant as he jerked to the side to change direction, his fist slammed into the kidneys, drawing a hard cry from his throat as Jordan took him to the floor his hand going for the weapon coming around on him.

Gripping the hand holding the weapon, Jordan struggled to wrestle it from his assailant before he could fire again.

"Bastard!" A harsh cry from the knee Jordan drove into his attacker's crotch as the gun went off, ripping along his side as Jordan snarled at the pain.

His fist slammed into a jaw as he jerked the weapon from the other man's hand and tossed it across the floor. He was going in for another shot when the bedroom door slammed open, flooding the room with just enough light to momentarily blind him.

He jumped in the direction of the weapon he had just tossed to the side.

"Clear." It was Micah's voice, icy cold and dangerous, that assured him the intruders were friendly rather than enemy.

Without hesitation, Jordan jumped to his feet and went

across the bed in a hard roll to come to a crouch where Tehya was supposed to be.

Instead of moving to a point of protection, she was finishing a quick knot to the belt from her robe around the hands of the first assailant.

She had jerked his shirt back on, two buttons secured just beneath her breasts. Red-gold curls flowed wildly around her shoulders, her cat's eyes glittered with rage and fear.

"Where are the others?" Jordan snapped as he jerked his pants from the bottom of the bed and quickly pulled them on, his gaze going between the two disabled men as Micah secured the second.

"Front room," Micah answered, his dark gaze piercing between the edges of the black mask he wore over his face. "We cleared the hall and the rest of the suite."

"Get these fuckers to the reserve suite." Rage was pulsing through him, eating at him as he turned, his gaze going over Tehya once again as she stared at the unconscious attacker at her feet.

Jordan had only disabled him, Tehya must have moved behind him and knocked the man out.

What the hell had made him think that she would actually move for safety? He wanted her safe. Wrapped in protective cotton, as she had said earlier. And God help him, he knew as long as this danger existed, there would be no chance of her ever knowing peace, or security.

Black-masked, moving with dangerous precision, Jordan's team moved in, gathered up the unconscious assailants and rushed them from the suite to the room next door.

Micah, Noah, and Nik had been staying there while John, Bailey, Travis, and Lilly had taken rooms across the hall.

The two couples were in the front room, faces unmasked, weapons held ready as they covered the opened, connecting door.

Watching from the bedroom door as the two men were dragged into the secured suite, Jordan could feel his teeth clenching in nearly uncontrolled fury.

The need to kill beat in his veins, threatening to override his control. He could tear their heads from their bodies. The thought of it had his muscles bunching, his fingers fisted as he fought to hold back the urge.

He turned back to the bedroom slowly, his fingers flexing on the side of the door. The hard, wall-vibrating slam of the door a second later sent an unconscious flinch jerking through Tehya's body as her eyes widened.

It was the first time she had seen his eyes since the attack. Tehya stared back at him, shocked.

She had seen him in a variety of dangerous situations. She had seen him when his nephew had been wounded, when his father had been hospitalized with a heart attack, and when his youngest nephew had nearly been killed in a car wreck several years before. She had never seen him like this. With the rage burning in his eyes like blue flames, his face was so tight with fury, so sharp with violence that the savagely hewn lines of his face were displayed in sharp detail.

"Get dressed," he growled, his voice a rumble of violence.

Tehya was moving before he finished speaking.

Jerking open dresser drawers, she had everything she needed within seconds. Less than two minutes later she was sitting on the side of the bed and tying the laces of her sneakers.

Beside her, Jordan was changing, taking more time to dress, taking the time to control the rage she had seen blazing in his eyes.

He wore jeans and a black shirt. His boots were still unlaced as he checked the clip from the Glock.

Snapping the ammunition into place, he sat down and tied the short combat boots he'd pushed his feet into. Rising, he turned to the pack beside the bed table, removed extra clips, and shoved them into his back pocket.

"If you go hunting tonight, then I go with you," she warned him as she stood, went to the dresser, and pulled a thick ribbon from the makeup bag that had somehow been knocked over and pushed behind the TV sitting there. Knocking it back along the dresser in frustration she stared at her expression, seeing the white, shocked color of her face and the brilliance of her emerald-green eyes.

She looked like death.

Dragging her gaze from her own eyes, she watched Jordan in the mirror as she tied her hair back, her eyes narrowing as she lifted her chin in determination against the dominant look he flashed her.

"I'm not going hunting tonight," he assured her.

Tehya forced herself not to flinch at the sound of his voice, a harsh, vicious rasp that assured her the rage was still in danger of escaping.

"You're not yourself yet." She swallowed tightly, terrified that once he faced the two attackers, he would lose the rational, logical control he was famous for. "You look like you're ready to kill, Jordan. I've rarely seen that look in your eyes."

He stared back at her ruthlessly.

"Look." She shoved her hands in the pockets of her jeans. "I don't want you doing something you'll regret because of me."

She could feel her heart racing out of control, the panic shifting from a fear of Jordan being wounded, or worse, killed, to the fear of him losing his control and perhaps blaming her for it.

"I'm fine." His hands swiped through his hair as a tight grimace crossed his face.

"Jordan . . ."

"I'm fine, Tehya." His voice sharpened. "I won't kill the bastards, no matter how badly I want to. Now if you want to be there for the questioning, you'd better come on. I want my chance to find out who the fuck they are before Noah cuts their throats."

He turned and stalked from the room, like a predator on the prowl, the air of danger surrounding him keeping her nerves on edge.

Jordan could feel her fear, her worry. His instincts were too finely honed, his knowledge of her too deep to escape it.

Just as his knowledge that he was the one now causing her wariness couldn't be escaped.

He would have to deal with it later. He would have to face the fact that he was riding a very fine edge of control because of the threat she was facing.

Stepping into the connecting suite he moved, or rather stalked to where the two men were bound in chairs, still unconscious.

"Who are they?" He directed the question to his nephew, still masked, his eyes a much darker blue and blazing with his own fury.

"We have John Frackle." He smacked the first man on the head, causing it to jerk to the side in unconscious response.

John Frackle was approximately six feet, his brown hair cut close to his scalp. Gray tape was still slapped over his mouth, effectively gagging him in case he awakened.

It would come off soon enough, as soon as he was conscious, and when it did, Jordan promised himself the bastard would talk or he'd lose his tongue. Or perhaps never have the chance to attempt to talk again.

"Frackle has a nice little history listed with several law enforcement agencies from what we're learning." Noah jerked his thumb over his shoulder to where Nik was at the computer pulling up files and printing them out. "It seems he likes to work for maggots who target pretty women. If they're not virgins when he kidnaps them, then he's known to rape them before they reach the men that hired him."

Jordan turned his gaze slowly back to Frackle and let his lips curl in anticipation.

"Killing him will be fun," he drawled.

Tehya flinched at the promise in his voice.

"And who is his buddy?"

"He's teamed up with Marco Fillipini. Good ole Marco may not know his partner well, though. This one, I know of. Marco's penny-ante, mainly sticks to France. I have a few feelers out to get his story, but I thought we might go easy on him if he talks a little bit for us." Noah smacked Marco a bit harder than he had Frackle.

288   LORA LEIGH

Both men were well muscled, likely well experienced, and in a world of hurt once they were conscious, if Jordan had his way.

"They were outside the party you attended tonight," Nik said from where he sat at the computer. "They're working with the same team that attacked Tehya's home. From what I've learned so far, they're mostly mercenaries, though Frackle and Fillipini were low-level soldiers in Sorrel's organization before he was killed."

Jordan lifted a brow as he gazed at Frackle, then Marco. His fingers curled into fists again. The need to see their blood was almost as strong as the lust that tormented him where Tehya was concerned.

That realization was shocking. He'd never allowed himself to become so involved with anyone, besides his nephew. He'd been angry over attacks against his men or wounds they'd taken, but never had he experienced this level of violence.

"Someone got them some pretty toys," Noah spoke behind him. "It took them less than three seconds to slip our security with ones they brought."

Jordan gave a brief nod of his head. "They have to be well-funded just as we suspected, with ties, or their employer has ties, to the military somewhere. That's the only way they could have acquired the technology needed to get through the security." His lips thinned as he continued to stare at the other two men.

"That technology is only available in a few countries other than America," Micah informed him. "You can't get that just anywhere, Jordan."

"I'm more than aware of this." Icy cold, emotionless, his voice was like a sibilant whisper of death.

"I want complete dossiers on them." He turned to Nik, his gaze meeting the other man's. "Everything. I want to know who they socialize with and who they work for. I want to know every particle of their lives."

"And you'll have it," Noah swore, "the moment it's ready."

And Tehya knew Noah. She knew the bond he shared

with his uncle. That information would be available very soon, if it existed.

With a jerk of his head toward the door behind him, Jordan indicated he was finished there and that the others should follow him.

Turning, he curved his arm around Tehya's waist and drew her with him back to the front room of the suite. He would give the two men time to awaken, then he would awaken them himself it necessary. Maybe. There were alternatives to interrogating men whom he knew wouldn't give him the answers he wanted. And he realized he didn't want to have to question them in front of Tehya.

He didn't want her to see the worst of him. In the years she had been at the base, she had never seen him interrogate an enemy, had never seen him kill.

He realized he didn't want her to see it now. And it was going to happen. Frackle and his partner had all but signed their death warrants when they came for him with the intent of taking Tehya. And if they didn't talk, if they didn't give him answers, then, Jordan promised himself, they would never threaten anyone, ever again.

CHAPTER 15

Tehya had thought she would know the two men when she faced them, that they would be men she had known from Sorrel's organization. She hadn't expected strangers. Men she hadn't glimpsed following her before. Men she knew nothing of.

It was so reminiscent of the years she had spent running from her biological father. Despite his death, he had reached out from the grave, determined to destroy everyone, anyone she cared for or who would attempt to protect her.

As she stepped into the main room of the suite, she wondered if perhaps Jordan wasn't right. Maybe love truly was an illusion. If it were real, wouldn't she have forced him out of the danger she faced? At the least, wouldn't she have run, or found a way to hide from him? To protect him. Wasn't that a part of love?

"Jordan, they're not going to talk." John stepped from the room, the others following. "They're not going to tell you why they targeted Tehya, if the information we're pulling up is true."

Jordan turned slowly to face him. "Tehya was the target once they killed me. And they will talk, one way or the other. I want answers John. They knew our security and exactly how to get past it, knew the lay of the suite and how to get to me. I want to know who told them."

"They knew which side of the bed you were sleeping on," Tehya pointed out, hearing the sound of her own voice, recognizing the dispassionate sound of it. "And it wasn't luck, because you rarely sleep on the same side of the bed two nights in a row."

It had driven her crazy since he had begun sleeping with her. She liked her side.

She liked Jordan alive.

She could feel herself freezing inside, feel the fear, the certain knowledge that in all the years she had been running, anyone who tried to save her died.

Could she bear losing Jordan as her mother had lost everyone she had tried to trust during the years she had fought to keep her daughter safe?

She couldn't. She knew she couldn't survive losing Jordan in such a way.

Oh God, she couldn't be the cause of the life being bled from those incredible blue eyes.

Tehya watched as the six men and two women exchanged looks.

"No one should have been aware of anything within this suite," Micah stated as he jerked the mask from his face and cast a disgusted look at the door they had just closed. "We don't allow staff or visitors in the room and Nik had the location of the furniture moved into the normal walk paths of the room before we arrived. No one could have known the layout."

"We're not fucking rookies, Tehya," Micah reminded her, his voice, his eyes icy cold. She had offended him and she hadn't meant to.

Tehya inhaled slowly. God, she didn't have time to deal with the male ego or tender feelings tonight. She'd had enough. Her fingers curled into fists as she fought back her own smart-assed response. The need to rip the eyes from the bastards that had attempted to kill Jordan was nearly overpowering.

They had almost succeeded in taking from her one of the few people she knew she could depend upon. The only man she had ever loved. The only man she hadn't been able to resist from the moment she had laid eyes on him.

Her point was the fact that Nik had reserved the room in his own name. At the earliest, they might have known she was in the room the day after. And as Micah stated, they hadn't allowed anyone inside the suite, even staff. Furniture in both the living and dining suite as well as the bedroom had been moved.

The only way any type of video or audio could have been placed inside the room was before they arrived. They had checked for surveillance equipment, though, she knew that. Hell, she had helped do it and they had found nothing.

Could the would-be assassins get that lucky?

No maids were allowed inside. Room service was never called, one of the men had gone out for food instead. Somehow, some kind of surveillance had to have been placed in the bedroom. It was the only way Frackle and Fillipinni could have known where Jordan was sleeping without the aid of night-vision equipment.

"Lights were left on here in the living suite," Jordan pointed out. Even in the dark it wouldn't be that hard to pick out the white comforter on the bed and the side the larger body lay on.

"What would be the point behind killing Jordan?" Noah asked softly, the quiet tone more indicative of the danger raging inside him than the icy control the other men displayed.

"He protects me," she said painfully. "That was Sorrel's favorite game. To kill whoever stood between him and his goal of acquiring me. Right down to my mother." She turned and watched Jordan, aching, filled with such regret that she could feel her stomach turning with the thought of the blood that had been shed when she was younger. "I killed Sorrel. How is he still haunting me?"

She remembered killing him as well as his son. She remembered seeing Raven and Sorrel's lifeless eyes gazing back at her. Blood had soaked their chests from the bullets they'd taken to the heart. She remembered it all, yet, it was as though they still lived.

Pushing her fingers through her hair, she turned away from the others as they gazed back at her silently, somberly.

She feared pityingly. She didn't want their pity and she had been cruel to accept their help.

They had lives, families. They had children, friends.

She only had them until she had moved to Hagerstown. And even now, she hadn't truly made friends. No one would miss her, save those who stood in the room with her now. And they would go on. They would remember her fondly. They would regret her death. But no one cared enough to truly grieve.

Perhaps not even the man sleeping with her. The man she had given her heart to.

She couldn't look at him. She couldn't face the danger she had brought to his life. And she had been too weak to run, too weak to remember the lessons she had been taught in the past.

Never make friends, because they died.

Never love anyone, because they were murdered.

Never, ever, dream of a life that could include a measure of security or of peace.

"Tehya." Suddenly, his arms were surrounding her, turning her, pulling her against the muscular strength of his chest.

He was warm, strong. He held her as though he could protect her against anything, anyone that would strike against her. He held her as though he were bulletproof, and she knew no man could make that claim.

"I wanted it to be over," she whispered as her fingers curled into the loose material of his shirt. "I just wanted it to go away, Jordan. It should have died with Sorrel."

"And it will," he promised her, his lips against her ear. "I promise you, this time, we're going to bury it for good."

She turned slowly.

She should have run, she should have protected him when she had the chance.

He was going to kill.

It was all Jordan could do to keep from stalking into the other suite and murdering the two men where they sat.

"You expected this," Noah stated quietly, accusingly, as he stared back at Jordan from the other side of the table.

"I would have been stupid not to." Jordan shrugged as Tehya finished bandaging his side more than an hour later, after Micah had been found to stitch it. "They just moved faster than I expected."

"I would have expected another attack to come outside the protected area," Micah inserted as he sat back in his chair. "It came too soon."

Jordan shook his head in denial. "The first attack was an attempt to take Teyha. Whoever's pulling the strings here wasn't aware she had friends willing to protect her." He glanced at John Vincent and Travis Caine. "Tonight's attack was the taking of an opportunity." He glanced at Teyha. "They thought they had the advantage so they took it."

He sat back, aware of the others watching him thoughtfully as he hid a mocking smile. There was a reason he was a commander in the Elite Ops unit. There was a reason he had been given more freedom than any other commander in the private covert operations organization.

Because he knew how to cover his ass, and he knew exactly how to push to achieve a reaction.

"We know whoever's been searching for her has a personal stake in it," he began.

"And how do we know this?" Nik was the one that leaned forward to question the observation. "I've gone over the past reports filed on her mother and the deaths of the men attempting to protect them, as well as the months Teyha was in France and the attempt against her there. I would say it's more likely one of Sorrel's partners attempting to punish her for killing Sorrel."

Beside him, Tehya flinched.

"I have to agree," Micah spoke up. "We've all been over the past reports, Jordan. How can you assume there's something personal involved, now that Sorrel and his son are both dead?"

"Sorrel's associates, friends, and even his enemies wouldn't play with her," he explained. "She's being toyed with, for whatever reason. Watched. Pushed to certain reactions. It's more a trademark of Sorrel's pattern when targeting a victim to kidnap rather than an attempt to extract vengeance for his death. The plan changed when the attack at the house didn't leave her on the run, vulnerable and frightened, because I was there." He glanced at the closed door to the suite where the two mercenaries were being held. "They were ordered to get rid of me."

Tehya sat silent, staring at the closed door, listening as he laid out, step by step, the actions that had taken place since he had arrived at her home.

And he was right. Even before he arrived, she had felt pushed, led, dragged into a situation she was helpless to avoid.

It was indeed a Sorrel trademark. Even as a child, Tehya had recognized the game that was played with her mother and the men who attempted to protect her.

No one could protect her. That was the lesson Sorrel had tried to teach her. He had been amused the few times he had managed to contact her. Once, he had even left a cell phone along with his number. And Tehya had called. She listened with a sense of unreality to the charming, caring voice of a monster so evil it had sent chills racing up her spine.

"How do you propose handling this?" Noah brought her attention back to the conversation going on around the table.

Noah's voice was deeper, darker for the fury burning inside him.

"I propose we let them escape," Jordan suggested, his lips curling in a smile. "Let them run back home to whoever Daddy is, while we follow and see who they're reporting to. Meanwhile, Tehya will be rushed from the hotel to Senator Stanton's estate, where we'll carefully arrange the rumor that our two erstwhile assassins actually managed to succeed in their attempt to kill me, but the bodyguards I had hired arrived in time to save Tehya." He turned to Noah. "John, Travis, and Noah will drag out my wrapped body and put it in the Conquest while Nik and Micah rush Tehya to the senator's estate. We'll drop Noah off to watch the two men as they "escape" while we collect the backup vehicles and follow them once they're on the move."

"Stage it first," Bailey suggested quietly. "Let them hear the argument when they awaken concerning the torture you're going to exact once you return from taking care of his body. Convince them Jordan is dead."

"And remember, I wasn't shot until the end, as I knocked Frackle out. They aren't aware where I was hit. It could have been a fatal shot."

Tehya sat silently and listened. The plan was simple and effective. A typical "Jordan" plan, while at the same time being in-depth enough to be completely convincing.

It was the reason why he had been so effective as a commander.

He left nothing to chance. Even the smallest details were taken care of, and each opportunity to put it to its best use considered.

"I can't believe you're totally dropping out of the game." Micah's gaze gleamed with amusement. "You realize we just laid in a plan that requires no backup support and eliminates ninety percent of the chances of failure, right?"

Jordan's expression was still tightly controlled. "It's that ten percent that worries me. Let's see if we can't get a little closer there."

Tehya got slowly to her feet. She felt stiff, old. As though the years she had spent running, plotting, searching for just a moment's haven to find some rest had prematurely aged her.

After the morning she had just spent, she definitely expected to find gray hairs.

"Tehya, are you okay?" Quiet, concerned, Jordan continued to stare up at her, the blue of his eyes darker than normal.

"I'm fine," she whispered as she extricated her arm from his grip and gave him what she hoped was a natural smile. "I do need to use the restroom though, if you'll excuse me."

Turning her back on them, she left the room quickly.

Her stomach was churning, and no amount of concentrating on others or distracting her thoughts was going to save her this time.

At the very thought of Jordan's life being taken so easily, the dinner she'd had last night was about to make a reappearance.

CHAPTER 16

Jordan was waiting on her as she left the bathroom, leaning against the wall, his arms crossed over his chest, his blue eyes narrowed as he stared back at her silently.

It would be impossible to miss the fact that she had been sick.

She'd washed her face, but she knew what it looked like. It was incredibly pale, her eyes appeared too large, her lips too stressed.

And he was taking in every inch of her face, her expression, whatever he saw in her eyes.

"You're not okay."

Duh. She'd just finished puking her guts up while escaping.

Thank God he had changed shirts and cleaned his blood up, but there was still a smear of red at his hairline. The sight of it had her stomach turning, as memories raped her mind.

"I'm fine now," she assured him, giving a brief shrug as she moved to pass him.

He caught her again. His fingers curled around her upper arm as her breath caught in her chest, and tears clogged her throat. The past was too close. There had been too many times that she had seen the results of Sorrel's horror. The pictures he had sent her. *See what you caused, baby girl? Come home to Daddy so he doesn't have to hurt anyone else.*

Sorrel had played with her. Just as someone was trying to play with her now. Who? He'd had no partners other than her brother.

"Tey?" His voice was a dark croon as his head lowered, his hand smoothing to her hip, fingers burning through the thin material of the short T-shirt dress she had changed into.

Her eyes closed as his lips pressed to the bared curve of her shoulder and he pulled the material to her side. When he placed her head against his opposite shoulder, she felt her breath hitch in her throat.

She could feel the warmth of him against her, his hand stroking up her back, then returning to her hips. The sheer gentleness, the tension of banked hunger, the need she could feel, unspoken and louder than words, surrounded her.

"Take me with you."

The plea escaped her lips before she could pull them back. She was terrified to let him out of her sight now. The panic building inside her threatened to send her running back to the bathroom.

She had spent so many years knowing each time she was separated from whoever attempted to protect her, they died. They were tortured, left lifeless after hours of pain.

"Tey," he whispered her name again, his fingers tightening on her hips once again. "Play your part, sweetheart. John, Travis, Bailey, and Lilly are going to rush you to the senator's as the others carry me out. I'll be there soon."

He moved to pull back.

"No, not yet." Her hands tightened on his shoulders, the need to hold him in place overwhelming now. "Listen to me, Jordan. Every time. Every time they left me and thought I was protected, they were killed." A sob escaped her lips. "You know they were. They were tortured. . . ."

It was all she could see. Jordan, his expression twisted in agony because he hadn't talked. Jordan wouldn't talk. He'd never tell anyone where she was if she were hidden. And they would ensure he died in agony.

"I've got this, baby." As he lifted his head, his hand rose and cupped her cheek, his gaze locked with hers.

This wasn't the man she had worked with. If she had dared express concern or fear for his life then, the ice that was so much a part of him would have kicked in.

It didn't this time.

His gaze actually softened, his lips quirked in tender amusement, but in his expression she saw his refusal to do as she asked.

"I've got this," he repeated, his lips touching hers, brushing against them. "When we're finished here, it's going to be over, and you're going to be safe. I won't have it any other way."

She had to clench her teeth against the urge to beg. This expression she knew. There was no changing his mind, and John, Travis, and their wives would ensure she was where she was supposed to be.

"Noah has my back," he promised her. "Nik and Micah have his. I'll slip into the senator's estate tonight, as soon as we're finished."

She tried to shake her head, tried to speak. His hand tightened on her jaw, his lips covered hers, and the kiss he gave her rocked her to the soles of her feet.

His lips rubbed against hers, stroked, and sent heat flushing through her system in a slow burn that, at first, seemed harmless enough.

The heat rose slowly, enveloping her, flowing into her blood and spiking it with a hunger she couldn't deny, or hide.

Her arms curled around his neck, her fingers feathering into the back of his hair as a moan whispered past her lips, and the need to hold on to him began to grow inside her.

She felt the hunger beginning to infuse both of them, his body tensing, his cock pressing more firmly against the juncture of her thighs as his hand slid up her leg.

His fingers played with the hem of the short dress, feathering against her thighs with a rasp of heat. She wanted to feel them moving beneath the dress. Her thighs parted further, a desperate moan in her throat as she arched against him.

One second she was in his arms, the next he was pushing away from her, his lips pulling away reluctantly.

"No." She fought to hold on to him, only to be left staring up at him, trembling with fear and need.

"John, Travis, and their wives are waiting on the other side of the suite. Once we're clear of the hotel and in position, they'll get you to the limo waiting outside."

She gave a hard nod.

"Our friends in the other suite are awake," he told her. "Once you're out, staff will come in and release them, aware of only the fact that we've checked out. We'll follow them from there."

She nodded again.

It was bad enough her nerves were back enough that she had begun throwing up again. She hadn't done that since the night before the operation to reveal the identity of Sorrel. The night before she had killed him.

"Come on, baby." Catching her fingers, he moved for the door. "Let's get this done."

Letting her go was the hardest thing he had ever done in his life. Jordan watched as the team surrounded Tehya and rushed her from the back entrance of the hotel to the limo the senator had sent to collect her.

He couldn't forget the look in her eyes. The fear had been so deep, so dark, he'd wanted nothing but to give her exactly what she wanted. To find a way to bring her with him.

Bringing her with him would have compromised the entire plan. They needed her safe, but they also needed her escape witnessed by the man Jordan was currently watching as well.

He'd figured the men that had come inside weren't alone.

"Lilly called as they were hitting the doors," Noah said as they watched the black Suburban from the cargo van they'd driven to the surveillance position. "She said Tehya was crying."

"Enough." The order was short, but not as icy as it could have been, because the thought of her crying affected him in ways he didn't want to look too deeply into.

"She's a friend," Micah spoke from behind him. "Having her safe and secure is all well and good, but leaving her without a future because her heart was ripped out wasn't in the plan when you told us what was going on."

Jordan could feel his teeth gritting as he turned to Nik where he sat in the driver's seat. "Where's your two cents?"

Nik's expression didn't change as he continued to watch the other vehicle and the driver in it. "Inflation sucks," he drawled. "The price is a buck fifty now."

Trust Nik to be the smart-ass in the group.

Propping his arm on the side of the door, Jordan rubbed the skin above his upper lip thoughtfully.

"Have you managed to ID him yet?" he finally asked the others. It was better to change the subject rather than continuing the course of the subject of Tehya.

"I have him," Noah said. "Another of those damned Sorrel soldiers turned mercenaries after his death. Wayne Trevits, former MI-6 agent discharged for theft and attempted sale of military weapons. He was sentenced to life in prison, but escaped after a year. He was with Sorrel for ten years before the op that took Sorrel out. It looks like Sorrel's boys have decided to go after a little vengeance."

That was definitely what it looked like, Jordan admitted.

It had all the signs of a group of Sorrel's former employees banding together to make Tehya pay for his death. Everything they had found led them in that direction.

"Maid's in the room," Micah announced, obviously watching the laptop displaying the room. "Ahh, there she is. Little old lady with gray hair and big brown eyes," he grunted. "And she's not moving to let them go."

Jordan waited.

"Ah, there she goes. She just pulled the radio from her pocket. She's calling security."

Jordan was prepared for that. He'd checked the staff out while they were there and reread the files once the plan was in place, to see who would be walking in on the little party Jordan had arranged.

He hadn't wanted anyone to get hurt, but he'd been certain this maid would choose the option of calling security versus releasing them on their own.

"And we now have two little weak-kneed security guards entering. They'll make mincemeat out of them."

It took only minutes.

"Yep, they're both down," Micah sighed. "They're alive, though."

"They're aware of the cameras in the hall outside the room," Jordan stated. "There's too great a chance of being identified."

"They're headed downstairs."

Jordan and his men moved.

Exiting the back of the van, covert mode intact, Jordan, Nik, Micah, and Noah moved to the appropriate, nondescript vehicles waiting in the parking lot.

Sliding into the Ford sedan, Jordan watched from above the rim of his dark sunglasses as the two men slipped from the same exit Tehya had used and moved quickly to the waiting SUV.

The assassins looked a little worse for wear, but satisfied. They thought they had achieved their objective. His would-be killers believed he was dead, and Tehya defended only by his men.

Evidently they weren't convinced of the danger posed by the men they would be facing. To this point, Jordan and his men had been playing, sitting back and letting Tehya's enemies hang themselves. Now, he thought he might help them just a bit with the rope.

The bastards had terrified her, and they had been aware of it. They had known what it would do to her. The plan would have been to take her while she was shell-shocked, while the realization of Jordan's death was still fresh in her mind.

She would have been more controllable and much easier to intimidate.

That would have been the plan. Unfortunately for them, it

wouldn't have worked so easily for them. He knew Tehya; and even more, he knew Tehya under pressure. His death would have destroyed her, but later. That shock they wanted so desperately would have been what had saved her life, and would have ended theirs.

As the SUV pulled from the parking lot, Jordan turned the receiver on in the sedan and smiled at the movement of the little dot indicating the tracker they had activated. The other assassin's bug hadn't yet been activated. He was the backup. The safeguard. Just in case.

There was a reason he had plans A, B, C, and D, with E, F, and G just in case. Sometimes, there were just too many bases to cover. And Jordan liked having all the angles worked out.

Work out the angles and you don't just protect yourself and your men, but you also protect the woman you had never been able to get out of your head and your heart.

He'd met Tehya eight years before, the night she had killed her father. From the moment he'd looked into those shattered, emerald green eyes, he'd wanted nothing more than to pull her into his arms and protect her from the world.

Unfortunately, it was too late to protect her by then. The world had already scarred her. Sorrel had already taught her to react first and grieve later.

And she would have grieved for him, he knew.

His men would have surrounded her long enough to attempt to convince her to hide, because it was what he wanted. She wouldn't have hid.

As he and Micah traded positions and the other men moved in behind the SUV in another vehicle, Jordan concentrated on the area around them. He made certain no one was following them as they followed their attempted assassins.

They traded places several more times before Jordan pulled into a parking lot across from a storage rental facility housed in an old factory. The units, Jordan knew, were temperature controlled, roomy, and free of those pesky surveillance cameras that turned most criminals off.

Slipping from the car, he joined Micah and Nik, and Noah

gave them a quick nod toward the warehouse. Using the available delivery vans, trucks, and occasional stacks of varied covered prepared shipments for cover, they moved into the warehouse following the beacon the tracker was giving off.

Minutes later, they eased in as close as possible, coming in together, weapons drawn as they moved in to watch the meeting.

The three men were waiting outside one of the rental rooms, heads down, leaning against the wall as shadows moved in the well-lit unit they were guarding.

They were talking, their voices too low to hear, and the satisfied demeanors of earlier had been dropped. They looked nervous and if he wasn't mistaken, quite possibly scared as well.

He'd read the dossiers on these men, and he wouldn't have believed anything could make them nervous, let alone have them looking like three teenagers preparing to face a disciplinarian.

As they waited silently, the shadows in the rental unit began to slow, and long minutes later another man stepped into view.

Gregor Ascarti.

Dressed in his trademark silk suit, his blond hair perfectly combed back, but with a limp Jordan didn't remember from that last operation against Sorrel that had reportedly taken Ascarti out as well.

Gregor Ascarti had been Sorrel's right-hand man after his son. He had been the logistical expert who had been damned near impossible to defeat.

And now he was back.

Somehow, the bastard had managed to not just survive, but apparently to live and thrive for the past eight years completely under the radar.

He moved slowly, the limp obviously hindering his movements, as Mark Tenneyson and Ira Arthurs, the mercenaries who had been watching the Taites, exited the rental unit behind him. Ascarti stopped directly in front of John Frackle.

Before anyone could guess what he would do, his hand

came back and a strong, heavy blow was delivered against the other man's face. Frackle was flung back against the wall, but surprisingly, considering his reputation, he didn't attempt to strike back.

Jordan saw the struggle in Frackle's face though, the tightening of his fingers as he made an effort not to make a fist.

Jordan strained to hear the conversation, but all he heard were angry murmurs. The combination of their automatic habit of keeping their voices low and the distance from the other men made the conversation impossible to decipher.

One thing was certain, though: Ascarti wasn't pleased. The fact that the men hadn't arrived with Tehya was likely the reason for Ascarti's displeasure.

Hell, he wished he could get fucking closer. If he could just hear what they were planning.

He wasn't aware how tense he was, how closely he was checking out the surrounding cover, until he felt Noah's hand on his shoulder in warning.

A tight grimace pulled at his face as he gave a quick nod, an affirmation that he understood the grip.

As Jordan continued to watch, Ascarti moved closer to Frackle, almost nose to nose, his finger poking in the other man's chest, though his voice never rose.

That was a conversation Jordan would give damned near anything to hear at this point. Though he was fairly certain he knew the gist of it.

They had returned without Tehya, and Ascarti wanted Tehya.

As Jordan had thought earlier, it had all the earmarks of a revenge strike.

But as he watched, eyes narrowed, events sifting through his mind, he couldn't help but suspect there was something more going on than simple revenge.

These men weren't having a love affair with Sorrel's memory. If Tehya happened to have dropped in their paths, then they would have struck out at her. But to still be searching for her after her disappearance?

It didn't make sense.

Suddenly, Ascarti moved again, the hand holding his weapon moving, the metal smacking into Frackle's face and knocking him to the ground. In the next breath Ascarti had his gun beneath Fillipini's chin, pushing it high and tight.

"Fucking stupid . . ." His accent was thick and dark with fury, the violence in his tone causing Jordan's brows to lift.

The voice lowered just enough now that only the tone could be heard.

Ascarti stepped back, watching as Frackle came slowly back to his feet, stumbling slightly as he braced himself against the wall.

"Imbecile. The next time, you . . . will . . ." The threat was clear as the muzzle of the weapon went beneath Frackle's jaw, lifting it as Ascarti leaned closer to finish the sentence.

With a final slap against the side of the other man's face, Ascarti stepped back, straightened his silk jacket, then turned around to face the mercenaries behind him.

The dim fluorescent lights above hit his face at just the right angle, giving Jordan a first, clear look at the other man's face.

His brows lifted.

The left side of Gregor Ascarti's face was horrendously disfigured. Scars marred the entire side of his face, twisting around his eye, giving his profile a grotesque appearance.

Jordan slipped farther back into the shadows as the Italian former smuggler moved with far less grace than he had in Aruba.

There was a limp to his right leg, an odd angle in the shape of his left hand as he walked away. Frackle and Fillipini followed him as Tenneyson and Arthur locked up and reset the alarm to the unit before moving quickly to catch up with the others.

The explosion that had targeted Ascarti had apparently not done enough damage. He was clearly as organized and just as dangerous as he had been while Sorrel was still alive.

Giving Micah a careful hand signal, he sent the other

man, along with Noah, to make certain Ascarti and his mercenaries were out of the unit.

It took long minutes for the rental storage facility to become deserted except for Jordan and Nik, allowing them a chance to slip from the shadowed area where the team had hidden.

Slipping a small leather case from the pack he carried on his back, Jordan quickly picked the heavy lock one of the Ascarti's mercenaries had secured before leaving, while Nik worked to disable the security inside.

It was apparent that Ascarti had no reason to suspect that Frackle and his partner had led Jordan and his team straight to them. Of course, why should he; they believed Jordan was dead.

As the heavy lock released, Jordan slid it free before slowly easing the door open, sliding the penlight from his pocket and stepping inside.

"Well, well, well," he muttered as he surveyed the contents of the unit before turning back to Nik, who had positioned himself protectively at the entrance.

The other man's pale, icy blue eyes narrowed as his expression tightened in lines of savage fury.

"What does the bastard have planned?" Nik muttered as they each surveyed the array of hidden weapons, ammunition, and surprise, surprise, several dozen handheld rocket launchers.

"I'd have sworn Sorrel was dead," Nik continued. "But this . . ." He shook his head slowly as he allowed his gaze to catalog each item there. "God, Jordan, this fucking makes me wonder."

"DEA would have a field day over this," Jordan murmured as he moved to several covered boxes, lifted a crowbar from one, and quietly eased open the lid.

The Russian-made automatic weapons weren't nearly as interesting as the weapons packed away, though.

A dozen Israeli corner shot automatic rifles were packed in the first box. Replacing the lid, he went to the one beside it. It was packed similarly, guns in the middle with boxes of ammunition packed around them.

Tehya's weapon of choice.

Easing one of the weapons from the bottom of the box, he carefully arranged the packaging material to hide the theft from a casual check of the inventory before doing likewise with several boxes of ammunition before handing it all to Nik.

He hadn't heard of the weapons missing, and they weren't available for street sale. They were strictly military weapons. He knew a certain DEA team commander who would be very interested in this facility and its contents.

It was also the weapon heading Tehya's "ask for from Santa" list. If possible, he would ensure it was given to her if he wasn't around later.

The thought had him pausing. As though there was a chance in hell that he was walking away from her. It nearly brought him to a hard stop. There had never been a question before of walking away from a lover. The only question had been how short the time he would be with her before he grew bored.

With Tehya, he couldn't imagine growing bored. He couldn't imagine a night, a day, a second of his life that he wouldn't want her.

He hadn't changed his mind about the illusion of love. What he had done instead was to convince himself that the illusion could be preserved, if only for a little while.

"We got a problem here, boss," Nik commented as he stared at the contents of the box. "If Ascarti has these weapons, here in America, then he could be planning more than simply getting his hands on Sorrel's baby girl."

Jordan turned an icy look on the other man.

"I was being facetious," Nik finally growled. "Hell, Jordan. You're going to have to either put a damned ring on her finger or cut the possessive crap. You can't protect her forever if you're going to keep walking away from her."

"I didn't ask your opinion," Jordan murmured as he turned away and glared back down at the weapons.

"I volunteered it," Nik assured him.

Hell, there was something to be said for being the commander while they were under contract to the Elite Ops. Now that they were free and clear, they thought it was simply fine to bust his ass whenever they wanted to.

He almost grinned. They had *always* thought it was perfectly fine to bust his ass every chance they found. Especially after Tehya had arrived at base and taught them exactly how to get away with it.

"Give our contact at the DEA a call," he ordered Nik. "Give him the information on this rental unit and who it belongs to. Don't give him the information on the mercenaries just yet. I want to find out what Ascarti wants from Tehya that's so important he's hunted her for too many years. Taking everyone out of the game won't give me those answers."

There was a long moment of silence behind him before Nik asked, his tone dangerously bland, "Are you setting our girl up, boss?"

His lips quirked, almost in amusement, at the question. He wasn't the only one protective of her; he was just the one determined to keep her.

"Aren't you the same man who just expressed his worry for her?" He turned back to Nik. "You can't have it both ways, Nik. Either I'm too possessive of her, or I'm setting her up."

Nik's gaze narrowed then. "One doesn't necessarily cancel the other out. Setting her up would be damned bad form."

"Then it's a damned good thing she's safe from it," Jordan snapped, his patience as well as his amusement exhausted with the subject. "Let's get the hell out of here, then make that phone call."

Jerking a heavy storage blanket from the corner, he threw it at Nik to cover the weapon he'd slipped from the crate, before turning back and replacing the heavy lid.

Seconds later, the weapon carefully covered, they slipped from the unit, relocked it, replaced the security controls, and made their way from the warehouse.

Noah and Micah were waiting at the entrance, their

expressions hard, eyes narrowed and emotionless. Jordan let his gaze meet his nephew's, seeing in it something he had hoped he wouldn't see again after the team had disbanded.

"He killed Frackle," Noah stated, his voice soft as he nodded to the large trash container just outside the door. "Put a bullet in the back of his head, then ordered his friends to toss him in it. Motherfuckers did it too." The heavy disgust that edged into his tone reminded Jordan once again that there was a reason his team had always been the best.

Their loyalty to each other. That loyalty had always assured they were watching each other's backs, just as it had always insured each operation was conducted with not just their success, but also their safety.

"Let's get the hell out of here," Jordan muttered as he watched the area outside the entrance. "I want this taken care of, and I want to know what the hell is going on, Noah. Ascarti's luck is getting ready to run out."

"Let's hope Tehya's isn't running out along with it," Nik stated behind him. "Or protecting her will become impossible."

Jordan's guts tightened at the thought, but Nik was right. If they didn't take care of this, and take care of it quickly, then he could lose Tehya in ways he had never imagined before.

To death.

CHAPTER 17

Back in the car, the weapon stored safely in the trunk, Jordan watched out the window impassively as Noah pulled from the exit of the storage warehouse and reentered the heavy D.C. traffic surging through the streets.

"We need to find someplace to lay low while we're considering our options," Noah proposed. "There's a hotel with suites just outside of town. We can get you checked in under an anonymous name. . . ."

"We're going to the senator's estate," Jordan broke in firmly. "Kell's throwing another party tomorrow night and I want to be in a position to protect Tehya."

"The team will be there, Jordan," Noah argued. "We can keep Ascarti at bay without you. If this jeopardizes her life, then you'll never forgive yourself."

But there was no staying away from her. Even now, every cell in his body ached to hold her close, to assure himself she was indeed safe and unharmed.

"The team will be there, and so will I." Jordan kept his tone smooth, and his decision firm.

In the rearview mirror, Jordan caught a glimpse his nephew's expression, the concern as well as the disapproval in his gaze.

"This isn't a good idea," Noah continued to argue, though his tone remained cool and unheated. "You could be seen by staff or anyone watching Stanton's estate after her arrival. It could endanger the plan to make it appear you've been killed."

Jordan's gaze met Noah's in the mirror for a second before his nephew turned his eyes back to the road.

The thought of not going to Tehya had his guts clenching in refusal. He'd be damned if he would let her sit there alone, allow her to sleep alone after experiencing the heat and pleasure of having her against him throughout the night.

"I didn't ask if you thought it was a good idea. I said do it." His gaze met Noah's again for a brief second, their wills clashing as Jordan set the tone of command at its firmest strength.

Noah grimaced and his gaze jerked back to the road, the muscles at the side of his jaw flexing angrily.

"She's getting to you, isn't she, Jordan?" Noah finally asked as he made the turn onto a bypass and entered the heavy late afternoon traffic as his tone sharpened with a flare of anger. "Are you giving in to the *illusion*?" he mocked.

"Like you and Sabella, Noah, the illusion is real for Tehya. Just because I don't believe in it doesn't mean she doesn't believe she feels it."

Or was there more to it? Jordan fought the denial raging inside him at the thought that love didn't exist. He had always believed it was an illusion. Since he was a teenager, since that first flush of love and the resulting betrayal, he'd refused to let himself believe.

And now he was beginning to wonder if perhaps he had been wrong. Tehya gave every part of herself to him when they came together, and he'd learned that each time he touched her, thought about her, ached for her, that the need became stronger, deeper, more intense.

"Doesn't mean you can't reap the benefits of it either, huh?" The disappointment in Noah's voice wasn't hard to miss, and it struck at one of the few vulnerable areas Jordan possessed. His affection for family, his need for that family's affection.

Jordan raked his fingers through his hair impatiently as

he met his nephew's mockingly angry gaze. "Just because I believe it's an illusion doesn't mean I can't claim the results of it," Jordan amended, his voice darker as a part of him cringed, or seemed to, at the illogical feeling of having betrayed Tehya somehow with that statement.

Noah didn't say anything further. His lips thinned, his expression became set in lines of disapproval, but he kept his argument to himself.

If only the others were so kind.

"Hey, Noah, did you notice he said *just because he believed it was an illusion* rather than *just because it is an illusion*?" Nik piped up from beside Noah, his voice heavy with amusement. "Maybe he's relenting just a little bit."

Neither Jordan nor Noah responded. Jordan could feel the heavy threat of condemnation rising from each of his men as they rode toward the senator's estate.

Noah had to fight to rein in the impatient anger brewing inside him.

Hell, he'd been around Tehya and his uncle enough to know that Jordan was determined to fight whatever he was feeling for Tehya. He'd been feeling it for six damned years now or more, and still, Jordan didn't dare mention the L word. If he acknowledged it, then he might have to admit it actually existed.

But if any man had ever been born to love a woman, then Jordan had been born for Tehya, just as Noah knew he had been born for Sabella.

It was the Malone curse, his grandfather had always said. Malone men were warned to love wisely, because once they loved, they loved forever, they loved deep, and they loved with a blazing heat that burned clear to the soul.

Jordan just didn't want to admit he was in love with Tehya. If he admitted it, then he had to face the fact that he couldn't exist without her.

And it wasn't a bad thing, Noah acknowledged to himself. He'd made mistakes with Sabella. He'd left her when he should have had her brought to him. He'd turned his back on his marriage, his life, his identity because of his own stupid pride and fear. But as Noah Blake rather than Nathan Malone, he'd returned, claimed everything that had ever belonged to him, and at the same time, Sabella managed to mark his soul a second time with a lash of delicate, feminine claws, female stubbornness, and raging hunger.

Hell, if he could knock some sense into his uncle, then that was exactly what he would do. Unfortunately, the more a man, or a woman, pushed at Jordan Malone, the more stubborn he could get.

Maybe, hopefully, this time Jordan would realize the gift Tehya had been holding for him all these years. The other men swore they'd seen it, eight years before. That first night they had come face-to-face in Aruba during the operation to identify and neutralize Sorrel, Tehya's father.

Noah prayed, for his uncle's sake, that he realized what he saw as an illusion was the only emotion that would ever ease that core of agonizing loneliness Noah glimpsed in Jordan's eyes. If Jordan let her go this time, if he walked away, then Noah feared there would be no going back.

Glancing in the rearview mirror once again, he glimpsed that dark, dangerous set of Jordan's face once again. He'd seen it too often, watched it growing over the years until Noah was beginning to fear that one day, it would become a permanent set to his face.

Until Jordan had come after Tehya. Only with her did he lose that look. Only when Tehya was around, did Jordan soften. She was Jordan's last hope, and Noah prayed, he prayed often, that this time she would break through shield around his uncle's soul and dissolve that core of dangerous darkness overtaking him.

If she didn't, then Noah feared Jordan would only return to the Ops, and if he did that, then it wouldn't be as a base commander. Jordan would take field command, and one day, he just wouldn't return.

As Jordan's gaze slid to the mirror, meeting Noah's as he glanced back again, Noah realized his uncle was riding a much finer line than he'd imagined. If the look in his eyes was any indication, if Tehya couldn't settle that darkness, then Noah feared he'd lose the uncle who had risked his career as well as his life, to save him.

Lightning flared across the sky, sharp brilliant fingers of electricity shedding its brilliant glow over the Stanton estate as it pierced the night. Thunder rattled and rolled and sheets of rain blew through the night, saturating the ground and lending a heavy sensual excitement to the air outside.

The storm vibrated with primal fury, pounding through the night as well as the senses as Tehya sat in the large, well-padded chair that faced the window and stared into the heart of the storm.

She felt isolated, alone. Fear and worry crowded her mind, turning her senses bleak and reminding her of the danger there seemed to be no escape from.

She was thirty years old. For twenty-five years she had been on the run in one way or the other, fighting to survive, clawing for freedom. And God, she was so tired. She was so tired of hiding, of watching over her shoulder, of knowing whomever she loved, whoever tried to protect her, would only lose their life for their effort.

Tonight, as she had so many nights before, she was dressed in borrowed clothes, a nightgown in this case, and sleeping in a borrowed bed. She was watching the night, knowing the monsters that existed there, knowing that any moment they could be watching her, coming for her. Just as they had so many nights before.

Or Jordan could be coming.

Tucking her feet beneath her, Tehya laid her cheek against her knees and stared into the night, feeling the storm raging inside her as well.

She wanted to run.

Oh God, she should have run the minute she suspected she was being watched again. Why had she become so stubborn when Jordan had arrived? What in God's name made her believe a house, a business, or friends was worth the risk Jordan and his men were facing?

Baby girl, all you had to do was come home. She would

have lived. . . . Sorrel had laid the blame at her feet. But a part of Tehya had known better. He had wanted both of them. He had needed both of them.

You and your mother were the key to my future, to Kenneth's future, he had sighed months before she had gone to Aruba. *Come home, baby girl. Let Daddy take care of you. I promise you, the embrace of your brother will be far better than what awaits you otherwise. . . .*

Running, hiding, losing friends, never knowing what true freedom was because she could never stop long enough to experience it.

It was still far better than the embrace of her brother.

She shuddered at the thought. When she had been younger, she had idolized Kenneth. When he would come to her and her mother's rooms, unlock the door and take her out into the gardens to play. When he would laugh with her, tease her, and tell her stories of what the world was like. The parties she would one day attend if she were a very good girl. The life she could have if she obeyed the rules.

If she would tell him or her father if her mother ever tried to escape. All she had to do was be a very good girl.

Her chest tightened as her stomach rolled sickeningly. She had never told on her mother, but her mother hadn't truly trusted her either. Tehya had been convinced the reason her mother had left her with Sister Mary was to test Tehya. And while running, Francine had learned exactly the danger she and her daughter faced.

A danger Tehya couldn't escape, even with Sorrel's and Kenneth's deaths.

She rocked against herself, her arms tightening around her legs as a knot of agony burned in her chest, the need to release it like a knife twisting inside her soul.

Thunder rocked outside, and lightning blazed with a power and brilliance that lit the world with nature's display of strength.

And how weak she was in comparison, not just to the storm, but to the danger surrounding her. The danger she had drawn Jordan and his men into.

The click of the bedroom door behind her drew her attention. Shadowed and dark, the tall, black-clad figure that stepped inside had her heart suddenly racing in much more than fear. Excitement and lust, emotions she had given up on fighting years ago, and a need for touch that threatened to leave her shaking.

The black mask covering his face didn't hide his eyes. The brilliant blue looked brighter, more sapphire, almost neon as he closed the door, locking it behind him before prowling across the room, dangerous intent marking every line of his body.

"The curtains should be closed," he informed her as he stepped around the chair, his back to her now as he reached up and jerked the heavy material across the floor-to-ceiling windows. "Anyone could have a bead on you, Tey."

Turning to her, he pulled the mask from his face slowly, dropping it to the floor as he stared down at her. His expression was tight, savage, and radiated pure hungry lust as he gripped the bottom of the snug black shirt and pulled it off as well.

Sensation punched through her womb, clenching it tight as she felt her juices ease along the bare lips of her pussy. The electricity of the storm seemed to sizzle over her flesh, tightening her nipples, her clit, and racing across her body with a sudden, exciting surge of sensuality.

Dominance radiated in his face, his gaze.

"Are you wearing panties?" Guttural, fierce, his voice echoed with the hunger reflected in his eyes.

The surge of electric sensation that pulsed through her pussy was so strong, so deep, it was almost an orgasm. Her heart picked up further in speed, racing, pounding with pure excitement as his hands went to the black nylon belt, moving slowly, with predatory intent, and released the catch.

Tehya swallowed tightly. "No."

Weakening sensuality swept through her at the smile that edged his lips. At the same time, he flipped the catch of his black pants loose, the edges spreading slowly apart as his cock sprang free.

Thick and long, the engorged crest had flushed a dark purple, moisture gleaming at the tip and over the tiny slit at the blunt point.

Heavily veined, wickedly erotic and explicit, the sensual demand apparent in the heavy stalk of flesh sent Tehya's senses reeling.

Slowly, she unfolded her legs, leaned forward, her gaze lifting to meet his as her lips parted, her tongue peeking out for a taste of the silk-covered steel throbbing demandingly before her gaze.

Male heat exploded against her taste buds. A hint of salt, a hint of spice. Addictive, intoxicating, the taste of him was a hunger suddenly exploding inside her.

Reaching for him, the fingers of one hand curled at the base of his cock, unable to surround it with her fingers, but her lips parted, taking the thick head between them, stretching around it to suck him inside.

The complete eroticism of the act was almost too much to bear. Her eyes closed, a moan trapped in her throat, vibrating there as she felt the hard throb of response against her tongue.

His fingers speared into her hair and clenched in the strands, tugging in sensual demand as she drew on the heated cock head, feeling his hands guiding her head, holding her in place as his hips began to move.

"Fuck, Tehya, I dream of this," he growled. "Watching my dick fuck your mouth again. Seeing your pretty lips stretched around it, sucking me deep."

She could feel her juices easing along the folds of her pussy, moistening her, preparing her for him.

She wanted him, with a desperation that clawed at her senses. His fingers flexed around the strands of hair he held, tugging at her scalp and sending an erotic fire radiating through it.

Pulsating need traveled through her senses. Flames of exquisite sensation raced over her flesh until she found her hands tugging at her gown, pulling it to her thighs as her fingers found the desperately aching bud of her clit. An agony of need filled her cunt, raging through it like a wildfire out of control.

A smothered cry escaped her as painful pleasure exploded through her. It wasn't as good as his touch; sometimes he seemed to know her body better than she did, her pleasure better than she ever could. But with his dick in her mouth, her fingers stroking her clit, she could still sense the impending explosion and the rapture that would surround her.

Inside, she heated and clenched as her juices began to saturate her fingers.

"Fuck. Tehya." The growl had her jerking in response as a shudder raced through her.

"Let me see, baby." He tried to move back, to pull free of the grip her mouth had on him. She couldn't allow it. She couldn't release him just yet, not as long as this pleasure was tearing through her.

His grip tightened, male determination apparent as his cock pulled from her lips and her eyes flared open in rejection.

"No. Not yet." She pulled her fingers from between her thighs, both hands reaching for him now.

"Let me watch." The order in his tone throbbed beneath the lust as he gripped her wrist and pushed her hand back to her thighs. "Let me watch you play with your pretty pussy, baby. I want to see it. Every stroke, every soft caress of your fingers."

Let him watch? Let him see the agonizing need tearing through her as her fingers played against her clit?

He went to his knees, and she admitted in that moment that she would do whatever he needed her to do. Whatever he wanted her to do.

One powerful hand gripped her knee, lifting it and guiding it over the arm of the chair as he continued pressing her fingers against her pussy until they moved.

She found her clit again, her head digging into the back of the chair as she felt herself rapidly flying into the center of the sensual, sexual vortex he was building inside her.

His gaze became darker, yet more brilliant, his expression

more savage as a reddish flush stained his sun-darkened face and his lips appeared more sensual, with a hungry curve.

"Oh yeah," he breathed out roughly, his eyes centered on her fingers as she circled her clit slowly. "Show me how you make your pretty clit swell, baby."

The hard bud pulsed and tightened further as Tehya felt her breathing escalate. The room suddenly became hotter, steamier with lust as his fingers slid up her thighs and parted the swollen folds of her pussy.

Sensation electrified her. It whipped through the sensitive bundle of nerves and left her gasping for breath as excitement tightened through her.

As his head lowered, his lashes lifting to stare back at her, she watched, entranced, as he licked through the saturated flesh, a low hum of enjoyment vibrating against her flesh.

Tehya jolted, a fractured cry parting her lips and she swore she lost her breath for precious seconds. Her hips arched forward, driving his tongue closer to the aching entrance to her cunt.

"I need you," she whispered, desperate for him, needing him now in ways she hadn't before.

Each time the pleasure seemed to be higher, hotter. It whipped around her with such incredible intensity that she wondered if she could possibly live without him or his touch now.

"Don't stop." His hand caught her wrist as her strokes eased, pressing them back to her flesh. "Let me watch you come, Tey. I want to see it."

The silky slide of her juices was caught by his fingers before he stroked the clenched opening, then with two fingers, began to penetrate the tender tissue. He parted her flesh, working inside her as her fingers began to move more quickly, more firmly against the sensitive bud now burning with the need for release.

"God, yes, Tey," he groaned as his fingers stretched her slowly, thrusting inside her with slow, deliberate movements. "Come for me baby. Let me see you. . . ."

"Jordan," she cried out his name, jerking as her body

tensed, tightened, and began to shudder with the orgasm suddenly tearing through her.

She was only dimly aware of his fingers sliding completely from her. She wasn't given a chance to miss them. In the next second he was stretching her further, the intimate flesh of her cunt burning with the sudden intrusion of his cock impaling her with strong, heavy thrusts.

Her lashes lifted as her hands moved with drugged weakness, her fingers gripping the strength of his biceps as his hips surged between her thighs.

The feel of his cock rasping over ultrasensitive tissue, stretching, creating a friction and pressure that sent electric surges of pure sensation tearing through her senses was almost too much to bear. Rapture exploded through her. Tender nerve endings flared with each pulse of her release as her pussy clamped down on his cock as though fighting to hold him inside.

Until he thrust in deep, his body arching, and the feel of his release suddenly spurting inside her intensified those last surging sensations rocketing through her womb.

His head fell to her shoulder, his mouth pressing to it for a second before they parted, allowing his lips to grip her flesh as a harsh male groan tore from his chest.

His pleasure combined with hers, whipping through her senses until she swore she could feel him moving through her soul, possessing her, owning her as nothing or no one else ever could have.

For Jordan, it was like suddenly waking. A part of him that he had never known existed flared to life. With his eyes closed, his teeth gripping her flesh, the taste of her, the scent of her overriding his senses, he knew some integral part of him had changed forever.

And it had happened the moment he saw her sitting before the window as though daring her enemies to strike.

The last ecstatic pulses of his release left him weak, pressed against her, fighting to catch his breath. It left him wondering at the sudden aura of contentment, of satisfaction that raced through his mind.

This was a part of pleasure he had never known before. It was an intimacy he couldn't have imagined existed.

The last surge of release shuddered through him as reality began to slip past the overwhelming sensations that had surrounded him.

Tehya rested against him, her arms draped over his shoulders, her breathing just as hard, just as rough as his own. Sprawled against the back of the chair, she held him to her, bonds of silk and feminine warmth locking him in place more tightly than chains ever could.

Moving wasn't something he wanted to do, it was something he made himself do. That inner voice of warning was screaming at him, alarms clashing inside his head at the realization that this one woman was beginning to mean more than any other in the past.

"Don't leave me yet," she whispered, the desperate plea in the words tearing through him.

"I'm not going anywhere without you, baby." As his flesh pulled free of hers and he rose to his feet, it was only to bend to her and lift her in his arms.

Cradling her against his chest, Jordan moved to the carefully turned-down bed and laid her in the center of the soft mattress before removing the rest of his clothing, her gown, and climbing in beside her.

There was no hesitation as she moved into his arms, her head lying against his chest as masses of red-gold curls spilled over his arm and stomach. The warmth of it was like silken chains wrapping around him, holding him in place.

God, what would he do without her?

For the barest second, his breathing paused at the thought. There had never been anyone in his life that he didn't think he could survive without, until now. And that was terrifying.

"Did you follow them?" Her soft voice pierced him with the underlying fear he sensed in it.

"We followed them," he answered as he smoothed his hand down her hair, finally allowing his fingers to tangle into the curls that lay over his stomach.

He didn't want to talk about this. He knew the past was

coming back to haunt her, that Gregor Ascarti had been one of the demons who had chased her since she was a child. One that refused to die.

"What aren't you wanting to tell me, Jordan?" The fear was gone. There was an edge of steel in her voice now, a determination he didn't particularly want to hear.

"Just lie here with me for a while, Tey," he sighed. "Let me just hold you for a minute."

He didn't want to do this to her. Telling her Ascarti was still alive would be nearly as bad as telling her Sorrel himself had risen from the grave.

"Senator Stanton has been on the phone with Elite Ops Command," she said, her voice quiet as she spoke of the shadowed group that governed the private multinational group they had been a part of. "He's trying to get a team out here to back you."

Jordan shook his head. "We have the backup team, Tehya. I don't need, nor do I want an Elite Ops team on this."

Hell, this was just what he needed, having his plans hijacked by a team that would do nothing more than clutter up the protection he'd placed around Tehya.

"Perhaps you should talk to him then," she suggested, the noncommittal tone of her voice causing him to wince.

That was the tone she adopted when she knew he wasn't telling her everything. When she knew he had one of his backup plans in progress and hadn't told her or the team.

"Perhaps," he answered as he frowned up at the ceiling. "The thing about the senator is that if I tell him to pull back, then, like you, he's going to know there's more going on than he's aware of. And the senator being the senator, he is going to apprise the committee. Then they're going to get their heads together and attempt to lay insurance that their ass is covered, forgetting in the process that I'm rather good at covering *all* our asses."

She was silent for long moments before he felt her breath whisper over his chest.

"Tell me who you saw, Jordan."

Keeping it from her wasn't fair. She deserved to know,

but hell if he wanted to see the shadows in her eyes after he told her.

"Jordan?" Tension filled the room, as did the memory of the girl he had met eight years before.

Eyes too big for her pale face. Hair that had been darkened from its natural color. And in those eyes, he had seen the fear, the courage, and the hopelessness she had begun feeling.

"It was Ascarti, Tehya. It was Gregor Ascarti."

CHAPTER 18

Gregor Ascarti.

He was a child's bogeyman. He was the voice from the dark whispering her name with vicious amusement.

Come out, come out wherever you are, little girl. Daddy's waiting. But first Uncle Gregor gets a sweet taste of you . . . and then laughter. That evil, demonic sound that she remembered echoing through her head as Boyd covered her mouth with his large hand, covered her young body with his own, and fought to protect her the only way he knew how.

The night they had been forced to run, they had nearly been caught. Tehya had been only twelve, gangly, always nervous, always certain the bogeyman was going to catch up with her.

That night, he had caught up with her, but Boyd had protected her. Less than three months later, Boyd had been dead, too.

Gregor was supposed to be dead.

For too long she had lived under the illusion of safety. And she was tired of the illusion. The weariness clawed at her, dragging her down, and reminding her, always reminding her like a sadistic whisper of evil in her head, that it would never be over. That she would never be free. That loving Jordan was the same as signing his death warrant.

She'd felt this in Aruba. That heavy, panicked uncertainty.

The knowledge that either freedom or death was just a heartbeat away.

"Answers aren't going to pop out of the shrubbery." Jordan stepped into the bedroom, his expression a dark mix of both hunger and chilling danger.

He was a hunter, and he'd perfected the hunt. He was waiting, patient, composed, giving his prey the perfect opportunity and the time needed to make their move.

But the prey was cunning, it was evil, and it had taken the lives of other strong men, men born to the hunt. Men who had thought they could protect her.

Slowly, the sage green coverings slid over the windows, enclosing them in a dimmer, sun-dappled room rather than the previous heated warmth that had spilled in.

"Have you learned anything?" She knew the others, Noah, Micah, Travis, John, and Nik were out plotting Gregor Ascarti's downfall. It couldn't come soon enough to suit her.

"We've contacted the appropriate parties and given them the location of the weapons." He checked his watch before his gaze lifted once more, sharp satisfaction filling it. "They should be hitting the warehouse any moment now."

"We have to find him to neutralize him, Jordan."

"No, our men have to find him," he retorted. "All you have to do is look very pretty, and very grief-stricken tonight at the party. Once he's certain I'm out of the picture, he'll plan his strike. That's when we'll have him, if we don't catch him at the warehouse."

Ascarti would never allow himself to be caught in that warehouse.

"Ascarti isn't that easy." She gave a hard shake of her head. "You should know that by now."

She knew it. She had fought to survive his search for her for far too long to consider him so easy to catch, to even allow herself to hope he would be so sloppy.

"I'm aware of that, Tehya," he growled. "I'm simply that prepared. There's no way he can strike without us catching him. There are too many eyes waiting and watching."

Tehya crossed her arms over her breasts, her gaze narrowing on the windows despite the fact that shutters now covered them.

Turning back to him slowly, she tried to ignore the heat that lingered in his eyes, the pure sensual, sexual interest in his expression as his gaze went over her, from head to toe.

"What do you have planned, Jordan?" He hadn't told her what he had set up yet. She knew he had been with Noah, Kell Krieger, and the senator for most of the morning, but she hadn't been invited to the plotting session. It had begun before she had ever awakened.

"The plan is exactly as it was." He gave a faint shrug of heavy shoulders beneath the dark gray shirt he wore tucked into jeans. "We wait."

Her eyes narrowed on him. That so didn't sound like Jordan, to simply sit and wait and watch.

"I'm not lying to you, sweetheart." Once again that faint smile crossed his lips. "There are times when nothing else but simplicity will do. This is one of those times." Then his head tilted to the side as curiosity lit his gaze. "Tey, darling, isn't that the same outfit that little old Indian trader in New Mexico made for you? The one with all the hidden weapons?"

Her brows arched. He remembered? She was certain he hadn't been paying attention the day she had ordered the clothing. The shopping trip had been a treat during the early days of her contract with the Elite Ops.

She had been frightened to leave base during those days, terrified she would be followed somehow. Jordan and Noah, along with the communication agent, Kira Richards, and her husband Ian, had all but ordered Tehya with them for a shopping trip, supposedly funded by the Ops to outfit her in more than the worn clothing she'd owned. She'd learned later that Jordan himself had paid for her clothes.

"It is." Her heart began to race. That something so small as the knowledge that he remembered that day should excite her, she decided, was truly pitiful.

He stepped closer, a predatory male animal suddenly

shifting into stalking mode, his expression tightening with lust, his gaze blazing with hunger.

"I shouldn't want you again so soon," he growled as he stepped in front of her, the backs of his fingers whispering over the leather that covered one breast. "But I swear, Tehya, the sight of you wearing leather and the knowledge that you could kill a man before he drew his next breath has my dick harder than hell."

And her pussy was creaming. Tehya could feel it, hot and moist, her juices saturating her cunt and preparing her for him.

"We could take a long break for lunch," she suggested, as the other hand curved around her back and drew her flush against his body.

"If I get you back in that bed there's no way in hell I'd go for the quickie it would have to be." His head lowered, but rather than the kiss she needed, all she received was a sensual nip to her lips. "When this is over, though, I'm taking you to a beach somewhere and I'm keeping you naked for a month. Naked and covering my body like a second skin."

The hard wedge of his cock pressed against her lower stomach as she tried to keep back the low moan of rising need surging inside her.

Laying her head against his chest and feeling his arms surround her, she wished there was a way to delay it, just for a little while longer. She would pay whatever price she needed to pay, kill whomever she needed to kill, for just a few more hours of security in his arms.

"When this is over," she repeated, her voice soft, her arms tightening around his waist as she felt that cold hard kernel of fatalistic knowledge harden inside her soul.

It would never be over until her own death.

"It will be over soon, baby," he promised as she pulled back.

Staring up at him, she realized the past eight years had only been the road to bring her here. She had been hiding, and a part of her had known it, just as she had known there would be a price to pay for it later.

"I love you, Jordan," she whispered before he could keep her from voicing the promise. "You don't have to love me. You don't have to keep me. Just always know, if I had known what was coming, I would have made certain I hid better. I would have kept this from happening. . . ."

"God, Tehya." His fingers were against her lips before she could finish the hastily whispered words. "Son of a bitch, baby, do you think in a million fucking years that I would even consider letting you face this alone? Do you think, Tehya, that I, or the others, weren't watching for a threat against you? That we weren't doing everything we could to ensure we were here if you needed us? Do you believe, for even a second, damn you, that I could have ever totally let you go?"

Frustrated anger, surprise, and a hint of amazement filled his voice now.

Jordan stared down at the little imp that had both tormented and comforted him for the past eight years. So delicate and tiny, he swore a good strong breeze could knock her over. She had a backbone of pure titanium, though, and a will that often amazed him.

"Teyha," he chided, his voice softening as he allowed himself the luxury of running the backs of his fingers down the side of her silken cheek. "I'm not a fool. I'm not one man trying to protect a mother and a child. I've told you this before. If you don't stop doubting me, sweetheart, then I'm going to become irritated."

"It's not you I doubt. Sometimes . . ." She swallowed tightly, fear flashing in her eyes, "fate—Lady Luck—doesn't often favor the good guy, Jordan."

He had to grin at that. "But baby, I'm Irish. Fate, Lady Luck, the Muses, *and* the gods. They love me."

And he was bragging even as he knocked on wood. It wasn't Fate, Lady Luck, or any other mythical force. It was preparedness, knowing what he was facing, and never taking things at face value.

"Do you expect Ascarti to be at the party tonight?" she asked as she moved away from him, no doubt to hide the hurt that he hadn't returned the words of love she had whispered.

His heart ached at the refusal. There were days, nights that he worried about the question himself, but refused to answer it.

He was prepared, but he also knew better than to tempt the future. He wouldn't make plans, he refused to delve too deeply into the unfamiliar emotions that sometimes assailed him. Not until it was finished. Not until he knew he wasn't going to lose her, or God forbid, that she, his men, and their families, were left without his protection.

He almost grinned at his thoughts. As though he could control any of it. But it sure as hell made him sleep better at night knowing he had done all he could to cover all the angles he could think of.

"I don't expect Ascarti to be at the party tonight," he finally told her. "He won't show his hand so easily. Nor would his handler."

"His handler?" She turned back to him, those thick, luscious waves of red-gold curls flowing around her as those mysterious green eyes narrowed on him. "Sorrel's dead."

Jordan gave a sharp nod as he moved to the bar, aware of her gaze following him as he passed her to prop himself on one of the bar stools.

"Sorrel's dead," he agreed. "But Ascarti isn't a man who can work alone, nor is he capable of leading his men effectively without a powerful commander."

Giving her that information wasn't something he wanted to do. Tehya, like anyone else, was more comfortable putting a face to the demons that chased her. Unfortunately, he couldn't give her that option yet.

She sighed heavily.

"I think I knew that," she answered, her voice bleak. "Then that leaves us wondering who the hell is pulling the strings."

He inclined his head in agreement before going to her again. This time, he didn't give her the option of pulling away from him.

Gripping her waist, he lifted her onto the bar and stepped easily between her hips. Her position was perfect to angle the engorged length of his cock against the heated mound of her pussy as her gaze darkened in immediate arousal. Her face flushed, her expression softening as the powerful waves of need he knew she felt began to wash through her.

He knew she felt it. He felt it. It was like tidal waves of hunger, almost impossible to resist.

Sliding his fingers into the heavy length of curls to cup the back of her head, Jordan held her still for his kiss. A taste of the perfection of her lips before he had to become a dead man and live in the shadows away from her.

To save her.

His tongue flicked at her lips, feeling them part as his lips slanted over them and he pulled her to him. The feel of her arms sliding around his neck, holding him to her as her fingers threaded through his hair, had his cock stiffening to the point of pain.

He'd fucked her most of the night, drowning his senses in every touch, every kiss, every whispered moan he could pull from her until they had collapsed in exhaustion close to dawn.

And still, he wanted her.

He needed her just as much as, perhaps more than, the first time he'd had her.

"Damn." Dragging his lips back from hers, he stared down at her, his breathing harsh, the impulse to pull her jeans to her ankles and fuck her like a man desperate for that connection was almost impossible to resist. And he had to resist. The party was only hours away and he would need all his senses intact to end this here and to ensure Tehya's future.

A future in his arms. The thought whispered across his mind before he could pull back from it. Before he could force himself not to consider the future or where either of them would be.

Don't jinx it, he warned himself. Only today exists. That possibility of tomorrow arriving was slimmer for men like him than for most. Especially now. And he couldn't allow himself to forget it.

"Your dress is on its way." He couldn't let her go, couldn't pull his hips from beneath her thighs. "The party's in a few hours. You'll be coming in with Kell and Emily. Watch for anyone too curious, anyone attempting to get too close to you or to draw you away. If anything, *anything* out of the ordinary happens . . ."

"Then I let Kell or one of the others at the party know." She gave a quick nod before her gaze darkened with concern again. "And you'll be careful?"

"I'll be careful. More importantly, Tehya, I'll be close. You won't be alone, baby. Never. I promise you that."

When was the last time anyone had worried if he would be careful? She made his chest get that funny melting sensation in it whenever she did something so female, and so incredibly caring as worrying about him. Even though the last thing he wanted her to do was worry.

As he'd told her, there were other eyes watching. He never placed all his bets on one plan, or one set of eyes. He'd pulled in friends, two teams completely unconnected to the Ops or anyone associated with them. Independent contractors in a manner, men he knew he could trust his life to. Even more, he could trust her life to them.

Glancing at the clock behind the bar, he restrained the sigh of regret that pushed at his chest.

"It's time." He kissed her gently on the lips before lifting her back to the floor. "The Senator's staff will be returning within the hour." And he had to be out of there before anyone saw him. Otherwise, the trouble they had gone to in setting up his "death" would be wasted effort.

He couldn't afford that. Tehya's life meant more to him than his own, and taking this threat out of it once and for all was more important to him than even she knew.

He lowered his head and his lips touched hers again as Jordan used every resource of control he possessed to keep from picking her up and lifting her back to the bar where he could love her in a way that would have her screaming when she came around him.

He contented himself with the knowledge that she had a bar at her own home, and he knew well exactly how to use it. He would have his chance once this was finished, and that was all that mattered.

Pulling away from her, he cupped her cheek for a moment, his lips quirking at the worry, the concern in her expression and the fear in her pretty green eyes.

"Smile for me, love." He gave his voice the faintest hint of the Irish that he'd picked up from his father.

Her lips twitched at the sound of it.

"I'll stop worrying if you promise to talk Irish to me the next time you make love to me," she offered.

They both knew she was lying, but hell, whatever it took to get her back in the bed.

"That's a deal." A quick kiss to her lips, just one more taste before he had to leave her and return to the dark shadows that awaited him.

A kiss into which he swore she fed all the love she believed she felt.

If the illusion was preserved, pampered, and taken care of, did it matter if it was an illusion, Jordan asked himself again as he slipped from the study and made his way to the basement, where Noah, Micah, and Nik awaited him.

With them was one of the two-man teams, his youngest nephew, Rory Malone, and a former Army Ranger with whom Jordan had worked in a few past operations overseas, Turk Gillespie.

"Commander." Turk nodded as Jordan stepped into the wine cellar at the back of the basement and closed the door behind him.

Low lighting and racks of wine stacked throughout the room gave it a shadowed atmosphere. At the very back, the door leading to an old tunnel and a hidden exit was open.

"Status?" He started with Turk and Rory.

"Casey and Iron are watching Ms. Talamosi," Turk answered. "The chip you placed in the belly ring she wears is working perfectly. Everything's in place if anyone makes a move on her."

"Ascarti's warehouse was hit and the weapons confiscated," Noah informed him. "Ascarti wasn't there, but we managed to get a jig on one of his bodyguards at a bar last night when he used his credit card to pay for drinks. He's currently sleeping off a hangover in a motel, so we haven't managed to follow him to Ascarti yet."

"I want Ascarti taken out at the earliest opportunity," Jordan informed him as he forced back the fury that rose each time he thought of the bastard still living.

"We already guessed that." Noah nodded.

"One of the mercenaries working with Ascarti, Mark Tenneyson, has made several drive-bys along the street in front of here," Rory reported. "We've tried to track him, but we keep losing him. So far, we've not seen anything or anyone to indicate someone else is pulling the strings."

"I agree with Jordan, though," Nik stated. "This setup with Ascarti is just a little too damned handy. Something isn't ringing right with it."

"John and Bailey, Travis and Lilly will be covering Tehya at the party," Jordan mused. "I have the tracker on her and we have every access to her I can come up with, covered. They'll move tonight, before they believe John and Travis can get a plan in place to have her covered. This is their best bet, there's no way they'll find a better opportunity to grab her, especially with the information both John and Travis have put out there."

Jordan prayed it would be enough. From the moment they had set this up, they'd pushed every contact they had and placed pressure at each pulse they could find leading out from the men they'd identified as a threat.

This party was the only chance they would see in the near future of grabbing her. Word going out was that a team would arrive in the morning to whisk her to an undisclosed location, where her identity would be so completely altered that there would be no finding her.

Whoever was tracking her, whether it was Ascarti or others, wouldn't want to risk being unable to find her, or identify her again.

"Our contact in Afghanistan also reported finally." Noah leaned against the wall, his dark face covered with a closely cropped beard to hide the scars he carried, frowned pensively as he crossed his arms over his chest. "It seems Tehya's identity and her location were betrayed by an anonymous party to a low-level criminal formerly in Sorrel's employ, Thaddeus Alchoni."

"Thaddeus is a French-born aristocrat identified as a runner and informant for Sorrel," Micah continued when Noah glanced at him. "Our contact there called me and reported that word went out to Sorrel's men within hours of his death ten years ago, that any information concerning the wife or the child that escaped was to be reported to someone they called the Marquis. Alchoni sent the information via a mail service Sorrel had set up years before his death for use by informants who couldn't meet with him. We have someone trying to track that now, but so far, there's no further information."

"Why didn't we know about that order when it went out?" Jordan questioned, his voice harsher than he intended at the thought that he had overlooked an important detail in Tehya's safety.

"Because it wasn't an organization-wide order," Noah picked the conversation back up. "That order only went out to a few of their higher-level informants. Those who weren't identified as part of the organization after Sorrel's death."

"It was well hidden, just as Lilly's mother and many of her fine friends managed to hide what they were doing," Micah growled.

It had amazed them, all the secrets they had learned once their operative, Nighthawk, had been allowed to return to her former life after she was nearly assassinated.

How the some of the impossibly rich conducted their personal lives, manipulated their bloodlines, and bought and sold their women as though they were no more than pets or breeding stock.

Men would choose their mistresses, future wives, or their son's playthings as young girls, then arrange with their fathers, or even their mothers, for specialized training or interests to be introduced into their lives.

The girls that rebelled were sent to a clinic in Switzerland that had often used torturous practices to ensure they never rebelled again.

They created puppets out of their daughters and monsters of their sons. And if the reconditioning didn't work, then men like Sorrel had arranged "accidents" so skillfully that even their parents never suspected, in many cases, why their sons or daughters had died.

Finally, Jordan turned to Rory. "You and Turk back up Iron and Casey from here on out. I want everyone ready to move on this if so much as a breath of wind thinks to blow the wrong way."

"You have a bad feeling about this, don't you, Jordan?" Noah probed.

His nephew had worked with him often enough, knew him well enough, that he picked up on it instantly.

"Something's not coming together," Jordan admitted. "I'm certain they'll strike tonight, but I'm damned if I can believe it's Ascarti." He gave a hard shake of his head. "I can't pinpoint it, Noah." And that was so rare that Jordan knew it was usually indicative of a mission going to hell at the last minute.

Noah's eyes narrowed. "We'll make sure we're all on our toes."

They would anyway, Jordan knew. But that feeling was never wrong.

Looking at the men watching him, for the first time in his career as a SEAL and then an Elite Ops commander, Jordan was second-guessing himself.

"Turk, you and Rory head out and meet up with Iron and Casey to coordinate your places. Be prepared for anything. I want, at all times, eyes on Tehya in some way. If, by any chance, she is taken, then I want to know where she's at every second."

Rory gave a sharp nod, though his gaze was concerned as

it met Jordan's, then Noah's. Rather than saying anything, he turned and he and Turk left the wine cellar quickly via the hidden exit that opened into a sheltered, overgrown ravine nearly a quarter of a mile away.

"Micah, you and Nik cover the gardens outside the ballroom tonight. Get in place so you have a clear view of the doors in case Tehya's taken out."

"We also have the gates covertly wired for security and wireless cameras covering the perimeter," Micah assured him. "We're prepared, Jordan."

Jordan nodded briefly. As they left, he turned to Noah, his second in command on this job.

He'd been tempted to take the women who, in his mind, were his wife, as Fuentes and Sorrel believed that if he broke the wedding vows he was known to cherish, then his loyalty to his country would follow.

But Noah, Nathan Malone as he'd been then, had never broken those vows. Even in the years after his rescue, before his wife had known he'd survived, after years of believing her husband was dead, neither of them had betrayed the vows they made when they married.

They were happy now. Their son, Riordan Nathan Blake, Nate as they called him, was six, in kindergarten, and driving his parents crazy. Noah lived and breathed for them.

"You okay?" Noah asked quietly, his darker blue eyes probing as he watched Jordan.

CHAPTER 19

The dress was absolutely beautiful, and Nik's wife Mikayla was one of those serene, at-peace souls who seemed to bring comfort to everyone around her.

Long, heavy blond hair was pulled back into a braid, her classically pretty face emphasized by the smile on her lips and the laughter in her eyes. And the sheer adoration present whenever she talked about her husband and their daughter.

Tehya knew Nik had lost his first wife and only child before he came into the Ops. The haunted pain she had always sensed in him had evaporated after he met Mikayla Martin, though. And now, she was still taken aback every time she saw him smile.

"I knew this dress would be absolutely perfect for you," Mikayla commented as Tehya stepped out of the large dressing room/bath attached to the guest room and let Mikayla see her creation.

The floor-length, tissue thin, dual-layer white-and-violet silk whispered from the shoulders to the cinched waist, where it then fell in soft clouds of material to her feet and the matching four-inch heels.

Tiny violet sequins were sewn in patterns of soft falls of intricate detail along the shoulders and again in a gentle wave to emphasize her breasts. More had been placed at the cinched waist at her hips and again at her midriff.

The bold splash of color drew attention to her eyes and the soft light tan on her skin. It also managed to give her an air of frailty, despite the height of the heels.

"Absolutely beautiful," Mikayla sighed as she moved around, bending and fluffing the material here and there as she checked for whatever it was a clothing designer and maker checked for.

Whatever she was looking for, she must not have found it. When she straightened and rose, there was a look of supreme satisfaction on her face. "I am proud." She sighed again as she fluttered her fingers against her chest. "You look like a fairy princess, Tehya."

"Well, I don't know about that." Tehya stared into the full-length mirror. "But the dress looks damned good, Mikayla."

Mikayla gave a little light laugh and a wink. "The dress complements the girl, is what I always say. It takes more than a pretty dress and a little makeup to do what you do to that dress, Tehya. And it takes a girl just as unique to catch the eye and the heart of the commander Nik and Noah feared would come home in a body bag if he went back into the Ops as a field agent rather than a commander, as he was considering."

Tehya ducked her head. She hadn't known he was considering such a thing. If Noah had discussed it with Nik though, then she knew for a fact it had been a possibility.

The fact that Mikayla believed Jordan was in the SEALs was besides the point. If he'd returned to the Ops as a field agent, rather than a commander, then the chances of that would be higher.

She knew Jordan. And she had sensed his discontent in his life before the Ops unit disbanded was riding higher than he let on. But she hadn't expected that decision.

"What makes Nik think I have his heart?" That question was uppermost in her mind.

Mikayla's smile was soft when she glanced back at her. "I've only seen Jordan a few times, Tehya. Each time I've seen him, until these last weeks, he's been tense, cold. But now, it's like there's something different about him. It's Nik's opinion he's in love."

No, he wasn't in love, but she wouldn't be the one to disillusion the little romantic.

Tehya looked into the mirror again. This dress was a beautiful confection of silk and dreams. It was the romantic heart that had envisioned it, that had created it.

But when it was all said and done, Jordan would walk away from her just as he had countless other women before her. He didn't believe in love. It was an illusion as far as he was concerned.

"You know, Nik hasn't told me what's going on."

Tehya's head lifted as she stared back at the other woman.

Mikayla gave a little shrug. "I don't just love my husband, I know my husband. He gave me a nice little story to tell anyone if they asked about the dresses I was making for you, who you were, who Jordan was, the whole nine yards." She waved her hand expressively. "Then this morning he gave me another story about someone close to you dying. He promised me when he retired from whatever it is he was doing, that there would be no more missions. Then he came to me and told me you were in trouble and he had to help. Whatever that trouble is, Tehya, I want you to know, I make a very good friend. And I know how to listen."

Tehya glanced away, her throat tightening with the tears she had refused to allow herself to shed.

"I had hoped I was hiding things better," she whispered,

"I doubt anyone but another woman who's in love, and feared losing that love, would notice," Mikayla stated. "We've only met a few times, but I've never looked into your eyes that I didn't want to cry myself. The worst thing you can do is cry alone. So, if you need a friend." She gave a little lift of her shoulder, an endearing gesture of a woman afraid of overstepping a boundary, but one whose compassion knew only one way.

"Thank you, Mikayla," she answered softly. "And I won't forget the offer."

She would never forget it, but she knew there was little

chance of being able to take her up on it. She couldn't allow herself to ever be caught again. That meant disappearing again and learning to ignore the hunger to put down roots, to own anything, to have friends, family . . . or the lover her heart longed for.

"Good. Now, show my awesome dress off tonight and tell everyone how totally unique and expensive I am." Mikayla flashed a warm smile as she moved to the bed, grabbed her oversized workbag, and headed for the door. "And don't be a stranger." She stopped after opening the door. "I'd like for us to be friends, Tehya."

Tehya gave a quick nod as she battled her tears again. She hated crying. She hated being on the verge of crying because it still puffed up her eyes and her nose and made her look washed out.

Which, she imagined, would be good for the overall impression of grief.

Breathing out roughly, she moved closer to the mirror, pulled at several curls until they draped over her shoulder from the jewel-encrusted clasp that held a mass of curls at the top of her head, allowing them to fall haphazardly around her head, to mix and mingle with the heavy strands that hadn't been pulled up.

Rather like a Grecian goddess, she thought, as her fingers trailed over the tiny sequins that ran along the bodice of the dress.

Glancing at the clock, she drew in a deep breath and searched for her courage. It was a trick her mother had taught her when she was very young.

She closed her eyes and imagined Jordan this time, rather than a bird flying free. His smile, the sound of those deep, amused chuckles, the way he touched her, the way he held her.

And she imagined his courage, just as her mother had taught her to imagine that bird's courage when it first took flight. How high it went, and how brave it must be. And how it wouldn't survive if it couldn't fly.

If she didn't fly, she couldn't survive.

And now, if she didn't have Jordan, if he didn't live and breathe, then there was no way she could bear life herself.

She would face whatever came tonight. She had no choice but that, to ensure Jordan survived. He had been targeted because of her. Someone had tried to kill him, and now he had to pretend to be dead.

Because of her.

Because she hadn't had the courage to run when she should have.

Because she hadn't had the courage to disappear in a way that would ensure Jordan never found her either. Now, tonight, she had to find the courage *not* to run, to walk into that party and to dare whoever or whatever had haunted her all her life.

She had never done that. She had always run, because she had always seen what happened to the strong, confident, self-assured military-trained men who had done just that in their attempts to protect her and her mother.

Her hand jerked up, covered her mouth and her nose as a sudden sob nearly escaped, as she felt something inside her beginning to crack, attempting to escape.

A vicious shudder raced through her, nearly obliterating her ability to hold back a wave of fury and blinding pain.

Where the hell had it come from?

Her breathing was shaking, almost shuddering through her as she seemed to gasp for breath.

She blinked desperately, finally, mercifully gaining control and unable to understand exactly what had happened.

It terrified her, though.

The sense of panic, of impending doom grew stronger, and finding the strength to gather her courage enough to walk out of the room took everything she had, because every instinct she had was screaming at her to run. To hide. To ensure no one else died because of her.

She felt like a coward. Like that little girl who had begged her mother to just send her back to her father so no one else could ever be hurt again.

Her eyes closed.

She hadn't remembered that, but now that event was so vivid in her mind, so fresh it might have happened only yesterday.

She remembered sobbing after she had learned Sister Mary was dead and how the Reverend Mother and sisters had died at the convent. Her mother hadn't meant for her to know. Tehya had slipped out of bed and crept to the top of the stairs and listened to her and Matthew Thomas talking.

Her mother had been crying, blaming herself, and Matthew had been struggling to comfort her when he glanced up and saw Tehya.

For just a second, she had seen a look of resentment, of accusation in his gaze. He had blamed her for the danger her mother faced, and the deaths that had followed them.

Tehya had broken down then. She had screamed, sobbed, demanded her mother call Sorrel to come for her. Demanded that they let her return so everyone would be safe again.

In a way, she felt as though she were now coming full circle, even though he was dead.

And she knew it would explode around her tonight.

She just prayed. She prayed as she had never prayed in her life, that no one died.

As she finally pushed back that terror and gathered the frayed threads of her courage together, a quick knock at the door had her flinching so viciously her teeth jerked together.

She was a mess tonight, and she knew it.

Moving to the door, she paused. "Yes?" Caution weighed heavily on her shoulders now. The knowledge that so many were willing to risk their lives for her made her second-guess every move.

"It's John, Tehya."

She opened the door slowly until she stared back at the handsome form of one of the men she had worked with for the past six years.

Dressed in a black silk tux and startling white shirt, he looked both dangerous and charming. Dark blond hair fell over his brow as he watched her with somber concern.

"I believe I'm escorting you to the party," he informed her with a quick smile.

She glanced behind him. "Where's Bailey?"

His wife was normally right at his side.

"She's waiting in the foyer just outside the ballroom with Kell and Emily," he informed her. "I'll escort you both in."

"I guess I'm ready, then." She knew her smile was tight, the tension radiating through her body not as well hidden as she would have liked.

It would lend weight to the illusion they were attempting to portray, though, she told herself as John held his elbow out to her.

Curving her fingers beneath his arm, she drew in a deep breath and turned with him to walk down the wide hall to the curved staircase that led to the foyer.

The dress whispered around her, sliding against her flesh and reminding her of Jordan's touch even as the derringer strapped to her thigh reminded of the gift he had given her several Christmases ago. Extra protection, he'd told her with a small quirk of his lips.

"Everything's in place," John assured her as they neared the stairs. "We have all our bases covered."

She nodded. She knew Jordan and his penchant for building in layers upon layers to his plans.

It wouldn't matter.

The thought didn't catch her off guard, though she would have preferred to escape it.

Still, it was the truth. It wouldn't matter. Tonight the culmination of a lifetime of running, of a mother's death and the destruction of friends and loved ones, would end here. One way or the other.

As they descended the stairs, she could feel the eyes on her. Dozens of guests were lingering in the foyer along with Bailey, Emily, Kell, and Senator Richard Stanton. She felt as though they were all staring at her, though she knew they weren't. At least not overtly. Just as she knew that the malevolent gaze that made her skin crawl couldn't possibly be in the foyer as well.

Still, she felt it, like a whisper of death over her flesh.

It was all she could do to keep moving forward, to hide the fear flashing through her from the man at her side.

"Okay?" John asked as they neared the marble entrance area.

"Fine," she assured him. She would pretend. She had been pretending all her life, practicing for this night.

"Courage is facing your demons," he whispered at her ear as they took those final steps. "We all feel it, Tey."

She didn't have a chance to argue the point. They stepped into the foyer and were immediately joined by Kell, Emily, Bailey, and the senator.

Bailey wore a deep emerald silk sheath cut high to the knee and revealing the chiffon confection of her slip. With her hair arranged into artful waves and emeralds glittering at her neck and ears, she looked sedately festive.

Emily's rich sunlit dark blond hair was pulled back from her face to reveal her graceful neck and high cheekbones. Her black silk strapless gown smoothed over her more petite form and emphasized her breasts. Black silken lace covered the bodice and fell in dark shimmering waves to her feet over the silk, while hundreds of tiny crystals winked within the delicate cobweb design. Between the gown, the heels that added to her height, and her diamond-and-sapphire jewelry, she looked like a soft midnight star, while the compassion and concern in her gaze nearly had tears filling Tehya's eyes again.

Both women had their own unique tastes that were excellently presented in their gowns, accessories, and kind demeanors.

Senator Richard Stanton, though nearing sixty, was still fit and handsome. The laugh lines at the corners of his blue eyes and the strength of his expression had drawn constituents to him for decades. Now, he was grooming his son-in-law for politics, and, Tehya knew, eventually taking his senatorial seat. It was the reason for the glamorous balls he'd been throwing for several months now. Allowing his backers, his business associates and friends, as well as other potentially powerful friends, to meet the former SEAL and, hopefully, decide to contribute to his run for office.

Kell would make a wonderful politician in some ways, she thought. He was a man who could command when needed and one who could lead effortlessly. He was also quite adept at seeing through the bullshit to the lies below and sidestepping them effectively.

"You look absolutely exquisite, my dear." Richard bent and kissed her cheek fondly before enfolding her in a quick hug. A major gesture in an atmosphere where affection was normally hidden.

"Thank you, Senator," she whispered, blinking again.

What the hell was wrong with her? Her stomach was trembling as though she had never faced danger before, as though this particular specter of evil hadn't been shadowing her for her entire life.

"Are we ready to make our entrance, then?" he asked the small group quietly before lifting his gaze to survey the foyer. "Most of the guests who have arrived are already in the ballroom, and I'd like my daughter and son-in-law to greet them and begin tonight's festivities."

His gaze was eagle sharp as he glanced back down at her, then extended his elbow to her. "Would you like to accompany me, Tehya?"

Tehya managed a small smile. "I would love to accompany you, Senator Stanton."

As they stepped into the ballroom, Tehya noticed the small amount of whispering. The rumors had already circulated that something had happened between her and her lover.

As they walked through the room, Bailey moved closer. "We just had a report from security that there was activity at the back gate," the other woman murmured in her ear. "Stay alert."

Tehya gave a small nod, very aware of the small derringer tucked into the specially designed garter belt that she wore around her thigh.

It wasn't much, but at close range it could mean the difference between life and death. Between captivity or freedom.

It had happened too quickly though, she thought desperately. The party hadn't even truly begun yet.

The band was still warming up in the center dais, the buffet tables were still fresh, and the men were lining up at the bar for drinks as champagne circled on trays carried by eager black-coated waiters.

The senator escorted her to one of the tables set up along the wall of balcony doors that led out to the gardens. The glass doors had been thrown wide, a gentle autumn breeze filling the brightly lit ballroom and whispering around the exquisite fabrics and gowns that filled it as conversation began to fill the cavernous room and the senator stepped up to the center dais with Kell and Emily following.

John, Bailey, Travis, and Lilly took their seats at the table with Tehya, their gazes seemingly inattentive, though Tehya knew better. She could see the signs of their suspicions, their careful regard of each and every guest.

"Ms. Johnson." Despite appearances and her demeanor of being less than cautious, Tehya still gave a start as Stephen Taite, his son, Craig, daughter-in-law Lauren, his granddaughter, Journey Taite, and the quiet, darkly brooding Beauregard Grant, stood just behind John's chair as he sat in a protective position. "I heard Mr. Malone's left. I had hoped to speak to him for a moment. Will he be returning?"

That was the cover story, that Jordan had left, only those associated with the assassin would believe he was dead.

That wave of agonizing anger and pain washed through her again, cramping her stomach and tightening her face.

She could feel her lips trembling as she tried to come up with a smile, too aware of the sudden interest when she couldn't control her response.

"I don't think . . ." she cleared her throat as her voice roughened.

"Mr. Malone was called away unexpectedly." John stood

and turned, his tone cool, brooking no questions. "Ms. Johnson is understandably upset that business concerns have dictated her inability to follow along with him."

She swallowed tightly.

"Tey?" Journey moved around John, ignoring the sudden frown on his face as he attempted to block her.

She merely gave him an irritated look as Tehya rose slowly to her feet.

So innocent, so ignorant of the pure evil they shared the world with.

"I'm fine, Journey," she assured the other girl, almost wishing they could go back to the day when their biggest worry was the landscaping scheme for a difficult client. "Jordan's departure has simply left me upset, I guess."

Stephen sniffed at her response to Journey. "A man has to do his business."

Arrogance filled his gaze; it was a natural landscape for his expression. Her grandfather, as her mother had described him, was much different. Bernard had been openly generous, warm and compassionate, where his brother was more prone to hide his emotions beneath that cool exterior.

Francine Taite had dearly loved her uncle Stephen though, as well as her first cousin Craig. Though Craig, Francine had always stated, may have believed in his own arrogant facade.

But before her death, during the times Francine and Tehya had had together, Francine had seemed to live on her memories of her family and the laughter she had once shared with them.

"We're not certain when he'll be returning," John answered for her. "I believe Tehya is actually considering joining him once her business concerns are taken care of here."

Stephen's hawk-like gaze swung back to her as a brooding frown centered his brows.

"You're leaving?" Journey's voice lowered until Tehya was nearly forced to read her lips instead. "I need to talk to you."

With her eyes, she gestured as though trying to glance behind her.

To Beauregard Grant.

He stood tall, brooding, and watchful behind the other girl.

Tehya glanced back at John. "I need a moment with Journey."

"Journey can wait . . ." Stephen began to protest.

"But I can't, Mr. Taite," she informed him.

Family or no family, she'd come too far in her life to ever bow down to his arrogance, or his sense of superiority. It was one of the things her mother had always seemed amused by, Stephen's sense of self-worth.

"I believe Journey has a previous appointment with me." There was a sense of desperation filling the younger girl's gaze and Tehya stared at him coldly.

"I really don't care." Keeping her voice soft she looked at his hand, then back to John with cool demand.

"I'm sure it won't take long." John turned to Beauregard, his expression confident that the other man would heed the order in his gaze.

And he did.

Beauregard slowly released Journey's arm, but not before he bent his head and whispered something in her ear.

Tehya watched as Journey seemed to pale, her gaze darkening in distress as her companion's head lifted and he stepped back slowly.

"Walk with me." She held her hand out to the younger girl, and waited until it was taken before turning back to John. "We'll just be a moment."

That didn't stop the two couples from rising to their feet and following behind her as she walked to the open patio. Stepping outside she turned back to them, refusing to be denied now.

"I think Journey and I can handle it from here."

John and Travis both stared back at her for a long, silent moment, obviously prepared to refuse the demand.

"I think I can conduct a conversation by myself," she stated. "I promise, we won't go far."

The group that stood just outside the patio didn't looked

pleased. Beauregard Grant looked frankly pissed, if the glitter in his gaze was any indication.

The cool solitude that awaited, just on the other side of the small grotto she led Journey to, would be a very welcome relief.

"What's going on?" Tehya asked as they stepped into the rose- and wisteria-covered sheltered area.

"I don't know." The stress in Journey's voice was apparent. "It's Beauregard, Teylor." Journey turned to her, tears glittering in her eyes. "I think he's involved in something very illegal, and I think he's going to attempt to force me to accept the proposal he made tonight." Her voice broke. "Teylor, what am I going to do?"

"And I think you may have been warned to keep your stupid bitch mouth shut!"

Tehya hadn't sensed anyone, she hadn't seen so much as a shift of a shadow, but she knew that voice. She knew the evil in that whisper and she knew, she'd just been caught by her enemies.

Her lips parted on a scream that never came. A heavy cloth came over her face, a noxious scent invaded her nostrils, and seconds later, darkness washed over her.

Chapter 20

Tehya came awake slowly to the sound of Journey gagging and coughing in reaction to her own return of consciousness and the effects of the chloroform used to disable them.

Sitting up from the thin mattress that had been laid over a rough low table, Tehya swung her feet to the floor as she swallowed tightly and forced back the reflex to gag.

It wasn't her first experience with the sleep-inducing drug. As she stared around the room, she was horribly afraid it wouldn't be her last.

"Teylor?" Journey's voice was weak, shaky. "Oh, God, what happened?"

"We've been kidnapped." Tehya stared around the room. It wasn't large by any means. The dim lights high on the metal walls were battery-powered rather than electric.

"Where are we?" Terror filled the young woman's expression as well as her voice.

Tehya breathed out roughly. "It's a shipping crate. The type they use for overseas shipping."

A sob echoed through the area.

Beauregard. She wondered if he was behind this. God, he had to be. But he wasn't old enough. He couldn't have been associated with Sorrel.

"Teylor, what's happening?" Journey whispered.

Tehya fought to clear her mind. She needed to think. She needed to figure a way out of this.

She remembered hearing Gregor Ascarti's voice as the cloth went over her face. He was involved, but he wasn't the one calling the shots.

As that thought went through her mind, she heard the sound of metal scraping against metal and the heavy door at the end of the metal shipping crate swung open.

"Let's go." Ascarti, Mark Tenneyson, and Ira Arthurs stood at the entrance, heavily armed.

Tehya stood slowly, her gaze locked on Ascarti.

He was frowning at her, glaring, actually.

"You were supposed to be dead," she whispered.

He grunted at that. "If you'd had your way, I would be. Fortunately for me, I think I might have actually survived." He smiled then. A reptilian smirk that sent a chill racing up her spine. "Unfortunately for you, perhaps. Now let's go." He waved the handgun toward the darkness outside.

"How did you get into the gardens?" she asked as they moved slowly from the crate.

"A little inside help," he revealed, his slimy voice amused. "Now, be a good little girl and let's finish our business. Then I can go about recouping my money from that little hit your friends made against my stash."

"What hit?" She played dumb. She'd perfected that illusion through the years.

He laughed, clearly refusing to believe her. "Let's go, Ms. Fitzhugh. Someone is very interested in talking to you."

Keeping Journey close to her, Tehya ignored the other girl's confusion as she followed Ascarti.

She was right, they had been held in a large metal shipping crate stored inside a warehouse on the docks. She could hear the sounds of the ships outside, voices calling out and machinery running.

Across from the crate, the doors to an office were thrown open, and it was there they were led.

Tehya stepped into the brightly lit room, her heart racing, fear drying her mouth and making her knees weak. As the men gathered there came into view, she felt something inside her soul wither and die.

At the same time Journey cried out in denial and confusion, then in fear as one of the men behind her all but threw her onto a tattered leather couch at a signal from her father as she moved to race across the room.

Stephen Taite, Craig Taite, and Beauregard Grant stood watching them. Stephen was propped against the edge of an old desk, his arms crossed over his tuxedoed chest, his expression hard and brutal. Journey's father, Craig, grimaced in disgust as Journey cried out to him.

Only Beauregard remained completely unaffected, cold, brooding as he watched.

Tehya sat down slowly at the other end of the couch, fighting to make sense of it, to believe what she was seeing.

"Ah, I remember that look." Stephen's smile was cold, cruel. "The same look your dear mother had when we caught up with her in Nicaragua. I believe she may have actually cried, though." The pleasure in his voice was sickening. "And I would have thought by now you would have explained who you are. The daughter of our dear departed Francine, Tehya Fitzhugh."

"That's not true," Journey cried out hoarsely.

"It's true," Tehya told her quietly, "and they're the reason Mother died."

"What are you doing?" Journey cried out before Tehya could speak. "Father? Grandfather? Have you lost your minds?"

Stephen flashed a hard frown at her.

"If she opens her stupid mouth again, gag her," her father ordered.

Tehya turned her head slowly, not wanting to face what she knew she would see in the young girl's eyes. She was only twenty-two. She might not have grown up with an affectionate father, but she had grown up with a semblance of confidence in the world and her place in it. That was being stolen from her grip now by the very men she trusted above all others.

"Will you gag me as well?" Tehya turned back to the three men.

Stephen smirked back at her, his lined face twisted in a parody of amused tolerance. "If I gagged you, dear, then I wouldn't be able to hear the answer to the question I have. And you will answer it, or Journey will pay the price."

He smiled benignly at his granddaughter.

It was Beauregard's reaction Tehya caught, though. A flash of something bitter, heated as he slowly tensed his arms unfolding and hanging, ready at his sides.

"*You* killed my mother." She felt numb. She stared back at Stephen and Craig. How horrified, how terrified she must have been when they caught up with her.

Stephen chuckled. "She thought we were there to help her. That her father had sent us after she contacted him." Satisfaction filled his smile. "She was rather upset to learn that wasn't the case." He turned to his son. "We did enjoy our last hours with her, though, didn't we?"

Craig's answer was a fond smile as Journey's smothered cry of horror sliced through Tehya's senses.

What the hell was she supposed to say now?

"Now, my dear, it's like this." Stephen's expression became hardened once again, the monster inside him gleaming through his eyes as they focused on her. "If you want to ensure your dear cousin Journey has a reasonably content life from here on out, you'll answer my question and do so without a fuss. Refuse me, or dare to attempt to lie to me, and she'll die with you."

"I'd rather die!" Journey cried out, her voice echoing with rage and pain as she tried to surge to her feet.

She was caught, and just as Craig ordered, the two men behind her fought to gag her. And they had to fight until Beauregard strode quickly across the room, caught her and jerked her arms behind her.

The cries, the hatred, and the fury that spilled from Journey's lips struck at Tehya's heart. The sound of the other girl's sobs was excruciating to hear.

Tehya forced herself to watch as, strangely gently, Beauregard bound her hands, then placed a wide strip of gray tape over her lips.

She was silenced, but she still cried.

Journey kicked out, striking Beauregard's leg with her shoe, though there was no reaction from him to even give Journey the satisfaction that she'd at least brought him discomfort.

"Now that we've taken care of that." Stephen sighed as he turned back to her. "Did you understand the rules to her continued safety? Or do you have questions?" His gaze sharpened. "Or do you want to be as stupid as your mother?" He spoke to her as though she were a moron, the superiority he obviously felt leaking through every pore in his body.

Would Beauregard Grant really allow Journey's family to kill her? He had stepped in to keep Ascarti's gorillas from hurting her. He'd bound and gagged her with gentleness despite her attempts to fight him.

"Were you behind my mother's kidnapping?"

Stephen rolled his eyes and shook his head as though amused by her question. "Let's get this out of the way, then, dear. I kidnapped your mother for Sorrel, but he didn't keep his end of the bargaine once he got what I wanted. He swore she was unaware of what I wanted when he was only attempting to steal it for himself.

"You worked with Sorrel?"

His smile was filled with pride. "I did. Though, now I will command as I should have been doing all along." He shot his granddaughter an irritated look. Now, does Journey live or die?

He wouldn't allow Journey to live. Beauregard might believe Stephen Taite would keep his word, but he wouldn't. Tehya could see it in his face. Journey would be lucky if she lived to see the next week out.

"What do you want?" She was at least curious why her mother had died.

"She gave you an account number," he stated. "A code of sorts. I want it."

Why hadn't she guessed? Why hadn't her mother guessed?

Perhaps the fact that her mother had never suspected her family was behind her kidnapping and the deaths of everyone who tried to help her, Tehya hadn't suspected either.

The shock was horrible. It lanced through her system, it destroyed parts of her she feared would never heal, and left her soul bleeding in agony.

Tremors raced through her, sobs catching in her throat, searing her chest.

"Money," she rasped. "This is all about money?"

"A rather large amount of money," Craig answered smugly. "To my calculations, minus the four hundred thousand your mother stole, it should now be close to three point two billion dollars in gold, cash, bonds, and yearly shares in Taite Industries. A legacy Bernard refused to turn over to the family until Francine's body was found. A legacy that was amassed over nearly a century of the Taites' superb business sense."

"As well as nearly a century of laundering the funds my father, his father, and his father before him made in the careful sale, trade, and trafficking of women Sorrel's clients preferred. And Bernard never knew; that legacy should have never been his. Should have never been given into his safekeeping at our father's death," Stephen finished, his voice becoming progressively furious until he was glaring at her in malevolent rage. "Taites and Fitzhughs have always worked together, but we were smart enough to keep from being caught."

All for money.

He had murdered everyone who had ever tried to help her mother. He had murdered everyone her mother had cared for, and everyone Tehya had cared for.

"Sorrel thought he could convince your mother to give him the set of numbers that would allow him to take possession of the accounts," Craig continued. "He promised your mother she'd have her freedom." He smiled. "She didn't trust him, I gather."

No, Francine hadn't trusted the man who had kidnapped her, imprisoned her, and raped her repeatedly for years. And Tehya had trusted him even less.

Stephen straightened from the desk. "Now, do you die alone?" He glanced back at Journey. "Or do you go with company?"

Tehya turned and stared not at Journey, but at Beauregard Grant instead. He was leaning against the wall, arms crossed over his chest, his gaze flat and hard as he stared back at her.

Once again she wondered if he would really allow Stephen and Craig to kill her and Journey. There was something about him that wasn't ringing true. She hadn't been looking closely enough at him, she admitted. She hadn't paid enough attention because he also wasn't aligned with Sorrel. He hadn't been around before Sorrel's death. He hadn't shown up on her background checks on Sorrel.

Who was he?

Her gaze slid to Journey. It wasn't fear in her eyes now, it was rage and pain. Tears washed down her face, but Tehya recognized the agonized demand in the other girl's eyes. A demand that Tehya give her father and grandfather nothing.

It was all for money, and the money wasn't worth protecting. Tehya had known about the legacy her grandfather had ensured her mother knew how to access since she was a child. She knew the set of numbers that would open a vault in a Swiss bank and give the bearer a fortune unimagined.

It wasn't worth dying for, but neither would she, could she, give them the satisfaction of ever acquiring it.

She turned back to the cousin and the great-uncle whose family she had once dreamed of being a part of. Ached to be a part of with a hunger that nearly had destroyed her.

"I never knew the key to the account," she whispered, and it was nothing less than the truth. "I couldn't remember it."

Anger flashed in Stephen's face. "Don't lie to me, bitch," he snarled, his fists clenching now as though the urge to strangle her was barely held in restraint. "She would never have let that fortune go."

"Because you wouldn't?" she whispered. "Her safety and mine was more important or she would have come home.

She would have taken what she thought was hers and she would have hired enough bodyguards to ensure no one touched her again."

So why hadn't she done it?

Tehya didn't have the key. What she did have was the safe deposit box where her mother had hidden the paper she had placed the key on. She made Tehya swear she wouldn't attempt to access the money until she knew that not just herself, but also the family would be safe.

Bernard Taite's death had terrified Francine and she had believed that the rest of the family could be in danger. She'd had no idea the family was in on it.

Stephen sighed before his fist clenched and he came closer.

Just that quickly Beauregard stepped in front of her.

"Journey's mine," he told the other man harshly. "I won't have what I want from her affected by your treatment of this one."

Amazement filled Stephen's face as Tehya tensed, preparing for a confrontation and, hopefully, a chance to escape.

Just as she thought she would have it, a heavy knock sounded on the door, jerking her attention behind the two men.

"What do you want?" Stephen barked.

The door opened and two male figures stumbled into the room and collapsed to the floor.

Tehya stared at them in amazement, blood clotting at the side of Rory Malone's face and at the back of Turk Gillespie's head.

"Who the hell is this?" Craig Taite stood almost frozen, amazement filling his voice as it filled Tehya's mind. "What's going on here?"

Stephen turned back to Tehya, and before Beauregard could stop him, before Tehya could guess his intent, he struck her hard across the face, throwing her back against the couch as hell seemed to explode around her.

The lights went out as flash explosions took out the far

wall and lit up the darkness outside. Shouted orders began to
echo around her as she jumped across the couch and threw
Journey to the floor seconds before she felt the bullets whiz
past them.

Stephen was screaming at Craig and Beauregard, demanding they get him out of there. As Tehya's eyes opened, though,
she knew her cousin wouldn't be going anywhere.

He stared back at her from his position on the floor as she
felt Rory and Turk suddenly moving.

Journey was lifted from the floor along with Tehya and
ran for the door.

"No! No, you won't," Stephen was screaming in outrage
as Ascarti suddenly stumbled in front of them, the handgun
he carried slapping against Tehya's head as Rory came to a
hard stop, his arms holding her tight around her waist as
Tehya clutched the derringer she had managed to slip from
the garter holster she had worn.

"Not her," Ascarti rasped, a crazed smile at his lips as
Tehya lifted the derringer to his chest and fired.

She wouldn't see another die. She wouldn't hear of it. She
wouldn't know of it. She wouldn't allow it.

It ended here.

She watched as a look of amazement came over his face.
Shock.

Rory knocked the gun from his hand and Tehya watched
as he fell, sinking to the floor as Rory and Turk rushed them
out.

Behind her, Jordan and his men and only God knew who
else were swarming into the office and kicking ass.

He had sworn he would protect her, and he had.

He had promised her it would end here, and as Rory
pushed her into the back of an Elite Ops med-van, she knew,
it was definitely ending here.

She watched as, a black-masked, medical operative cut
the bindings from Journey's wrists and pulled the tape gently
from her lips.

Their gazes met.

Journey was shell-shocked. Silent.

Her gaze dropped to her fingers as they twined together and Tehya watched the tears begin to fall again.

Tears she couldn't seem to shed. A raging pain she couldn't free.

And the fear that nothing would ever make sense again.

Jordan left the warehouse behind the federal operatives who were pulling a screeching Stephen Taite from the melee that had erupted inside.

He'd had men outside the warehouse before Jordan had called for the advance. Nearly a dozen hard-core mercenary soldiers had been taken down within minutes by Killian Reece and his team.

After the years of manipulating everyone around him in order to see to their safety and their happiness, Jordan had finally been on the receiving end of it.

One of Killian's operatives had leaked the fact that Tehya wasn't dead to a known Sorrel associate. An associate suspected of being linked to a shadowy figure rumored to call himself The Marquis, a name French authorities had found in a single file belonging to Sorrel. The single reference had hinted at Sorrel's fear that the Marquis would find Francine or Tehya before he did.

That someone else, according to the file, was determined to find Francine and Tehya. Just as Joseph Fitzhugh had been determined to keep him from gaining the "key" Francine Taite held.

The information Killian's team had been working on since the death of Killian's wife stretched back more than a decade. Killian had refused to let the investigation go, and Jordan hadn't known about it.

Until the other man had walked into the Senator's house just minutes after they'd realized Tehya had been taken.

"Jordan, wait up." Killian turned Stephen Taite over to one of the authorities before moving quickly to his side.

"We don't have anything to say, Killian," he snapped. "Get the fuck out of my face."

Killian's expression registered surprise, but only for a second. His gaze darkened and then his lips quirked with somber knowledge. "I knew you loved her. I told you that when I came to base last year, didn't I?"

Jordan jerked back. There was a part of his mind that watched, completely unsurprised as he grabbed Killian by the front of his mission shirt and slammed him against the metal shipping crate.

"You told me she would fucking kill me," he snarled. "You didn't trust her, Killian. You didn't give her a safe haven. You fucking turned your back!"

Killian's eyes widened for a second before he sighed wearily. "She always had safe harbor," he finally said softly. "I always knew where she was, and my men were always watching her." For a second, agony flashed in his eyes. "I lost the woman that owned my soul, Jordan. You're the only fucking friend I ever had; did you think I would let this world take what means the most to you?"

He'd known Killian for far too many years. He'd known the other man's demons, he'd known his rage, and when he was telling the truth.

He was telling the truth.

Jordan released him slowly.

"I had to let her think I hated her," Killian sighed, still facing him. "I had to let *you* think it. If even once, she'd turned those haunted eyes on me in friendship, I'd have never been able to do what I knew Elite Command was going to have me do."

"You could have told me," Jordan raged.

Killian shook his head. "If anyone came to me and told me they were going to use Catherine in that way, I would have killed them before I allowed it. You would have never let it happen."

No, he wouldn't have.

Jordan was smart enough to admit that to himself. He would have run with her. He would have hidden with her. He would have never allowed her past to touch her in this way if he had been forewarned.

"I could kill you for not coming to me, Killian," he rasped as he pushed closer, feeling that need for violence ripping through him. "And I wouldn't feel any guilt. I wouldn't feel a moment's fucking regret. Do you know that?"

"Jordan . . ." Killian spoke softly, warningly.

"My fucking woman," he snarled, the fury snapping through his mind. "She was mine and you knew she was mine."

Killian's brow arched, some gleam of unholy amusement in them searing the fury only growing inside Jordan now.

"You weren't claiming her," Killian reminded him. "You let her go. Maybe, if she was your woman, you should have given a man a clue so he'd know how to proceed."

"I told you and every other man that came around her to stay the fuck away. I warned, I threatened, and when I had to I intimidated, so don't fucking tell me I didn't claim her."

"You never said you loved her," Killian pointed out.

Jordan's lips parted, the stunned at the accusation that came from Killian's lips.

God, he did love her, he realized. There was no fucking illusion, there were no attempts to deny it any longer. He'd stopped denying it the second his brain had processed the information that Tehya had been taken.

"I shouldn't have had to say shit," Jordan snapped. "By God, you should have known."

"And perhaps you should have said something."

Jordan froze.

His gaze jerked to Killian's and found smug satisfaction quirking at his lips. An amusement tinged with a haunted pain, a memory of what he himself had lost.

He turned slowly.

The shoulder of her dress was ripped. It was dirty, streaked with dirt and smoke, tattered at the edges. She was barefoot, her stockings shredded, and her hair was in disarray around her shoulders.

And still, she was the most gorgeous creature he'd ever laid his eyes on.

"Perhaps someone should have enlightened me when I started making a fool of myself denying it," he told her softly.

Her face was tear-stained, pale, and her gaze was still bright with unshed tears and pain.

Moving to her, he reached up, his thumb smoothing across the tears only to find others taking their place.

"Jordan," she whispered, her lips trembling as he slowly pulled her into his arms, a wave of agony sweeping over him at the thought he could have lost her.

"I have you, baby." His arms tightened around her. "Right here, I have you."

"It hurts." Her breathing hitched as her hands suddenly clutched at his back. "Don't let me go. Please. Please don't let me go."

Let her go? He'd tear his own heart out of his chest before he even considered such a villainous act.

"Come on, baby." He picked her up and carried her to the waiting car that Nik had driven in. "Let's go home."

Where he could hold her. Where he could hopefully help ease just a small part of the horror she was feeling.

As he passed the medi-van, in the shadows close to the opened doors at the front of the vehicle, he caught a figure moving.

The form wore the familiar dark mask, and rather than a tuxedo, he was pulling on the utility belt that went with the mission clothes he had obviously changed into.

He hadn't known who or what Beauregard Grant was until Killian had met him at the warehouse. He'd had no idea Beau had been doing the same thing Jordan had done more than fifteen years before.

He was creating a background, an identity, and a history that would put him in place where the Elite Ops needed him most.

He was a dead man walking. But if the way he was staring at the young woman sitting on the van's gurney with her back to him, her eyes closed, tears still whispering down her cheeks, then he was a haunted man.

Jordan could hear Stephen still screaming at Journey from the car he'd been placed in. Furious, filthy curses and accusations as the young woman appeared deaf to the words.

But he knew she wouldn't be.

Placing Tehya in the car, he turned to Noah as he loped over and nodded to Stephen's granddaughter. "Get her out of here. Send her to Ireland until this blows over. Let her stay in the castle. She's going to need time."

"Where are you heading?" Noah tilted his head to stare at Tehya sitting silently in the back.

"Home," Jordan breathed out, suddenly feeling the tension easing inside him. "I'm going home, Noah."

As they drove away with Nik at the wheel, Jordan sat in the back, his woman cradled in his arms, thanking God for her safety.

Noah couldn't help but grin, even as thankfulness swept through him with enough force to weaken him.

He had a feeling that for the first time in far too many years, Jordan had found home.

What was she supposed to believe?

Tehya watched Jordan, desperate, terrified to believe he truly loved her as he carried her into the bedroom of the suite Nik had escorted them to.

He kicked the door closed before lowering her slowly to the floor and locking the door behind him.

Her lips parted, the question she needed to ask almost falling from her lips before he laid a finger over them.

"Not yet." His expression was fierce, demanding. "Not yet, Tehya. Let me know you're still living, that you're still here with me first. God, let me get that nightmare out of my head."

His lips covered hers.

Shock vibrated through her at the agony, the pure emotion that filled his voice before he kissed her as though he were dying for her.

Deep, drugging, his arms surrounded her, enfolded her as he held her to him, his lips slanting over hers as his tongue licked at hers.

The remnants of her gown were dealt with quickly, the material falling at her bare feet as he shrugged his jacket from his shoulders.

Suddenly hungry for the feel of him, Tehya pulled at the buttons of his shirt, several snapping free and falling forgotten on the floor until she could spread the edges apart, her fingers finding warm, hard flesh.

Hunger rose between them like an inferno, blazing across their flesh, searing their emotions as they hurriedly undressed each other.

Tehya breathed out roughly as she felt him lift her, the strength in his arms making her feel dainty, helpless, and protected as he laid her back in the middle of the bed.

Reaching for him, Tehya drew him to her, her breath hitching in her chest; the overwhelming feeling of complete absorption coming from him was intoxicating.

It was different. Each touch was laced with something that hadn't been there before. A tender possessiveness he had kept leashed until now.

His fingertips stroked along her breasts, following the curve, feathering against her nipples and tightening them further as she arched to him.

His lips sipped at hers, strong teeth nipping, catching her lower lip and worrying it before his tongue stroked over it with a hungry lick.

Broken moans filled the air as he came over her, strong knees pressing between her thighs as his lips released hers and moved down the line of her throat, following the taut arch until he laid quick, heated kisses on her breast.

His tongue licked over a tight nipple as he moved between her thighs, his fingers stroking over the wet curves of her pussy before they parted the sensitive folds.

"Jordan." Desperation filled her as she felt the thick, broad width of his cock press against her. "Jordan, please."

Heat speared through her, circling her clit before whipping through her body, as he began to penetrate her with tight, slow, shallow thrusts.

His lips lifted from her nipple and moved back to her face.

"Look at me, Tey," he groaned, his voice tight, heavy with hunger. "Let me see your eyes, baby."

Her lashes lifted, lips parting at the brilliance in his eyes.

"No illusion," he whispered then, his tone tight, guttural. "I love you, Tehya."

She froze beneath him.

"What did you say?"

His fingers stroked down her side to her thigh before his hand cupped beneath her knee and lifted her leg higher, over his head, he seated himself deeper inside her.

Stretching, burning, pleasure rippled through her flesh in a wave of such intense sensation she cried out with it. Arching, her legs lifting, arms holding him closer, Tehya held his gaze and let herself be taken by him.

However he wanted to take her.

With his body. His hands. With deep drugging kisses as her lashes feathered over her cheeks and she lost herself to each sensation.

The hard, powerful thrusts of his hips, the wicked, heavy strength of his cock impaling her, taking her, marking her in ways she couldn't have imagined she could ever be marked.

There, in the darkness, their moans rising, heat building between them until felt herself exploding in such intense ecstasy that she could only cry out his name and hold tighter to him.

"I love you, Tey," he groaned at her ear as he fucked her, thrusting deep a second before she felt the hard flesh tighten further and the eruption of his release suddenly filling her.

As though her soul opened and he filled it, light flooding her entire being as she cried out in his arms.

She was home.

For the first time in her life, Teyha was home.

Her eyes opened, lifting languorously to stare up at him.

Perspiration beaded along his forehead, his shoulders. His gaze was drowsy, black hair falling over his cheek and forehead.

"Jordan," she whispered, her heart racing, suddenly terrified she hadn't heard what she thought she had heard.

"I love you," he whispered again. "I've always loved you, Tehya."

The warmth was brilliant, racing through her, flooding her being.

"I love you."

The dream she hadn't wanted to admit to was suddenly real. It was there, in his gaze, his touch, his kiss.

For the first time in her life, Tehya belonged.

Alpine, Texas

Riordan Malone, father, grandfather, Irish stock, and a man who longed to join the woman who held his soul, sat at her graveside and stared into the night.

He could feel it. His Erin had always laughed at him when he looked at her and told her when he felt his sons and his grandsons.

He blinked back his tears and reached out a gnarled hand to touch his wife's headstone, feeling the warmth of the marble as he fought to imagine it was the warmth of his beloved Erin.

She'd made him swear that if she went before him, he'd stay long enough to see her babies wed and happy.

There would be another wedding soon, he thought, then he'd just have to wait on his namesake, young Rory, to find his future.

Damn, that boy could be slow, though. He'd never been one to move fast on anything, and he didn't seem to be in a hurry to settle down anytime soon.

"What are we gonna do with him, my Erin?" he sighed into the night. "He's too slow, and I'm tired of waiting. I'm ready to come home."

Home. Back to his wife's loving arms.

And God he missed the warmth those arms held. The gentleness, the acceptance.

He missed his Erin.

Bending his head he kissed the top of the stone, touched his forehead to it for a moment, then rose from the bench he'd placed there.

He was getting too damned old to kneel the way he used to. But he couldn't miss saying good night to his laughing lass. To the woman who had completed him.

"Good night, my love," he whispered. "We'll work on young Rory soon, I promise," he sighed. "Just a little more time to finish growing the boy into the man, then I'll be comin' home to ya. Ah my Erin, I can't wait to come home to ya."

He patted the stone, turned, and walked back to the small home he'd shared with her, the one he'd raised his boys and his grandsons in, where he'd grown old, grown tired, and now, moved ever closer to leaving to his boys.

Soon, he could go home.

EPILOGUE

Two years later
Alpine, Texas

The house was full.

Jordan watched as his nephew, Noah "Nathan Malone" Blake and his wife Sabella laughed over the antics of their two-year-old daughter, Mira Paige, while their eight-year-old son, Noah Nathan, rolled his eyes at his sister and his parents. Little Noah was content being the "big brother," but told anyone who would listen that she just simply refused to listen to her elders.

Micah Sloane stood beside his wife, Risa, their younger son exchanging an animated conversation with little Noah. Nik Steele and his wife Mikayla sat close by, a delicate little blond girl perched on his knee as she watched everyone shyly, obviously entranced by the antics of the boys a few feet from her.

Travis Caine's other half, Lilly, sat beside her husband, holding her child. At eight months old, the surprise package still had the power to bemuse her parents.

Likewise, the son John Vincent and his ex-CIA wife had given birth to almost a year before, was often regarded as a miracle by the parents who had believed they would never be so blessed.

The men of the Elite Ops had come full circle, from "dead" men without lives, to men who enjoyed living far more than they had ever imagined they could.

Joining them were the men and women who had followed them through eight years of operations and two years of learning how to be simply husbands. Simply men.

They were all there. Laughter filled the room as the children, Joseph McIntyre, Kyle and Elissa Chavez, Jessica, Laine and Little Macey March, along with the much younger Lincoln Richards joined in to create a laughter-filled, harmonious event.

The christening of Erin Elizabeth Malone, the newest addition to the extended family, who watched the world with bright, Irish eyes.

His daughter.

Jordan stood behind his wife of two years, Tehya Malone, and couldn't help the smile that curved his lips or the pride that filled his soul.

And the love.

This was no illusion. It was no desperate attempt to justify anything. It was pure, rock solid, and it filled every particle of his being.

He was a husband, a father, a friend. He was a man that awoke each morning to the warmth and the pleasure of the one woman who completed him as nothing ever had in his life.

As he glanced around once again, he saw that same love, that same remarkable miracle of salvation that bound the men he had once commanded with the women who had fulfilled them.

Women who had turned dead men into fully living, loving, laughing husbands and fathers who would die to protect what they held dear.

This was living, and Jordan knew life had never been so good.

"Hey, Jordan, come over here and tell Reno exactly how you managed to come up with that plan to flush Orion from his hole," Micah called out to him, his expression much different now than it had been the night Jordan had first met him, just days after the assassin Orion had destroyed his life.

His hand stroked down his wife's curls as he bent and kissed her temple lightly. "I'll be back," he promised her.

The smile that beamed up at him filled his soul.

"And we'll be right here waiting on you," she said, the promise in her gaze one Jordan knew he could depend on.

She would be waiting for him. In life, or in death, holding the vows they had made, close to her soul.

Always his and always loving him as she had since the day they had met.

A love to match his own.

"Thank you," he suddenly whispered.

"For what?" Her smile was like a blessing, a warmth that would always fill him from the inside out.

"For showing me it's not an illusion."

With a final kiss on her sweet lips, he moved across the room to remember, to give thanks they had survived intact.

It was his daughter's christening, but it was also his and Tehya's. The affirmation that love existed, thrived, and that they weren't alone.

The men and women who had followed them in battle, who had laughed with them, pushed them toward each other, and conspired to see Jordan happy and safe in the arms of the woman that loved him, were celebrating as well.

They had all found their homes, in the hearts and in the arms of the women and the children who loved them.

Wild Card

Navy SEAL Nathan Malone's wife, Bella, was told he was never coming home. But if he can get back to his wife, can he keep the secret of who he really is . . . even as desire threatens to consume them? And as danger threatens to tear Bella from Nathan's arms once more?

Maverick

The only way for the Elite Ops agent to uncover an assassin—and banish the ghosts of his own dark past—is to use Risa as bait. But nothing has prepared him for her disarming blend of innocence and sensuality, or for his overwhelming need to protect her.

Heat Seeker

John Vincent has every reason to want to remain as dead as the obituary had proclaimed him to be. He'd left nothing behind except for one woman, and one night of unforgettable passion. Now, both will return to haunt him.

Black Jack

The Secret Service can't control him. The British government can't silence him. But renegade agent Travis Caine is one loose cannon you don't want to mess with, and his new assignment is to die for.

Renegade

Elite Ops agent Nikolai Steele, code name Renegade, is asked to pay an old comrade a favor. This friend swears he's no killer even though he's been mistaken as one by Mikayla. Nik goes to set her straight, but the moment he lays eyes on her, he knows he's in too deep.

Live Wire

Captain Jordan Malone has been a silent warrior and guardian for years, leading his loyal team of Elite Ops agents to fight terror at all costs. But Tehya Talamosi, a woman with killer secrets and a body to die for, will bring Jordan to his knees as they both take on the most deadly mission.

🐟 ST. MARTIN'S PRESS

Midnight Sins

Cami lost her sister in the brutal murders that rocked her hometown so many years ago. Some still believe that Rafe Callahan, along with his friends Logan and Crowe, were involved. But how could Rafe—who haunted her girlish dreams, then her adult fantasies—be a killer?

Deadly Sins

A newcomer in town, Sky O'Brien is a mystery to Logan Callahan. Like him, she is a night owl. Like him, she is fighting her own demons. Like him, she hides a secret in her eyes—a fire that consumes him with every glance. Could she be the one to heal him?

Secret Sins

Sheriff Archer Tobias has watched the Callahan family struggle to find peace and acceptance in the community—despite the murders that continue to haunt them. But he is torn between duty and desire when Anna Corbin becomes the next target.

Ultimate Sins

Mia, left an orphan after her father's death, was raised amid the lies and suspicions against Crowe Callahan. But nothing could halt the fascination she feels for him, or the hunger that has risen inside her.

St. Martin's Paperbacks   St. Martin's Griffin

Sizzling erotic tales from
New York Times bestselling author
LORA LEIGH

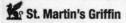 **St. Martin's Griffin**

Available wherever books are sold

www.loraleigh.com